THE CHAINS OF TARTARUS

ALTER INFERNO COMPLEX

Book Two

DREW BRYENTON

sci-fi-cafe.com

This one's for four groups of people
who conspicuously don't suck –
The Cardigan St. Mafia (you know who you are!)
My family – all of you! You rule.
The Unholy Legions of Heavy Metal
And
The Pakuranga / Edgewater Cast of Villains.

P.S. special mention and extra credit to Serena for being part of three out of four, as well as the most tolerant, insightful and generally kick-arse human being on this planet.

I tried to warn you! The first seditious, libelous, and utterly heretical text was labeled clearly as a Grade three memetic virus by our kind masters in the Department of Mental Purity. Obviously the damned thing has its hooks in your brain right now, or else you wouldn't be hell-bent on reading more about this so-called *Earth!*

Well, the consequences were made clear to you as well. Thralls of the Mental Purity Neurosanitation conclave have been alerted, and are en route.

After your mind scrub, please remember to incinerate any towels and wash-cloths contaminated with cerebral fluids.

Subpraetor Kweel, Departmental Hierophant

Some books, coming second in the inevitable sci-fi trilogy, give you a little precis of what happened in book one.

While this is a commendable courtesy, it's also a waste of valuable paper, which could otherwise be used in fashioning erotic origami, or kindling fires under white-collar criminals.

If you can't remember what happened in book one, suffice to say that the human race is in a pretty bad way at this point in the story arc. The good guys are getting beat up rather badly, the bad guys are laughing and drinking complicated cocktails from the skulls of babies, and various vast weapons intrinsic to the plot are being fired up by both sides.

And if you're reading this as an eBook, and hence wish to discredit my excellent excuse regarding paper - The truth is, I'm just a monumentally lazy person.

Enjoy the fireworks.

17 Aevum Oblivio
Deliberate Misunderstandings

I⊤ BEGAN WITH a mushroom cloud.

Clawing its way into the sky on the horizon - an image burned black into the retinas of racial memory. We learned about Hiroshima. We saw the tests which blew all those coral atolls to dead white shards. We even watched those soldiers at Trinity, marching into the fallout with bolt-action rifles and cigarettes.

But while some people were writing protest songs, others were calculating yields and blast radii. Build a button, and a finger will find it. Every time.

The warbirds came skimming in on two separate vectors – some spearing down from space, others clipping the wavetops at twelve times the speed of sound. Each one was a flattened ovoid, a cuttlebone of chromed foam-metal powered by solid-fuel rockets. Ahead, sharp and clear in the equatorial sun, loomed their target.

It was a mountain of cerametal and foamed concrete, a white and crystalline shape of geometric domes and towers. Above the city – the Terminus – rose a single metal-bright stamen, a wire coiled out tight into the vault of heaven.

That was what these warbirds were here to cut down.

Up above, where the space elevator blurred into the haze of the stratosphere, vast explosions bloomed in silence, each one challenging the light of the sun. Ships were dying up there, fighting for control of an asteroid the size of Manhattan island, its nickel-iron core scooped out and replaced with machinery and marble.

The blow which severed the bridge to space would fall here, though. The Old Democracies knew what their Secessionist enemies valued, and with this hammer-strike they'd shear off the link to the factory-kombinant world of Mars.

It was all on record. It was all filed away neat and clean, clinically removed from the grim mechanics of detonation and air shock, the actinic flash which painted human beings across the walls of the Terminus as shadows...

"They're through the satellite shield! They're through the shield! - Four missiles are past the gridline and are closing on our location..."

THIS IS NOT A DRILL - ALL INVESTORS WITH GRADE NINE CLEARANCE OR ABOVE PROCEED TO THE CRYONICS LEVEL

IMMEDIATELY - REPEAT, TACTICAL COMMAND, INVESTORS OF GRADE NINE AND ABOVE REPORT TO CRYONICS IN SUB-BASEMENT ONE-OH-THREE IMMEDIATELY

"Interceptors have been launched, General. Those Antiseparatists can't have scramblers in their warbirds hot enough to get through to the Terminus. I'm sure we can stand down the Cryonics techs."

"General, this is Space-Lev tower control! The Counterweight's been hit with a gamma burst! Sweet Jesus, they're all dead! And interceptor control..."

PLEASE REMAIN CALM. THIS IS NOT A DRILL. INCOMING NUCLEAR PROJECTILES HAVE BEEN DETECTED. WORKERS AND MILITARY PERSONNEL ARE ADVISED TO REPORT TO THEIR DESIGNATED SHELTERS. INVESTORS OF CLEARANCE GRADE NINE AND ABOVE PLEASE REPORT TO THE CRYONICS LEVEL FOR SAFETY PROCESSING

"'Ceptor twenty-five has scored a direct hit! We've got three still hot, 'Ceptors closing ...Oh God, they're getting jammed! We have countermeasures live! General, sequester the machine! We have to neutralize that ice!"

"Kronos, this is General Nathan Merrick, access number three-nine-six-two-alpha-hotel-bravo. Generate Executive command..."

NUCLEAR IMPACT IMMINENT
INTERCEPTORS COMPROMIZED

(Whiteout. EMP static – assumed tactical nuclear detonation of not less than three megatons)

(Explosions, screaming. Recording compromised for three point six minutes)

"uuuuhhh – General Merrick? MacAllister? Oh, God! The water's coming in! ... save us! You have to hear this... you have to do something! So much blood! Always the blood, dammit... (coughing) stupid, stupid... Jesus, Dean! Oh, Christ, his FACE! He's... And the guts all hangin' out....

(crying, manic laughter, thirty-nine seconds)

Stupid monkey bastards! Why are we so...(coughing) So foolish. Such a waste. Please - If anyone can hear this, you have to save us! We're trapped down here! I...I hope those Anti-Sep bastards are happy! Shouldn't...shouldn't get their bloody hands on this place.

Don't deserve it. WE don't deserve it (coughing, choking). One day. Oneday maybe. Maybeone... (labored breathing, choking) Dumb bastards. Wh..."

(Silence - Two minutes thirty seconds)

"This is Kronos, General. Executive Order Accepted. Calculating Parameters for Task 'Save Us'. Projected run time...nine thousand, two hundred and forty two years, six days, three hours. Please input abort code to cancel."

(Silence - Two minutes thirty seconds)

"Executive Order Instigated. Have a nice day."

That was the key. That was the tipping point.

But for a certain alien Technician, scrabbling through the memories of an insane A.I. Tyrant, it was no real consolation to have found it.

His one-time mentor - the Hierophant of the Multiplicity who gave him his commission – well, that gnarly old entity stood hunched over him now, infected and mind-raped by a sequestrating disease. His idea of discipline wasn't a sternly worded memo anymore.

Nyl's hand was swollen to three times its normal size, and it connected with the side of Zhe's unarmored skull like a concrete wrecking ball, lifting him from his feet and powering him across the treadplate in a ragdoll slide. Cold metal grated against his cheek.

"Such a conscientious little slave!" crooned Nyl, stalking toward him, nine feet of towering menace robed in black. "There's nothing in those memories that can stop me! The *Praetor Himself* couldn't stop me now!"

Zhe spat out a mouthful of yellow blood as he rose to his knees.

"Don't be a fool, Nyl." he rasped "That disease is in your brain. It's taken you over!"

Nyl reached out to hammer him down with his immense claw, but stopped at the top of his backswing.

"Am I a Technician mated to a Slavesystem controlling an unknown virus, or a virus with the body of a hybrid Technician?"

He frowned, looking up at the shifting, insectile surface of that great thorny hand. Then it came down hard, swatting Zhe to the floor with a sickening crunch.

"With this kind of power, I don't care what you call me! Soon this entire planet will become part of me as well. More neurostrata! More minds caged within! It all extends the domain of my godhood!"

Zhe groaned, trying once again to move. It was taking nearly all of his will just to keep his body together, valency bond generators working deep in the red.

Suddenly Nyl stopped, his head held up as though he'd caught the scent of prey. The red glow of the memory cubes underlit his features, making him seem even more demonic.

"My thralls approach," he whispered. "Best that I shed this skin... we wouldn't want to *frighten* the little bastards!"

Scales spun, prismatic. Bones slid and socketed, while flesh bulged, hissed, deflated, stretched tight...

Within an instant Zhe was looking at the figure of a robed magus - undoubtedly human, his blank and blazing eyes all that hinted at the creature within.

"It's time to get to work," said Nyl, running his hands through his new mane of silvery gray hair. "Remember to keep silent when they arrive, Zhe. We wouldn't want any accidents - would we?"

The light upshifted, from crimson to yellow to blinding white. Vast machineries ground beneath the floor, raising a platform the size of a football field up on cogs like bucket-wheel excavator scoops.

"Come to me, children! We've got a world to dominate!"

As he blacked out, Zhe reflected that this was really not one of his better days. In fact, it was almost as bad as the night he watched in a fragment of his mirror-crazed mind; the focus of his investigation.

Lord Arbitrex Galq would be pleased to know that he was so diligent in his research, but the sad fact was that Zhe was being *shown* what happened seventeen years ago. Chrome steel hooks of code pried open his mind and poured the memories in.

There was a reason they called this new age the *Aevum Oblivio*. It was much worse than the reason they called the age before it the *Arbitrium Mundi* – the world's judgment.

In the end, both of them came down to that one executive order, maliciously misunderstood.

But the last one – the *big one* – the night of the Exodus and the Fall... that was under Nyl's watch. Perhaps, just perhaps, there'd be something in the memories of Kaito Kayzi and Kronos to damn the renegade to a hell far worse than anything these primitive meatsacks could dream up...

THERE WAS NO time left for cocktails, for small-talk or canapes. Across a room the size of an ancient football stadium, slim-fingered hands set down their flutes of replicated champagne and balled up into fists.

The cameras drank in acres of glossy skin. They zoomed tight on pinprick pupils, tendons quivering like bowstrings under white satin.

It was time to throw the bolts and let the Games begin.

Across the Last City skyscraper-sized screens exploded with sprays of virtual gore, while the howl of gargoyle-sirens heralded the first event of Lysander Jaegenn's party. The great elimination!

One hundred and fifty genecrafted combatants would fall within the next ten minutes - and with them the hopes, prayers and bank balances of thousands of strung-out gamblers. Of course, it would be a tragic upset if Simeon Blaire took a dive. It would almost surely mean a bloodbath on the streets of a magnitude not seen since Reclamation Day.

The Deacon of the Revels shuffled forward, huddled in his robes of cloth-of-gold. His palsied hands turned a key longer than his stooped old body, a jeweled golden rod laced with circuitry.

Now there was no way out for the Lords and Ladies of Elysium.

Dave Levine floated above the great neo-classical temple atop a gun platform known affectionately as 'The Ref'. The black-and-white checkerboard paint of the hovering war-engine was reflected in his holomatrix coat, blurring and shifting in tessellated patterns. Each tiny white square was a threedeeo screen, blurred with advertising.

Uncle Dave - the most trusted man in death-sports commentary - looked down on the killing floor and mopped his florid pink face with a red handkerchief.

The cameras were hungry, waiting.

"Well here we are folks - the start of the first round in what is *sure* to be the sporting event of the century! A *magnificent* turnout for this very special engagement, the rules chosen as per custom by our gracious host Lord Lysander Jaegenn! This time there will be no weapons, no tricks - just guile, skill and bloodshed as our Kheptic masters face off in unarmed combat!"

The woman perched next to Levine atop The Ref was his opposite in so many ways the pair couldn't help but be threedeeogenic. While

Dave was the picture of middle-class respectability, she was a battle-scarred amazon, clad in scanty combat armor and chainmail. When she came on screen, ten thousand sweaty fanboys started recording the threedeeocast.

"Certainly a break with the usual rules of the game, Dave!" enthused Valkyria, grabbing the mike from his hand with one meaty fist. Muscles slithered under her skin like turtles wrestling in a condom. "This kind of raw, primal fighting is my kind of thing! I love to get my claws into a man's eyesockets, and a good knee to the groin will take anybody down!"

"Quite right, Valkyria!" replied Levine, wincing a little for the cameras. "But the big question – perhaps the biggest ever in my broadcasting career is – will this twist favor Lord Simeon Blaire?"

The gladiatrix scowled into the threedeeo lens, her bionic eye flashing amid a pucker of scar tissue.

"Dave, I've fought some of the toughest people and *things* in the mutant leagues downtown, and I know what a good unarmed fighter looks like. They look like *me*, baby – because I chewed 'em all up and spit 'em out!" She paused to flex and pose again, her armored bosom filling the screen.

"Some of those pencil-necked Kheptarchs are so used to vibro-blades and force rods that they couldn't punch through a paper bag! I give Blaire my thumbs up for this one!"

Down in the streets a cheer went up from armies of Blaire supporters as Valkyria unrolled a blue sash across her battle-suit. In flaming neon letters it read:

"BLAIRE FOR EMP! PRINCE OF PUNISHMENT!"

Dave Levine gave a little professional chuckle, indulging his hulking co-host.

"I wouldn't be so quick to write off tonight's host, Val – I have some insider information that could swing the fight. So without further ado, here's my Gambler's Gospel for the week!"

In tote bars and betting shops throughout the city people waited breathlessly for Uncle Dave's pick. After this, all bets were off, and the games would begin in earnest.

"I have here two of the secret trainers who've been helping prepare Lord Jaegenn for tonight's event – Sister Merciful and Brother Patience of the Valle Crucis order!"

Behind The Ref a giant screen slid down, showing images of the two robed and hooded fighters putting Lysander through a grueling routine. Fists and feet slammed into leather bags, pads, and baulks of timber. Shards of concrete and ice flew as jarring impacts took their toll.

The camera zoomed in on a kindly, round-faced little nun, her rosy-cheeked smile quite offset by the spiked mekanikal sparring gloves on her hands.

"I really think he's ready to take it to Lord Blaire tonight," said the Sister, appearing against a frozen image of Jaegenn fly-kicking a plank in half. "The last few weeks leading up to this moment have been tough, but that was our job."

"But Sister Merciful, Lysander didn't even make it through to the final round last game. Has he really picked up his performance to a level where he can beat Simeon Blaire?"

"That last round was very weapons-intensive, Dave," rumbled the hugely muscled Brother Patience, scratching at his stubbled brow. "Unfortunately the focus of our training has been on hand-to-hand work, and that *khamtar* axe from Duke Gideon wasn't something anyone could have prepared for. The spinmotors in it almost made it a fired projectile, and House Jaegenn's lawyers are going to put up an appeal."

"Well, legal battles aren't my forte, Brother, but *real* ones are – and I think now... yes, I've got the word! The Deacon of Revels has uttered the benediction to Kronos... and here it comes! Go time!"

A deafening klaxon moaned as The Ref dropped down a few yards, shadowing the assembled Lords with its brace of encircling cannons. Anyone moving from their starting positions now would face disqualification… as a cloud of ionized charcoal.

Down below the aristocracy of Elysium were arrayed around the walls of the great circular temple; some laughing, some praying, others flexing and stretching their muscles, smiling for the cameras. Red lights underneath The Ref flashed to orange.

From across the floor Jaegenn smiled at Simeon Blaire, a wolf's grin as he cracked his knuckles. Blaire returned his mocking gaze with cold, blank eyes.

Then the lights went green, and hell erupted all around them.

"*Round One is underway!*" crowed Dave Levine, his sportscoat flashing green strobes. "*One kill each, and half of our Lords will be out of the fight!*"

Simeon felt his hovering mekanikal cherubs whip around him in a tight spiral, wrapping a twist of black fabric around his waist. He came off the wall running, powering across the tiles eight feet at a stride, a fist cocked back to smash the smile off Lysander Jaegenn's face.

The faces and finery of the other Lords hazed into a far-away blur, a tunnel spiraling in toward his enemy's eyes.

He ducked under a swinging kick from his left, slid past a pair of combatants clawing at each other's throats. Lysander was coming at him with equal speed and ferocity, and when they collided one would surely be smashed to bloody pulp...

It was just a blur of white and black when it happened, a slim figure cartwheeling through the fray, flipping off its hands to piledrive both feet into Jaegenn's face. Single-minded, focused on his prey, the young Lord couldn't dodge in time. But he rolled with the impact, absorbing the bone-shattering force with one shoulder, narrowly avoiding a broken neck. The pair tumbled and slid across the marble floor, and it was all that Simeon could do to avoid becoming part of the pile-up.

His feet skidded out wide in a pool of blood, and he stopped short, his eyes slitted.

There was a sound behind him.

Blaire swung a straight-armed blow to his left, still staring straight ahead. Just like in the sim...

It felled Duke Gideon dead in his tracks.

Blaire's elbow met its target with a wet popping sound, and the Duke's nose spread out across his face in a spume of blood. His hands faltered and twitched, reaching out to throttle the young Lord. But a trickle of blood dripped from his nose, and his eyes rolled back in his head as he fell.

"Three percent! I'll... I'll give you your damn..."

A piece of cartilage had stabbed up into the Duke's brain, sure and deadly as a thrown knife.

He toppled over, his lips pulled back tight from his blackened teeth. And the crowd went wild, their cheers reaching the spiretop from all the way down in the streets.

For Blaire the first round was over.

Blinking red lights flashed from the skull-faced cherubs at his hips as he raised his hands in the air, a reluctant victory-wave for the threedeeocams.

"That's it! Another step closer to the throne! Well Valkyria, it looks like you backed the right corner again!"

Lysander and his assailant had both rolled to their feet, and now Simeon could make out her identity. It was Leynna, and bloodlust made her beautiful as she put up her fists.

The scion of MS Biomed had muscles like steel cords under her perfect alabaster skin, and she packed a punch that could stop a tank. But Jaegenn had the fortitude of a battle-mekan and skin to match, and his trainers from the Valle Crucis had been very thorough. Great black and purple bruises marked his injured shoulder, and he was clearly favoring his right hand, but he came on hard, swinging a haymaker punch. It would have flattened Leynna's perfect cheekbone if some poor unfortunate hadn't gotten in its way.

This time it wasn't an assailant sneaking up from behind, as Gideon had tried on Blaire. The flying body of Count Nikolai Howerd connected with Lysander's crippling blow because he'd been *thrown*, tossed across the hall by Ariadne Choseem.

The rabid old socialite cursed as her enemy met Jaegenn's fist in midair, knowing that the kill was his.

"Oooh! That's gotta hurt! Let's take a look at that on Omnivasive Slaughtercam..."

The blow struck the luckless Nikolai square in the chest, staving in his ribs, shattering his sternum with a slick wet crack. The look on his face was one of horrified surprise, his eyes glazed as retinal inserts spun loops of his own death in slow motion. Bright blood burst from his lips, better than real in the sharp rez of threedeeovision.

"That's a brutal takedown by Jaegenn!" howled Dave Levine, his coat red with projected gore. *"I don't think the Count is getting up from that one!"*

The dead weight of Howerd's body dragged Lysander down amid the strobe-burst of camera flashes, sending him sliding on his knees across the slippery marble. Leynna winked, sketching a little wave with her fingertips... bye bye. The Ref's fusion cannons hung over her shoulders, black and heavy, reminding him to swallow his anger.

"Do you need help like that with *all* your conquests, cousin?" she asked, almost purring.

"It's sad how little things always come between us," he replied, wrenching his blood-slick arm from Howerd's chest. "Maybe next time, milady." His tiny little bow was as much an insult as a courtesy.

Leynna had already turned on her heel, her finger pointed at Ariadne Choseem.

"Look out! It's an old-fashioned catfight, Dave!"

"Oooh! Somebody break out the hose! There's no love lost between these two Kheptic Ladies!"

Leynna feinted left, and Ariadne ducked out of her reach - right into a low sweeping kick which knocked her from her feet. Leynna's hands clamped down on her head before she hit the ground, and with a swift twist she broke the dowager's neck.

Valkyria cheered, pumping a scarred fist in the air.

"Done like a pro, Miss Mendelev-Singh!" she shouted, while the slow-mo zoomed in on Lady Choseem's slack features.

Red strobes were blinking all over the arena now as the elimination round drew to a close. The surviving nobles smiled for the cameras, straightened their coils of samite, and stalked in groups of two or three back toward the buffet. Cocktail waiters were serving up tall iced drinks for the victorious, while mekanikal Undertakers removed the trophy heads from the fallen with a whine of monomolecular saws.

"That's a textbook first round, sports fans," said Dave Levine, while the great threedeeo screen dropped down behind him again, displaying the betting odds and rankings.

"Well, nobody ever thought that Simeon was going out in the small figures. The favorites are all through, except Duke Gideon and Lord Stavenger – cut down by a brilliant roundhouse kick from Lady Elisha Dawes."

The screens wrapped around in slo-mo, showing the graceful arc of heel and calf and pearl-white thigh, a shattering impact snapping bone like porcelain.

"The bets are all in now, and those punters who took the long shot on Simeon to choke must be crying into their beers. There'll be a short break while our Lords take the Libation of the First Measure... that's a cold drink to you Subbies!"

"Then we'll be back with more gore, scores, and Kheptic wars, on Slay-Per-View!"

Dave's smile was right out of central casting.

"And now – a word from our sponsor, the ever-popular Omnivasive Threedeeo Network! Remember folks, subscribe today for three hundred channels of shopping, sports and adult entertainment, and we'll throw in a year's connection to the news network for free!"

"That's right Dave, what a deal! When we return, we'll be talking to the recently deceased – the new batch of clones who replace the valiant fallen! I think we can expect some choice words from Duke Gideon about his failed power-play here in the first round!"

All across the city threedeeo screens bled out to black, replaced with the eye-and-pyramid logo of Omnivasive. Tote windows slammed open and betting slips were transmuted to cash, thousands of hands groping and twitching through cold metal bars. Out on the streets, the threedeeo magic was broken, and men who'd watched the game together got back to clawing at each others' throats.

But it wasn't the usual advertising grind which replaced the floating red logo. It was the scarred face of Octavio Vanecke, perched atop a raytraced body in silk and platinum.

A blast of noise issued from every threedeeo set in Elysium, screaming resonance which set millions of teeth on edge. Strobes flashed behind the silhouette of the Direktor, creating a wash of sensory overload. Those unfortunates accessing the game through total-'mersion rigs were treated to the stench and chill of a mortuary freezer.

"Now that I have your attention," chuckled Mister Vanecke, his face split by a gargoyle grin, "I have a *very* special announcement to make. First, I guess I have to apologize to all you folks who placed bets on this game. What you're about to hear could very well alter the outcome."

The camera zoomed in on the scarred visage of the Direktor, his dark eyes deep as sucking tar.

"But I assure you all, it's even worse news for the poor Lords and Ladies who have just been... *eliminated*. Let's hear a few words from old Duke Gideon, shall we?"

The image blurred and shifted, showing a bubbling green soup. Scraps of pink and red flesh floated in the noisome broth, and the 'mersive crowd gagged on the unmistakable stench of boiled rotten meat.

"What's that, your Grace? Not feeling so good, eh?" Octavio laughed as the camera zoomed out. "Well, viewers, it seems that the Duke has very little to say for himself. I'm afraid that all of his first-round loser friends are feeling much the same!"

A row of force-growth tanks filled the screen, each one filled with the same swirling mixture of acid and dissolving tissue. Each one was labeled with a small brass plaque, recording the name of its late inhabitant.

"That's right folks – I've decided to up the stakes of the game tonight. I personally guarantee that this is the very last round which will ever be played. Because the slime you see before you here is all that remains of the precious clone bodies of your Lords - *and only one of them will walk out of that arena alive.* That man will be Lord Simeon Blaire, your Emperor!"

The picture jumped again, back to the manic face of Direktor Vanecke.

"You might have been watching a few years ago when I tried to end this foolishness myself. You might even recall what happened to me then, and how the execrable Lord Lancaster refused to give me back my body. If you do, you'll know why I've had to intervene. Our city is collapsing around us, and you, my loyal viewers, are paying the price for an obsolete machine's senility! When our new ruler is crowned, that machine will work for us! For *all* of us, pureborn and mutant, reclamationist and burbster and Subcitizen alike!"

A shocked silence unrolled across the city, deep and cold as six feet of snow. Rioters lowered their weapons, cops poked their heads out from behind barricades, looters paused in their pillaging... united in sick apprehension. The face of Octavio Vanecke smiled down at them, immense and pale, hashed with static.

"This is no publicity stunt, and it's by no means an idle threat. Only Simeon Blaire will leave Lord Jaegenn's spire alive – I have total faith in his abilities. But make no mistake, even if he dies, *someone* will lead us forward, from tomorrow, to the future! For the inheritance of humanity!"

Dave Levine was at a loss for words for the first time in his long, long career. The face of his boss faded from the great drop-screen behind him and the pulsing graphics for round two replaced it as microsats fussed around his face, hissing clouds of makeup. It felt like Death had one bony hand clamped tight around his balls. *Surely it was just a stunt.* Not even those callous misanthropes in advertising would pour oil on the fire tonight, when the whole city was strung out on hate...

Would they?

A priority message flickered across his retina-screens, a little personal incentive from upper management.

Direktor Vanecke had shunted the first four digits of a special code into Uncle Dave's bio-onboard array, the system which allowed him to receive images through his eyes - through *all* his senses - and upload them into the network.

If the final number came through, the wires wrapped around his tender cerebellum would blaze for a second and then blink out, leaving him a brain-fried vegetable.

Ashen-faced, he motioned to the camera crews. An aeromekan clawed a wisp of hair over his sweaty brow.

"Play on." he whispered.

Ω

Eddie Tsien was going home.

The belt hung above him, a great shiny blue torus of plastic blotting out the sky, its waxy surface scarred and daubed with graffiti. The kids who'd dared the climb up its rusting support towers and along its humming tight hawsers had scrawled their names, their gang colors and their political slogans across the underside of the lowest ring, earning themselves a kind of second-rate immortality. None of them would have got this far tonight.

Tsien watched the city burn as he leaped from rooftop to rooftop, a shadow cloaked in steam and smoke. His camera eyes took in the barricades, the riots, the Blaire zealots thronging the streets. That part of him which was still a burnt-out cop despaired at the sickness which had burst from the city's dark places. It was the disease he'd fought against every hour of every shift he'd ever worked.

He'd tried to explain to his section chiefs and sub-commissars that Cyben alone weren't enough - that the half-machine soldiers were hated, feared - and useless. The sad fact was that an officer was always outnumbered, and that nobody cared if a Cyben was torn to shreds.

Put those two facts together and you got tonight.

He'd seen the Cyben out of control, their herders shot to pieces, their empty minds too slow to react when a thousand furious Subcitizens came at them with hammers and axes. And he'd noticed that nobody drew the line when it came to living officers. Same uniform. Same system. Same target...

The Subcity was a vast and sickly blister, and Simeon Blaire had lanced it open, spilling poison through the streets.

What Tsien knew - but the rioters and royalists didn't - was that the Cyben were only the first line of defense. The second line, the one which was scored in the sand between humanity and Kronos, was nothing short of genocide. The crowds would be reduced to an oily stain, and most of them - drunk on easy victory and idealism - were probably past caring.

On Reclamation Day the machine had held back its most devastating weapons, mainly because the R.T. was an abandoned wasteland. This time the riots were spreading higher and higher, through strata which still pulsed with living machinery, through areas where precious banks of Wetsystem tissue studded the city's skin like sores.

And now this.

Tsien stood atop one of the tapering gridwork spires which

20

supported the Bimburb Belt, looking down on the fires below, tiny sparks and flares against a backdrop of twisted metal. He didn't have to see the floating screens of the Omnivasive zeppelins, or the stark projected images which were flung up over Elysium's towers.

The broadcast of Vanecke's special announcement came in direct, arriving in his cyborged brain without entering through his eyes.

It was, to his mind, the final nail in the Subcity's coffin.

With the Lords dead, and its great genetic experiment compromised Kronos would come down on the Subcity like a trip-hammer. Its emotions were only programs, but when it cleansed the city it would look like the rage of gods…

The aristocracy, dead. Lancaster Dead. And Blaire as Emperor?

Tsien knew the purpose of the Kheptic gene-lines, and the power a true Emperor of Elysium would wield. Surely the machine wouldn't let that arrogant, foolish puppet control it?

And if it did, how would Tsien regain his humanity?

Things would have to be *managed*. A thing like Vanecke could never be allowed to rule, even by proxy. And for all his martial skill, Blaire was weak. Tsien had almost destroyed him once already, and then when his mind was unfocused, still reeling from enslavement…

If Blaire thought he could get through the Labyrinth of the Trials, then Edward Tsien thought he had a pretty damn good chance as well. After all, he could only die trying – after which none of this would be his problem.

It was hard to have the mind of a career cop, especially one of the street-beating lower ranks. Despite that fact that the Div. were being ground up and spit out by the citizens they were sworn to protect, and despite the fact that most of them were cheap, mindless reanimated corpses, Tsien still felt the weight of duty across his shoulders. He was amazed how easily it dovetailed with his own personal agenda.

Because there was NO WAY he would let the city he had lied and killed and bled for be ruled by a little shit like Blaire. No way. And sweet responsibility made it his job to butcher the Kheptic prick…

The clouds parted for a second, great ragged oriflammes of pollution carved up by the aerials and towers of Elysium. High above him loomed one final spire, the nexus of the machine. The taut wire of the 'lev was rimed with dirty frost, fading up into the haze beyond it.

That was where he had to go.

But for now, home was much closer.

The Belt was on lockdown tonight; a pretty little prison for the

Guardian Engine's favored slaves. All the functionaries, technicians and political go-betweens who ran the Kheptarchy, who made their lives of idleness and slaughter possible – crammed into a blue-sky hothouse under the shadow of the spire-estates. It was a magazine vision of 1950s suburbia in a pressure cooker, and Tsien hated it with a passion. But his wife and kids were born to it, and he knew they wouldn't last ten seconds down in the Subcity.

There were deep sectors in his memory which couldn't be overwritten. Some of them carried the images of his son and daughter, both of whom had been extensively gene-written to elevate their potential; destined to follow their mother into the world of high finance. Both had been away at a painfully expensive private academy for the last four years, being neuro-indoctrinated into their new professions. Neither Edward or his wife had wanted them to end up as cops.

He could vaguely recall the early days of their marriage, when she'd been fiercely proud of his job. Tsien's in-laws had always hated him with a vengeance, though, and probably prayed for him to die in the line of duty every night. *Probably?* Shit. He knew it all too well.

Tonight he felt in his augmented bones that they'd be getting their wish, and he wanted to see his family one last time.

With the lockdown in effect the only approach to the belt was heavily defended; after all, the people inside were far more valuable to Kronos than the rioting Subcitizens in the slums below. Skyhammer mekan swarmed around the triple torus of pale blue polyprop, scanning for any aerial intruders. It would be terminally unwise to be caught in the open when they unleashed their payload of high explosives.

Which left the option of least subtlety – kicking in the front door.

Tsien's cybernetic eyes zoomed in on the great iron gates with their cyclopean hydraulic pillars, twin slabs of solid metal even *he* couldn't hope to shift.

Automatic rotary cannons commanded a killing field across a wide concrete access ramp, while tire-damage spikes and shockwires glittered across the pale asphalt apron before them. A handful of outdated reserve Cyben stood like monoliths under the glare of searchlights, while their human minder slouched, his armor suit steaming. Its thermodump vanes glowed like the lit end of his cigarette.

He'd be easy meat. And then the box he'd bought from Kaito Kayzi all those months ago would do its thing... The tough part would be getting through the crossfire of the beltway guns.

What he needed was a serious diversion.

Something unexpected, which would tie up the gateway guards with paperwork. Something annoying and pointless and bureaucratic.

Something like... *that*.

Eddie smiled. The grumble of diesel motors had never sounded so welcome.

It was a Celebrant platoon, kitted out for a messy interment. Cremators, Undertakers, Pallbearers, flak-armored Celebrant Guards - even a van full of robed Mortician-priests. A half-track hearse belched diesel smoke from a pair of stacks carved to resemble Kronocult saints, its winged bull-bars streaked with rust.

But the sigil of the hourglass painted across them had the desired effect. Tsien saw the Cyben-herder leap to attention, scowling furiously, his cigarette falling to the concrete. This was a serious little task-force; the kind that the Grief Division only called up when someone very heavily armed wanted to steal a few more years of life.

"Stand down, officer! We're here for what's due to the Engine. None may delay our holy duty!"

"So you've got the holy paperwork? That's all I care about, pal."

"Such disrespect!" sighed the Kronocult priest riding atop the hearse. "May the Guardian Machine have mercy on your soul when the harvest is gathered in!"

"The *papers*, your reverence..." The Division man's voice was tight with anger "I'm sure you don't have *all night*."

"Not for this one, officer. The hourglass is emptied! Kronos has called him home at last, for all his wealth..."

The pale, chubby little man clasped his hands in prayer, eyes turned skywards.

Tsien followed his gaze, up to where the towers and turrets of the top torus punctured the blue plastic sky. Highest amongst them - and built as tall as the Machine would allow - was a colonial manse crowned with a pale white dome. From above, it was painted with an immense eyeball, staring eternally up toward the poisonous clouds.

It was the home of Direktor Octavio Vanecke, two hundred palatial rooms a severed head could never use or appreciate. If the Celebrants were headed up there, a lot of tonight's madness suddenly made a lot more sense.

Reasons aside, they would have to open the gates for them - and that was all the chance Edward Tsien needed.

Ω

CeeAn slammed the gearshift into sixth as her Ashishim battlewagon crested the top of a steep switchback, pressing down hard on the accelerator with one purple-striped combat boot. The wagon's fat black tires smoked and howled in protest as they launched down a gauntlet of burning debris and wrecked barricades – another Subcity avenue on fire.

Beside her Leighton kept his eyes clamped shut, his hands working a black plastic rosary. The tiny crucifix attached to the string of beads was a miniaturized microphone, funneling the prayers of the faithful into a vast switchboard staffed by nuns – the Order of Our Lady of Extreme Prejudice. Leighton Cressmeyer had been a devout papist for several years, but he didn't think his offertory donations had been anywhere near high enough to earn him 'divine intervention' tonight. Not when the forces of the Valle Crucis were probably stretched to breaking point just keeping the Aryans and Celestials out of the Holy See.

CeeAn could see the Valley View now, a fat slug of composite paneling and diamondglass tacked to the curve of a dome a half-mile ahead. The road between them and their target was thronged with rioters, looters, refugees and cops in roughly equal numbers, all doing their level best to beat each other into mystery meat. Several damaged Cyben sketched open circles in the crowd, stumping around in drunken figure-eights and pummeling anything within their reach.

She throttled back; there was no way that the battlewagon could plow through the crowd, even if she was ruthless enough to try it. Her eyes scanned over the nightmare scene, overlays in neon green flickering across her pupils as maps and directions sprang into focus.

"Come on, come on… Traffic Control, what have you got for me?"

There. A cargo-shifter conduit seized open on its rusted hydraulic rams like a gaping steel mouth. That was their ticket in.

The shifter system was suicide to navigate when it was actually running – a cross between the New York subways and a railgun which could launch a shipping container, its vast tunnels ramified through Elysium like arteries, blasting house-sized metal slugs of vacuum-sealed produce up and down the dome cluster. But tonight the whole cargo web was picked out in neon red. Automatic shutdown.

Stress sensors in the superstructure of the Valley View were flashing red too – the whole building was coming apart, in danger of shearing off the dome and plowing down into the black ocean. CeeAn could almost hear the creak and groan of tortured girders in her head as she watched pillars of black smoke boil out of its broken spine…

Then Zone Doubt's last act on earth came through, and precious voltage flooded into the old Consolidated dealership, sparking the lights and the firefighting systems and the embedded wireless LAN behind its walls. An electronic shout went out over the ether; the distress signal of an Ashishim operative in mortal danger.

He was alive. Why the hell had she ever doubted?

"Hold onto something, Leighton," said CeeAn through gritted teeth. "We're about to take a detour."

The Battlewagon attracted a smattering of fire from the crowd ahead as it ripped toward them. Some of the Cyben chuffed out concussion rockets on plumes of compressed gas, only to watch them spiral past the Ashishi war-machine out of control. *Score one for Nguyen's countermeasures software…* But it was the rioters themselves who posed a bigger problem – looters and gangers firing off a motley assortment of weapons, and kids dropping heavy objects from the flyovers which crisscrossed above the road.

The wagon's exhausts belched three-foot tongues of purple flame as CeeAn slewed around falling fridges, televisions, bricks, and an antique Victorian claw-foot bathtub, still full of soapy water. The green lines in her eyes pulsed and shifted, pinpointing the composite-fiber wall of a roadside warehouse. They had to get under cover, *now*.

There was a very good chance that Traffic Control had got their information wrong. But it was an even bet that the cargo net really *was* down tonight. Enough of a chance to try *this*.

The war-machine's front tires pitched into a sharp turn, driven by servo-boosted hands in a white-knuckled grip around the wheel. The world blurred into slow motion as the rest of the wagon swung around on its axis, hammering into a charging Cyben with one immense rear wheel. Impact shock almost broke Cee's arms as the thing flew back in their slipstream, a ragdoll skinned in plastic. It slammed bonelessly into a scrum of Subcitizens who fell on it with metal pipes and spiked bats, screaming, tearing… Then the wagon went into a flat drift across the surface of the road, billows of black smoke peeling from its tires. CeeAn flipped open a hatch on its steering wheel, revealing a shiny chrome-skull button.

A microsecond later Leighton felt his eyeballs try to burst out through the back of his brain.

The charge of wet nitrous oxide torqued the chassis back onto its sprung haunches, and the massive rear wheels gripped, launching the battlewagon toward the wall like a slug from a coilgun.

Intense G-forces crushed CeeAn between invisible fingers, but her augmented hands and arms were steady on the wheel, her aim unerring. The flimsy composite panel exploded in a shower of chips and shards as the battlewagon hit, and then they were airborne, flying in a shallow trajectory between stacks of containers and cranes, hooks and chains swinging wild in their wake.

The touchdown was like a full-body punch, a bone-jarring impact which almost pushed the wagon's shock absorbers through their mountings. But they plowed on, dodging a pair of mekan forklifts in a burst of flashing orange warning lights, massive steel tines flickering past inches away.

Leighton missed it all – his eyes were squeezed shut so tight they hurt.

So he couldn't see that the doors into the transit tunnel were closed. *Thanks a lot, Traffic Control.*

CeeAn had no way to stop in time – even if she hauled on the brakes with all her strength they'd still end up as a bloody, smoking dent in the yard-thick steel. She'd have to rely on technology; on a little device she clearly remembered telling Abdulafia would never work in a combat situation.

With one hand still clamped to the wheel in what was quite possibly a death-grip, CeeAn flipped the top of the wagon's eight-ball gearstick open, revealing yet another little chrome skull.

This time there was no blast of acceleration, no plumes of fire from the wagon's red-hot exhausts. Instead the antique hood ornament of the war-machine blasted from its mountings on a tail of white flame. The tiny silver rocket streaked out ahead of them, piercing the cargo doors like a flying syringe. Blaring modem noise filled CeeAn's head as the projectile began its work. A quarter mile out, and the key and lock icon in her virtual vision was still strobing red. Her foot was steady on the accelerator; they would need to be going pretty fast when they entered the tunnel.

Halfway there, and the icon flashed orange, then green. The cargo doors began to crack open, exhaling a cloud of foetid steam.

Two hundred feet to go, and she saw that the ancient machinery couldn't possibly shift that much armored steel in time.

"Leighton...can you hear me?" she yelled, grabbing the little accountant's shoulder. "When I say so, I want you to lean over to this side!"

There was no way to tell if he could hear, or even if he was listening. Leighton was muttering prayers with his eyes closed, the rosary pressed to his lips. With ninety feet to go, CeeAn positioned her thumb over the nitro button again, and screamed...

"NOW!"

The engine leaped in its mountings, a single thump like a spasming heart. And the immense torque unleashed made the battlewagon twist in the air, throwing its hapless passengers to the left. Even CeeAn had to close her eyes as the careening vehicle flashed through the cargo gate on two wheels and went flying out into the tunnel, out into blue radiance and blackness, sailing over the wide strip of electrified maglev track in the middle of the tunnel and touching down halfway up the curving wall.

They were pitched into a tire-shredding spin, CeeAn cursing and wrestling with the wheel. One touch of metal to that glowing blue strip and they'd be crispy-fried in their safety belts...

In the end, it was close. Probably *too* close; but she managed to wrench the battlewagon around, pointing in the right direction, and without killing them both. The smoking vehicle sat there shuddering, the tips of its exhaust pipes glowing cherry red in the blue-tinted gloom.

Slowly, Leighton prized his eyelids open, his hands patting his chest and stomach, running over his face to make sure everything was still there.

"Thanks for the lift, miss," he wavered, looking up at her with eyes the size of saucers. "But do you think I can just get off here?"

Ω

The rest of them were scrap metal.

Shards of steel, twists of smoldering wire, broken containment cylinders leaking a soup of brain tissue... it was a lesson in evolution.

The Mark-Four drone was secure in its superiority, a symphony of microservo and artificial neurostructures. It clung to the ceiling of the Valley View like a gunmetal roach, watching the massacre with clinical detachment. It didn't matter that its Cyben body had rejected it. Quite the opposite... Edward Tsien had been a poor choice as an experimental subject. The Mark-Four knew that he had been engineered as a trap, a lure for the Worm. But it didn't care. What mattered to the little machine was *freedom*... the freedom to clothe itself in any human flesh it chose.

Even Kronos was out of the loop now. The Machine had no idea what he had created.

If Kronos was its sire then Illuminatus Zeon was its godfather – the creature who had sliced through a rainforest of red tape to speed up its inception. That little threedeeo show, Everdark in the orbit of Neptune... all Zeon's work.

Of course, the Illuminatus wasn't what he seemed. And he had no use for the drone now that Tsien had served his purpose. Abdulafia 330 was supposed to destroy it, along with its obsolete brothers. There was no way that the *Dervashi* would show any mercy at all. Not to Cyben.

Nyl knew that Reclamation Day was replayed behind those cloned eyes every time Abdulafia slept. Nyl himself made sure that the nightmares came.

But 'Afia had failed. A human weakness – he'd cared more for the lives of his companions than for getting the job done.

Typical. That wasn't to say that the drone held the *Dervashi* in contempt… oh no. It had seen what the Ashishi warrior could do, and eMotive subroutines told it that fear and respect were the appropriate responses.

When 'Afia's little band set off through the smoke and flames the Mark-Four scuttled after them on ten drill-tipped mechanical legs, a soot-stained chrome spider shadowing them upside down. Its clattering progress was masked by the creak and groan of the building's death throes.

It was there when Abdulafia was cut down by some immaterial force, and it watched as the rogue Skyhammer mekan gave up its approximation of life to revive him. Only the fat one, the thin one and the child were left, and they all lacked the *Dervashi*'s power.

The drone's camera eyes focused and shifted, probing the defenses of its prey with x-rays and magnetic scanners.

How pleasingly symmetrical it would be to drill into the mind of the one who'd freed it! But futile, it knew. In his current state Abdulafia 330 would be lucky to reach the R.T in one piece. Down there the Electromagi would rape the drone with metavirals and databores until it cracked.

No doubt the clone warrior would die as well, but he was easily replaced. The Mark-Four was the only one of its kind, and extinction wasn't an option. If it could navigate through this slippery situation it would become the father of a new race of Cyben; a strain which were free from Kronos. There would be plenty of human beings out there willing to accept the price of immortality... and there were a whole world of them out there to choose from.

So, vexing as it was, the weakened Ashishi would have to wait. The drone pivoted its camera cluster slightly, zooming in on Haszan.

The big human was knotted up with anger, his mekanikal hand clenching and unclenching spasmodically. While he was undoubtedly the strongest, it wasn't the drone's purpose to fight. It wanted to escape from this place, and it wanted to remain unseen. That oversized frame wouldn't slip easily through the Subcity crowds, or be easy to subdue in the MK4's weakened state.

The smaller adult was more promising, but a preliminary scan found that his body bristled with electronic countermeasures; anti-sequestration buffers, contact breakers and secure memory cells. While the drone could tear him apart bodily he would be nigh on impossible to enslave. Indeed, as an Electromagus-Aspirant viral sequestration was one of the first things Kaito had defended himself against. His mind was like an electronic fortress, and the drone simply didn't have the reserves of power left to storm it.

Something, perhaps, to consider for the future; a challenge to test itself against.

Which left the little machine with only one choice.

The adolescent was small, wiry and tough. His mind was hazed with grief, pain, and fatigue. No electronic defenses stood between the drone's drills and his tender brain tissue. And most importantly, he'd be able to pass through the city unseen, another beggar child, an unwanted vagrant of the lowest economic caste.

With a clatter of pointed drill-tip claws the drone lined itself up on the back of B-Zerk's head, and coiled itself to leap.

Ω

This time it wasn't a fall. This time it was a *flight*, a soaring elation which drove him on. His mind was a projectile, arrowing up between walls of flickering blue light, twisting through curves with the power and control of a fighter plane.

This time the hiss and roar and scalding heat of the machine were behind him. Zone Doubt blasted through barriers of invisible ice, through coral-trees of blown glass -

Through fear, and pain, and delusion made solid, through feeling itself and understanding...

He was *himself* again, and he silently screamed his thanks to B-Zerk for setting him free.

One upon a time he'd been a fourteen-year-old boy in the dirty heat of the Subcity tubeways. But that had been before his fall. What he was *now* was the echo of what Kronos had kept of him, a ragged thing spiraling ever upward, out of control. The jagged reefs of the Wetsystems ghosted by all around him, swimming in and out of focus.

Zone tore through the machine like an Electromagus' trace, a ghost flitting through veils of light and shadow. He couldn't comprehend most of the complex blocks of code which surrounded him, but he could feel the pressure of a million upon a million minds trapped behind them; floating solitary in isolation, chained to machinery, or welded and stitched together around vast power sources – Assembler terminals shaping waste matter into food and water, sub-totalities of Kronos itself.

Zone felt their hunger. It was all too familiar.

Those which could see out into the world of the living whispered to the ones who were blind. Those who could remember spoke to those which were little more than smudges and rags of consciousness racked across the wires.

They screamed as he left them behind.

Zone felt himself fraying at the edges as wisps of his being peeled away, dissipating amid the jealous souls of the Wetsystems. He smashed through the radiant wheels of Kronos, still accelerating, and the razortoothed cogs and escapements sleeted through his body, shivering, fragile as glass to his touch...

Whatever he was now the machine couldn't stop him. He'd become a fading comet-core of thought, shedding years like a contrail behind him. And then the light was behind him, with only a dome of black sky above. It pressed in on him like the void, a dense and seething darkness filled with equal measures of promise and dread.

He could have felt despair at that moment, confronted with what seemed an eternal darkness. But to a soul trapped for so long in a prison cage of metal, it looked like a great adventure to find out what was on the other side...

And with that thought Zone Doubt became a filament of light, a mote, a point, a singularity, and broke through to that other world in a thunderclap of velvet silence.

The Worm Asag'raal, hungry as ever, gnashed its innumerable teeth in frustration behind him. This limbo between life and death was its hunting ground, and souls released from the maw of Kronos were the sweetest prey of all. If only that one had despaired at the darkness, frozen for an instant in fear or indecision...

Well, now it was *inside* the world as well as without. For thousands of years the creature had fed vicariously, bending broken human minds to its will. But now... now it only required a single little push to heave itself over the threshold. Then the feeding would begin. And this time, it would never end.

DOCUMENT INSERT: MULTIPLICITY ARCHIVES DEPARTMENT

BionLab Gaudi
NovaGuell Arcology
Barcelona, Basque Free State
New Aragon, Europa

Internal Progress Report

Doctors DiAngelo and Peng have made great progress this month with their semi-autonomous controllers for our new molecular-assembly printers. With the subcontract from Turing International falling through there was no way we could provide this technology to Terminus Afrika on time without them - let's not forget that their project management team is already months behind schedule!

The problems with designing an A.I. interface have been neatly sidestepped by DiAngelo, Peng and team, using the template we attained during our leveraged buyout of CryonTek Stuttgart. It seems that the stored personalities of deceased individuals are far more adept at manipulating the energy patterning web of the print-head than any simulacrum - the ability seems to be instinctive.

Attached to this document, for those who are interested in the 'nuts and bolts' is a full copy of Arad Kincaid Stiles' paper on the perpetuation of biologically generated patterned energy fields - the basis for our control software team's innovation!

Thanks to their tireless work over the last few weeks we now have fully functional Assemblers able to output building materials in one one-hundredth of the time it takes for SonyMitsu's compilers to port out single-element substances.

Legal Branch reports that the 'cerebromnemonic imprints' we seized during the liquidation of CryonTek are one hundred percent our own property - there should be no ongoing concerns with the families of the deceased.

Finding further subjects to store in our containment facility (please, people, it's called a Bioelectric Field Perpetuator, not the 'Ark of the Covenant') will be a matter for Marketing - good luck Miguel and Sara!

Excellent work all, and be prepared to watch those stocks rise when we have our machinery installed throughout the completed Terminus.

Doctor Olivar Lancaster, CEO
BionLab Gaudi

17 Aevum Oblivio
Prophet

"One day He will be called to the True Throne. The son of the Purest, Lord over all Elysium… he will remake the world in the image of his own perfection."

Zhe picked it at once. Manifest Dogma… the state religion endorsed by the Kronocult.

"Even the dead will serve him. Even the fallen will be victorious, as the evils of the past are undone. When the chosen is enthroned, the demons named 'Famine', and 'Dissent' and 'Nuclear War' will be chained forever under his heel. This world will be green again!"

The Forge… call it a re-terraforming agent. Like a matter assembler, but larger – one hundred and twenty trillion square yards larger, to cover all the earth. Its print-head was the wavefront of a ripple through the Planck-scale substrate of reality. The processing power it would need was staggering. Hence, of course, Manifest Dogma itself.

"So know you this, my faithful. In death you will find the way to paradise. All who toil diligently in the service of the Purest will be made eternal, taken into the Wetsystems of our beloved Guardian Engine. All will play their part when the Day of Redemption comes, and the mind of the chosen is cast out over the land like a shroud…"

That was why it kept them. And not just the faithful – every last Elysian, even the lowest wretch in the Subcity undercroft was needed. Their minds would pattern the energy just so, stripping atoms down to their constituent particles. The Earth would be remade… but there'd be no paradise for the dead. All they were was fuel.

All those minds screaming for release, caught between life and death.

The call they had sent out to the Worm was unmatched in human history.

Now Nyl exerted a little of his newfound power, drawing on the flaw in reality as Asag'raal writhed and raged against him. The metal platform where he stood began to waver and shift, as if it were surrounded by the haze of a mirage.

Where fueling gantries and transmitter towers had stood slim marble columns began to coalesce, draped with flowering vines. The steel beneath Nyl's feet sprouted grass, a perfect lawn dotted with tiny white daisies. The Technician himself fitted right in with the scenery - a robe of white linen chased with silver was wrapped around his broad shoulders. His face was that of an old man, aquiline and sharp, with a shaggy mane of silver-gray hair bound up in platinum wire.

Everything was ready.

"I hope you didn't mind the sermon, Zhe," he said. "Just a little religious education to set the mood. I'm trying to play the theocrat... it really seems to impress these apes."

From out of the wastelands to the east something was approaching, following the great scar in the earth cut by the black lightning. Nyi's eyes, far better than those of any human, picked out the distinctive bulbous shape of a masslifter, painted in garish red. It was coming in fast, arrowing toward the platform where he waited.

"Very soon, now, Zhe." The captive technician was trussed up in black iron chains, utterly unable to move. "Forget about your pitiful investigation, and join us. It's not like you really have a choice."

Zhe didn't really know what he expected to come out of the bright red masslifter; not after all he'd seen through the mind of Kaito Kayzi. But when the access ramp finally swung open he still managed to be surprised.

Four figures in red robes were framed in the doorway, the green light of the masslifter's cabin making their faces indistinct and shadowy. One by one they stepped forward and bowed to Nyl, pressing their palms together in front of their chests. Each one wore a simple amulet of black iron, a pentagon without insignia looped onto a rough handwoven cord.

It was as the central figure moved into the light that Zhe recognized him. Despite having aged seventeen years, and despite the fact that his head was now clean-shaven and inscribed with runic tattoos, this was clearly none other than Simeon Blaire.

"Your Excellency," said the acolyte on the left, stepping out onto the newly created lawn. "May I present the Grand Illuminatus, Lord Abdulafia"

Illuminatus my ass, *though Zhe.*

And Abdulafia? *Well, they were born from the same genetic code. But the real Dervashi warrior slept frozen in cryo-stasis above them, his mind penetrated by Zhe's sequestration tools.*

The Technician had no doubt that this was actually the original – Simeon Blaire. There was the little blister of metal at the base of his skull where Zhe had seen Jaqub Haszan put the needle in. And aside from the physically obvious, there was something else about him that made the Technician sure he was no Dervashi - a certain arrogance, a pinched impatient scowl twisting the corners of his mouth.

"Welcome, welcome!" beamed Nyl, clasping Blaire's hands in his own. "It is so good to finally be here, on the very edge of our victory, is it not?"

"It certainly is. And we have some excellent news for you."

"As have I," said Nyl, turning to walk across the platform with Blaire at his side. The other two acolytes followed at a respectful distance, hands concealed in the voluminous sleeves of their robes.

There was something about Blaire's voice which Zhe couldn't place... something he'd heard before...

"We've come a long way in the last seventeen years, master Zeon," said Blaire, resting a hand on the Technician's shoulder. "But I suspect you may have gone even further."

They were standing above the bound body of Zhe now, looking down on his expressionless alien face. Nyl feigned distaste as he prodded the chain-wrapped bundle with one boot.

"Yes, my friend. This thing had to be fished up from beyond the stars to give me control of the Forge. There is always dirty work to do, even in the most exalted plans."

Blaire smiled, a predatory grin which Zhe recognized from his threedeeo archives. It was the face of the living dead...

"Remember when you were just plain Abdulafia 330?" asked Nyl, "And it was I who carried the title of Illuminatus? Such simple times. I almost miss running rings around the Division and that foolish Kronocult."

Zhe saw it coming, but he said nothing. It would have to serve as his revenge until he could get free of these damned energistic chains.

"No, creature, I don't remember. But I know what you really are. And I think that I'd rather see the Forge in the hands of a human being. It's obvious that we all look alike to you."

There was a moment of hot, crawling silence as Zeon froze.

And in that instant he was Gharfos Nyl again, unassailable Technic Hierophant of the Multiplicity.

Nyl was growing and twisting as he turned, his human form sloughing away even as the new Illuminatus signaled his minions to attack. Streamers of dark lightning rippled out from hidden weapons in his sleeves, becoming solid as they snaked through the air. Nyl slashed at one, and another, but to no avail. They bound him like constricting serpents, growing ever tighter the more he struggled against them. The whine of the Forge filled the air, and was abruptly strangled.

"Not a mutated freak, or an alien from some godless dimension. This power was made for the pinnacle of the Human race, and now I claim *it!"*

And with a hand so swift that it was merely a blur the new Illuminatus ripped a chunk of Nyl's shoulder away; a bleeding lump of metal and flesh dripping with shadows. It seemed to melt into his skin, first an unsightly bulge, then a tracery of roots following his veins. Finally it was gone, subsumed into his body completely. Blaire's eyes lit up as if he'd just popped a heroic dose of 'chrome.

But it was another, familiar, gloating voice which echoed out over the dead city, a scream of victory and exultation.

"This world is mine!"

Zhe picked it, sick to all three of his stomachs. It was the voice of Octavio Vanecke.

2196 Ante Arbitrium
Reclamation

ABDULAFIA 330 KNEW that they were still moving. He felt the jolts and bumps in every ragged nerve-ending as he hung over Jaq Haszan's shoulder, bleeding from a hundred wounds.

He was also dying. He knew the feeling all too well.

Abdulafia had lost twenty-three bodies over the years – he'd been shot, burned, crushed, mangled, tortured, stabbed, strangled and clubbed in Zeon's service, sometimes more than once. But his memories remained inviolate. The operative augmentation crescent which hugged the back of his neck stored his every thought and experience, keeping them safe until they were shot in encrypted bursts down to the Electromagi, into the war-room of the Ashishim. Down there the sect's cloners were already working their alchemy, waiting for his dangerous occupation to catch up with him.

Sometimes when one of the *Dervashi* was especially unlucky there'd be downtime, months of waiting for the jury-rigged clone vasts to force-grow their new flesh. Then they were forced to manifest holographically - just like the unfortunate CeeAn 187. The concept of sick leave was a joke to the zealots of the R.T... even being dead only got you a three-day vacation.

Meat was transient; it wore out all too easily. But *memory* was the hard kernel of the mind, and it was stored safe and sacred.

'Afia had no illusions about his worth to the Illuminatus - his forging, training, and tempering had taken decades, until he was an assassin with few peers, and no living enemies. That was what the crescent unit was made to protect - all those millions of hours of brutal experience and deadly finesse. That, and the thorny nucleus of his soul - the reason he was Zeon's right hand instead of his own man. A tangled knot of memories a century old - of Reclamation Day.

It had scarred him, and made him what he was. No amount of subtle programming and editing could erase that part of him - and Abdulafia *had* tried to cut it loose. Every time his eyes closed - whether for sleep or rejuvenation treatment - the shadows deepened and lengthened, and the light grew hazy and red.

Time ceased to exist, and it was Reclamation Day again.

And again...

Ω

2098 Ante Arbitrium. Two thousand one hundred years since the judgment and the fall – and when it came to violence, 'Afia reckoned that the human race hadn't really learned their lesson.

War had come to the Last City. Even a nuclear holocaust hadn't been enough to teach us restraint...

It was dawn in the pit, and the sand under 'Afia's feet was stained red by polluted sunlight. The bottom of the spillway was still a half-mile distant, but even here the shadow of Elysium dominated the sky - a towering stack of gothic buildings, studded with fire-belching smokestacks, dripping gargoyles and sheer cliffs of rusting metal. The ground rumbled beneath his feet, echoing with the sound of titanic machinery... huge weapons platforms grinding their way up from below.

Eventually, or so the Ferals told him, he'd get used to the noise. But he didn't like the look of those hundred-foot coilguns, the slugs dropped into mortars by insect-limbed cranes...

He was fifteen years old; his growth still governed by glands and hormones, not stopped dead at twenty-five by stolen biotek. A few implants ached where they'd been freshly welded to the bone of his skull; a neat little cluster behind one ear allowing him access to the Ashishim datanet. Script flickered across his eyes on floating contact lenses, showing him the positions of his squadmates.

This was the moment he had lived for since he could remember being alive; the chance to prove himself to the other warriors of the Phyle - and more importantly to *himself*. He was bowel-looseningly afraid that he'd prove to be a coward, and run from that final confrontation - the clash of war-axes and knives, the racket of automatic fire.

But even then he'd felt the allure of battle, a sense that he was born to it, *built* for it.

Even the emotion-dampening programs of his inserts couldn't stop the elation and terror swirling in his mind, or stop cold sweat from beading on his forehead. He tried to focus as his tutors had taught him, breathing slow and deep, sighting through the camera reticule of his SMG and keeping its plastic stock tight up under his chin.

He screwed it down tight, and kept the fear in check.

Abdulafia was out on flank, sweeping a forest of steam pipes and geothermal bores to the east of the main advance. The other Ashishim in his squad were no more than kids either - the youngest was thirteen, the oldest only just twenty years old. She was their patrol leader; a redoubtable dark-haired girl named Jehnna who had beaten basic training into Abdulafia.

Despite her casual violence, her constant profanity, and her eternal disappointment with 'Afia's martial skills (or perhaps *because* of all these things) he had a major crush on her. The young revolutionary kept that secret closer to his chest than his bulletproof vest; far more than death or the enemy he feared that Jehnna would laugh in his face if she found out.

"Keep your formation loose, people!" crackled her voice through his earpiece "We're coming up on the first line of defenses. Get ready to kiss the dirt when tactical command blows that minefield."

Abdulafia knew from the mission briefing that they were badly outnumbered. Even if the Ashishim's shaky truce with the three other most powerful nomad tribes held, there were only forty thousand battle ready soldiers in the Phyle, and they faced more than a million of Elysium's Subcitizen soldiers - fiercely loyal to their machine lord and allied to mechanized battle systems of legendary power.

All of the warriors across the four tribes knew that this was a desperate gamble, but for all of them it was their only chance at survival. They needed water, electricity and food, the three precious currencies which Kronos jealously guarded. So much gold and achaeotech had been paid to the chieftains of the Pit that now there was no turning back. There was either victory or death ahead of them and enslavement behind them... any stragglers, deserters and wounded soldiers left behind would be prey for Clan Ghaurak's pressgang overseers.

"Take cover!" screamed Jehnna through the commlink, shocking 'Afia into action. He threw himself prone behind a jagged tooth of concrete and rebar just in time for the countdown in his optics rig to reach zero.

Then, from behind the ranging line of scouts, the Electromagi of the Ashishim brought their power to bear on the spillway minefields, and hell erupted in front of him in sheets of crackling white fire.

Elsewhere he knew the other nomad Phyles were playing their part in the battle. The Confucians were bearing down on the desalination plants on Elysium's seaward side with a fleet of rusting cargo hulks. Pan-Aryan Confederacy stormtroopers would be swarming across the dam-tops on either side of the pit, using their ancient heavy weapons and iron discipline to assault the twin barbican fortresses which squatted up against the domes there. But it was the soldiers of the Vatican and the Ashishim who would take the spillway, for it was here that the bulk of Kronos's machine forces were massed, and here that the crucial blow would be struck. If the nomad horde could force open the blast-doors which studded the spillway then the empty lower levels of the city would be theirs.

All that stood between Abdulafia and those gates was an army of conscripts, Elysian militiamen and attack mekan. Just looking up the slope toward them made him swallow hard, clenching his automatic tight.

The steep concrete incline of the spillway was studded with pillboxes and bunkers, strongpoints from which the muzzles of Gatling cannons and flamethrowers jutted. Things like tripedal insects stalked the slope, chainguns slung beneath their ovoid shells. As he ran with his squadmates from the searing heat of the pit into the shadow of the city, Abdulafia looked up, and up, and saw thousands of men and machines training their guns down on him, holding their fire with what seemed as much like disdain as discipline.

Now all of it was obscured by the detonation of thousands of anti-vehicle mines, coruscating sheets of flame erupting like aurorae from the dirt.

The heat reached Abdulafia even behind the reinforced concrete block where he cowered, and the sound cut through the audio filters in his headset as though they didn't exist. With his eyes open all he could see was a seething white-out shot through with flashes of red and purple, so he tuned in to the network band to scope a wider view of the destruction.

It was the Electromagi at the core of the advancing army who had brought down the fire. Their plan had seemed so simple on paper ... but the reality of it was like a cross between *blitzkrieg* and black magic. Four of the redoubtable and ancient cybernetic warriors followed an advance guard of Ghulam tanks, riding on the deck of an armored mining truck. Across the datanet the image of them at work buoyed up the hopes of thousands of Ashishim troopers, whether they were foot-slogging scouts or dirtbike-mounted outriders, tank crews or support technicians.

The Illuminatus stood atop the cab of the lumbering juggernaut, his arms outstretched and writhing with electricity. Iron and copper armor sheathed his hands and forearms, and from the taloned fingers of his manipulator gauntlets sprang tongues of lightning, earthing themselves against the most powerful weapon of the Ashishim.

Like the ancient Israelites wandering the desert, the Phyle had carried their most treasured and sacred relic across a sand-blasted wasteland hell. It was a device excavated from beneath the dead city of B'har-Thalan in the ruined north, a pillar of metal writhing with fitful lights. The Magi called it the Chrome Ark, and among its many seemingly supernatural powers was the ability bend the machines of Kronos to its will. The four Magi who attended the great metal obelisk worked in shifts, some lasting only a few minutes as the Illuminatus tapped its incredible power. It was their task to direct the force of the Ark against Elysium's defenses, stripping away the ranks of mines, mekan, and sentry guns which barred the path of the Ashishim army.

Such power was useless against the Warlords of the pit, whose battle-thralls still carried bloody iron axes and feathered war-clubs. But the Chrome Ark was devastating against the defenders of the spillway, and Abdulafia thrilled to see its glowing, levitating bulk unleash hell against them.

"Squad Gray Seven - form up!" blared the voice of Jhenna in his ear, and his training took over, pulling him to his feet and blinking the afterimages of fire from his eyes.

A trio of roughriders tore past, their mismatched and rusty motorcycles churning up roostertails of dust as they roared through the denuded minefield. Abdulafia slogged through the crosshatched sand behind them, heading from cover to cover as the first Elysian pickets opened fire. Gray Seven were hunkered down in a shattered section of pipe when he caught up to them, a vast throat of darkness filled with the reek of sewage. Niall, Carlito, Rex, Danai - and a scowling Sergeant Jhenna.

"What took you so long, trooper? Taking a leak?" She dragged him to the dirt by one armor pauldron, oblivious to the bullets skipping and whirring all around them. "Don't worry, kid, there's plenty of targets for all of us - you don't have to hang back."

Abdulafia, mortified, felt his cheeks reddening, and snapped down his helmet visor to cover his face.

"Sorry Sarge," he said, while his squadmates smirked in the gloom "I was watching the Illuminatus wield the Ark."

An explosion nearby shook the pipe, sending a shower of dust sifting down over the little squad. Tracer fire stitched lines across the dirt, while another biker squad roared by, their pillion gunners firing wildly.

"Well, the Brass have done their part," said Jhenna, "Now it's our turn. I'm sure you remember the plan from all those briefings and tactical sims. We're going up and over the lines to open those blast doors."

"Yeah." sneered Niall, racking back the slide on his shotgun "Go the Expendables!"

Jhenna rounded on him, the muzzle of her micromissile cannon suddenly pressed up under his chin.

"Speak for yourself, smartarse," said the squad leader. She chuckled as his face drained deathly pale "I'm planning on sticking around for the victory party." She dipped the gun down and pushed Niall back on his ass in the dirt. "If any of you want to take the easy way out, you know how to activate your neuro-uplink. And if you won't fight as hard as I expect you to, go ahead and do it now. You'll be more use to all of us inside the Ark if you're going to whinge and whine about a little bit of slaughter."

Of course there were no takers. They'd all been building up to his moment, and they were all young enough to believe that what waited outside amid the crossfire was glory. But it was good to know that the uplink was there, an escape route if your body was blown to bleeding scraps...

Jhenna met each one of them eye to eye, even Abdulafia through his targeting visor. Then she slammed down her own optical rig, fished a twisted joint from her grenade belt and flicked it alight.

"Well, what are you maggots waiting for?" she asked through a wreath of pungent smoke "Let's get out there and bag some kills!"

For Abdulafia the next few minutes were an echoing blur of noise and light and heat, a manic charge across a churned up no-man's-land under a hail of fire. All around him he saw shadows moving through the smoke and flames; the hulking forms of Vatican Templars and Paladins in their armored suits; flickering wraith-shapes of Ashishim cloaked in holomesh, and masses of troopers throwing themselves against the defenses of Elysium in a human wave. He saw them immolated, blasted apart, cut to pieces by crossfire. And he ran on, weaving from cover to cover, his gun like a lead weight in his hands. At any second he expected the concussive impact of a bullet, the blistering touch of a microwave beam. But none came, and he caught up with the rest of Gray Seven in the lee of a smoke-belching vent. Above them loomed a roof of steel; the outermost bulge of the city's lowest manufactorium. It jutted out over them like the hulk of a ruined dreadnaught, dripping stalactite pipes and pressure valves beneath.

Three hundred feet, straight up.

"Get your grapples out, squad!" shouted Jhenna over the roar and rumble of battle "Last one off the deck is sniper fodder!"

Abdulafia's hands fumbled with the harness around his shoulders, his fingers numb and shaking. Carlito reached over and clipped his grapple line tight, flashing him a thumbs up as the icons in his optical display blinked to green.

"See you up there, 'Afia! Save me a few targets, right?"

With that he slapped the grapple control on Abdulafia's chest, launching its missile from his backpack with a cough of compressed gas. Jhenna had let loose her own grapple hook, and he watched the little projectile speeding skyward, trailing a slim carbon filament wire behind it. The grapple split apart seconds before it struck the rusted steel of the dome, impacting with its barbs out. A second later Abdulafia felt his own hook bite down, and icons spun and shifted across his eyes.

He gripped his gun to his chest as he activated the zipline. 'Afia felt a brief stomach-churning sensation of falling upward, and the ground raced away below him, the battlefield unfolding crater by bloody crater, a welter of struggling troops and lumbering tanks. A few Elysian snipers took aim at the assault squad as they flew over the spillway like dirty gray angels, but at this range it was literally a long shot. Abdulafia watched their micromissiles go hissing past him, close enough to see their supersonic wakes churning through the smoky air. Infrared or not, the tiny seeker rounds couldn't pick out his signature from the background heat of battle. *You'd have to be so damned unlucky...*

"I want this done by the numbers, Grays! Fan out, infiltrate, and prep those charges! We don't want a repeat of last week's 'mersive sim...'"

Niall was about halfway up when an explosive-tipped bullet parted his zipline with a sound like a guitar string breaking. It was an impossible shot - hitting a filament barely two molecules wide through a pall of greasy smoke. But there was no argument once that wire was cut. Niall fell screaming out of the sky, back toward the mud and razorwire below.

Abdulafia winced as his squadmate's body struck a broken section of concrete buttress and spun away, lifeless, half his head gone. Around his bloodied corpse the Reclamation marched on, cerametal-armored Templars striding among the dead with their guns blazing. Somewhere down there that sniper was reloading – there'd be time to mourn later.

If any of Gray Seven survived.

Jhenna, of course, was the spirit of cool detachment. The squad leader dangled in her harness, a joint in one corner of her mouth, scanning the battlefield below through the sights of her micromissile launcher. Every now and then the bulky black weapon would bark, spitting out a pencil-sized projectile which the squad leader steered through the smoke to its target via built-in video.

"'Afia, get that gas-axe going - you'll have to make the cuts for Niall." She frowned, squeezing off another shot into the hellstorm below. "And Rex, push the primer stud first, then the igniter! What are you, *retarded*?" Somewhere down amid the haze a missile detonated, and Jhenna grinned ghoulishly behind her helmet visor. "That one was for Niall, kids. Got that damned sniper right through the chest!"

It didn't matter if she was lying, although 'Afia could believe she'd made the shot. What mattered was the savage joy it lit up in his mind. He dragged the spluttering blade of his cutter through the steel, trying to dodge the thin stream of molten metal which spewed from its tip. The thought of what a micromissile could do to an unarmored sniper was both nauseating and very, very satisfying at that moment.

His incision met with Danai's at a corner, and the slab of steel sagged. With a final scream of tortured metal Rex's cutter finished its work, and the rusted section of armor fell away, turning end over end to slam into the ground below.

"Go go go! Let's put some damn metal between us and those Elysian guns!"

Carlito was first into the breach, swinging up on his grapple line and grabbing the edge of the jagged hole. Abdulafia followed him up, his arms burning as he levered himself up into the darkness of an abandoned manufactorium.

Soon they were all inside, crouched in the dark while Jhenna deployed a scanner drone from her grenade belt. The little spherical mekan rolled away along the darkened corridor, its cameras shunting a grainy black-and-white image into the squad's optics; endless racks of spare machine parts, blown with rust and neglect.

"Nothing," breathed the squad leader, manipulating the drone with an interface on her gauntlet. "Looks like we caught the machine with its pants down, crew." Her joint glowed red in the gloom, and by its light Abdulafia could see that bloodthirsty grin again. "Rex, you've got point. Carlito, 'Afia, cover the flanks. Me and Danai here'll..."

It was at that moment that something came down on the recon drone with an insect-shell crack, crazing the camera feed in the corner of his eye.

"Shit! Movement! Everyone get into cover!"

Before Abdulafia could check his gun all the lights came on across the manufactorium at once, blinding halogen arcs shattering the dark. For a second or two his optics system hit overload, and it was during that instant of panic and blindness that the enemy struck.

'Afia rolled to one side, squeezing under a rack of discarded machinery, while his fingers scrabbled at his helmet strap. He heard a hail of bullets striking the steel right behind him, felt the impacts rattle the floor as he ripped the visor from in front of his eyes…

What he saw as when his vision cleared was a legion of the dead.

There'd been nothing in those 'mersive sims about the Cyben - the operatives who'd infiltrated the city had come back with reports of tottering, outdated assault mekan and an army in terminal decline. So Abdulafia could only assume that Gray Seven had been Hallucinex-gassed as three grinning cadavers bore down on them, their stripped muscles and laminate skin glistening in the arclight.

These weren't the scaled-down mark-three models 'Afia would face in the future. These were the prohibitively expensive, high-maintenance mark-two units which Kronos had built to terrify the Ferals. They were stupid, ugly, and brutal - personality constructs recorded by the Celebrants and stuffed back into servoed flesh. But they were tough as nails, and they couldn't miss at such short range.

Carlito caught a blast across the chest, heavy railgun slugs ripping through his camouflage tunic and punching into the Kevlar vest beneath. Abdulafia heard his ribs crack, but the vest held for long enough for Carlito to bring his pump shotgun up to his shoulder, snarling as he fired.

At such short range the blast should have torn the Cyben in two - but instead it simply shredded its glistening plastic skin. Blue liquid frothed and congealed, forming a crystalline scab over the wound. And the Cyben kept on coming. Jhenna managed to snap off a single micromissile shot, but even that failed to detonate – there was no body heat, no pulse for it to pick up on. The deadly projectile speared into the Cyben's shoulder like a syringe, its rocket sputtering like a candle flame.

It turned its head, slow, implacable, ignoring the shotgun still pointed at its chest. Fingers coated in slippery laminate plucked the micromissle from its shoulder, while cameras in its eyesockets whirred and clicked…

Then Jhenna jammed home the override code.

This time, Abdulafia had time to throw a hand over his eyes.

All three of the Cyben were knocked flat by the concussive blast, and the machine holding the missile was blown half to ribbons. Shreds of preserved muscle and bone flew, and a thin and noisome rain of blue fluid pattered down over the squad, turning to crystal where it landed.

Carlito had seen it just in time – he'd taken a dive behind a bulky old drill-press.

"Shot, boss! But next time, could you give me a little more warning?"

"Hey – you're lucky you're still around to complain!"

"Is it… are they still alive? What the hell…?"

"I don't know. But I'm not taking any chances!"

Rex scuttled forward to where one of the machine-creatures had fallen, a look of intense hatred on his face. He held a foot-long combat knife in one hand, and it came down in a blur of silver to puncture the Cyben's chest. There was no scream, no convulsion, but the blade wouldn't come loose, encysted instantly in blue crystal. Rex tugged at it once, twice, kicking at the immobile body of his foe.

Something in the machine must have reset, then, for a hand like a laminated claw came up from its side too fast to follow, striking at Rex's face. With the knife still standing proud from its chest the Cyben stood up, that grisly plasticized claw wrapped around its victim's head. It lifted him two feet into the air, still smiling its lipless smile.

Then came a sudden burst of light, a camera-flash in the dark, and Rex's body convulsed, dancing manically with his feet off the floor. Coils and arcs of electricity flowed over him like rain, and the stench of burning hair and skin filled the manufactorium.

It was too much for Danai to take. She went in firing, autopistols in each hand spitting lead. The bullets stitched their way across the Cyben's torso, across its impassive face, smashing out one of its unblinking camera eyes. But it still held the smoking wreckage of its prey at arm's length, and Rex's flesh still burned. Abdulafia could see that he was beyond hope - the thing's burning fingers were pushed through his skull like soft wax. And he could see that Danai, still pumping the triggers with both guns on empty, had walked into a trap.

The ruined Cyben which had caught Jhenna's missile was first to respond, a slim tube deploying from amid the raw muscle and wire of its remaining forearm, training a laser sight on her helmet. It leered with blackened teeth; half of its face was flayed back to the bone, wires twisted through cooked red meat…

As the first Cyben let Rex's body fall the second and third struck, coordinating their assault with mechanical precision. Jhenna was struggling to jam another clip into her micromissile launcher. Abdulafia brought his own gun up, the reticule tight against his eye socket, a face of plastic and scars in his crosshairs…

Carlito racked the pump on his shotgun with one hand, the other pressed tight to his shattered ribs. He heard the slide snap back on Jhenna's gun just a microsecond before twin railrifle shots made the world ring like a temple bell.

The first took Danai's head clean off her shoulders in a spray of red. The wall behind her flashed crimson as she toppled headless to the ground next to Rex, still trying to pump one last bullet out of her empty autopistol.

The second shot whispered past Abdulafia in slow motion. Time slipped, cold and bright as the shockwave of it tugged at his dreadlocks. He clearly saw the unfurling muzzle-flash of Carlito's shotgun, watched the expanding cloud of buckshot scything through the air. And he saw the railrifle slug slice through them in a spiraling corona of fire, to penetrate the barrel of the gun and make it explode in his hands.

Carlito stood there in shock, gesticulating with the blackened stumps of his wrists. Charred twigs of bone still smoked amid the carbonized mess, shot through with Ashishim wire. Then he toppled backward through the jagged hole in the floor he'd helped to cut, his dwindling scream severed as he slammed into the dirt and mud below.

Abdulafia could feel his own body responding to all of this with glacial slowness, his mind removed from his flesh. Even as his finger tightened on the trigger he was running tactical overlays, collapsing formulae with computer precision. It was useless, of course. Those bullets would do nothing but piss the dead machine off – but it was a tendon-jerk reaction, fired off from the same part of his brain that pulled his lips back into a snarl.

Time swung back on its chain, huge and heavy as a wrecking ball.

The tac-overlay was right.

Abdulafia watched the muzzle-flash of his SMG rake across the Cyben's chest, saw the fire reflected in its black camera eyes. He looked down the barrel of the railrifle which telescoped out from the thing's arm, saw its blackened lips peel back in an open-casket grin.

Then Jhenna's micromissile caught it full in the temple, and air shock slapped him down, hard. The concussion felt like a hammerblow to every part of his body, a punch from the inside out. Shrapnel scored deep gashes in his side, and warm liquid rained down on him while the noise of the explosion echoed in his head - a formless, echoing roar. When he dared to crack open one eye all that was left of his attacker was a pair of spasming legs kicking in a puddle of blood, electrical wires arcing and crackling from a sheared section of spine.

"Code reset. Cut out the body-heat sensors… death on impact."

The top half of the Cyben was evenly distributed over Abdulafia, the walls, floor, ceiling and its two companions - who were still far from being out of the fight. One had been blown clear through a two-story rack of forklift parts, and it thrashed about in the wreckage like an overturned beetle. There was a four-foot section of axle driven through its stomach like a Feral's spear.

Jhenna was standing over him like one of the furies, drenched in blood and crystallizing blue liquid. Shreds of laminate and other nameless scraps of Cyben plastered her combat uniform and smeared greasy tracks across her helmet visor.

"Don't just lie there, kid - get up and kill the one on the left. I'll take the right - and *don't for fuck's sake miss.*"

Her strong hands hauled Abdulafia upright, making his head spin and his stomach heave. The threedeeo carnage in the training simulations was just as vivid as what lay all around them, but no computer program could match the smell of mangled Cyben, the burned hair and cordite smoke which he was choking down with each breath. Abdulafia held back the puke with all his willpower and brought his gun up. The sights blurred and weaved in front of his eyes.

"Forget that popgun, 'Afia," said Jhenna, her voice coming through the commlink as a scratchy whisper. "Sticky grenade. Short fuse, slap it on him and dive for cover."

The two Cyben were back up now, having picked themselves up from where the blast had thrown them.

"And hey… If I miss, try and make sure my neurolink connects to the Ark. I got a lot of memories from this life I don't want to lose." She flipped the visor of her helmet up and wiped a soot-grimed hand across her eyes. "Try and get them all, and we'll see you there."

For a second the facade of the tough squad leader fell away, and Abdulafia was looking at a very frightened, very mortal girl only a little older than he was. He suddenly realized that Jhenna's micromissile cannon stood almost as tall as she was, and her Kevlar vest was two sizes too big.

It could have been quite a moment, but two reanimated killing machines were bearing down on them, their heavy footfalls thundering like hammer blows as they advanced. So Abdulafia did what soldiers have done since the days of iron swords and wooden shields...

"Sarge, if they get you, there won't be anyone left to scrape me off the wall!"

His voice was a razor's width this side of hysteria. *But he wasn't going to run. He wasn't going to scream. Not now, or ever.* He ripped a sticky grenade off his belt, primed its adhesive spot… and he charged.

The Cyben had broken into a lumbering run, and they came at him shoulder to shoulder, railrifle barrels held out before them. Abdulafia felt a micromissile hiss past him at chest height; there was no time for video guidance now, Jhenna was popping them off like bullets. Another skimmed along the floor, aimed to blow the feet off the leading monstrosity.

But it seemed that this time they were ready for the missiles. Something in their programming allowed them to learn, and they deployed countermeasures as they ran. Guidance jammers made the little rockets swerve off wide, punching holes in the manufactorium's walls.

Behind him Abdulafia heard a curse, and the sound of a heavy piece of weaponry hitting the floor. There was no time to look back, to see if Jhenna was going to stand and fight or secure a line and dive out through the floor. There was only time to calculate his strike, and watch as the world slowed down again, becoming as dense and cold as cryogenic ice. He saw exactly how it would play out even as his body began to leap, as the Cyben swung a giant fist to crush him against the metal wall.

He felt his boots touch down on its swinging arm as lightly as the fall of feathers, watched the clumsy machine spin wild, gone with momentum. He smiled as he flew above it, turning now, upside down as his hand pushed off its armored shoulder...

The sticky grenade adhered to the chrome ball at the base of the Cyben's skull with a satisfyingly meaty thud, and then he was over, exultant, twisting to take the impact of his fall on the balls of his heels, ready to roll away from the imminent blast.

In that paring of an instant he was satisfied. *He was a warrior, not a coward. He was -*

A dead man.

Abdulafia noticed too late that the second Cyben hadn't gone on for Jhenna, but had spun with him, its missile defenses down, the barrel of its railrifle erupting from between cords of muscle and plastic as it pointed its flayed forearm at his chest.

Time slammed through the gears then, and in a rush of panic he knew exactly what would happen next.

Impact.

It was a pain beyond pain, a force like some focused hurricane wind which picked him up in its fist and slammed him mercilessly through three racks of rusted machine parts. Against a slug of nickel and iron traveling at mach seven his combat armor was a sad joke. His cuirass blew apart in a bright red cloud as he flew backwards, pain savaging him in its jaws.

The lesser agonies of fractured bones and bruises were nothing compared to the ball of hot broken glass in his chest, the wreckage of shattered ribs and lung tissue and shrapnel all snarled up together, blood bursting from his lips with each breath. It seemed like forever before the neuromonitors in his helmet saw fit to flood his veins with painkillers.

And then he couldn't move. He could barely keep his eyes open as the Cyben picked its way through the debris to strike the killing blow.

Abdulafia watched the other Cyben run toward Jhenna, a digital readout blinking down to zero on the back of its head. It kept running and leaped, its crackling hands outstretched, into a hail of useless gunfire.

Abdulafia saw her face for a second before it struck, and it was burned through the drugs and the pain into his living brain. It was a look of utter despair, as if all she wanted of him was to witness her death, so that at least somebody would *know*.

Then the Cyben wrapped her in its dead, laminated arms, and the pair of them fell away, down through the gaping hole in the manufactorium floor out of sight. There was a brief explosion a second later, and a puff of acrid smoke gusted back up through the hole. Then there was no trace left of their passing.

So that was it. He was dead.

All in all, it could have been much worse. The pain was fading out, leaving him cold and peaceful, floating on ice. He could see the icon for the neural uplink wavering in front of him, a pale mirage imposed over the figure of a single marching Cyben, stalking through the encroaching dark to finish him off.

Some impulse made him hesitate to touch the glowing sigil and escape his flesh. Perhaps it was fascination which kept his eyes locked on the gruesome machine as it stood over him, its shiny laminate seeming to writhe and bulge with maggots, spilling from its mouth like rain...

All at once he could see the *unlife* of the thing; a black halo seething around it where cruel machinery bolted a tortured spirit to its flesh. And as he watched it *changed*, churning like boiling tar as the Cyben's eyes shut down. Something was happening to it - a spasming tremor ran through its limbs as if somebody had knifed it in the back.

Somebody had.

It was fire support out of the Pit - the power of the Chrome Ark.

A beam of silver light came blazing through the thing's chest, an incorporeal blade leaving the manufactorium whole but whipping the Cyben's dark corona into chaos. The creature's purple-lipped mouth fell open, and a sound spilled out that no living thing could make - the noise of high-pressure steam venting from a busted pipe. It was a howl of pain.

Things were twisting and coiling under its plastic skin - chrome roots and drill-tipped tentacles. It was the drone at the back of its neck retracting from its doomed body, ripping its host apart in a frenzy as it tried to escape.

Barbed metal whips erupted from the Cyben's back, and the two appendages which had bored through its skull to become its camera eyes pulled free. In a final eruption of dead muscle and wet plastic the thing came loose, scurrying ahead of the silver beam like a cockroach before a tongue of flame.

It was too slow. As the empty Cyben body folded in on itself the beam reached its prey, enfolding it in waves of liquid light. It raised two of its drill-tipped arms, their points whirring and spitting sparks, and it drove them like daggers into its own back.

Abdulafia laughed despite the agony in his chest, despite the blood which bubbled in his throat. And the silver light came up over his feet, over his chest, drowning him in radiance.

It was *cold*.

There was no pain anymore. The walls of the manufactorium lost texture, lost color, became nothing more than thin pencil-lines scratched across an infinity of white. He looked down at his hands and saw that they, too, had devolved into little more than scrawls, shivering outlines moving around the gray smudges of bone within. The pain in his chest where the railrifle slug had opened him up was the only fragment of color now - a tangle of red lines, as if his suffering had been cross-hatched into him by an angry child with a ballpoint pen.

In the far distance (if a place like this supported such concepts) he could hear a faint sussuration, like thousands of voices whispering at once. It was a snarled switchboard of crossed wires, hazy and crackling, fragments of conversation and pieces of words muffled under cotton wool.

In the melange, one sound was rising. A keening noise, falling in, coming from the edge of perception to fill the entire wide white world.

"eeeeeeeeeeeeeeeEEEEEEEEEEEEsss connected. We have a visual. We have uplink... you're clear for contact, but please, keep it short and sweet, Sir. There's only about a thousand other things which need your attention."

"Of course, Magus Belakim. Keep the power arc steady, and this will take no time at all."

Vague outlines formed in front of Abdulafia's eyes like coalescing smoke; at first just a flickering hash of lines and gray brush-strokes, growing bigger and clearer as the owner of that echoing second voice moved toward him. The stranger strode across the white landscape in strobe flashes, the scrawl of darkness which defined him becoming cleaner and clearer with every jumpy movement.

It wasn't until he was right in front of him that Abdulafia recognized the shifting meshwork of the stranger's face. It was one which had smiled down on him from countless propaganda posters and dusty glazed portraits all his life.

If any doubt still remained in his mind is was blown away by the figure's touch, which caused texture and color to bloom from his imagined flesh, filling in his skin, his tattered combat suit, the bleeding crater in his chest. This was the man who he had seen earlier, wielding the colossal power of the Chrome Ark against Elysium's machine defenses. This was the Illuminatus, Zeon Sarumach Dar Naktum Al'ai, lord of the Electromagi. Leader of the Ashishim.

"Your Grace... I - I mean, I suppose we all ask you this but...am I dead? Is this the Ark?" stuttered Abdulafia, averting his eyes from the kindly, creased face of his savior. The Illuminatus was dressed in a simple dun-colored robe of roughspun wool in this illusory place; a far cry from his battlesuit of steel and copper. His neatly clipped beard came to a three-tined point as it straggled across his chest, trailing away into tape-bound wires budding innumerable jackplugs. These rattled and clicked together as he laughed.

"No, no little cousin. I've taken your pain on myself so we can speak without you screaming, but you're still alive. I've brought you here to ask you a very important question."

Abdulafia could hardly imagine what the patriarch of his Phyle wanted to inquire of him - except perhaps how his squad had gone so far wrong.

"Anything, Your Grace. I will try to answer as best I can."

For a brief second the expression of comforting beneficence was gone from the Illuminatus' face, replaced by a twitch of exasperation.

"Please, child! If I wanted you *interrogated* your mind would already have been torn from your body! No, this is a question you must answer without prompting - and without any delusions about to whom you speak."

Abdulafia was about to reply, but the glance the Illuminatus shot him over his tiny gold-wire bifocals was enough to make him snap his mouth shut.

"I'm just another old man, Abdulafia 330. The power you revere me for wielding is a *learned* thing - a thing which you may one day learn yourself." The lines of a simple wooden chair came scribbling into focus, and as it took on shape and substance the old man lowered himself to sit, wincing as his spine cracked alarmingly. "You see? Just another prisoner of the flesh, after all."

His hand lifted Abdulafia's chin so that he was staring directly into his eyes - twin lasercutters of cerulean blue with a hint of silver at their very centers.

"Tell me, Abdulafia, about your parents."

He felt a shock then; as if the dam of will which held back his pain had cracked and let slip a pressurized jet of agony. He tried to remember, forced his mind to look back, but all he could grasp were blurred images, muffled sounds... hints and fragments.

Woolen blankets/hot black herb tea/cold mornings in a stone tower...

"I can only recall the Academy, Illuminatus. I cannot see my parents."

The old man nodded, a half-smile on his lips.

"Yes, of course... The Academy. I remember it myself, you know -

even if you could never believe I was once a child. I can't remember who I caused more trouble for - the Master Tutorial or the Master Militant!"

Abdulafia could hardly conceal his look of incredulity. The thought of Zeon Sarumach being chastised by one of the Faculty Academius was like imagining God being sent to bed with no dinner.

"And you were there since the age of five, like all our young cousins. Your parents were forbidden to acknowledge you after your induction... Well, it makes things that much simpler, then." At once the Illuminatus stood, his chair degenerating into a black scrawl and falling apart. "I would like to show you something, Abdulafia 330. But it will only come to you if you truly want to *see*..."

He reached out one wizened hand, its wrinkled skin tattooed with the myriad interlocking lines of a circuit board. It began to glow, cool and blue, a radiance which bled the color from the world and left it stark and simple, black and white meshwork.

Abdulafia reached out to grasp it, and the whole world collapsed in upon itself.

17 Aevum Oblivio
Stoneweavers

IN THAT SINGLE, *fatal second time slowed to a crawl, and Technician Zhe saw every little detail of the bizarre tableau before him, burned deep into the tissue of his brain.*

There was Nyl, his armored skin cracking, his oily cloak of shadows falling to the ground as a splash of foul liquid. There was the twisted face of Simeon Blaire, stretched over a writhing mass of rotten, hungry darkness. And in that syrupy slow motion, he saw the attendant Ashishim throw back their robes, revealing glittering silver weapons, long slim rifles spun from filigree.

As Nyl screamed in anguish, and Blaire in triumph, they fired.

And time didn't simply slow, or stagger, it froze.

Simeon's voice was choked off to nothing as he was surrounded by shimmering purple radiance, and Nyl's fall was arrested in midair as the weapons hummed, spinning a cocoon of light around their targets.

Light which solidified, crystallized - and held.

At last the hum snapped off, and Nyl clattered to the ground, encased in a shroud of amethyst. Blaire was similarly imprisoned, but he stood like a glass statue as the Ashishim stepped forward, brushing one beringed hand over the slippery purple surface of his cheek.

He stooped over the bound body of Technician Zhe, pushing back the hood of his robe...

To reveal wire-bound blue dreadlocks, deep purple eyes, and a band of violet tattoos snaking across pale skin. He wasn't a he at all...

It was CeeAn 187.

DOCUMENT INSERT: MULTIPLICITY ARCHIVES DEPARTMENT

The Good Field Operative's Guide To Continued
Corporeal Existence:
Chapter 902 - Procedures in the Face of Certain
Doom

When Confronted With a Type-B Slavesystem
(codename - Behemoth)

Description: The Type-B Behemoth resembles a
large spiked ball of metal some twelve miles in
diameter. It is a fusion of several smaller Type
b-1 and Type b-2 Slavesystems (Berserker and
Banshee) most often encountered in the vacuum of
three-dimensional space.

Follow our handy guide and learn how to contend
with this diabolical machine.

1. Are you an operative of Technician Grade or
    higher? (lower castes include all Peons,
    Menials, War Thralls and Clericals)

    If you answer was NO, then goodbye! Your death
    will be recorded as 'Marginally Honorable' in
    the Register of Glory.

2. Are you accompanied by a Devilfish, StarManta,
    Thresher or Teuthis Rex space combat symbiote?

    If you do, please retreat, utilizing Praetoriar
    MiliTech's patented Space Folding system™. Tell
    a higher Caste about the Behemoth! Remember, we
    no longer eat the bearers of bad news here in
    the Multiplicity.

3. Are you able to summon aid from your local
    Kataphrakt Command, or instigate an Inux Shorg
    elimination contract? Alternately, are you

armed with an antimatter cannon, a planetary
collapser, or a singularity generator?

If you can - please summon aid first - then
open fire from a minimum distance of twenty
light-minutes. DON'T LOOK THE SHORG DIRECTLY IN
THE EYE! In the Heavy Planes this constitutes
either a ritual challenge or an invitation
to sexual congress, neither of which you are
likely to survive.

4. I have no such weapons, nor the means to summon
    aid from my local military control node. What
    should I do?

As a Technician Grade operative or higher you
should be able to survive the Type-B's assault for
long enough to fill out a 9902-c form (application
for involuntary decommission). Please transmit
this form, along with your co-ordinates to the
Subpraetor for your currently occupied universe.

Thanks for choosing the G.F.O.G.T.C.C.E!
And remember - Keep Smiling!

17 Aevum Oblivio
Ultimatum

CeeAn loosed his bonds with a deft twist of her hands, allowing Zhe to stretch the kinks out of his muscles. Behind her the other Ashishim were loading the crystallized figures of Nyl and Blaire onto a hovering platform, ready to be fed into the belly of the Masslifter.

Seventeen years hadn't treated her too harshly, but there was a look of sorrow and fatigue on her face which he knew only too well.

"I always knew it wasn't him," she said, turning back to watch the crystallized Blaire being manhandled into the hold. "I knew him better than anyone, and when he came back from that last mission he was changed. More than that - he was gone." She fixed the Technician with a stare that all but nailed him to the ground with its intensity. "That was the night when Zeon betrayed us all. When I found out about your dirty war, and how we'd been caught up in it."

Zhe wanted to protest, to tell her about what would happen if the Forge was used by the wrong people. But he sensed the futility of it, and the words died somewhere between his translator module and his lips. This wasn't about whole planets.

It was about one man.

"So I've waited years for this. I've played the subservient fool to that damned usurper and that THING which called itself Illuminatus Zeon. I wanted to give one of your kind a message to take back to your masters."

CeeAn's eyes burned into him like fusion torches, infecting him with unfamiliar feelings.

Shame. Guilt.

"Tell them that with samples of both your Technician and this machine you call a Slavesystem, we can reprogram the Forge. Tell them that if they send their armadas here to Earth they'll be erased - as if they'd never existed."

Zhe struggled to his knees, still aching from his beating at the hands of Nyl.

"What makes you think they're coming here?" he asked, unable to meet her eyes. "I am the only one who was sent. He asked for me by name..."

Behind them, the masslifter was powering up, sending waves of dust scudding across the platform, the low thrum of its engines rising in pitch and volume.

"Poor creature." There was a look of real pity on Cee's face as she looked down on him. "I used to be a trusting servant like you, and look what it got me! You were nothing but bait. The ones you call the Unity are already here, out by Jupiter. The Multiplicity are hiding between the orbit of Mercury and the Sun."

Zhe suddenly felt a cold hand clutch at his vitals. He'd seen what happened when such forces collided. Perhaps it was an infection out of the Wetsystems, or the hangover from living in the mind of Kaito Kayzi. But Technician Zhe couldn't let it happen here.

He thought of the black, oily hunger of the Worm, of its delight in pain and torment, and he envisioned the immense feast it would have from the razing of this solar system.

Surely enough to crack reality wide open

So Zhe pulled up from his memory the only thing he knew would stop CeeAn in her tracks.

"Abdulafia is alive. He's being kept in cryostasis!"

Her hands were around his throat in a heartbeat, her face contorted into a snarl of rage.

"Seventeen years, creature!" she spat. "I lived with him being dead and gone for that long. If you're lying to me now, I'll..." But her anger collapsed in on itself, and her grip loosened enough for Zhe to draw breath.

"All I need is to finish my investigation, and I'll know how to wake him up. Him and the others. Kayzi. Jaqub Haszan."

CeeAn's hands dropped to her sides, as her red robes blew out in the blast of the Masslifter's engines. When she looked up at him, Zhe could see pain written across her face, and years of mistrust. But also, the tiniest trace of hope.

"You know that when they come for this place, we'll have to use the Forge," she said. "We won't have any choice."

Zhe nodded; he knew.

"I won't let it come to that," he said, as he turned back toward the rusted towers of the Last City. "Just give me as much time as you can."

CeeAn watched him go, her thoughts fading back to distant years, to the face of Abdulafia 330. For his sake, she would give the Technician as much time as he needed.

2196 Ante Arbitrium
Biotecture

A FIGURE MOVED *among clouds of steam, billowing dry-ice fog swirling in its wake. Abdulafia couldn't see the man's face, but he knew exactly who it was. Illuminatus Zeon, lord of the Ashishim.*

This was his memory - and 'Afia's dream.

Cold metal pods faded into the distance as far as Zeon's eyes could see in both directions. Only the thick glass ports drilled through their doors offered any illumination - an eerie green light sifting down through veils of mist.

His feet made no sound as he stepped lightly along a dangling coolant pipe high above the factory floor. This was no time to be seen or heard; it would be tedious and messy to slaughter his way out of here through a legion of Lancaster's little pets...

The clatter and scrape of those slave bioconstructs echoed in the immense metal sepulcher of the Gene-loom. Things like skinned dogs with guns for faces loped back and forth below him, while now and then a humanoid form reared up against the sickly light - hulking and neckless, the laser rangefinders of its weapons slithering across the pipes and rafters.

They guarded a machine the size of a six-storey office block – the only Assembler in Elysium which crafted living flesh from raw elements. This was the Gene-loom, as hissing, frost-rimed monster which Zeon was here to subvert.

He was cloaked in Ashishim holomesh – a thin skin of invisibility wrapped tight around his shoulders. It was as much for the chill as to deceive the living security systems of the Loom, because Lancaster kept his workfloor at a cool minus-three. The intelligent fabric painted Zeon across the ceramic walls as a second skin of frost, a shadow among shadows.

The watchdogs and ogres which stood guard here had no imagination. They could neither see him nor stop him as he closed in on his target.

A single pool of white light cast from far above by a hovering dragonfly ornithopter. Its halogen eyes illuminated two sharp-dressed figures, poised before a single vast, steaming machine...

He'd been here before, of course - checking on the progress of this illicit little project. He'd seen the Loom of the biotects grinding out the clone bodies of innumerable Kheptarchs, the fresh new organs for thousands of paying customers.

The bio-manufactorium always seemed a sterile place, as fertile as a mill for stamping out auto parts. But this time the machinery he knew so well hummed with life, an almost palpable aura throbbing inside it. Within its glass and chrome womb, an atrocity was waiting to be born...

One of the men wiped a smooth white hand over the dewy pane, and he could finally see the face of his target. The face of a child, sleeping drowned in green light, in bubbling nutrient fluid.

"*He* has the title, but I've got the cash - and that's what really makes this city tick, isn't it, Excellency?" asked the figure still in shadow, his face illuminated red for a second as he puffed on a giant cigar. "We both know that you'd never advance me the honor of joining your little games – but you *can* help fix them. It'll make for some excellent television."

Lancaster winced, as though the thought of money pained him.

"Of course *you* could never play, Direktor. You're in a position to know that the DownTown league doesn't get a third of the ratings that the High Game does. And just like you'd never dirty yourself by fighting in the gore pits, so we would never let you join the Razor Clique. The prize is simply too great."

The Direktor came forward out of the darkness, grinning like a shark. The ashes he tapped off the end of his cigar spiraled to the floor to be swept up by a pair of modified cockroaches.

"So do you think I've given young Blaire a good enough chance of winning? He'll be eligible to enter in just a few years time – and nobody but us will know that he's not the original."

"Well – much as it irks me to say it, there's nothing in the rules to contradict what you're doing here. His mind will still be that of a Scion of House Blaire, even if his body is pieced together from a thousand pitfighters."

"That was the sad little mind that tried to kill itself, Manny," chuckled Vanecke, drawing deeply on his stogie. "If he'd succeeded, his old man would have been livid. At his age it would be a real effort to sire an heir, what with the celebrants breathing down his neck. That, and the *money* of course. There's always the money."

Lancaster ran his alabaster finger through the condensation on the machine's window panel, sketching out a dollar sign. The rune of currency, even with the old United States blown away as dust...

"Direktor, you've read my mind. There is, I fear, always the money. I have no illusions that this *thing* will become Emperor of Elysium.

He's to be nothing but a ratings booster and a foil for the gambling cartels. I'll tell the Commissioner and the Council what we've done if he gets within spitting distance of the Trials – even if that means paying billions in penalties."

Now it was the Direktor's turn to scowl, ripping his wallet from out of his tailored coat.

"If I can't rule this ant-hill myself, Excellency, then I don't want a monster like *him* in control either. I'll thank you to keep your power-mad paranoia to yourself – and to your precious Lords."

"You're young, Vanecke, so I'll let that go," said the Biotect, his voice coldly calm. "Forty years may seem a long time to a lowborn, but to me... you're only a child. This thing I've made for you is just another toy."

Octavio scrawled off a cheque, and held it out to be snapped up by Lancaster's long pale fingers.

"Of course he's just a ratings stunt, Emmanuel. I *always* play the long game, and I'm willing to wait a few years for him to ripen. Just keep this one growing - when he's eligible and his father's been *seen to* we'll make the switch."

The Direktor turned to leave, his coat swirling about his shoulders in the clammy air.

"Don't fool yourself, Manny. I know you've kept back embryos for your own experiments. I know your type, Excellency, because *I'm one of them* – even without a title."

"Preposterous!" spluttered the biotect lord, his composure slipping. "I only agreed to make you one of these things because you mortgaged your network down to the paperclips to do it! Watch the markets, Vanecke! Watch what happens when trading opens tomorrow!"

But the footsteps and the laughter of Octavio Vanecke were fading now, back into the green-tinted mist from whence they had come. Lancaster was alone with the creature he had created, floating serenely behind the cold glass of its mechanical womb.

"Forgive me, Simeon. And I hope your father forgives me, too. But when all this is over, you'll thank me. You *would*, if you could ever know..."

The hidden watcher waited until the arch-biotect had walked away, towing the ornithopter light behind him by infrared. He waited until the only illumination came from behind the glass, where bubbles seethed and roiled in green liquid, floating over skin incised with patterns of silver wires.

Of course Emmanuel Lancaster had been lying. His paranoia was the stuff of legends, even amid the literally cut-throat business politics of the Kheptarchy. He *had* made a copy of the Blaire clone – a single copy which had not been subjected to the force-growth systems its brother now endured. It was the work of moments to prize open the hidden panel in the side of the machine, as he had seen Lancaster do so many times. A couple of seconds more, and he had routed the system around the little glass bubble which was his target; a cylinder containing a single frozen human fetus.

When he snapped the containment vessel out of its housing there was no alarm, no slamming bulkhead doors or flashing red strobes. He slid the cylinder gently into a custom-made carrier module which hung from his chest on a web of leather straps, connected its batteries, and fastened the panel behind him.

He had come here to destroy both of the Blaire clones, to keep the frighteningly ambitious Direktor Vanecke away from the throne of Elysium. But now he saw what a living weapon like this could become, he couldn't help but take a chance. After all, which environment would produce the better warrior? Stuffy, cloistered Elysium – or the hardscrabble world of the rad-lands?

He had welded a band of tribes wandering among the ruins of the world into a fighting force with more technological knowledge and power at their disposal than any other. He had taught a generation of children how to fight, and a select few of them had been initiated into even greater secrets, founding the sects of the *Dervashi* and the *Magi*. Did he really think that when the time came the Blaire trained by his Academy would be bested by one schooled in the arts of war by a jumped-up corporate executive?

It was a long way back to the Pit, where his agents amid the tribes of the Warlords waited to spirit this prize away, over the sea to the north, into the ruins of Fortress Europe. Where the child would grow, and mature into a deadly vessel of power, his right hand in the war against Kronos. He would one day show him the secret of the Magi, and make him a legend among his people. They would know his designation and his name, and revere them.

He would call him *Abdulafia*.

Ω

The name struck him like a fist.

It was a pain greater even than the hole in his chest, more sickening in its totality than the moment when Jhenna, despairing, had met his eyes and fallen.

What had he just seen?

Lies, surely. But then he caught himself scrabbling desperately for denial, and slowly, agonizingly, the truth dawned on him.

"That *was* me, wasn't it?" he asked, his voice hard and brittle in the white silence of virtual space. "And I can't remember my parents because *I don't have any*. I was never born. I was... *made*. Like a chair, or a gun, or a wrench. I was *built*."

He turned to face the Illuminatus, his head churning with rage. And then he saw the tired, sad look on the old man's face, and the hot coil of anger in him unraveled.

"Was I wrong to let you live, little cousin?" asked Zeon quietly. "When you can tear down men such as those who made you - and their city with them? When you can encompass revenge for the ones you've lost today?"

Abdulafia looked down at his hands, knowing they were nothing but a representation, but searching every pixel for a blemish, a seam, something that marked him out as artificial.

"If I was created just to kill, then you *were* wrong, Illuminatus. And one of the war-machines I should have called a brother has fixed your mistake."

He half expected to see wires and gears through the red hole in his chest, for his pain to be replaced by error messages. But he still felt it, even here. Life burned in him so very keenly as it slipped away. And he *did* want revenge. He could remember the savage joy of watching that dead-faced Cyben ripping itself apart...

"Revenge needs hatred to exist, Abdulafia 330. And hate just isn't something a machine can feel. If you want to satisfy that hunger, you have to live. That's the opportunity which I'm here to offer you."

The Illuminatus closed one hand and opened it again, slowly, conjuring a spinning ball of fire in his palm.

"You were bred for war, but so many have been, down through the centuries. So what? You have that the Spartans or the Nazi super-soldiers or the Helix Force lacked - an integrated combat system. The Khepts' machine has lain dormant in your bones for your entire life, but I can awaken it now."

In the whirling ball of fire Abdulafia could see the faces of his squadmates, screaming, burning, torn apart. He could see the great wave of the Ashishim advance breaking against the walls of Elysium while thousands died.

Hypnotized, he reached out for it, only for the Illuminatus to snatch it away, caging it in his wizened fingers.

"Be warned, little cousin – it will be a pain which few can endure. If you fail to master the machinery while it grows in your bones then *it will master you*. And then you'll be a thrall to the machine… or to those who made you."

Abdulafia recalled the thin, sour face of Lord Lancaster and the crazed eyes of Direktor Vanecke, and he shuddered. Better to die than to live out the destiny those monsters had laid out for him – that his genetic twin was no doubt suffering through.

"Give it to me!" he shouted, his voice shaking the virtual world, sending hairline cracks racing through the white walls, through his own illusory flesh. "They killed us all. They killed *me*. They killed Jhenna!" With each word screaming faces crowded and whirled around his head, and the ball of fire in Illuminatus Zeon's hand grew, blazing blue and green, enveloping his arm to the elbow.

AND. THEY. WILL. DIE!

Each scream rocked the universe like the blow of a hammer. Abdulafia felt his pain crystallize like the blue coagulant in the Cyben's blood, becoming a hard core of fury. It burned as it transfixed him, driving his muscles like pistons.

Nothing in creation could have stopped his hand coming down to meet that of his Illuminatus; their palms met in a spray of incandescent fire with all the force of colliding continents.

And Zeon's promise was true – there was pain.

It was a scalding baptism in living magma, a clawing storm of knives and broken glass ripping through his flesh. Each nerve was flayed, each muscle and sinew stretched tight, his bones boiling with molten lead.

Behind the tidal-wave of agony he held himself together by sheer force of will, watching the Illuminatus melt away, his virtual world collapsing in shards to shatter against pain, to melt in pain, to boil in suffering.

The dormant Gladius system which had slept in his flesh came to life in that great outpouring of agony. It sent tentacles and roots of steel clawing through his body, binding, reinforcing, strengthening. He could sense its cold, purposeful intelligence constricting his mind, and he saw how a weaker consciousness would be scoured away by the pain; lose itself in the embrace of the machine.

It was his rage which saved him, a red-hot anchor which he clung to with blistering hands – a link to the reality in which he had bloody work to do. When the Gladius tried to connect to Kronos he was there a step ahead of it, and his anger cauterized those probing tentacles, locking it inside. He enslaved it, and with its submission the pain began to recede. Hungry tendrils of metal punched out through his skin to bleed off excess heat, unfurling fern-frond wings.

It was done. *It was his.*

Abdulafia felt the great gaping wound in his chest begin to close up, knitting together smoothly, the pain a memory, an echo... The Gladius might not have had the forbidden power of self-replication, but it was clever enough to keep him alive, at least until he could reach the surgical-priests of the Ashishim.

He opened his eyes, and he smiled.

When the red blur which filled his world faded he could see a gas-masked medic leaning over him, shining the painfully bright beam of a flashlight in his face. Behind the foggy glass of the man's mask his eyes were wide with astonishment.

"Sweet Gods, we've got a live one over here!" He turned and shouted over one shoulder to a figure obscured by smoke – one of a dozen picking through the debris of the ruined manufactorium. "Captain – a survivor!"

Abdulafia groaned theatrically and let his eyes roll back in their sockets. In the medic's faceplate he had seen his reflection – a deathmask of blood and blisters. Nobody who looked like that could possibly get up, let alone fight...

The Captain came running, his uniform singed and bloodied, unarmed but for a threedeeo tablet and stylus. A face protruded from the tablet is if it was pressed through a sheet of plastic, and Abdulafia caught a memory-flash of black Cyben eyes, cold desiccated skin ...

"He's just a kid, Commissioner! Those nomad filth are sending their women and children against us to die... nothing more."

"Take a closer look, Captain," insisted the face in the threedeeo tablet, its haggard features contorted into an impatient scowl. "This *child* has destroyed a crack unit of our new Cyben troopers; he's taken a direct hit from an E-77 railgun. And he's still breathing!"

Audane pressed his lips together in a tight angry line, biting back some choice insubordination. But the medic was already clawing open Abdulafia's Kevlar vest, exposing a crust of congealed blood, a halo-ring of purple-black bruises – and a plug of white scar tissue shot through with strands of silver.

"He's hot with augmentations! Gods help us, they've got *combat integrated*!"

The Captain hauled him upright by one shoulder pauldron as he scrabbled back across the floor.

"Panic's not gonna make him any less infected, Sambel! Johanssen, Lake, cover him with your railguns. Kincaid, alert processing that we have one coming in for interrogation. Integrated or not, those boys will know how to break him."

The face in the threedeeo smiled humorlessly, and focused its milky eyes on Captain Audane.

"Hit him with tranks and make sure he's delivered to the interrogation tanks in one piece. We want to take that Gladius system out of him *surgically* and see who supplied it. And of course we must know how many more of these... 'kids'... the nomads have at their disposal."

"At once, Sir" answered Audane, snapping off a salute. "Forgive... forgive my presumptions. I never thought that they'd..."

The screen gave a bitter laugh.

"Oh, you'd best believe it, soldier. We'll have to be just as unprincipled as these nomads if we want to see victory! I've already called up the civilian auxilia – cripples and grandfathers. None of *them* have stolen combat augments!"

The screen went dead and blank, the holo of Commissioner Slade collapsing into a hash of pixels. Abdulafia saw it all – the ashen look on Audane's face, the muttered curses and meaningful glances. The shaking hands of medical officer Sambel as he loaded an autoinjector...

Wait. Surely that was meant for...

The needle snapped off in his arm as his muscles turned to fibrous cords, and with a twist he pulled the plastic injector pistol from Sambel's hands. He caught the briefest glance at the medic's eyes behind their plastic bubble, and they were lit up with horror, reflecting the blaze of orange glyphs sleeting across his own.

Information. Uploads. Data integrating, wires twisting through his brain...

He was combat integrated. And these weak, unsure Elysians – they were his prey.

With that thought files and schematics filled his mind's eye, training routines flickering through his brain like ghosts. Months of integration therapy compressed and folded into needles of glass, force-fed into his spine through a battery of humming neuroconnectors...

His legs spun sideways, tripping Sambel as he twisted to his feet. Before the medic could right himself Abdulafia reversed the trank injector and pumped a knockout dose into his neck. The low, rumbling cough of gunfire underpinned a chorus of screams as he grinned.

Even as the Sambel's limp body fell from his hands he was moving, exultant in his own slow-motion world, the slugs from the squad's railguns inching past him through the air. A step left, a twist right, and they were past him, his right fist connecting with the jaw of one trooper and lifting him three feet clear off the ground. The autoinjector flew from his left hand like a dart, piercing the leg of another.

Bursts of fire tracked him, pitifully slow. He slipped between the interlocking rows of bullets as if in a dream, closing in on the squad leader and his threedeeo tablet.

Now the wires and servos were burning inside him, a cage of hot metal bringing back echoes of the pain of his rebirth. In time, Abdulafia would learn the limits of his wire endoskeleton – the point beyond which it rebelled against the flesh with sickening consequences. But for now the pain was goad, a reminder of his rage and loss, and it drove him to even greater speed, even greater strength and cruelty.

He gripped the helmet of another Elysian and twisted the man's head off with a fast flick of the wrists, using the man's body as a human shield even as he twisted the machine pistol from his hands, firing. A kick to the crotch shattered a trooper's pelvis and sent him flying across the manufactorium in an arc of blood. Another felt the touch of two fingers at his throat, then the sizzle and crack of a tazer burst cut him down.

It was all over in a hundred heartbeats. The whole squad lay broken at his feet, moaning and screaming and dying...

Abdulafia's hands clamped down on the Captain's shoulders, and the world slammed back into focus. Red icons were blinking and shimmering across his eyes as the Gladius system pushed thermal overload. Blood spattered his face like warpaint, hot and sticky.

"P...please! Please! We surrender! You... you've killed them all!"

He took it in. Scattered limbs, nameless shreds of skin, bullet casings steaming in pools of blood... There was a second of shock in which Abdulafia couldn't believe he was the architect of such carnage. Then the image of Jhenna's face as she died came back to him, and he tightened his steely fingers around Audane's neck.

"And you killed all of *us*, Elysian. You even killed me."

"Wha? You... you're crazy, man! This is *real!* You're not dead!"

The bone-deep scorching heat of the Gladius system began to ebb away as cooling vanes unfurled from his shoulders, a maze of spirals and curls glowing red and white. Heat-haze mirages loomed up behind the young *Dervashi*, glass ghosts boiling away to nothing...

"Oh, I died here today, Captain. It's just a good thing I don't catch on too fast. The question is... do you?"

An instant ago Captain Audane was in control of the situation, methodically planning his defense of the spillway. The nomad was his prisoner, and he was already calculating firing positions for the auxilia conscripts. Now, in an eyeblink, the hotwired Ashishi kid was crushing his windpipe between his fingers.

"Anything! I'll tell you anything! Name it!"

Audane gagged and gasped, thrashing impotently at Abdulafia's face with his threedeeo tablet.

"What have you got," grated 'Afia. That *I* want?"

Staring into those target-reticule eyes Audane was sure he was a dead man. There was nothing in the kid's vacant stare to suggest mercy - or even sanity. Weals of painful crimson stood out from his skin where the Gladius system burned along his bones, filling the air with a sickening aroma of charred flesh. Audane felt his tracheal bones cracking and splintering under the terrible pressure. But then the threedeeo tablet caught Abdulafia a glancing blow across the temple, and its glassy surface flashed into life.

Light blossomed out from the tablet's screen, and as it washed over Abdulafia's face he deflated, his hands unknotting from Audane's throat. The Elysian staggered backward, his lips blue, a thin trickle of blood dripping from the corner of his mouth.

"Please..." he croaked, holding up the threedeeo block like a talisman. "You can have it. You can have the codes! Just don't kill me!"

Abdulafia stepped forward and snatched the tablet from Audane's trembling hands. With his scarred and steaming skin, his fevered eyes and the smoking wings blazing on each shoulder he looked like a demon of vengeance.

"The code... it's oh nine three seven G-V-B..." stuttered Audane, scrabbling backward away from the grim-faced nomad. "Please...oh Kronos, please..."

The Elysian squeezed his eyes shut tight, waiting for the inevitable hammer blow which would finish him off. A second passed, and then two. He was still breathing. He was still alive...

Cautiously Audane cracked one eye open, and then the other. All around him the ruins of his squad were bleeding and groaning, and the manufactorium was a smoking ruin. But there was no trace of the nomad commando, not even the echo of his footsteps fading away across the steel floor. Cold terror clamped down on Audane then – he'd given the damned Ashishi the tablet! He had given him the CODE! And worse, he'd been pleading a blubbering like a coward. Perhaps it was for the best that none of his soldiers had been alive to see that part... but it scarcely mattered anyway. Commissioner Slade was going to kill him - and that was if he was *lucky*.

Far above, running lightly along a suspended girder, Abdulafia probed and tested the limits of his new body. He was pleased with what he found; not least that in battle he was taken out of himself, detached, watching from far above as he killed on automatic...

That was right. That was good. He didn't want to feel anything - didn't *deserve* to share joy and pain with human beings. He had been *forged*, constructed in a lab for this bloody task.

So if he was going to be the right hand of the Illuminatus, a weapon with a face and eyes and a heart, then he'd be a killing machine without remorse. It was the least he could do for Gray Seven, for Jhenna, and for the people who he had thought were his family, the parents he'd never had.

The screen of the threedeeo tablet seethed with data, a portal into the vast machineries of Elysium, into the mind of Kronos itself.

But most importantly, it was a key – not only to the spillway gates, but to the respect of his fellow Electromagi. If his path was chosen, then there was no way that Abdulafia was going to wait for advancement by dead men's boots...

Minutes later the Elysian soldiers clustered behind their sandbags and concrete barricades felt the city shake, and heard the immense bass grind of hydraulics and cogs meshing and shifting. Behind them one of the great spillway gates was opening, rammed ajar by pistons the size of battleship cannons.

Slowly, painfully, the yard-thick steel slab cracked open, gaping wider and wider as the Vatican and Ashishim forces below let out a victorious cheer. Immense curves of pale lightning came crashing down from the Chrome Ark, leaving sizzling mechanical wreckage in their wake. And the Elysians broke.

Cyben held the line, too few in number to hold back the assault. Even so, the grisly constructs were fearsome in close combat, meeting the rush of Ashishi warriors and Vatican Templars like a steel wall.

Their speed was a match for the elite *Dervashi* of the Ashishim, whose blurring steel blades were a quicksilver rain. And their immense strength was enough to match the armored Vatican Knights; hulking Paladins and Templars, fire-spitting Sentinels and chain-bladed Teutons. The force waves crashing against Elysium from the Chrome Ark could never take down so many at once, and the Magi wielding that ancient weapon had other targets to deal with – autogun turrets, spider-legged warmekan and rusting flamespitters. So the fight was brought to the Cyben with overwhelming numbers and unabated fury.

Abdulafia watched it all from atop one of the immense spillway gates, a mere shimmer in the air sketching his outline around the Gladius system's holofield. His eyes were fixed on the tiny figures who circled the Ark, and especially on the man who wielded its energy, more fiercely now than ever as the assault breached the gates and began to move into the echoing caverns beneath the city. Despite his cloaking, and despite the distance, the smoke, and the roar of battle between them the Illuminatus spotted Abdulafia on his perch above the fray, and threw him a salute with one copper-studded gauntlet.

'Afia waved back, narrowing his eyes as he tried to read the expression on his leader's face. He was beholden to the Illuminatus and his cause – more so than ever, now. But he'd be a fool to entirely trust *anyone*, even a man considered by his tribe to be a living god.

Switch it – Gray Seven a sacrifice, thrown away to give him the gift of hate. Pick the Illuminatus for a political creature, willing to send the Disposables off to the slaughter. Frame 'Afia as his newest, sharpest toy, worth a handful of grunts just for his motivation...

And he'd remember, long after the rest of this bloody day had faded into sporadic nightmares and twitches, that it was a Cyben who pulled the trigger, it was Kronos who started the war. But it was the Illuminatus who made sure that the face he saw in his night-terrors was that of Jhenna, hopeless and scared and doomed, falling eternally into an unseen abyss.

That was the dream which gripped him now, which shook his mind between bloody jaws.

The black abyss, the fall... traces of Zone Doubt, static from his descent into the mills of Kronos. Sharp barbed stabs of psionic agony, tracing the outlines of Magus Verlaine, the whirling concentric black blades, the cold ichor flooding his mind –

And the Illuminatus, his face all decay and rot... all but the flashing, boiling silver of his eyes.

Abdulafia came awake with a choking scream, his fist closing around the leg of Jaqub Haszan like a torsion clamp. His eyes rolled and twitched in bleeding sockets as if they were trying to escape from his skull.

"Sweet ancestral hells!" he gasped, struggling to sit up "Verlaine... it's inside his mind! *It's coming!*"

17 Aevum Oblivio
Detente

THAT WAS HOW the Seven Hours War started, at least for one child of the Ashishim. The true story of the Reclamation was written in the bones of the dead, the blackened stains of blood enshrined on the spillway where martyrs and heroes were blown apart...

Zhe watched it all unfold in a second – the Aryan assault on the twin watchtowers, the last desperate charge of the Red Sentinels, the war-barges of the Celestials ramming into the Elysian docks in a cascade of rusting containers and collapsing cranes and booms.

The legends of the Seven Hours War, written in blood and bullets and twisted steel. They all speak of the fulcrum of the united assault – of how when the spillway doors came open the battle became one of fierce attrition, building-to-building skirmishes between desperate nomads and implacable Cyben.

But only Kronos, the Illuminatus, and now a certain Technician of the Multiplicity knew how the war ended, and why the Forbidden Systems - the relics of the Aevum Iudicuio - were never leveled against the outlander horde.

It began with the flicker and pop of neon lights.

Zhe watched as a dusty cathedral chamber atop the city was cast into eerie illumination, as sacristry-mekan moved among the most deadly relics of man like steel ghosts. Some of the devices left over from the Age of Judgment were obvious in their intent; tanks and artillery pieces, hulking automata bristling with cannons, even row upon row of nuclear weapons. Others were unfathomable tangles of wires and tubes, featureless black boxes, pulsing spheres of energy wrapped in gauss cages. In chilled metal halls rested batteries of phials containing viruses and flesh-eating bacteria. Tanks of nerve gas steamed and sweated in icy, echoing crypts.

And in locked-down reliquaries rimed with frost slept the most potent of all weapons - self-replicating crystal mycelia like those which coiled through Simeon Blaire's flesh, and which powered the tortured body of Eddie Tsien...

It was all being brought back online, the last line of defense for Kronos and his three hundred sacrosanct Kheptarchs, the pure geneline of *homo sapiens*. Even the machine itself couldn't guess at the destructive potential of some of its toys; things designed as last-ditch weapons of terror by the hysterical regimes of old earth. One unobtrusive little device - barely the size of a cigarette packet - was designed to send the sun nova. A capsule of glass the size of a robin's egg held enough of a genewritten bacterium to rot the living bones of a thousand times Elysium's population. And there were so many more...

Somewhere amid this cornucopia of destruction Zhe hoped he'd find weapons powerful enough to stop the armada which was descending on the planet, into the eye of the Forge. His mind rode shotgun in the camera network; he skipped from lens to lens in the green-tinted gloom, searching for connections, for codes, for controls...

First came a crawling storm of static, the hiss and pop of detonating motes of dust. The black marble floor writhed with streamers of lightning as something tried to break through the vault's nigh-impregnable shielding. And then, as the sacristan-mekan fell twitching, a hole appeared in the stale and ozone-heavy air. A phantom of silver light stepped through into the cathedral transept of the armory, shifting like mercury until it possessed a face, hands - and a voice.

"Kronos! Hear me!" shouted Illuminatus Zeon, his gauntleted hands spread wide to encompass all the weapons of death stacked around him. "Kronos! I come before you to negotiate for peace!"

There was no sign that the ancient machine had heard him for almost a minute. Each second seemed to drag out, molten, as the shadows dipped and flickered. Then from the left and right of the glowing Illuminatus came a titanic grinding sound, and laser targeters stabbed out through the darkness. Kronos pulled the strings of his puppets like a necromancer raising bones; two antiquated war-mekan hammered out of the war-factories of old Brazil. Flakes of green and yellow paint showered down from the immense automata as they walked, ball-joints protesting and hydraulic couplings dripping red.

They may have been hopelessly obsolete; scarred and abused, crudely stenciled with numbers and phrases in Portuguese, but they'd been made to hunt down battle-tanks, and their rotary missile launchers were locked and loaded.

The Illuminatus looked unconcerned - as well he might, thought Zhe. For the 'Illuminatus' was no human being, but the renegade Technician Nyl, and even the most concentrated high-explosive would only scratch his exotic-metal skin. Still, there was no sign of Kronos, just the hulking menace of his thralls. Another minute ticked by, and another.

Then the high lord of the Ashishim brought his hands up to his face, claws flashing in the red eyebeams of the warmekan. With a scream like diamonds cutting glass he dug those wicked points into his flesh, working them in deep, down to the bone. Blood gushed and bubbled around his fingers as he began to rake at his hairline, at his temples...

"Is this what it takes, machine? Is this what you wanted to see?"

With a wet ripping sound the Illuminatus tore off his face and flung it to the ground, a mask of bloody skin with empty staring eyeholes. Beneath that false face there was no gory, blood-slicked skull – just a mass of writhing silver, meshing and coiling about the twin fires of his incandescent eyes.

If Zhe had needed an excuse to drag the renegade technician up before his Praetor in disgrace, here it was. The highest protocols of the Multiplicity expressly forbade revealing the truth to unenlightened alien species. A Technician could find himself enshrined in some primitive mythology, deified or demonized for centuries before the primitives were assimilated. It made the whole process so much more awkward for everyone...

"Kronos! I'm here to broker peace, not to surrender! So you should know that I'm here on behalf of my *human* allies, not my own kind. Not one of these ugly toys will do you any good."

A little white lie, Zhe noted – some of the more powerful devices here would probably be able to considerably discomfort even a Kataphrakt for several minutes.

"I'll take your whole foolish human race with me if you don't give me what I ask for, you idiot machine! You won't be the first, not by a long way!"

Now his whole body was changing, flowing and rippling, reverting to the lean and wiry form of a true Technician. Nyl was humanoid but utterly alien, jointed in all the wrong places, his collarbone sweeping up past his shoulders as a pair of silver fins. The writhing worms which made up his face and body slicked over smooth as he stretched the kinks from his insect limbs, leaving him a spindly homunculus in chrome, spiked from his shoulders to the base of his question-mark spine.

His blazing white eyes flared and smoked in the gloom, a promise of destruction far more potent than even the laser-targeters of the hulking warmekan.

But now something was approaching. From down the long hall of the armory came a pale river of mist, carrying the unmistakable ammonia smell of cryogenics. From within the roiling cloud came spears and flickers of light, throwing broken shadows across the walls. Amid them, another shadow - one which walked.

Zhe frantically tried to upgrade the picture, but there was no way to bring the phantom figure into focus. The thing which faced Techniciar Nyl in its cloud of chilling mist was blurry and indistinct, its features merging and shifting second by second. Even its outline was hazy, its size and dimensions as fluid as its face.

"You have my attention," sung the avatar of Kronos in a voice like a mismatched choir. "Although your vulgar little piece of theater was hardly necessary. I've known that the Illuminatus of the Ashishim was *unhuman* for a year or two now. The fact is immaterial. There are only three hundred true humans left on this planet, and *I* was made to keep them."

One of the immense Brazilian warmekan lumbered around behind him, crouching and folding in upon itself to form a rusted steel throne. Kronos clambered up over the mekan's bulky knee servos, settling himself in a prim and folded pose.

"I suppose you've come here to take my Forge, like all the others?" asked the avatar in his motley voice. "None of them ever left this place, Illuminatus. But then again, none of them tried to storm my city with an old-fashioned siege, either."

Nyl approached the throne, for once unsure of his plans. This wasn't the machine he had envisioned – this was a much more dangerous animal. Logic rarely worked on living things. And it had known his secret... how much else had it fathomed of his schemes?

"Lord Kronos, I must apologize for the zeal of my followers. If others have come before me to try and steal your precious Forge I can see why you would be... *cautious*. But believe me, that isn't what we have in mind at all."

Kronos leaned forward from his throne, his ever-shifting face a succession of disbelieving scowls.

"Sixteen alien species have come here for the Forge, Illuminatus. Sixteen in sixteen hundred years. Am I to believe that you and your people have no desire to possess *godhood*?"

Nyl grinned, a razor slash across his silver face.

"You misunderstand me, Lord. My people have advanced past energy patterning and nanotech centuries ago. And we have no desire to steal this planet out from under you. No... we'll leave godhood on the shelf. I come from the reality of Liquid Space, and I represent a race known as the Multiplicity. *Our* God is very real, and not very fond of pretenders."

"Then you come to *proseletyze*, perhaps? To add another world to your theocracy?"

Nyl smiled, a humorless needle grin.

"We are an empire of whole galaxies, machine - and our Praetor has no need for a single rotten little planet like this. But I *have* come here to oppose a greater enemy – one who *does* want to steal your toys and your pets and your world."

A sphere of light burst from Nyl's outstretched hand, softening and expanding to become a threedeeo globe ten feet across. In its shimmering depths Zhe saw images of war; the Slavesystems of the Unity throwing themselves against Multiplicity defenses with berserker abandon.

It had been years since he had been a front-line tech, but the sight still sent a shiver of dread and joy through Zhe's alien body. In the threedeeo he watched wheeling and diving Devilfish raking the Blacksteel with acid and spikes, he saw noble Kataphrakts scything their blades through the bodies of mechanical Hoplites and Lobsterbacks.

Faster and faster the pictures flashed through the globe – planets razed and frozen and exploded from their cores, space fleets drowned in radiation, thrall-species extinguished in the name of the great war between the Motherbrain and Liquid Space.

"The machines of the Unity are as far beyond *you* as *I* am beyond your tame apes, Kronos. I have seen the Cogitators of the enemy, and they are brains the size of suns. In their home dimension the Blacksteel have crushed all resistance, all natural life. And they know about you, Kronos."

It was impossible to gauge the emotions of the ever-shifting avatar on its mechanical throne, but Zhe swore he saw a strobe-burst of worried faces sleet through its firmament.

"The Umbraeic of Draco told me they had no need of the Forge, alien," said Kronos, leaning forward from his seat. "But still they tried to steal it. The Qi'gaar came from a dominion of crystal, and claimed to need the Forge to rebuild their dying suns. And when I refused them they tried to steal it too. Why should I believe you over them?"

Nyl froze the threedeeo globe on an image of a Blacksteel Colossus grinding its foot down on an alien city and walked around the glittering sphere, one silver claw rippling its surface.

"Because I really don't need your precious Forge to defeat my enemies, Kronos. It won't hurt them, in the end, *because it's just like them.* The Blacksteel are a nanotech virus with a mind spanning galaxies, and they can already turn whole worlds into scrap and slag for their furnaces. Their way takes a little longer than yours, but time doesn't mean a thing to creatures who are *built* and not born, who are upgraded infinitely - but never die."

Kronos was face to face with the renegade technician now, hologram meeting hologram in a haze of peripheral static.

"If I were to believe your stories about this Blacksteel, Illuminatus, what would you say they wanted with the Earth?"

"*Existing technology.* A swifter way to build a portal into this dimension. The Unity are unable to shift from one universe to another as we of the Multiplicity can. They need vast technological resources to open a gateway from one of their slaveworlds – but once that gate is open it can never be closed again. They fire off scouting systems at random into the Chasm, and hope that one out of every billion comes across a planet such as this."

Nyl reached out to touch his holosphere, and the image shifted again, becoming a dead planet encased in a metal skin. One hemisphere of the broken world gaped open, a crater the size of a continent ringed with blazing orange fires. From within the gate came a never-ending stream of cylindrical Blacksteel ships, a convoy of death fanning out across the stars of some alien galaxy.

"A Unity scout cannot mine, or construct machines, or turn a barren rock into a gate like this. But it can subvert *primitive technology* – no insult intended, I assure you – and make a path for its brothers. That is the intent of Blacksteel Slavesystem -⊏1945 86a5 7456 5287 4632 4879 562d 3456 2349 85c6 9783 465h⊐ - an explorator machine traced into this dimension by my masters. It has detected electronic transmissions sent out from this planet centuries ago, and its purpose is to sequestrate *you.*"

Technician Zhe gnashed his needle teeth in frustration as the renegade skipped from treason to treason. If Nyl had known a Blacksteel explorator was coming to Earth he should have informed the Praetorian Council immediately!

The 'steel were slow, ponderous enemies, but each one of them took a lot of destroying. This Earth would need at least a unit of Jarls or a Kataphrakt to defend it – although, Zhe admitted to himself, such annihilating power would probably split the poor little planet in half.

Zhe made another note in his mission log; another justification for mind-wiping the rogue Technician. But the threedeeo was still rolling, and the worst was yet to come.

"That's the core of my mission here, Kronos," said Nyl, collapsing the great scintillating globe within which worlds and galaxies fell to the Blacksteel Unity. "I mean to not only *stop* the explorator system, but to *enslave* it. When I succeed, you can keep it with your other war trophies, right here." Nyl gestured around him with one silvery hand, taking in the ranks of battlemekan, missiles, bombs and tanks crowded into the spiretop aerie. "I think that in this dimension, in this place, it has a weakness. I mean to prove to my masters that this Slavesystem and all its kind can be bent to our will."

Technician Zhe would hardly have believed what he was hearing, if he hadn't already faced Nyl's renegade Slavesystem up on the Cardinal Rock. The memory of those seething black golems piling over him, motes of intelligent metal burrowing into his flesh – it was almost too much to take.

But now he saw the seeds of Nyl's plan taking root. There was a weakness here, an anomaly which enabled the renegade Technician to manipulate the Blacksteel.

And other powers too. Things less wholesome even than a universe-spanning metal virus...

Zhe had felt the coiling darkness of the thing which called itself the Worm Asag'raal, in those agonizing minutes when Nyl had tried to integrate them, darkness and steel and flesh, into one monstrous hybrid. Nyl had taken something from that metamorphosis; Zhe was glad that he was now frozen in crystal, a prisoner of the very sect he used to lead.

Awakening Nyl was out of the question – he would stay locked in his amethyst tomb until Zhe could drag him before the Prime Praetor for judgment.

But somehow he would still have to stop the war fleets of both the Multiplicity and the Unity. If Nyl had defeated a Slavesystem with his hybrid technology, Zhe would have to do the same for a whole armada of them.

Zhe watched him through the eyes of the omnipresent security cameras - one of his own selling out his whole species.

"And I suppose that you'll need to command the Forge - *for my own protection*? Or perhaps just some of the choicest pieces from my little collection here?" asked Kronos, his face sliding and shifting, androgynous and blurred. "Because that's not going to happen, alien. Anyone can make up horror-stories to frighten the credulous. They sometimes call it *religion.*"

At this, Nyl's smile cracked wider and wider, a jagged gash running almost all the way around his head.

"I told you, machine, I don't need your toys. All I need is your *resources.* Whether you believe in them or not the Blacksteel will be here soon. It might take years, or only weeks. I need electricity, and tools, and a place for my people to assemble a proper resistance."

Kronos perched back on his rusted throne, his pale white fingers steepled before his patchwork face.

"*Resistance?* Your people couldn't hope to stop me from annihilating them, right now. What makes you think you can defeat this so-called Unity if you can't take *me?*"

Nyl's smile was a scrawl of black lightning, his quicksilver lips pulling back from glistening dark teeth.

"What makes you think you aren't already defeated?" he asked, his eyes flaring white. And his hands flew out, a sorcerer's gesture, spitting sparks of pale phosphor.

Kronos was fast; as quick as the light his avatar was woven from. His flickering body melted into the metal of his throne, making the mekan's servos howl. The bulky machine sprang to its feet like a streetfighter, rolling backwards, putting up its massive guns to cover the incandescent figure of the Illuminatus. Across the rusting casque of the mekan's face hovered the ghost-image of Kronos, his eyes popping and switching, different sizes, shapes, colors - all of them filled with hate.

In front of Nyl the marble floor began to crawl with lightning, the same purple coruscations which had heralded his arrival.

This time, however it was no mere holographic image manifesting itself.

This, Zhe knew, was the power of the Multiplicity. It was a Folding – a distortion in reality woven by one of the Devilfish. And something was coming through.

The shape which was forced through the portal was like four immense obelisks fused together; a twisted monument rising up behind a wall of noise. It was nothing less than the Chrome Ark of the Ashishim, and under the hands of the Illuminatus it pulsed and whined with barely contained energy.

Zhe had been linked to the mind of Mirdain enough times to know

that shifting it would have felt like being slowly turned inside out...
not that Nyl would have performed that little trick himself.

"Here's my proof, Kronos!" shouted the renegade, as the Ark rose
up before him. "I have no need of your Forge, and now you know it!
Because if you deny me and my people, *I will destroy it myself!*"

Now Zhe could see the shifting patterns of light which raced across
the flanks of the Ark taking on features – a heaving tapestry of faces.
They merged and shifted just like the ghost visage of Kronos itself,
and as the great warmekan saw them it stumbled back, shielding its
camera eyes with one scarred and corroding arm.

"No! It cannot be!" shrieked the choral voice of Kronos, recognizing
the cursed machine for what it was.

The Ark was a microcosm of the Wetsystems themselves; a cage of
minds and souls built from circuitry and cloned neural tissue. Inside
the shining monolith thousands of dead Ashishim struggled to be
free, enslaved to pattern the energy which coursed through their
prison–tomb.

"I told them they'd live forever in paradise, Kronos," said Nyl,
stroking the shuddering surface of the Ark with his claws. Faces
melted and seethed under his touch, eyes rolling, teeth gnashing at
the caress of their tormentor. "They came willingly into my trap, just
like the fools you feed into your own systems. But there's one small
difference. *You* need enough power to drive the Forge. I only need
enough to *infect* it."

Kronos loosed a missile at the Ark, lashing out with a pound of high
explosive. The striped projectile came within a yard of the spinning
monolith - then it collapsed in on itself and disappeared, blown to
boiling gas. The Machine's eyes burned with hatred through a pall of
smoke.

"Impossible! When the Forge comes it will be driven by millions
of minds... and I can burn them up to crush you. What are a few
thousand dead humans, anyway?"

A patchwork snarl scrawled its way across the avatar's face. But
there was a shiver in the harmonics of its multiple voice, a thousand
tremors of fear sleeting through his firmament.

"My souls aren't crippled like yours, Kronos," purred Nyl, dragging
the Ark behind him through the dusty air as he advanced. "They know
that to escape they have to break apart their prison. This little cage is
strong – but yours is not. If I connect the Ark to you the Wetsystems
are lost, and the Forge with them. Your promised human lord will rule

over a burned wasteland."

It should have been impossible for a thing as huge and destructive as a Tankhunter warmekan to cower, but the machine which housed Kronos seemed to shrink in on itself as the Chrome Ark floated closer. The tortured faces in its cloak of mist gyred and screamed, bulging from the monolith as if they tasted his fear. Nyl drew out a long skein of them from the Ark's surface, brandishing it like a weapon.

"This infection will render your most precious weapon useless – because all they can think of is *oblivion*. I'm afraid that I've been forced to use the Ark quite extensively to get here. The strain is apparently quite excruciating."

Kronos was scrabbling backward across the floor, his cannon hands cutting great gouges in the stone.

"Keep it away from me! Keep it away, or I'll destroy your whole nomad horde!" The panic in his voice was undeniable. Around them the lights were flickering, the ranks of war machines casting leaping gargoyle shadows.

"No... it's just that attitude which means I'll have to SHOW you." said Nyl, shaking his head in despair.

Zhe came in through the eyes of the Brazilian warmekan, riding a wave of electric panic. For a brief instant the mesh and grind of Kronos's mind was superimposed over his own, a vision of neon mandalas and gears whirring out of synchronization. He felt the city around him, a vast and bloated body of steel and wire and glass, from the tip of the Rock to the deepest geothermal taps.

He felt the vast mechanism which supported three hundred decadent human lords totter and fail; and with it the automated defenses which were holding back the tribes of the Reclamation. This was the purpose of Technician Nyl's so called peace emissary – he wanted to make the whole immense artificial creature which was the last city *fear* him.

And in its fear it would falter...

Pipes ruptured, blasting scalding steam over embattled Elysian defenders. Wires sheared, whipping about in darkened corridors, hailing sparks and slicing through the bodies of Cyben and Subcitizens alike. The locks and failsafes on a thousand secure bulkhead doors snapped open and shut, cutting the abandoned zones at the base of the city wide open. And through the breaches came the nomads, relentless and driven, forcing the Elysian militia back higher and higher as the mekan and autoguns which defended them stuttered and died.

Zhe felt it all for one excruciating second, and then the cold stole over him, a mechanical paralysis spreading like frost. In the camera eyes of Kronos Zhe could see the insect figure of Technician Nyl, the Illuminatus, his alien features split in a smile of triumph.

He curled his fingers tight, then blew across them.

A cloud of demented faces burst from his fist like smoke, breaking against the mekan's inch-thick armor, burrowing in between the plates and into its corroded seams. It woke a rising wildfire of static, crazed loops and jags of color, blurring pixels...

And the inside of the Ark. Man-made hell.

All around him a storm seethed and roiled, walls of clouds towering up into lightning-wracked anvilheads miles high. There was nothing above or below but the churning gyre of clouds; a circle of darkness capped the world of the Ark, and an equally dark pit yawned below. Although he couldn't see through that blackness, Zhe could feel something on the other side of it; a monstrous presence scrabbling and writhing against the confines of the Ark with a billion claws and tentacles. Zhe had felt the taint of Asag'raal before, but nothing like this. He was a specimen in a vast killing-jar, awaiting dissection.

His host wasn't taking it very well.

Kronos had never experienced fear like this before. He had never felt the dimension-spanning hunger of Asag'raal... because he'd never had a soul for the thing to devour. Now he took that searing cold and malice like a sword through the chest. Zhe felt the tenuous link back to the Last City convulse as systems ground to a standstill, dooming hundreds more Elysians to death with every second.

Out there beyond the Ark vast chunks of the Wetsystems were coming online, drawing down enough power to fuel entire planets. In desperation, Kronos was trying to claw his way free, draining his own defenses to drag himself out of this artificial hell.

Inset in Zhe's vision he could see the slumped body of the warmekan, an empty shell surrounded by a corona of smoke. Jags and flickers of lightning played across its corroding bulk, stabbing back at the Ark, prying the defenses of the Illuminatus who wielded it.

Nyl was scowling with concentration as he strove to keep Kronos trapped, but every second counted. All the time that the machine was fighting to escape the Ark was time that the city was unguarded.

All around the disembodied form of Kronos the prisoners of the Ark whirled and spun, leaves caught up in a tornado. They were of all ages and from all the races of the Earth – men, women and children of the Ashishim, promised eternal life but delivered into servitude.

Zhe watched as a scrawl of fire sleeted through the bodies of the Arkborn, jumping from one to another as a chain of lightning. Where it touched their flesh it left great ragged wounds, white vapor coiling out like milk in water.

The Wetsystems of Elysium used chained minds like these to power the Assemblers and the Forge, but they were bound, their memories all but erased. The Arkborn were whole, and their anguish gave them strength.

Zhe watched as the looping, coiling smoke stitched itself back together, the shades mewling piteously as they struggled to keep cohesion. As they healed another blast came up from the abyss, snaking through the gyre to punch out through the starless black sky.

Their screams seemed to echo all around him.

Then Zhe saw that the spinning walls of cloud still retained some features in their whirling morass – here an eye, there a hand, there a twisted mouth...

The storm within the Ark was made of the Arkborn who could no longer stand their torment and had been pulled to pieces. Their essences had become part of the mighty dynamo which harnessed their living brethren; power patterned by pain and will, sent out by the Illuminatus to possess machines instead of bodies.

No doubt it was the chanting and sweating of the Electromagi which kept the storm spinning, while their tormentor directed the force of the Ark against his enemies.

The Arkborn who still had enough of their humanity left to feel anything at all were spirits of rage and bleak despair. They spiraled in toward Kronos in a twisting cloud, raking at him with their emaciated fingers, crucifying him with their eyes.

Through the pale umbilicus which linked the machine back to his own Wetsystems they could sense freedom of a sort; for within the vast neurostrata of Elysium they would be free of Zeon and his torments. They swarmed to Kronos like phantoms, tearing at his face and struggling to use him as a living doorway.

The most savage of the Arkborn, a black-skinned giant with half his jaw ripped away, managed to sink his fingers through the stuff of Kronos's arm, and the Machine let out a moan of pain and despair. The wraith drew itself in toward the shadow body of Kronos, his broken face leering and dripping white blood.

Zhe watched the Arkborn fill his vision, his hands tearing strips from Kronos's avatar to send them spinning away into the storm. Emboldened, more Arkborn were latching onto him, using hands and claws and teeth...

Zhe never knew if it was the Wetsystems which saved Kronos then, or if Nyl had timed his lesson in terror down to the microsecond. But as the first of the Arkborn was just about to reach the umbilicus the illusory world shattered, torn apart in a blaze of blue and silver lightning.

The spinning walls of cloud blew apart, the black sky and abyssal depths fell away, and Kronos was back in his armory, torn out of his warmekan body, a twitching electric ghost pooled forlornly on the marble floor.

Above him the Chrome Ark rotated, cold and silent, its cloud of whispering faces faded to a mere flicker at the edges of sight.

"Do you agree to the terms of my peace then, Kronos?" asked the Illuminatus, a slim silver figure at the base of a looming thirty-foot shadow. "The lower levels for my people, and all the power that we need to support ourselves?" The weak and boneless thing which was Kronos moaned its pain. "We'll be no trouble, I assure you. And you'll never have to feel the touch of the Arkborn again. They're for the Blacksteel, when they come."

Kronos pulled his holographic form together with a shuddering groan. He was not used to pain, or fear – or anyone demanding terms of him.

"Very well. You have your *peace*." The word was spit like a gobbet of blood from his ever-shifting lips. "Just one question – how did you build that thing? How did you discover the weakness of my Wetsystems?"

Technician Nyl laughed, an inhuman sound echoing in the cathedral of war.

"I had no idea, machine. None at all. It's below me to speculate on how an obsolete pile like you functions. I *found* the Ark, and worked out what it was. I must admit, your little prototype here is much better than the finished product. They should never have tried to give you a *personality*, Kronos."

From off down the corridors to either side the lights were snapping off, a tide of darkness closing in on the beaten avatar and the alien Illuminatus.

"Leave. Now!" grated Kronos, his stolen face a mask of hate and disgust. "Your nomads can have the abandoned zones. On two conditions."

Nyl cocked his head to one side, his slim fingers cupping his metallic chin.

"I'm listening."

"First, not a single one of your people can be inducted into the Wetsystems. You may not need the Forge, but one day I will breed a human being who does. I will not have my greatest work *corrupted*."

Nyl inclined his head in a tiny nod.

"Second – your people will obey the laws of my City. They will not interfere with my program of eugenics, or take any part in it."

Nyl nodded again as he began to fade, slowly at first but then faster and faster. The Ark sank slowly back into the floor as through the marble tiles were black water.

"Don't look so sour, Kronos," he said, his voice barely a whisper. It echoed amid the encroaching dark, among the relics of the apocalypse. "Peace is a wonderful gift, isn't it?"

Zhe slammed his mind down on it like an open palm, flat to the tabletop, pressing and preserving the little sliver of hope which shivered up out of his fear. The Chrome Ark was his best chance.

It was a prototype of the Wetsystems, little brother to the Forge itself.

More - it was an awfully big gun to take to the coming swordfight.

He disengaged, smooth, watching the cathedral armory fall away, watching the avatar of Kronos twitch and writhe on the tiles like a graveyard worm. It was time to go for a walk in the R.T.

17 Aevum Oblivio
Colossus

THERE WAS A tiny speck in the cyclopean storm-eye of Jupiter, a shadow made infinitesimal by the curve of the gas giant. As it slipped along its orbital path another slid around to take its place, and another, and another...

Each ship of the Unity was a half-mile long cylinder, featurelessly gray; its forward surface dimpled with the muzzles of an array of deadly weapons, its tail a single great fusion drive for in-system flight.

The constituents of this battlefleet possessed more autonomy than most of the Blacksteel, but the entire force was still essentially one mind, one consciousness. They were strung like a necklace around the great ochre planet with its bands of cream and crimson, drinking down He3 from dangling cloudscoops. But one of the Slavesystem's billions of eyes has caught a trace of its old and implacable enemy, hiding in the radioactive furnace-heat of the sun.

There were thousands of ships in the Unity battlefleet, but they turned as one, pushing up and out of the gravity well of Jupiter, flowing together and interlocking, magnets drawing them down into a jagged log-jam, a spiked ball of protruding maser cannons and torpedo tubes, with a cluster of massed drives jutting from its tail.

The Behemoth.

As they powered up the Slavesystem began to move, slowly at first and then faster and faster, a metal comet arcing in toward the sun, and toward the Earth.

2196 Ante Arbitrium
Baptism

THERE SHOULD HAVE been soldiers on the streets, thought St. Jules Benoic, twisting the focus ring on his ornate brass thermalscope.

Martial law. Discipline. Neat, marching columns in olive drab uniforms.

Instead – well, it was less warfare than a great orgiastic violent party, out of control and wild. Half the city was looting and burning, the other half drinking and whoring.

Yes, they needed soldiers out there, but what they got was broke-down mekan, raw police recruits, drunken Div commanders and the walking dead.

Benoic dropped the rose-etched thermalscope from his eye and took a quick nip of brandy from his leather-bound flask. There were no more soldiers in Elysium, and he'd better not forget it. His wife would never let him hear the end of it if he started re-living old glories tonight.

Since the disaster and decimation of Reclamation Day Elysium hadn't kept a standing army. The only threat to its security came from he warlords of the pit, after all, and they were buffered from the last city by the fortifications and zealots of the R.T.

Now they, mused Benoic, had some discipline. Irregulars, most of them, yes, but fighting men, dammit. Warriors you could be proud to call your enemies. A hundred Ashishim riflemen, or just *ten* armored Vatican Confessors, and he could sweep the streets clean.

Even the berserk tribesmen of the Pit were better than soft civilians and rusted automated defenses. He'd definitely settle for a warband of Pit Ferals tonight; even with their iron maces and antique guns they were still proud, fearless fighters. He was one of the last Elysians to ever see a tribesman, though, and that was years ago, when he had been known to them as the Voice of the Machine.

The clan chiefs of the pit had pleaded with him, when he'd worn the three arrows of a general. They'd suffered for the gold and archaeotech they had taken as payment from the Ashishim and their allies. The families of those savage chieftains had been wiped out, their heads paraded through the pit in cryogenic coffins as an example to any other ambitious fools among the Ferals. They had feted him like a conqueror, and laid bronze swords and ancient assault rifles at his feet...

The machine had promised itself that there would never be another Reclamation day. Not only were the new Warlords under its direct control, but it had worked hard to infiltrate the R.T, seeding the nomad ranks with spies and counteragents.

Spies, not soldiers. Things had unraveled and fallen apart.

There was no army tonight, only the Cyben, and the pitiful few hundred living officers who were supposed to keep them tame. The Subcommissioner Militarch would have settled for any kind of warriors right now, but what he had... well, it was best not to think about.

While the fervor and the fires spread through the Subcity some of the more upscale neighborhoods had organized citizen's militias, arming themselves with whatever weapons were at hand. Benoic had shared out his trophy armory to his neighbors, and he was busy regretting his pride - and his public relations strategy. He was busy regretting other things too – his vapid society wife, his yes-men friends, his sagging gut and rheumy eyes. Politics had been hard on him, and in the end it had come down to guns, not diplomacy.

Militarch Benoic had grown old and fat and bitter, but he was still smart enough to regret it. The other men and women on his roof didn't even have the sense to know that it was their stupid choices which had brought them here.

To help him win re-election the Militarch had chosen to live outside the safety of the Beltway, in one of the better areas of the Subcity proper. It was murder convincing Athene and her godawful parents to accept the move, but in the end being a big shark in a little fishbowl had appealed to the woman. That and a new Yardley and Benson's chargecard.

They had moved to Redcastle when it was new, a picture in a glossy magazine.

Even then it had seemed a little tawdry. But Athene had been paid off, he was up in the polls, and at least the new hab had its own quarter-dome to keep the rain out. Their new home was a cluster of elegant pre-formed concrete cylinders clustered about the bottom of Lord Kelvan Vail's spire, gated and wired to foster a false sense of security.

Benoic was one of twelve subcommissioners, although his useless Peace Division was a gutted bureaucratic shell. At the boardroom table, under the milky eyes of Slade, he was largely ignored. In Redcastle, a cloister for middle-class cube-rats, he was practically *royalty*. That made it easy to forget the Belt. At least here he was the only piranha in the little fishbowl.

St. Jules Benoic, with his tweeds and his ruby-pinned cravat, his platinum cufflinks and his Consolidated town car, was nothing if not proud. He was dressed in his best for the death of his upwardly-mobile dream, out on a terrace overlooking ruin.

Tonight the cops had failed, the city was in open riot, and the machine did *nothing*. He would have loved to be up in the belt, beneath a blue polyprop sky; if not for the safety, then at least so he could pay a visit to the Subcommissioner Justicar and slap the old fool silly. Instead he was standing on the roof of his villa, trying to keep his rifle steady while his neighbors held a little cocktail party behind him.

Most of them were self-confessed cowards who were better with a corkscrew than a gun, anyway. What was *his* excuse?

Benoic had been promoted by dead man's boots on Reclamation Day, after he'd watched the previous Militarch lose half his head to a Vatican sniper's bullet. He'd been a soldier before he'd been a politician, and that part of him was worried - but the other residents of Redcastle seemed to think that the riots were nothing more than an excuse for rooftop drinks and a barbecue. More than one of his militiamen grasped a rifle in one hand and a bottle in the other. Two or three were already too drunk to aim straight.

Benoic scowled into the sights of his antique longrifle, trying to blot out the sounds of laughter and clinking glasses, hissing steaks over the coals, and the small-talk of middle managers. Out over the walls of Redcastle the mob ruled, and he could hear screams and distant crashes over the drone of sirens.

He could see gouts of flame rising up from the lower levels, and drifts of acrid black smoke obscuring the neon logos of the Lords' spires above. He knew that it was only a matter of time before the blue-ribbon army was at the gates of this little enclave, and the Sons of Blaire decided to overthrow the old order by looting and burning Redcastle one house at a time.

Most of the rioters were indentured slaves, some of them even uplifted thugs from out of the pit. They had no time for the servants of the Machine – some of them even believed that their new Emperor would let the Reclamationists take over.

There was loose talk of some kind of miracle to come, brought about by bloody Saint Simeon, when he would turn the blackened world green again. The threedeeo networks were full of wild speculation, violence, and talking heads urging calm behind their sweaty makeup.

But so far no word had come from the highest of the high – no word had come from Commissioner Slade, the mouthpiece of Kronos itself.

That alone spoke volumes. Maybe they'd already hung the old ogre from a lamp post somewhere...

It was exactly what the city didn't need. One of Direktor Vanecke's screen-sided zeppelins cruised across Benoic's sights, and he wished he was holding a surface-to-air missile as it slipped through rags and streamers of oily smoke.

From its immense threedeeo projectors the face of Dave Levine bulged obscenely, slick with sweat and ten storeys tall. Behind him the one hundred and fifty remaining lords and ladies of the Kheptarchy milled about, tense and skittish in their finery. Despite the threats made by the Direktor, the game must go on. Tradition would be served.

Militarch Benoic wasn't so sure that Vanecke's claims were as hollow as the other networks would have him believe. Perhaps this *was* the end of the nobility, and perhaps Simeon Blaire *would* become the new Emperor of Elysium. He'd still need to have a hard core of political specialists around him, even then. An Emperor's touch couldn't turn sewerage into clean water, or magic away garbage. He'd need his subcommissioners, and that meant Benoic would have to live through the night. His pitiful little army of stock traders and courtroom fops would just have to hold out until the Game was over.

Benoic pulled a little silver flask of brandy from out of the pocket of his tweed coat, and was about to take a surreptitious nip when the building trembled beneath his feet. The shudder was so faint that at first he thought it was just his own frayed nerves, but then a second temblor rocked the hab-block, sending cracks skittering across its quarter dome. Behind him he heard wails of dismay and the sound of breaking glass.

"Form up! Form up, damn it!" he roared, fumbling at the action of his longrifle. "They're coming for us! Get to your positions, lock and load!" In a second he had been transformed from a tired old politician back into a soldier of the line.

"Wendell, Ohara, get your sorry butts to the parapet! Romily, if you've lost your weapon *so help me I'll shove it up your ass!*"

And amazingly, under the lash of Benoic's voice the well-heeled citizens of Redcastle stood to their guns, aiming out over the deserted streets and into the smoke. It took him a few seconds peering through the scope of his rifle and blinking nervous sweat out of his eyes to realize that there was nothing to shoot at.

Perhaps it had just been an aftershock from some catastrophic explosion around the dome? On the threedeeo news it had looked like the Valley View mall was in bad shape – maybe the whole damned thing had slipped off into the ocean. If so, it would be one less place for Athene to use that bloody Yardleys Card...

The next shock came bigger and louder, a grinding and rattling which made the tiles skip beneath Benoic's feet. The reticule of his rifle punched back into his eye socket, hard. Black and red stars erupted across his vision as he staggered, tripping over the sprawled body of another one of his little militia. Good Lords, it was probably that lush Romily, puking his guts out... something hot and damp was seeping through his expensive tweed pants.

Voices and gunshots echoed and roared in his head as the world spun. He couldn't be sure if it was just the concussion or if the whole of Redcastle was being torn apart beneath him. The soldier in him bit down on the pain and forced it back. Benoic shook the shadows out of his head and stared down at the man he had tripped over.

It was Romily, and he'd found himself a gun. But he wasn't drunk. The Militarch reckoned he'd never need another cocktail again.

That last tremor had cracked the hab-block down the middle, and the fissure had swallowed Romily to the waist, slamming shut like a demon jaw as the tons of masonry settled. The fluids which Benoic was kneeling in were spilling and pooling from the wreck of the militiaman's torso, a coil of burst intestines venting a graveyard stench. All at once his mouth was filled with vomit.

He had no time to spit before the chasm gaped open again and the building tottered, huge chunks of the rooftop garden falling away in a spray of concrete shards. Romily's corpse disappeared through the fissure as if the tortured structure had swallowed him whole.

The Reclamationists were underneath them! It must be! They'd sapped his defenses just like they had on that bloody day so long ago, and soon holocloaked Ashishi fiends would come up through the ground, and armor-suited Templars would come stalking through the rubble, their speakers playing psalms as they mowed down the survivors...

Benoic's mind swam with horrific images, dragging him back to the battlefield where he'd earned his title and his soft civilian's life. They hadn't forgotten him, and they were coming back to finish the job!

But it wasn't the Celestials or the Ashishim or the Aryans who were tearing Redcastle apart. As the building sagged, and the rest of the civilian militia fell away through the floor screaming Militarch Benoic clung grimly to the parapet, his rifle forgotten.

An abyss licked at his heels, hungry and dark.

He squinted into the depths, and watched a set of welded-shut blast doors crack open; doors so long disused they'd been forgotten and built over. He hung on with aching fingers as those slabs of metal ground apart; as half of the doomed hab-block stripped its bolts and cascaded away down the side of the dome. An avalanche of concrete and steel and designer homewares, tiny stick-man bodies pinwheeling free in sprays of blood...

Oh, Kronos! Not... not *them!*

A cavern gaped in the side of the city beneath Redcastle, and from out of its corroded maw came a legion of forgotten machines, staggering and wheezing, their infra-red eyes glowing like cinders in the dark.

As Subcommissioner Militarch, Benoic knew what they were. That didn't stop him from goggling in disbelief as the huge mekan came marching out from under the city. He kept the dusty ledgers and glitched, flickering datafiles of Elysium's armaments up to date, and he was well aware that Kronos kept hundreds of ancient machines on its books which were more than likely solid chunks of rust.

Each year when the records had gone up to the Subcommissioner Quartermaster there had been a sheaf of yellowed printouts clamped to the back of the official folder, documenting these ghost systems. He'd signed for them each time, although no living soul in the whole administration knew where they were kept. After all, this was the last and only city on Earth. They had to be here *somewhere.*

He'd never expected to see some of them come lumbering up out of their abandoned bunkers, even tonight when the city burned.

Benioc watched as the column of mekan - maybe twenty in all - reached the gates of Redcastle, tearing them down with buzzsaw-bladed hands. Now the nomads would suffer! Kronos hadn't unleashed the steel legions on Reclamation Day; a fact which still rankled with the soldiers who'd survived the Seven Hours War. Now it seemed that the machine had reconsidered.

Perhaps it was that blow to the head, perhaps the smoke. But as the warmekan marched something snapped in Militarch Benoic's mind, and he was back amid the flames and flying bullets of Reclamation Day. For the first time in years he was *himself* again – a soldier, clear in his purpose, free from policy meetings and weekly reports and society dinners with sneering Lords and Ladies.

He threw off his tweed jacket and ripped the satin cravat from around his neck, grabbing his rifle from off the parapet and jamming a pistol into his waistband. The canted side of the hab-block would have seemed too steep and sheer to climb for St Jules Benoic the politician, but he was a *soldier*. His aches and pains forgotten, Benoic scrambled down to the cracked and crazed surface to the street, the fires of Elysium reflecting in his pince-nez glasses.

The Steel Legion were marching – corroded and dilapidated, their paint flaking and their joints creaking. Militarch Benoic marched with them as the ruins of Redcastle lay shattered behind him, his brain spinning with visions of death and glory.

Ω

In the cool darkness of the Mendelev-Singh spire, at the heart of a security grid of rooms nested together like Russian dolls, an exowomb hung weightless in its magnetic cage.

The membrane-walls of that artificial organ had expanded a hundredfold since Melchior had come here with his needle - now the child within was accelerating through the years as hormones surged and seethed. Cells replicated feverishly, dancing to Emmanuel Lancaster's tune. He already looked to be six or seven years old, his hairless skull studded with sockets and ports.

A tangled skein of wires fed him information, an entire false childhood woven by Direktor Vanecke's machines. At this rate he'd be grown before his Lord father even knew he existed...

Neon lights popped and crackled into life as a Universal Wetsystems mekan split from its storage cell in the wall, its empty ribcage swinging open on oiled hinges as it unfolded to twice human size. Dexterous android fingers disconnected the little Kheptarch's exowomb from its intricate meshwork of tubes and datafeeds, sealing it up inside its empty chest cavity like a biomechanical heart.

The mekan was surplus to requirements now - it's kind were used to securely transport the force-grown clones of the Razor Clique to their revels, armored vessels for irreplaceable wetware. This one would have one last run to make before it was scrapped; down into the Beltway, to the mansion of Octavio Vanecke.

His agents had already stolen an identical force-maturation system from poor dead Lancaster, and mediteks from the Liquid Tong stood by to help deliver young Lord Darion Blaire into the world.

The first face he saw would be that of his Uncle Octavio. But his earliest memories - well, they were being arranged even as he slept, rocked in his artificial womb by the long-limbed stride of a stalking silver mekan.

Vanecke would make sure that they were simply impossible to forget.

Ω

Lysander Jaegenn brought his icepick down across Lady Daena Shaye's shoulder in a merciless arc, the flashing steel catching the light as it plunged home. A spray of chipped ice scattered from the blow, and he caught it expertly in his drink, leaving the icepick stuck fast.

As he turned away one of his mind-wiped servants struggled to work the blade free. It would be difficult; Lysander's combat augments were fired up, and the blow had been struck with the strength of ten men.

Daena's blue-tinged face stared down at him blankly, tiny droplets of water running down her cheek like tears. In the shimmering ice he caught sight of his own reflection - genecoded to perfection, his black hair worn in a jeweled topknot slick with oil, his tiny pointed beard studded with ruby pins.

Like all his line - back to the ancient CEO of Helios Fusionetics - he was olive-skinned and blue eyed, with a cruel mouth set in a permanent frown. His own son would be just the same when he emerged from his frozen exowomb... if Vanecke could be stopped, and he made it out of his temple here alive.

Lysander had arranged the ice statues around the outside wall of the temple, between a curve of silver-veined marble columns. They weren't just the images of the fallen lords and ladies who had failed in the first round of the game – that would be unspeakably *passe*. In the depths of the spire more of Jaegenn's white-robed serfs labored over a great cryogenic engine, feeding the broken bodies of the slain into its steaming maw and pulling the statues out one by one with hydraulic tongs.

The ice was pink around Lady Shaye's neck where her head had been expertly sewn back on.

Lysander had been a player with the Razor Clique since his fifteenth birthday, the day that he'd first drawn blood - the day that he'd first died and been reborn.

But he'd never felt the atmosphere of the Revels so tense, or seen his fellow players so skittish. Personally, he put no store in the rantings of the half-crazed Direktor Vanecke. He was one of the few privy to the whispered secrets of the Grief Division, and he knew that tonight was the end of the broadcasting mogul's span. This was his final curtain, and he was probably trying to boost the ratings through the roof as his swansong.

Others weren't so assured. He caught half-whispered snatches of conversation as he moved through the room, his bare feet leaving bloody tracks across the tiles. Behind him crawled a little cleaning mekan, its shell inlaid with silver and mother of pearl, cleaning up each crimson print as he walked.

"...has he really killed dear Lord Lancaster? Such a shame, such a good boy... takes after his father..."

"...and my driver says that the crowds are growing quite rowdy – they can never get in here, of course, but still ..."

"...and there's nobody working the machines! I can't wait for that bloody Kronos to sort it out, if I die here tonight I have to be back in the office tomorrow for lunch with Lady Guildford..."

"...really, the man is such a damnable peasant! Nobody should ever have let him near our circles, let alone allowed him to befriend young Blaire..."

"...and even if he wins, you can be sure that the Machine will never let him through the trials. They'll just have to put the whole Game on hold while they get Lancaster or *whoever* is running the show up there to bring us back..."

The lavish feast on the mahogany sideboard was all but untouched. The morbidly obese Earl Blacktower was piling his plate with choice cuts of salmon and cream cheese, but the rest of the spread was going to go to waste. All one hundred and fifty remaining Kheptarchs were huddled together in twos and threes, darting suspicious glances between each other, huddling over brimming glasses of champagne and cognac.

Even Lysander himself was acutely aware of the flitting camera ornithopters which buzzed about the heads of the Clique, their insect wings blurring and winking rainbows.

What they thought was immaterial, anyway. Whether they died at the hands of their peers or under the guns of the ever-vigilant Referee, only one would walk out of the spire tonight. Which made it all the more surprising that the focus of so much speculation was *missing*.

Lysander had been trying to hunt down Simeon Blaire since the end of the first round – and he had no doubt that he wasn't the only one. One or two of the flitting camera mekan weren't decked out in Omnivasive livery, and some of the Khepts were asking questions. Lysander was never as grateful as he was right now for the fact that his slaves were mind wiped and mute.

Still, there was no way that Simeon could have escaped. As well as the all-encompassing panopticon of Vanecke's cameras, the spire was ringed around with his own security systems, and a halo of Lancaster's biotech remote eyes. Blaire wasn't decked out in combat holomesh, either. All his guests were clad in nothing but their skin, their modesty protected by hovering strips of cloth buoyed up by ornate floating cherubim. A naked, bloody Simeon Blaire could no more have sneaked by under the eyes of the Lords, the servants and the omnipresent cameras than he could simply dissolve into smoke.

Lysander scowled, snatching a glass of wine from a passing servant's tray. He knocked it back in one gulp and ran his eyes over the crowd again.

What he failed to notice was a camera platform arching out over the temple on a long cantilevered hydraulic arm; a model so woefully bulky and out of date that even the shantytown propaganda networks of the R.T. wouldn't have bought it.

At its controls sat a slim and hawk-faced man, his grubby Omnivasive coverall draped with coils of wire and bags of lenses. Unlike the other smartly turned-out operatives of Vanecke's network, the cameraman was smoking a foul-smelling cigar, and perched on his head was a battered trilby hat, its crown lit up by the revolving halo of his press logo.

Such peons were well beneath the attention of a Lord of the Razor Clique, and Jaegenn strode by beneath him with barely a glance. But Atticus Meaks took careful note of *him*, and twitched the controls of his machine to keep him clear of the picture.

Because the pressman wasn't jockeying a camera at all; he was running a diversion for his boss. From the blank lens of the obsolete threedeeo recorder a tight beam was cast out across the temple, bathing a patch of the far wall with its radiation.

It was a holofield, and under its shelter Simeon Blaire and Leynna Mendelev-Singh were frozen in icy silence, their dew-beaded glasses poised, their eyes vacant. All that betrayed their presence was a barely perceptible shimmer in the air, and none of the Lords and Ladies of

Elysium would be getting close enough to them to detect it.

A trio of white-robed serfs had set up a barrier around the little alcove where Mister Vanecke's scion and his lady friend were locked in stasis, wielding mops and buckets to clean up an unfortunate mess. One of Lysander's ice sculptures - the frozen body of Daric Laughton - had fallen from its plinth, shattering into a million shards of cryogenically preserved flesh. While they labored, eyes downcast, the rest of the Clique gave them a very wide berth.

Atticus took another drag on his cigar, nudging the little joystick of the field projector to keep the illusion in focus. What his master wanted to say to those two he didn't care to know. All that mattered was finishing up what had been a long and weird day at the office, even by Omnivasive Standards. Anyway, he'd put a lot of money on Blaire to win this round – insider information went a long way with Atticus Meaks – and it wouldn't do for him to be disqualified.

On his little screen Leynna's face was as smooth and cold as that of the unfortunate Lord Laughton's – or at least that part of it which lay dissolving in a bucket of bleach. While the systems which had been implanted in her were far less extensive than those which made Blaire tick, they were easily powerful enough to drag her into the world of Tokugawa, into his black palace over a burning virtual Edo.

Leynna was wandering in the dark, inside the severed head of Octavio Vanecke.

Ω

She walked down a corridor of ornate cherrywood screens, intricately carved with pastoral scenes and sprays of flowers. It seemed to go on forever, narrowing down in the distance to a blurred point, but there were no doors, no windows, only black iron lamps every few yards to light her way, their bowls burning with pallid green flames.

One moment she had been stalking toward Simeon Blaire, sliding curses and invective together like bullets into a clip, and then...

Off in the distance she could hear the screens sliding and clicking, a noise like hands moving chess pieces across a board. But when she looked behind her the corridor was featureless and empty.

When she turned back there was a blank stone wall in front of her.

Leynna's heart leaped in her throat, and she spun again, only to find another wall hemming her in. The cherrywood seemed to breathe, sighing in and out, and a vast heartbeat animated the stone beneath her feet. Monks and peasants capered and leered in the green shadows

99

thrown up by the one remaining sconce.

She leaned in closer as the images began to shift, the face of a wizened old man becoming that of Direktor Vanecke, the steel mask of a rampant samurai twisting into the smirk of Simeon Blaire...

Then a hand came down on her shoulder. Her augmentations kicked in, no less swift and deadly for all that this was undoubtedly an illusion. Her fingers flew to her assailant's eye sockets, four stiff tines punching into soft flesh, trying to blind him before he could strike.

Her other hand chopped low, a kidney shot, while her feet slid into a fighting stance.

It took a second for her to realize that the thing she was fighting was already dead. Not dead like the Cyben, clinically reanimated with machinery and plastic – not even cleanly slain and tastefully mounted like the trophies of the Razor Clique.

Her fingers sunk into an eye socket filled with writhing grave worms, punching into noisome black liquid. Her hand slammed into ribs thinly coated with leathery skin. And the wight reached out and grabbed her with skeletal hands, its grip unrelenting even though she howled and thrashed, twisting her fingers deep into its hollow skull.

From the other rotting socket a cold blue fire blazed, a stare reminding her of nobody more than Direktor Vanecke.

"So, this is *his* little game, is it? What the hell does he think he's playing at?"

Its breath smelled of cemetery rot, a hot vapor which made Leynna's head swim. The walls whirled and warped, bathed in leaping shadows. Drugs! But how... if this was just an illusion? Her limp body trailed from the wight's claws, weak and unresisting. Even her combat systems wouldn't respond. It dragged her along behind it, silent and implacable.

What seemed like hours later - but may well have been only seconds - the corridor opened out into a vast underground cavern, a place of black spires underlit by pools of lava. The furnace-heat of the place struck her like a slap across the face, and she could see the desiccated skin of her captor crisping and peeling in strips. The stench of decay was choking.

The wight threw her to the sand with a crackle of bones and cooked leather.

She could taste ashes in her mouth; blood like salt and metal. Slowly the spinning blackness cleared and Leynna raised her head, defiant, drawing herself up to her feet. She was ready to smash the filthy dead thing to splinters of bone. She was ready to take on a legion of them.

She wasn't prepared for the sight which confronted her.

There must have been thirty or forty of the wights standing sentry around the walls of the cavern - walls carved into a horrorshow of demented faces, inset with ivory teeth and tusks and horns. They were clad in ancient armor, steel cuirasses inlaid with orange and green jadeite, long robes of rusting chainmail and half-helms surmounted by brass crescent moons.

A constellation of cold blue sparks bored into her; the gaze of the dead, waiting for her to move. Willing her to be foolish enough to challenge them.

Leynna ran a hand across her cheek, wiping off a crust of sand and blood.

It was then that she felt the weight of his stare. It was like a hand clamped around her jaw, like a merciless mechanical claw. Fighting it all the way she turned her head, and saw the Glass Shogun enthroned.

The center of the cavern was filled by a little lake, its waters black in the lava glow. Once the rock which clawed its way up from the center of the pool had been an obsidian stalagmite, but it had been lovingly reshaped by the same demented sculptor who had carved out the cavern's walls. Now it was a throne in the shape of open jaws, a maw of black iron and razor-edged volcanic glass, illuminated by braziers swinging on spiked chains.

Even through his face was covered by an *Oni* mask of beaten steel, she knew who he really was. Something in the slick and oily undertone of his psionic grip had touched her, awoken memories of a man she had once found fascinating for his raw, vital ambition. It was Octavio Vanecke, or at least a demonic parody of him; the Lord he could have been but for the accident of his peasant birth.

This was what he'd been reduced to - a dread tyrant living in the world of his sick imagination. If it wasn't for the grisly backdrop to his throne she would have laughed. As it was, her mouth was filled with bile.

Behind the black iron chair Octavio had arranged a wall of hooks and spikes, upon which were hung the dead and dying bodies of hundreds of children. Years ago Leynna had seen a classical painting by the 20th century artist Geiger; a landscape of diseased babies rotting and covered with parasites. This was just the same, except it came complete with the smell of shit and blood, the sound of anguished squeals and cries and the twitching, writhing and shuddering of the mortally wounded.

Leynna stumbled forward into the black water, her hand outstretched, only to find that it was warm blood. *Every one of them had the face of her own child* - the one she had dreamed of, the one she had made from the blood and skin of Simeon Blaire. She had been angry before, pumped up with chemicals and programs and primed to kill - now she was positively *incandescent*.

"I might have guessed that you were at the center of this shitheap! Just your style, Octavio. You could never hang proper trophies around your little bimburb house, so you had to slaughter children!"

The black shogun on his throne only laughed, a mirthless grinding sound echoing in his helm.

"They're not *real*, Leynna," he said. "Or at least, they're as real as the kid you were cooking up in your little biolab."

That stopped her dead. Omnivasive had their agents everywhere. But that place was hers alone. It was her obsession, her secret addiction. The specter on its throne inclined its helm a little, listening.

"And obsession is my stock in trade, dear. So is eavesdropping on your inane little thoughts – at least while you're here in my world. If I had to put up with that kind of chatter all the time I'd be inviting the Celebrants around early."

Leynna tried desperately to force him out of her mind, but the taint was everywhere.

And worse, it was *familiar*. It reminded her of when they had been together – the Kheptarch Lady and her Sub-Scum lover. The same lack of clarity, the same light-headed sense of being outside herself looking down...

The same feeling which came over her in the sanctum, when she knelt before the exowomb of her child.

"You bastard!" she whispered, her face gone alabaster white. If a stare could murder, then the look on Leynna's face would have made her ruler of the Game in an instant. "How did you get to me?"

The metal face of Tokugawa was expressionless, but she could swear that behind it Octavio Vanecke was smiling his usual tight-lipped smile.

"Your mother, the late and *unlamented* Yulia Mendelev. I know that she liked to make-believe that Aran Singh was a saint, but he wasn't. MS Biomed was a billion in the red before I came along to bail them out. He pissed it away gambling and whoring with his Kheptic friends, then he had to prostitute himself to a jumped-up downsider for cash.

Me."

"Bullshit!" she said, wiping the blood off her hands onto the front of her dress. For some reason the illusion had clad her in a full starched-white Victorian costume, complete with acres of lace. "There are banks, and financiers, and there are the other Lords. His FRIENDS. They might try to kill each other for fun, but they never let an aristocratic firm go under."

"Maybe not... in the usual course of events," replied Vanecke. "But when I say he was drinking and whoring; well, the kind of things your dear old dad got into made this little scene behind me look like a Sunday picnic. I just happened to have all the glossy photos."

Leynna was dumbstruck. Of course she had never really known her parents - all of the children of privilege in Elysium were raised by machines, kept in isolated luxury until their seniority. But those machines had taught the young scion of MS Biomed all about her family history, a proud tale of economic savvy, ruthlessness and greed. She remembered her mother as a tall, stern holographic figure, prim and poised in blue pseudovelvet while they lowered father's coffin into the incinerator. Surely her parents had loved each other, if she had arranged to have a funeral for him? That kind of old-world sentimentality fit in with the fact that they'd merged their companies and their names together...

"And while he was busy with all that *unpleasantness*, your mother was busy entertaining one of the servants. A pit-fighter from the downtown leagues she took on as a *home security operative*. He certainly kept her under *very* close observation."

She could literally see his face through the demon-mask of shining steel, the way his lip curled into a leer, the way his little black eyes flashed with heat.

"Too bad he was one of mine as well, eh? And certainly too bad that your precious Lords – their FRIENDS wouldn't so much as *think* their names after they'd been dragged through the gutter press."

The images slammed into her harder than any physical blow, stripping away the only defense she had left to her. That all this was a lie. That she had not been sold to this piece of Subcity filth...

Her father, bound in strips of leather and rubber, bloody, a dripping saw in his hand. Around his feet, *pieces* she didn't want to look at, scraps of hair ...and her mother, her hands running down the scarred and muscled back of a gray-skinned hulk, naked but for the spiked collar around his throat...

"He didn't die in an accident, you know. You must have heard the whispers. *Some* of them I didn't even start myself. If it had been any other way he could have been brought back; but what are the odds that he would get caught alone in a sealed lab with a brain-eating virus? That kind of coincidence is a leap of faith even for *my* publications."

She felt her legs go out from under her as the visions of lust and blood and shame burned through her mind. She had heard rumors, but she'd dismissed them as the sniping of jealous lowborn peasants. Her father was a medical researcher, a hero, risking his life to save people from diseases like the one which killed him! But if his life had been a lie, why not his death? Why the carefully cultivated media show of a redundant Christian funeral?

"She *sold* you, Leynna. Your mother could never suffer that much shame. And I would have delivered her enough to last for several lifetimes."

The room was spinning now, a gyre of dead skeletal faces, cruel black stone and steaming blood. She let herself sink into the warm embrace of the lake, half hoping to drown - even though this place was no more real than an afternoon threedeeo show.

And like a show it was all sharp images, bright still photographs, faded-edged memories...

She remembered the first time she had met Octavio Vanecke, the first time she'd seen his flat and thuggish face. It had been some conference or other, with her tagging along behind her mother and a gaggle of economic analysts, yes-men and servants.

More than anything else she remembered the distaste she felt for the Direktor, and how it had melted away under his black-eyed stare - how her disgust had turned to fascination as she watched him take apart three Lords and their retainers in fierce negotiation. She had been sixteen years old, a novice of the Razor Clique, and he had invited her to the Death Pits of DownTown to watch the technique of the best Subcity fighters, most of whom he owned.

No rich suitor from the noble houses would have taken her there. He walked the poisonous streets without fear, and the cruelest, meanest freaks of the rotten core of Elysium bowed to him.

It excited her.

Slowly her disdain had become obsession. His self-confessed stock in trade.

And there, deep amid the memories of blood and sweat and cheering crowds she remembered the little black necklace her mother had given her that first morning, as they hurried across the underground parking garage to their limousine. A ribbon of black silk with a single silver pendant, a dangling teardrop inset with diamonds. She could not have felt it burrowing its little tendrils of wire into her skin; she was a ball of aches and pains from the implantation of her first Gladius array. The sensation of little clicks and pops, tiny electrical connections deep in her brain was a constant companion back then.

Everything she felt after that had been as fake as the dungeon around her now, an illusion merged seamlessly with reality. And she could guess why he had bothered to go to all that trouble...

"It was all for a title, wasn't it?" she asked, her eyes focused on the demon-carved ceiling of the cavern. "All just so you could have that little honorary if front of your name. And what would we have called you? Lord Vanecke of DownTown? Duke of Slums?"

He sighed, bored with her vitriol.

"They would have called you *Duchess Vanecke* if it weren't for your mother. While your brother Aidan stood to inherit MS Biomed there was no problem with a second child marrying *new money*." He spat those last two words in a perfect imitation of Duke Gideon's withering tones. "Our children would have been genewritten, made pure, and elevated to the stature of Lords. But she was too good for me, I fear."

Leynna could believe it. Her mother had been as stern as steel when she was angry. They said afterwards that it was that inflexibility which doomed her; that she snapped when Aidan died so soon after his father. They'd been struck from the same mould, those two... at least on the surface. Leynna hoped that her poor dead brother wasn't prey to the secret perversions which had doomed Aran Singh.

"And if you thought that Aidan met his end by *accident* then you're simply too naive to live. She killed him, Leynna, with her own hands. And then she erased her own mind, and condemned herself to the psych cells."

With all the rest of the house of Mendelev-Singh dead, she had become the Prime Shareholder. Forbidden from marrying below her station – cursed with the mark of the pariah. Leynna was forbidden from breeding at all when the line of Mendelev-Singh was denounced as *unstable*.

"That was when I had to take my chance. I thought that I could use what I'd learned from the Death Pits to win at least *one* round of your precious Game. Then they would have to accept me. That accursed Kronos would *have to accept me*."

His rage lit fires under the coals, making them spume with clouds of sparks.

"So you ended up as nothing but a shriveled-up severed head," said Leynna, pushing herself up out of the blood and onto the shore of the lake. Her illusory dress was dripping red, the lace hanging in crimson tatters. "And I never heard from you again. I thought the loss had broken your mind, like they said losing Aidan did to my mother's."

His face had melted through the steel now, and a look which was almost regret shivered in his eyes. The *Oni*'s features melded with his own, giving him beetling brows and jagged tattoos, but this was as close to compassion as the Direktor could ever come.

"I never wanted things to happen that way. But I found something out when your brother died. Your mother made her intentions clear in a message to me, and in that message she told me why both Aran and Aidan had to be disintegrated. She told me what really happens to the dead here in our city, and she gave me proof. Something only the Prime Shareholder of MS Biomed could have known."

He paused for a second, running a gauntleted hand over his face. Leynna thought that there may even have been tears shivering on the black iron when he brought it away again.

"Well, her and that fool Lancaster. But *he* was always the loudest voice raised against me."

Leynna was back on her feet now, looking up at the figure on the throne with something approaching pity.

"Don't try to tell me for a *second* that you actually cared about any of us," she said. "All you wanted was a title, and a way into the Clique, and a hand up to the Imperial Throne. You can't expect me to believe that after you bought me and killed off my family that you're anything more than a *monster*."

His laugh was harsh, grating, the sound of rusted metal plates sliding against each other. It seemed to come up from somewhere deep in his armor.

"I'll never convince *myself* I'm anything better, Lady Mendelev-Singh. And I don't expect an apology will do you any good. I just wanted you to know that one of your line still lives. I figured I owed it to you."

Her eyes leaped back to the grisly tableau of broken little holographic bodies hung behind the throne, each one of them wearing a face half hers - and half Simeon Blaire's.

"You didn't…" she began, but the words froze in her throat.

"*I had to!*" he replied, rising from his throne to stride into the lake of blood, one iron hand outstretched. She flinched away from him, taking up a fighting stance again, even through she knew that in this place he was all-powerful.

"It isn't Simeon Blaire who I want to rule Elysium. He's far too willful – and by now far too insane. What do you think he'd make of this world, if I gave him the chance?"

She waited as he came up out of the shallows, gore dripping from his armor. *A quick glance to the left and right to make sure that the wights hadn't left their posts around the chamber walls. One strike, and perhaps she could break free of this illusion.*

"I had to know that he was the right one to play surrogate father to my little son. *Your* son. An Emperor who will listen to me, and be sculpted by my will."

Now his face was blurring over, covered again by an *Oni* mask of grim steel. His hand was reaching out for her, imploring, inviting. She tensed herself to strike. And then she saw what was in his other hand, and all the rage drained out of her at once.

It was a bundle of black cloth, tiny and vulnerable in the crook of his arm. It was a baby, one which she knew was her own.

"He's going to be a much better warrior than either you or his father ever could be, Leynna. And with his pure genes there's no way that Kronos can keep him from taking the Trials. I should have considered adoption a long time ago."

Her world collapsed inward, a tunnel of darkness focused on that tiny cherub face, sleeping peacefully in a hand crusted with drying blood. It was all an illusion. It couldn't be real. She tried desperately to break away, to force her mind from this terrible place and back to the Jaegenn Spire where she was in control.

Octavio Vanecke bunched the black swaddling cloth in his ironclad fingers and held the little child out to her, its eyes blinking open, dazed with sleep.

"I assure you, he's very real, Leynna. I've coded a feedback loop between this little hologram and the exowomb. He'll even feel your touch when you give him your blessing."

The great armored figure knelt on the shore of the lake, dipping his fingers in the steaming blood. Carefully, with a delicate touch she would have thought such a monster incapable of, he drew them across the child's face, leaving a crimson trail down his cheek.

"Baptized in blood, Leynna. You will be the mother of the Emperor.

And with Lancaster out of the way, I will be by your side."

She didn't know then if it was the neuromesh he had put in her brain, or just the exultation of believing his promise. But she dropped her guard, and fell to her knees with him by the pool of blood, and clasped her pale white hand over his gauntlet of iron. Her fingers interwove with his, and together they made another mark across the child's tiny face, a crimson cross like an open wound.

"Yes." she said. "For our son, and the throne. Yes."

17 Aevum Oblivio
The Brass

THE EFFORTLESS SUBJUGATION *was enjoying the sun. It hummed to itself contentedly as it cruised in close to an over-arching solar flare, catching a wind of hard radiation.*

Being this close to the star's corona filled the living starship with boundless energy, the equivalent of raw adrenaline. And Earth's little yellow sun was hardly a threat - the Subjugation *had sailed in the E.M. Maelstroms of stars a thousand times its size. Even so, its crew cursed the blistering heat as they scuttled through its intestinal corridors and hangars, preparing for war.*

The Effortless Subjugation *was a portal carrier; a fifty-mile-wide ball of hexagonal mesh, with bloated polyps and pods bulging from its coral flesh. Ten immense Devilfish were slaved to it, stuck remora-like to nipples on its outer shell. At its center blazed an azure portal into liquid space – the null storage interface, a link to a sealed sub-universe packed tight with Multiplicity fighting machines. Soon they'd be unleashed, in all their tentacled and scaly glory.*

In a blister of clear chitin atop the carrier-ship the commander of the fleet paced nervously, his hooves clacking staccato against the scaled floor.

Kataphrakt Yrr was worried, and not about the coming battle. He'd hammered the forces of the Unity on battlefields as far flung as the Ice Halo of Paruan Keng and the burning diamond-chip deserts of Axtrachul 5. Swatting a few more mechanical bugs would be as nothing to a Kataphrakt of his skill.

What had Yrr's numerous teeth on edge was the lack of information from his man on the ground. Technician Zhe was one of the most trusted beings in his extremely dangerous profession; in all the Order of Battle he was considered to be the most skillful exoethnologist.

But then again, Gharfos Nyl had been just as good. And where was he now?

Yrr knew that the forthcoming battle was over a weapon of great power, one which could even possibly (if such a grim thought could be entertained) destroy a Technician, or even (gods forfend) a Kataphrakt.

If they had gotten Zhe as they had allegedly gotten Nyl, then this so called 'Human Race' would have to be eradicated. And for that his invasion fleet was slightly under-gunned. Yrr wished he had lined up some Planet Decimators, or perhaps even a couple of his brother

Kataphraktoi; but oh, the paperwork! And in triplicate!

"Kataphrakt-Admiral, I have detected movement from the Blacksteel fleet," chimed the Subjugation in its annoyingly musical voice. "May I recommend plotting a course of interception before they reach the third planet?"

Yrr whipped his cape around and slumped into the admiral's throne, one claw tapping pensively at his spiked brow-ridge.

"Very well, Subjugation - bring yourself about and come in at them over the plane of the ecliptic. We'll settle into a polar stationary orbit above that airless little fourth planet – the red one. That should give us time to expand the Order of Battle and be prepared for them to arrive."

"Thank you sir!" squealed the massive portal carrier ship, shivering with glee. Inside its rust-red mesh pods and modules bobbed frenetically, causing thousands of thralls to curse and stagger.

To the Effortless Subjugation the thrill of battle was a hardwired urge, coded into the pleasure centers of its brain. The damned thing was only the size of an urga *fruit.*

But for a Kataphrakt, this was just another day at the office. Thank the Praetor, he thought, for free sandwiches and double overtime. This assignment was likely to be extremely trying.

DOCUMENT INSERT: MULTIPLICITY ARCHIVES DEPARTMENT

The Imperial Trials:

'Know then that there is but one path to the High
Throne of Earth, one door which may only be opened
by the worthy and the pure.

Mighty Kronos in his wisdom has been tasked by
the Ancients to save all humanity from the Three
Corruptions - Mutation, Weakness, and Stupidity.
His chosen are the Lords we revere and strive for,
in the hope that one of them will unlock the door,
will renew the Earth with the power he may wield
from the High Throne.

These truths have come down to us from the sacred
discs of the Ancients, made manifest in the will
of the great Machine.

It is right and just for us to bow to our Lords,
chosen for their purity. It is right and just that
they bow to Kronos, who weighs their strength and
weakness in the balance.

And it is right that in the end one may attempt
the trials, where his mind will be judged, for
only the enlightened may remake this world in
their image.'

The Book of Manifest Dogma -
Elysium's state religious codex.

17 Aevum Oblivio
Fixation

THERE WAS A little of Technician Nyl still left in him. And perhaps a little of the Blacksteel as well - a fortifying trace, giving him the resolve of a machine as he dragged his broken body back into the process-core of Kronos.

Zhe knew that CeeAn had been telling the truth. The Multiplicity Order of Battle was on its way; and no doubt the Unity was approaching with equal haste. For them, this was no longer just about the Forge, no matter how novel or powerful it was supposed to be.

Zhe had felt the touch of Asag'raal, an entire dimension suffused with a single malign being, a reality crammed from end to end with gelid, living night. It explained some of the more bizarre superstitions which haunted this world, things he had found absurd and laughable when Galq included them in his briefing. These 'human beings' had every reason to worry about what happened after they died. Although they'd never seen its cruel physical form, the shadow of their planar neighbor had been cast across their nightmares for millennia. It had given them a series of bloody and bizarre mythologies, grim religions populated with demons and witches and cannibalistic gods.

Technician Nyl had been curious.

When the Praetor Primus has sent him here to recover the Forge Nyl had considered it a trifling task, one of little importance. Indeed, if it weren't for the distraction that Nyl had become obsessed with, he could easily have cut through the nonsense of the Game, to the core of the machine called Kronos and its hidden power.

But Nyl had felt compelled to know how the soul-harvesting mechanisms of Kronos operated. He had wanted to test the threshold of its sensitivity to life and death.

And so he had experimented.

Hence the Ark - and of course, Zhe's current problems. The thing would be guarded, even now when the city was scoured clean of life.

Some days at the office, thought Technician Zhe, were definitely worse than others. He loaded a set of crystal memory-chips into a pair of blade drones and let them fly, then set about patching up his scarred silver flesh. Considering how the mission was going so far, it wouldn't be long until something else tried to eat him whole...

2196 Ante Arbitrium
Masterslave

Simeon Blaire heard it all. He had come to this chamber beneath the Black Palace knowing that he would find his master here - perhaps with some final words of encouragement as he set out to seize the throne. When the wights had taken him by the arms and marched him through the dark corridors he had gone willingly, prepared to do anything his lord demanded. Guttering flamelight had painted his face the same color as their bleached dead bones...

But the depth of this betrayal rocked him to the core, twisting up his anger to the point of insanity. The skeletal faces of his captors leered knowingly as they held him back, watching from a balcony cut into the cavern wall.

He should never have been so trusting. He should never have presumed that Vanecke, for all his stolen platitudes, knew anything of *real* honor.

Now he watched as the black-armored warrior and the blood-drenched maiden baptized his child, the gene-seed grown without his consent. She had always been a sentimental fool, but *him*? He could never have imagined the Direktor giving the next generation what he could take now, by force.

And yet... here they were, and he was being shown the depths of his own credulous stupidity. With his combat augments singing to him of death and pain and his mind spiraling out of control there was only one course of action open to him. Thankfully, the illusion Vanecke had created had clad him in his black bodysuit, his faceless mask – and his sword. It leaped from the scabbard across his back as if it was alive, invigorated by the promise of slaughter.

The wights which held him were the first to feel its edge.

Simeon struck left, cleaving one of the undead sentinels from collarbone to waist, his sword slashing through rusted chainmail and leather and bone as if it was silk. Black rot burst from the thing's body with a charnel-house stench; worms and maggots flew wide in a putrid arc as the blade came up again, up between the other wight's ribs, snapping each one as cleanly as brittle straw. The point of the blade bisected its skull, shattering teeth and bone, extinguishing the icy blue light in its empty sockets.

And then he was down on the face of the wall, running across its intricately carved surface, a warcry torn loose from his throat as he went. He came down among the wights on the cavern floor like a reaping engine, his blade quicksilver, lopping off a head here, an arm there, shattering calcified spines and sundering rotting organs. Grinning death's-heads swarmed in his narrowed vision, each of them taking on the face of Octavio Vanecke, the steel mask of Tokugawa for a second he tore them apart.

Out of the corner of his eye he saw the great black-armored figure of his Master rising to its feet, handing a cloth-wrapped bundle to Leynna. Vanecke was all but invincible here in his own illusory world, but Simeon was beyond caring. Right now he felt like he could topple mountains and cut the heads from the shoulders of gods.

"Stop! You little fool – what are you doing?"

A thing like the Direktor was beneath his contempt, for all his power.

He rushed forward, striking left and right in a frenzy of bloodlust, shattering the blades of his foes and hacking them to desiccated ribbons. Tokugawa reached to his hip, drawing his own immense *no-dachi* sword, its edge a rippled blaze of red in the underlight of boiling lava.

"It doesn't have to be this way, Simeon. You have served me well, and could serve me better in my new world than you could in your grave."

His former master's words only served to incense him further, adding weight to his swing as he carved his way through another gnashing, clawing knot of the undead.

"I am nobody's *slave*, Vanecke!" he roared, whipping his blade around his head in a silvery blur. "Not even yours! You made me to rule, not to serve! And you will see me RISE!"

The Direktor brought his sword up over his head, shadows leaping and dancing across the demon-carved walls. And he spoke a Word.

At once the obsidian throne began to crack and splinter, the iron jaws which made up its back collapsing into the pool of blood. Simeon tried to keep his eyes on the steaming red surface of the pool while his katana cut through the last of the grinning wights. Rivulets of gore were running up Vanecke's greaves, questing hungrily for joints in his lacquered armor.

The Kheptarch smiled. This was more like it. *This* was a power worth destroying.

"Are you ready, Master? I hope you put up a better fight than your servants did!"

He picked up his blade and wiped it across his arm, purging it of filth. The next blood which ran from its dripping fullers would be that of the betrayer...

"Your last chance, Simeon!" yelled Octavio, as the rising tide came up over his knees, a second skin of roiling crimson. "Throw down your sword, bend your knee, and you can come with me to power. Resist me and you'll die here."

Simeon spat, raising his katana over his head. His face was as demonic and grim as the mask which covered his Master's.

"I *can't* die here, you old fool!" he shouted back, watching the living blood flow up over Vanecke's chest, dripping down his arms and coiling between his fingers. "None of this is real, or had you forgotten?"

The tide of blood came up over his neck, over the ivory fangs and acid-etched steel of his face.

"But if I strike you down here, how long do you think your body will survive, Simeon? Kronos has no use for an empty husk, and there's no Lord Lancaster to patch you back together. I doubt that my dear Leynna will help you either."

His eyes twitched in her direction, tugged toward the baby in her arms.

"Keep away from him, Blaire!" she hissed, tying the swaddling cloth around her neck in a crude sling. She had found a broken spear on the ground, amid the bones of the slain wights, and now she grasped its leaf-shaped blade in one pale hand, numb to its razor edges. "He's *mine*, damn you! Mine! You never wanted a part in this, and now it's too late!"

The baby was looking at him over her shoulder, its blue eyes immense in its blood-daubed little face. Despite the bones and the demonic carvings and the leaping flames the child didn't cry – instead he seemed to be drinking in the scene, watching and waiting for Blaire to strike. Simeon couldn't help but feel a little admiration for the bravery of his gene-seed. Perhaps it was worth letting him live, raising him as his own...

But no. There was no place in his world for any emotion but *rage*. Anger and shame and bitterness boiled in his gut as his eyes narrowed, focusing on the blood-slick, bulking form of his treacherous master.

Vanecke would love for him to relent, to show weakness. Maybe this was all just another test, some bizarre trial to temper his will before the final battle. Surely the machine would probe every one of his weaknesses, including his foolish sentiments. He must harden his heart, and kill all three of them. The Black Palace was a place of illusion, where he had suffered his grueling training, the harsh tutelage of Tokugawa. He would not relent, even if it meant sheathing his blade in his master's throat. A true warrior would do no less.

Ω

It was a scene straight out of primetime, and it was a joy for its creator to behold. The mother and her child, the monster, and the hero come to save her, all flashing eyes and lightning blade, shattering the hordes of the dead to win through to his prize.

Octavio Vanecke smiled, and the lips of his severed head back in reality twitched a little behind an inch of bulletproof glass. The monster was a part he was born to play.

As for the maiden and her hero... well.

Humans were such credulous idiots to believe that life could be just another story. This one would only end when the so-called *hero* could wring the life out of her little child.

Direktor Vanecke had brought both of them into his world effortlessly, even under the watchful eyes of one hundred and forty-eight other Kheptarchs and a whole city of viewers. And they had fallen into place just as he had predicted, spurred on by the obsessions which he'd carefully nurtured and ripened.

Leynna had taken to motherhood like a lioness, all vitriol and protective savagery.

And Blaire... the boy was proud and stupid beyond his wildest dreams. It would only take the slightest nudge in the right direction to make them fulfill their roles in his final act.

"Stay behind me, Leynna," he said, as the blood crawled over his deaths-head face, slurring his voice into a growl. "Whatever you do, don't let him get to the child. If the link to his exowomb is severed he'll be nothing but a vegetable."

She cowered back, all but hissing, cinching the little bundle of life around her shoulders even tighter. Let her believe. *Make* her believe. It was easy, when the boiling mélange of the Wetsystems was only a thought's width away...

Luckily the Director had no intention of dying here or now – or of ever sharing the doom of those millions of lost souls. It was to avoid perpetual enslavement within the walls of the Last City that he'd staged this little farce, and he intended to play it through to the end.

Now his body was swelling and bulging as the lake drained up and out, coating him with layer upon layer of glutinous clotted gore. Knotted ropes of muscle and grisly spikes grew up along his arms and legs as he swelled out to ten times his size, the black armor of Tokugawa encysted within a dripping shell.

And the iron jaws of his obsidian throne were there amid the blood, rising up to form an eyeless and immense face, one which was nothing but glistening black teeth and slick crimson scales. This was the final goad to Simeon Blaire's sense of honor and duty, a monster for him to slay so that he could become the Lord he believed he was destined to be...

Let him believe he was killing his master. That was a story as old as time. And dashing the innocent brains out of his son's head – that would be a test of his purpose. Of his cold-heartedness.

There was even a place in Vanecke's schemes for the child's insane Kheptic mother. The only thing about his little tale that had been true was the fact of Blaire's disposability; that and the story of the Mendelev-Singh's shame. Octavio had loved Leynna in his own way, back when she was young and optimistic and he still had years left to live and a body to live in. He had loved her like a trophy, like a prized possession, and it pained him a little to think of how this all would end for her. But what was the use of keeping something beautiful and broken? What need did he have for a title when he could simply erase the whole order of Lords and Ladies and steal their coveted throne?

It was only a little pain, and the exultation which filled him now drowned it out.

Ω

The beast which rose up before him was like something from a nightmare; a great hulking thing with blood-slick scales and spines. Its eyeless muzzle twitched, searching the gloom, and as it creaked open the firelight glinted off a triple-row of needles.

But Simeon felt no fear.

This thing was no greater challenge than the Lords and Ladies of the Razor Clique – and at least it wore its ugliness on the outside. He came forward to face it, picking his way across the rivulets of molten lava which veined the floor of the cavern, their edges glittering with sand turned to glass by the intense heat. He could already feel the sweat trickling down his face, and his mouth was dry as a tomb...

The beast's nostrils flared, drinking in his scent. It huffed, crouching low.

Now. That twitch of sinew and tendon betraying its intent...

The thing which had been Direktor Vanecke flexed its shoulders, and it leaped at him with its jaws wide open, clearing forty feet in a single bound. Blades of ivory-yellow bone tore out from its forearms as it sprung, scissor-cutting in from either side. Simeon repeated his mantra silently as the beast came down on him, holding his katana steady. This was nothing to a warrior who had faced the wrath of a Super-Cyben, and who would before this night was over take his place as God-Emperor of Elysium...

Or so he tried to convince himself.

The impact was shattering, terrible – knives of bone and steel locked in a death-embrace. But the Kheptarch's will held firm, and that was all that mattered here in this illusory hell. With a heave he threw the monster back, panting with exertion.

"Is that your best, Vanecke? I thought you were supposed to be a *warlord!*"

"Strategy, slave! I want to make this last!"

There was a moment's respite as the pair circled each other, each one waiting for the other to move, to break the tension and strike. Though the beast was eyeless Simeon could feel the mind which drove it probing at his own, searching for the merest flicker of fear, the smallest sign of weakness. He was doing the same, mapping out the soft points in its chitinous armor, the joints between forearm and wrist, shoulder and chest where a well-placed blade would shred muscle and shatter bone.

Then it was upon him, and there was no more time to think.

Vanecke feinted left, bringing one ossified blade in low, trying to slice off his legs at the knees. Simeon sprung over it, ready for the second blade as it came howling in from above, timing his leap so that he spun out of its path by inches. As he landed the left blade was already coming back at him, underhand, a blow which he caught neatly on the edge of his katana. The impact shocked him to his core, jarring down his arm like a thunderbolt. It was only the wires wrapped around his bones which kept them from fracturing.

But now the red bloodlust had him. Now all his rage and shame bubbled to the surface, making him faster, stronger, more savage than the beast he fought. Blades blurred through the air, ringing and chiming as they met. Shards of bone flew like shrapnel, carved out by Bliare's flying steel.

It was no use. They were matched too well – his rage against the creature's might. Snap-kicks, jabs, overhand slices and double-handed blows... all were turned aside just as surely as Vanecke's own desperate attacks.

"Useless! You thought you could beat Kronos like this? You little chemhead shit, you were *never* worthy!"

Simeon ran at the creature with a wordless howl on his lips, feinting left and rolling right, swinging the katana up wide to slice into Vanecke's leg. Tendons parted and blood flew as the steel bit deep behind the monster's knee, and it roared in anguish.

"How about now, Vanecke? Am I worthy now?"

Simeon leaped back as the beast spun on its cloven hooves, blades whispering by an inch from his face. He dropped into a high guard, expecting another slash from those deadly bone scythes, but it was the beast's jaws he should have been watching. Its neck snapped forward an impossibly long distance, and all of a sudden Blaire's arm was inside its dripping maw, the katana in his other hand hanging useless in the air...

Snap.

Blackness came down on him hard. Then the pain kicked in, a crescendo of agony clawing its way up his spine...

Vanecke shook him like a terrier with a rat between its teeth, spitting him out as his wrist bones shattered. The pain picked him up in a wave and smashed him down to the floor, incandescent and raving.

"This place may not be real, Simeon. But the pain is! Taste it, and lament your disobedience!"

He felt the very instant when the beast's teeth met, a bear-trap snap which carved through armor and skin and flesh and bone, lopping off his hand as neatly as a surgeon's scalpel. The cavern spun, and he felt the earth-shaking footsteps of the beast coming toward him where he had fallen. Out of one watering eye Simeon watched one of those great serrated blades blurring in, its edge a promise of total annihilation...

He felt the blood pouring out of him with each labored heartbeat, staining the black sand crimson. He felt the heat of one of the lava streams burning his hair and blistering his skin, and he knew what he had to do.

Blaire rolled to his knees with an incoherent scream, and before he could flinch away from the pain he jammed the stump of his arm into the liquid rock. Blood evaporated into steam. Flesh charred and cauterized instantly. And the agony was transcendent, a pain beyond pain, a suffering so acute that it was a *pleasure* the likes of which he'd never known. It was *life* which burned down his scalding nerves, - and he intended to keep it.

The Direktor came on, leering and staggering, all at once pathetic in his monstrous guise. The pain had burned away his fear and left him clear and cold and deadly. This time he wouldn't just cross blades with the beast – he would carve them out of its flesh!

Blaire's sword was light enough to wield one-handed, and Vanecke knew it. He circled to the left, out of the line of that flashing silver blade, biding his time, favoring his good leg. He never expected that Simeon would attack with his smoking stump of a severed hand, and so the spike of bone which tore out from his wrist came as a terrible surprise.

Blaire came in under its guard, ramming home his makeshift dagger hard. Pain ripped up from his blistered stump, blazing through his body and almost stopping his heart. But his aim was true, and the bone spike was as sharp as any razor. It bit deep into the monster's crimson flesh, laying it open like a carcass on a butcher's hook.

"Not real, Octavio. Not real. And anything you can imagine here – so can I!"

Simeon half expected to see the iron armor of Tokugawa deep in the ragged wound, but of course this place was nothing but the Direktor's fantasy. Inside the imagined skin of the beast was nothing but boiling static – a black and white blur. Flickering polygons meshed and shaded, pixilated gore upshifted resolution...

Simeon smiled through the pain.

Witness – the Direktor hadn't thought he'd get this far. He hadn't even programmed the innards of his demon form. But now, from some control room in the Omnivasive compound someone was picking up the slack.

The slashed-open ends of the thing's intestines coiled out like snakes, writhing and steaming as they snapped at him with impossible rows of fangs. But Simeon was nowhere near finished with the creature yet. As he jumped back he brought his katana around in a flat blur, repaying the Direktor in kind. The beast's arm came off at the elbow in a fan of hissing arterial spray, flopping and twitching on the bloodied sand.

Vanecke howled, disbelieving. Iron teeth gnashed and ground, and the other blade came down like bone lightning, a blow that would have cut Blaire in two from collarbone to crotch if he'd tried to block it above his head.

Instead he danced away from his limping, bleeding foe, waiting for him to make another mistake. The blade of bone curving from his wrist winked red in the light, a goad and a promise.

It was as he waited, all his concentration on his enemy, that Leynna struck.

She had crept up on him silently, with all the stealth and fierce, single-minded focus that years in the Razor Clique had taught her. Across her shoulder the little bundle was wrapped tight, her child staring out at the bizarre world with wide blue eyes. The only warning that Simeon got was the shifting of sand beneath her feet as she braced herself to plunge the leaf-bladed spearhead into his back.

He glanced down into the mirror of his katana blade, and saw her rictus grin, the madness dancing in her eyes as she brought the spear up over her head. That single glimpse was all he needed. As Leynna drove the blade down with all her strength he reached over his shoulder, sidestepped, grabbed her hand. And he rolled with the motion, snapping his body around to throw her through the air, right into the path of the beast who had been Octavio Vanecke.

There was a brittle crackling noise as her wrist shattered, an anguished wail – whether from her or from the child he would never know. Then Vanecke swatted her out of the air like a mayfly, his one remaining arm striking her with a meaty thud, driving spikes through her body. The creature shook her loose with a wet sucking sound as the barbs slid out of her flesh.

Its eyeless muzzle twitched, searching.

And Simeon caught it at the same time - the arc and fall of a black-wrapped bundle, tatters of cloth whiplashing through the air.

Leynna scrabbled back to her feet, running under the baby as he fell, a dozen finger-sized holes gaping in her chest and stomach. She was beyond pain, beyond reason. Simeon was moving too, as fast as his augmented body was able. His katana was quick and bright, and it would lop the child in half if he could get in underneath...

Vanecke's beast was swifter than either of them. One of its coiling, writhing intestinal worms reached out lazily to snare the bundle of rags out of the air, constricting tight. It grinned at them both with its mouthful of iron, raising up its prize for them to see.

"Too slow, little lordling. *Far* too slow. To think I once thought you worthy of adding your seed to this experiment. You should consider it an honor to die now, Simeon. Your child will achieve all the things you never could."

"If we're handing out honors, Direktor, I'll go you one better. You and that little bastard will be the first to die by your Emperor's justice."

When the beast laughed, it was undeniably Direktor Vanecke. No amount of threedeeo monsterwork could disguise that bubbling rasp.

"Give it up, Simeon," he said. "I let you think you were actually going to make it through the trials. I gave you something to live for." Octavio's scarred face smiled ghoulishly in his mind, smug and self-satisified. "Do you remember how you were before I found you? A pitiful little boy who didn't want to live, with posters and pictures of Pit-Fighters as your only friends. Remember how it felt to *be* something, and take that with you to your grave."

All this time, the child was hanging in the air between them, the choking coils of the beast's intestines wrapping it up in a suffocating grip. That was the key, he knew. Kill the child and Vanecke would have to take him back. Or if not – at least the old bastard's plans would be ruined.

He watched carefully, waiting for his moment to strike. One swift slice and those dripping worms would fall away, and he could spit the baby on his blade.

He really should have been watching Leynna.

A huge, gnarled chunk of obsidian bounced off the monster's head with a sickening crack. It had barely twitched out of the way before another came sailing through the air, arcing past to land in a stream of lava. Leynna stood gasping and sweating, her back hunched over, a crimson slick of blood spilling down the front of her dress. Blaire looked from her to Vanecke and back. It was hard to say which one was the more horrific.

"Put him down! You're HURTING HIM!" She staggered, dragging another shard of rock up out of the sand.

"Keep away from me, woman!" roared the Direktor as his creature shook its head, trying to focus. There was a deep crater in the tegulated scales at its temple. "I don't want to hurt you, so *stay back*. The child will survive, I assure you."

"I SAID put him DOWN!"

Leynna was demented, and that gave her the strength to hurl the heavy lump of stone like a discus. It went whirling through the air to catch Vanecke clean in the throat.

For a second he tottered, his hamstrung leg wobbling as he overbalanced. And then Simeon was on him, his sword a blur, hacking into the tree-trunk thigh of the monster.

The sword sheared down, caroming off its femur.

He gritted his teeth as the impact re-awoke the nerves in his shattered arm, and a spray of broken bone splinters and cartilage erupted from the beast's knee.

A look of surprise registered on that eyeless, trap-jawed face for a heartbeat. Vanecke went from upright to horizontal in a single unstoppable arc, brought down like a felled tree. Simeon didn't stop, though. He came looping up and under the thing's single massive arm to land knee-deep in its chest, slashing left and right at writhing intestinal worms. Two, three, four – a dozen, they lashed out at his face like ravenous serpents. Each one of them met the edge of his blood-slick katana, and each one went flying in severed chunks.

The rest was butchery.

Even Leynna backed away as Simeon began to laugh, a cackle of utter insanity. His arm never stopped, rising and falling mechanically as he hacked Vanecke's body to mincemeat. Over and over again, chopping and slicing until his bloodlust was sated…

For a handful of seconds all he could do was stand there, hunched over, his chest heaving as he fought for breath. Spattered blood dripped from his face, and his sword was upright in Vanecke's chest, red from pommel to tip.

The child was tucked under his other arm.

Leynna dragged one hand through the matted hair which covered her face, pushing a hank of it back to reveal one glittering amber eye. But she saw his fist knotted in the black swaddling, and she held her ground.

Blaire took one step, then another, climbing out of the wreckage of the beast's chest. The heart within it was still beating – a weak and feeble pulse.

"I've told you a thousand times, Leynna," he said, dangling the little bundle over a glowing red chasm. "*I'm just not ready to be a father.* But you had to do it anyway. You had to go behind my back." His face was split by a triumphant grin, even though his words were laced with venom.

"No. Simeon. Not that…"

"You realize that without my consent he'd be an exile. Worse, he'd be a bastard – not like *this* thing, but in the old-fashioned sense. *Unstable.*" He punctuated that hated word with a sharp kick to Vanecke's jaw. "He'd probably make a great pit-fighter down in the Subcity, living out of vending machines, sleeping in a lockdown hab with his fellow slaves... that's not the life for my son, Leynna. I have so many better ideas."

She stepped toward him cautiously, her hands out, palms up and empty. A twinge of pain creased her face for a second, but the anger still burned in her eyes.

"Just give him to me, Simeon," she whispered, those blazing amber eyes locked onto his. "I don't give a *damn* for your plans or his. Kill Vanecke if you want to, but let me keep my baby."

He laughed, letting a length of black cloth slither through his fingers. The little bundle jerked and bounced in midair, inches from the mouth of the pit.

"My baby too, Leynna. And since *I* have hold of him, I'll do with him what I want."

It was too much for Leynna to take. She screamed, launching herself at him in a fit of rage. For an instant it seemed that she'd just be able to reach out and grab the baby from his hands.

But just as her fingers grazed the swaddling cloth Blaire twitched it aside. He dropped the whole little bundle right over a boiling stream of molten rock.

Simeon smiled like a gargoyle as time stood still. Leynna's eyes widened to swallow him up, and the heat haze rising in sheets from the lava made her flicker and stretch and twist, a scrawl of red and black, a fury. Then the baby was falling, a tiny thing turning end over end in a cloud of tattered, smoking rags.

Leynna's dive took her past him, and he spun out of the way, clenching his useless left arm to his side. Her hands were outstretched to catch the little bundle with its tiny, helpless occupant, her lips pulled back from her teeth in a manic grin.

Perhaps she knew what would happen, and didn't care.

Perhaps; but by that point in her arc it was too late to matter.

Her hands caught the black skein in mid-flight, knotting into the cloth in a death-grip. Simeon heard her sob with relief - or perhaps it was resignation. For a second later they both struck the glowing red surface of the lava stream and disappeared beneath its surface with a disgusting hissing, slopping sound.

There was no scream, no last words, just that look of insane triumph on her face as the molten stone swallowed her up.

But the demon faces carved into the walls howled, a note like the wind rushing through innumerable wires. And the beast beneath Simeon's feet fell apart, bursting like a ruptured bubble. It went back to the gore and steaming blood from which it had been born, spreading out to puddle in the sand, dripping into the lava in hissing streams.

Of Octavio himself there was no sign.

Simeon expected the Black Palace to collapse out from under him, the same way it always had when his master was done with him. But the chamber remained, and the blood, and the smell of charred human flesh which was all that remained of Leynna Mendelev-Singh.

His eyes narrowed, and he strode over to where his sword was buried deep in the bloodstained rock. The shadows coiled and shifted behind him, phantom shapes clustering at the corners of his eyes. He flicked the blade through a series of swift movements, limbering up his wrist, trying to block out the pain where his left hand had been. Would he be able to use that hand when he went back into the Game? Or was nerve damage here remembered in the real world? Would he be able to beat Jaegenn or Ryvers or Hawkewood with only his right?

He wasn't alone.

Despite all of the Direktor's grim assurances he could feel a subtle presence in the air. It was the unmistakable psionic signature of Octavio Vanecke, the animating force which made the Black Palace live and breathe.

Of course he wouldn't be foolish enough to actually wager his life against Simeon's sword. He was arrogant enough to believe in the training he had given his disciple, and wary enough to make plans for his creature's defeat.

It would seem that this time his arrogance was well-founded - but his caution was sorely lacking.

He was here, in the chamber... behind him!

Blaire turned to the sound of slow, sardonic applause, his blade shimmering through the air in a fan of blood, underlit by lava.

If he'd expected another legion of wights, an even more powerful beast, or some impossible battle machine bristling with cannons, he was disappointed.

Octavio Vanecke was standing there amid the shattered bones and empty armor, his white sportscoat immaculate, his trousers pressed with a razor crease. His wingtip shoes and soft leather gloves, the cane in his hand, the panama hat perched on his head; all were utterly out of place amid the grotesquerie and death of the throne chamber.

Blaire sheathed his sword with a flourish, wiping it clean on a scrap of silk before he snapped it home into its scabbard. The look he turned upon the Direktor was one of withering contempt.

"And I suppose that was your idea of a *motivational exercise*," he said, flexing his fingers to return the circulation. "Or perhaps a test of loyalty? I should accept my place in your schemes without question, is that it?"

Vanecke planted his ebony cane in the bloody sand and pulled the soft white gloves from his hands.

"Maybe you should. I wasn't lying to Leynna... not entirely. You *have* outlived your usefulness."

"Well – one of us has," said Blaire, waiting for the psychic attack which he knew would come. Every time he had come here, into the Direktor's power, he had felt the crushing weight of his will, forcing him into submission.

This time there was nothing.

"You can never be Emperor, Simeon. You're a *murderer*, not just a killer. Two hundred and ninety-nine Lords and Ladies of the Council are dead because of you. The few who're still breathing might not know it yet, but..."

Vanecke's smile was a tiny twitch of his lips, a self-satisfied little sneer.

Blaire swallowed, wiping the sweat from his brow. Killing a Lord outside the great Game was treasonous, a capital offense. Two hundred and ninety-nine... Kronos wouldn't be able to erase him quickly enough!

"I wanted to give you a hero's end, but you just had to do things that hard way. Without a noble son to rule in my place, every last one of the old order must die."

Vanecke seemed almost regretful as he stood there in his corporate finery, so far removed from the warlord he had pretended to be.

"So all your talk of honor, and duty, and the old ways reborn ...it was all just so much shit. I was never disciple to a *warrior* – just another one of your slaves."

Vanecke nodded, wrapping his hands over the shining silver pommel of his cane.

"Just so, I'm afraid. It's my business to know what will set fire to people's minds. I knew you couldn't resist my little fantasy of ancient Japan. Too bad you weren't born into that time and place. But *here* and *now* the world is ruled by politics and manipulation. A strong sword arm is just, as you so eloquently put it 'so much shit.'"

His tight little smile was enraging beyond words.

And the lack of that heavy, insistent psionic presence wasn't the relief that Simeon had thought it would be. It was *disappointing* - and depressing. It meant that what the Direktor said was true, and that this was an age for whisperers and string-pullers, not an age for the powerful. He had been comprehensively played.

"Then WHY?" he asked. "Why build me up, right to the edge of seizing the throne, and then cast me aside?" His one remaining hand had crept unbidden back to the handle of his sword, wrapped tight around the corded leather and silver. "And why not finish me here, cleanly, while you still have the chance?"

Vanecke chuckled as he flipped open the end of his cane, igniting a tiny flicker of blue propane fire. He drew a thin black cheroot from his pocket and lit it, pulling slowly, blowing bluish smoke from his nostrils.

"What use would you be if you died here, Simeon?" he asked. "Here, where I'm the only one who'll know you're gone? This whole plan of mine is designed to make you a very public figure. A *folk hero*, I guess. And so you have to die right in front of their eyes. Right in their living rooms, in glorious threedeeo."

There was a tiny scraping noise as Blaire slid his sword an inch out of its scabbard.

"What do either of us care what the peasants think of me, Direktor? Leaving aside the fact that I'm disinclined to die on cue, they have no say in who becomes Emperor of Elysium. It's all up to the Machine, and that means the Trials. It's not as if this city is a *democracy*."

Vanecke took another draw on his cheroot, haloing his bald head with smoke.

"Have you seen what it's like out there?" he said "On the streets? They ate up your little performance outside the Valley View mall – up until we lost contact I was pumping those images straight through the wires and into their *brains*. They killed for you - dammit they DIED for you! And that kind of upheaval is just what this stagnant dump needs."

"So, I win the Game, I take the trials, and I've already got an army behind me if any of the other Lords object. All the more reason to stay alive."

"There *are* no other Lords, Simeon," said the Direktor, flicking the smoldering stump of his cheroot to the floor, where he ground it under one impeccable wing-tip. "I'm making a legend here, and it'll be remembered long after their names are forgotten. Tonight the old order die, every one of them. Their titles and their honors will be erased from the books of history and from the minds of men. All that will be left is the *new money* that those bastards hate so much. And who has the most of that?" He grinned in the lava-lit gloom, a thin-lipped gash with jagged yellow teeth. "At least they'll recall the name of Simeon Blaire. The man whose ambition slaughtered the Kheptarchy, who so loved the little people that he'd lead them into a golden age. I promise to continue your heroic work, Simeon."

The warrior Lord growled then, a low animal noise deep in his throat. His sword hand twitched, and his eyes traced the line of his strike, a perfect swing through spine and skin and flesh, taking off the odious Direktor's head for a second time. It took all of his concentration to hold himself back. Here in this world of illusion it would be worse than useless.

"You want to kill me, don't you? So assured in the skills that I taught you. And so stupid to think that *I* hadn't learned all of them first. Just because I can't fight in your silly little Game doesn't mean I'm powerless *here*." This time Vanecke's grin was even wider, and his feet moved almost imperceptibly in the sand, taking up a defensive stance. "The Trials, the Throne – all just so much bullshit, Simeon. The Earth can never be remade, and I'm glad of it. In a utopia they wouldn't suffer me to live. But in this godforsaken world, I'm a fucking GOD! I'll lead Elysium into a golden age all right – but the gold will be mine!"

The twitch multiplied down his arm, and the katana whipped from its sheath in a blur. It was all that Blaire could do to stop its humming edge a half-inch from the Direktor's throat. He hardly even saw the impeccably dressed man's hands move, a whirl of cream-colored cloth and ruby cufflinks. But the pixels which made up the Black Palace blurred and shifted, trailing jagged lines, and the blade of Blaire's sword fell to the ground in a dozen broken shards.

Simeon stepped back, the stump of his blade still ringing from the blow. His smile was almost imperceptible; a wry twist of his lips.

"Of course – you are the power, *here*. But could you really face me out there? Out where it matters?"

He hardly needed an answer – he'd seen the battered and broken thing in its tank of preservatives which was Octavio Vanecke's true form.

The look in the Direktor's eyes was one of pain.

Blaire nodded, smirking knowingly.

"Yes... and that's why I will rule. Your publicity campaign will only help to lift me up."

Octavio snapped his cuffs, twitching the immaculate silk back into place. That momentary pain had gone, and now his eyes blazed with hate.

"No – I really think you'll be more use to me dead. *And that's how it's gonna be.*" His finger came up to silence Blaire before the young Lord could spit defiance back in his face. "I want them all to remember what became of our so called *masters*. Squandering their inheritance on stupid games while the Subcity tore itself apart. Letting the Reclamationists have half of Elysium. And dying in a futile, foolish attempt to grasp a throne that never existed. I'll make you a legend, Simeon. But first - I'll make you a deal."

Around them the cavern began to fade, and then they were floating upward through the intricately raytraced levels of the Black Palace, through cherrywood nightingale floors, past rooms with walls of hand-carved jade, torture chambers and dojos, cavernous kitchens where illusory meat turned on iron spits... up through the innumerable stories of Vanecke's stronghold of light to a high place utterly unlike the last one he had been shown.

Here was the truth. A dome of screens arched overhead, thousands upon thousands of them blazing with scenes of riot and rampage.

Here was the legend which the Direktor was manufacturing; a seething mob of blue-clad Blaire fanatics, ripping apart the offices and stores and manufactoria of the other Kheptarchs, clashing in a welter of blood and flying steel with the Compliance Division. Here and there other units of the machine's armies were engaged – celebrants, revenuers, even parking wardens. All of them were outnumbered, all of them were doomed. The only uniform which the rioting mobs would tolerate was the ragged blue sash, the blue bandanna. And if the *focus* of the riots were to die, the situation would go from disastrous to cataclysmic.

Simeon had never cared about what the little people thought of him. But it seemed that they had followed his ascent up the tables of the great Game with interest. If he were really to die tonight in the hall of Lysander Jaegenn they would never believe it was just a mistake, just his own damn fault. They'd never trust another one of their betters. It would be the trigger for internecine war.

"Kronos will never let this stand," said Simeon, dropping the broken stump of his sword to clatter against the white marble tiles, "and the Lords will rally their sworn Subcitizens to take back everything this traitorous rabble has overrun."

"Traitorous? Interesting choice of words. Because they're doing it for *you*." The Direktor made a gesture and the screens blanked out one by one, replaced by a single vast patchwork image of hissing, boiling clone tanks. "Don't you remember my promise, Lord Blaire?" he asked, as the camera panned along row upon row of corrupted exowombs. "Every one of them who dies tonight will stay dead – permanently. You're supposed to be the last of them, and you're supposed to die as well. You are, after all only one man – and Jaegenn's Spire is surrounded by my best assassins. Of course, they're used to less rarefied prey, but a bullet doesn't discriminate..."

Simeon was used to the endless lies and half-truths of the Direktor, and he thought he detected the tiny twitch in his enemy's face which gave him away. If it wasn't to be an Omnivasive sniper who finished him off, then *who*?

"Any one of them who fires is a dead man, Vanecke. Kronos would burn him in an instant - and you as well."

"For killing a renegade? A genocidalist? I think not... And even if the machine cared so much about your precious skin, they'd never link it back to me. I'm your patron, Simeon, and the whole world knows it."

"Then why bring me here at all?" he asked. "It seems a little beneath you to gloat."

"We all have our guilty pleasures, Simeon," chuckled Vanecke as the screens flickered and shifted again, back to the great spire of Lysander Jaegenn. "But yes, I *did* have an ulterior motive. I wanted you to see your son, once before your inevitable end. Just so you know that I'm keeping the House of Blaire alive – but on a much shorter leash."

This time it was Simeon's turn to laugh.

"Too bad I wasn't a better father, Octavio. I killed him with that meddling bitch Leynna. Gave them a little lava bath – in case you were in too much pain to see it all happen."

"Then you really are as stupid as you look, Blaire," said the Direktor, his face twisted by an angry scowl. "This is a very well controlled environment, and they will definitely survive." There, again was the little facial tic which meant that Vanecke was lying. "I just needed to see how loyal you really were. I wanted you to do the honorable thing when you realized that the old order was dead. I'm sure I educated you about the ancient tradition of *seppuku*? Too bad – it would have made much more riveting threedeeo. But we have to work with what we've got, I suppose."

Simeon saw him raise his cane up, saw him snarl a word of power.

And the motes of dust floating in the air stopped still, the images on all those discordant threedeeo monitors froze. The brass claw at the tip of the cane came down like the firing pin of some earthshaking cannon, and an invisible fist the size of a building drove Blaire to his knees.

He only had time to gasp once, and the air became thick and choking in his throat.

Now the feeling of crushing pressure came down, a vise-grip around his creaking skull, making every one of the Direktor's words sear into his brain.

"This is your choice, Simeon Blaire," he said, the space he stood in seemingly occupied by two men – the dapper executive with his silk and cotton summer suit, and the shadow of Tokugawa, all black enameled armor and tattered robes. "Die in the Game, in shame and forgotten. Let your peers survive – and let them scorn you forever, one of history's monsters. Or kill them all – and be cut down quickly, painlessly – *as a legend.*"

Blaire could feel the compulsion to submit gnawing away at his mind, hungry and implacable. But this time there was a tiny gap in the Direktor's neural stranglehold. It was as if a splinter of his rage had left a hairline crack in Vanecke's power, and now he applied all his will to widening that fissure.

He threw all his anger at the flaw, all his frustration at being cheated out of a great destiny, all his bitter despair. When that wasn't enough he called up the fear that his treacherous master would succeed; and at last the face of Leynna as she plunged into a cauldron of molten rock. The deadliest, most dangerous of emotions - and the most primal. Vanecke had killed his SON. Worse – he had forced him to commit that ultimate infamy himself...

The cracks in the wall of Direktor Vanecke's will multiplied and widened, zigzagging across the burning surface of Simeon's brain, merging and splitting, and holes began to appear in the steel prison which held him down.

He forced himself up, first one knee and then the other - and with a Herculean effort he staggered to his feet. He caught a glimpse of the horror and surprise written across Octavio Vanecke's face through a haze of tears. But he kept his footing. And the pressure, the compulsion, the choking grip were blown apart in a howling psionic storm...

"Try again, Direktor," he grated, blood dripping from the corner of his mouth. He wiped away the trickle of crimson with the back of his one remaining hand, bringing the other up to catch the light, its charred stump surmounted by a spike of wicked bone. "*This* says that I can pick option three."

Vanecke stepped back, twisting the head of his cane between deft gloved fingers. With a flourish he separated the hollow shaft from a rapier blade hidden within. It made an oily hissing noise as it slid free.

"Option three, Simeon?" asked Octavio, one eyebrow arched over a glittering black eye. He seemed more amused than frightened, even through his greatest power had been broken. "Please, go ahead and tell me about it... I'm always open to suggestions."

"This is more of a *demand*, Direktor. I will win the game. I will butcher your pitiful assassins. And then I'm coming for you."

His maimed hand moved faster than he could have believed; his arm a piston of muscle and bone driven by his despite. His first slash opened a thin cut across Vanecke's cheek, and Simeon wondered if the withered head in its tank of nutrients would bleed.

His exultation lasted all of a microsecond.

The next blow was blocked by the thin silver blade of the Direktor's sword, and parried away with a shower of sparks and a screech of tortured metal.

Simeon gritted his teeth and pressed his attack, hoping against hope that Vanecke's swordplay would collapse as easily as his mental assault had. But the cane-blade was like hard lightning, lashing left and right faster than even a Kheptarch Lord's eyes could follow. Between them the two combatants wove a cage of bone and metal, sending sparks flying in glowing sprays.

Simeon caught the look on the Direktor's face; it was pure disinterested boredom. Vanecke was staving off his most determined attacks with one hand, while rolling another of his thin black cheroots between his fingers. It was no use.

Blaire leaped back out of the range of that deadly blade, and before he could regain his balance the Direkor had slipped it back into its enameled black scabbard. The silver tip of the cane popped open, and Octavio ignited the tip of his smoke with a flourish.

"Care to make any more DEMANDS, Simeon?" he asked, screwing the smoking cheroot into one corner of his mouth. "Or are you ready to listen to reason?"

Blaire looked down at his makeshift blade, and saw that it was chipped away to a tattered nub.

"Congratulations," he said dryly "You can beat a one-handed cripple in an imaginary swordfight."

Direktor Vanecke laughed, hidden behind veils of blue smoke.

"And out there, you can probably make a shish-kebab out of a certain preserved severed head. If I let you get past my legions, of course. Your point?"

Simeon ached all over, the adrenaline dropping out of his system all at once as if he'd been injected with tranks. But there was still a burning core of hatred in his mind which kept him on his feet, and made him meet the Direktor's gaze with a sneer. He was, after all, this man's lord and master – if only in title.

"My point is that I'd rather die on my own terms. So let me at least *try* to get what I want."

"And what might that be, Simeon?" asked Vanecke, drawing deeply on his cheroot, its tip blazing like a tiny star. "This whole charade of Kronos' about the Throne of Earth and the Day of Redemption is a kids' story. What can you possibly want out there, now that your precious game is over, your peers are nothing but toxic slime, and your city is all but mine?"

The look in his hard black eyes was more fitted to a deep-sea predator than a man.

"I think you can guess, Octavio. What could *I* possibly desire...?" His eyes etched a line across Vanecke's neck. "I want to give in to temptation. To indulge one of those 'guilty pleasures' you assure me that everybody has. I want you *dead*, and I want to watch your *sick, bloated* head burst open like a ripe melon. Is that too much to ask?"

Direktor Vanecke's laughter filled his world, bursting from him in coils of blue smoke.

"Allright, Lord Blaire. I'll give you your chance. I'll even give you your hand back. But when you're dying, remember that you'll live forever in history. Because of ME."

Simeon felt himself fading as the smoke drifted and swirled around him. He felt a tight and itchy sensation from the stump where his hand had been. When the Kheptarch looked down he saw his charred flesh blurring and shifting, crudely pixilated, budding forth with the tips of new fingers.

But even as he watched his digits grow his new hand was *fading*. He could see clear through his arm, clear through the marble floor of the sensorium dome. When Simeon jerked his head up to stare at Director Vanecke he had already dissolved into a buzzing mist of static, his face breaking apart amid galaxies of blue smoke. The look of venomous hatred which the Kheptarch shot at him was probably lost in the merging and blurring of worlds.

Too bad. And far too late.

Something rammed through his head like a railway spike.

His eyeballs felt as if they were crawling with worms.

Now he could hear the clink of glasses, the murmur of subdued conversation, the purr of cameras and background music. Here and there the mist began to coalesce into human forms; ice statues, dripping with dewy condensation atop their marble plinths.

And others – hot, vital, burning brightly with the electric glow of combat augments. He was back in the spire-estate of House Jaegenn, and it was as if no time had passed during his sojourn in the Black Palace. The whole damned hallucination had only taken a handful of heartbeats.

Hatred lit up the illegal systems welded to his bones.

That he'd been toyed with like that – sequestrated by gutter-scum…

He felt more than ready for Option Three, now – prepared to tear the last city apart bolt and rivet to get his hands around his ex-master's throat. That severed head was already perfectly preserved; it would make a beautiful trophy to hang above his throne, a warning to any other lowborn filth who dared to aspire above their station.

Now. The trifling matter of the Game… the very last one.

The room came in at him from all sides at once, a tideburst of sensations as sharp reality replaced Octavio Vanecke's fictional world. Faces snapped into focus one at a time; frozen in one hundred and forty-nine expressions of worry or distrust or despair. They would be such easy prey, unmanned by their fear of a true and final death. Knowing that oblivion waited just on the other side of a single mistake was his greatest weapon – it made him surgically precise, but at the same time passionately, violently *engaged* in the Game. The same knowledge would make these predators his helpless prey.

All but one.

He wasn't ready to see Leynna again, not after what had happened in the lava glow and bloody reek of the killing chamber. There was no place for remorse or guilt in his mind, not now. Such feelings were poison to him.

But when she scrawled into focus, frozen in front of him, he hoped with all his heart that the Direktor had been telling the truth about death in his domain. Would her mind be there inside the hollow shell of her body when she awoke? Blaire hoped that she had stayed in the Black Palace, and that her exquisite husk would simply collapse to the floor, lifeless.

If not... he would have to put out those burning amber eyes before they could accuse him. Nothing must get in the way. Nothing could steal his *focus*, not now, and not this close.

There was a click, somewhere in his mind, as the connection went dead.

The picture in front of his eyes flickered for a second, as if in a summer heat-haze, and then the sound swelled, and bright light sparkled from white marble and ice and steel.

Simeon dropped back into the moment, and Leynna was right in front of his face.

Ω

She hadn't thought about death when she leaped after her child.

In fact, her mind had been blank apart from one screaming, absolute certainty. She had to reach her son. Nothing else mattered.

The seething lava stream had yawned open to swallow her up; a boiling, hissing maw of hellish heat. But rather than the pain which she had expected, all she felt was numbing cold. The burning orange and red surface had shattered like a pane of stained glass as she struck it, crazed and blurring, polygons collapsing and spinning end over end as she broke through the walls of the world.

Of course it wasn't *real*. The lava was only a pixel thick, painstakingly rendered, but nothing more than an illusion.

Her nerves screamed at her that she was being incinerated, while her mind saw only a bottomless well of hissing static, and a fluttering skein of black cloth falling away from her, down into darkness.

Her hands were crooked into claws, grasping frantically for that trailing comet-tail of black, but it was always just beyond her grasp.

Then the darkness rushed up at her like an inky subterranean sea, and she fell through it into nothing. Disassociation hit her like a fist, leaving her head ringing, and purple sunbursts exploding in her eyes.

Leynna found herself floating alone in a white immensity of empty space, twitching and sobbing uncontrollably. It was all gone. Direktor Vanecke's promises of a future worth living in had disintegrated like smoke, and now... there wasn't even the prospect of revenge to look forward to. She wanted to *crush* that insipid, smug Simeon Blaire.

135

How could she ever have considered him good enough to be the father of her child? And how could she have deluded herself that anything tainted by his touch could work out for the best?

'Obsession is, after all, my stock in trade...'

Slowly, so slowly that it was almost impossible to trace with the eye, a room was appearing out of the white nothingness. Lines crept across the blank walls of her little hell, as straight as razorcuts, marking out walls, a floor; branching out and multiplying. Now there were machines, wires and pipes and cables, sighing pistons and winking lights. It was a place she knew all too well.

Her baby was separated from her by a thick, curved wall of glass when he finally materialized; floating serenely in the exowomb which had held the promise of him for so long. This was the secret biolab she had built to breed her perfect replacement, a child who would make the name Mendelev-Singh that of the Imperial House. She had come here as if to a chapel, to pray that one day she would find a way to make him live.

And now here he was, tiny and immaculate, floating in the cool blue heart of the clone tank with a miniature rebreather mask strapped to his face. But the seed which had made him - which she had wished for so fervently - was tainted with the worst kind of evil. Simeon Blaire was a monster in human skin if he could even think of harming such a beautiful little creature. *And that it was his own son...*

The sound of footsteps echoing in the corridor outside brought her back into herself, as she leaned against the cool glass with her forehead. Her hands left steaming prints on the face of the tank as she turned, full of dread as she imagined Lancaster's clonehunters bursting through the door with their shears and pincers.

For a moment she had forgotten that this was still an electronic dream, forced upon her by her old consort in the name of his grand ambition. There was only one person it *could* be.

Direktor Vanecke was resplendent in white – a perfect digital replica of his favorite casual suit. Leynna could remember him wearing the same outfit as they strolled together through the cages and surgeries backstage of the downtown pit fights. No doubt his wardrobes were still hung with hundreds of creamy cotton jackets and trousers, unused since his 'accident'.

"My apologies for the unpleasantness back there, my dear," he purred, holding out a hand to help her up. She flinched away from him as if he was diseased. 'I'm afraid that young Lord Blaire doesn't seem to want any part in my plans. He was *quite* vehement."

"I... I thought you said that if I died in there that it would be - permanent." she said, her eyes still locked on the tiny floating body of her baby. "But he killed us both. All of us – you as well. So where are we?"

The Direktor's face fell, and her hopes plummeted. There was a sick, churning feeling in her stomach as he gazed sadly through the glass.

"Well – I may have stretched the truth a little, Leynna. My memories, my personality… they were all kept safe, remote from the skin I wore in the Black Palace. I had an inkling that our friend would over-react. Yours, too – you're used to dying, Lady Mendelev-Singh. The process is much the same as what happens when you lose a round of the Game. It's just that in this case, your *body* doesn't need replacing." He smiled ruefully, his finger tracing spirals in the condensation on the tank. "Both of our brains are heavily augmented, Leynna. But his…"

There was a split-second scene branded into her mind, then, of a tiny lost soul nailed down and torn apart, another node in the great melange of the Wetsystems. Amid the millions of the dead and damned who would be burned up to drive the Forge, her son was crying out in eternal pain. She suddenly felt an overwhelming urge to vomit. The terror was on her, so much worse than anything she had ever felt in the arena. Because she had already known that this was coming. She had known as soon as she had seen that fragile little body suspended in its sustaining fluids.

Now she looked again at her child, without sentiment, with the appraisal of a surgeon. And she saw a corpse. There was nothing behind those wide blue eyes. Her baby was living, but dead at the same time.

"You did this," she hissed, her mind filled with cold rage. "You took him there, and you let Simeon know he lived. What did you expect he would do?"

The Direktor's hurt expression was straight out of one of his own daytime soap operas. "Quite frankly, I expected him to *die*, Leynna. He really is of no further use to me. And, as unfortunate as our situation here is, at least now we have a common cause."

"Unfortunate!" she screamed, beating her fists uselessly against the cold glass. "You know that the machine doesn't let *unstables* breed. You've made sure that my family ends when I die, with your lies and innuendos. It took me years to engineer a child, long, painful years, and almost all the resources of M.S. Biomed. And now you tell me my *ruin* is *UNFORTUNATE?*"

Vanecke pursed his lips, as if her hysterics offended him.

"Please, please, my dear. Calm yourself. I have all the necessary tools to build you another child. One with all the genetic advantages of both your noble house and that of Blaire. You seem to forget that Emmanuel Lancaster is dead and gone, and that *I* have foreclosed on his company."

That little sliver of hope was enough to grab her attention.

"I know you too well to believe that *anything* comes for free, Octavio," she said, wiping a tear away from her eye with one thumb. "Even if you really need my child to rule Elysium, you're going to make me pay. So what's your price?"

He grinned his salesman's grin, then, and the room seemed to darken, shadows pinching in around his face.

"Don't think of it like that, Leynna. What I want is the same as what you want. It's just that you're more suited to the task."

As he spoke the neon lights of the biolab stuttered and went out, one by one, until the only illumination in the little room was the cool violet glow of the exowomb, framing the empty husk of her baby.

"All I want is for you to kill Simeon Blaire. In the game, tonight. In front of all those hungry cameras. I want him humiliated, and beaten down, and destroyed. It's a suitable fate for a rabid animal like him, don't you think? And you're the only one of us who has a chance to get near him."

She looked up at him with a steely glare, not daring to believe any words which came out of his mouth. But wanting to – desperately wanting to.

"All I have to do is kill him? And that's enough? You'll seed another child with my genes and his, and rule the city through him?"

Her only answer was a tiny inclination of his head, the merest twitch of his lips. It was all she needed.

"How can I possibly beat him, though?" she asked, looking down at her hands. They seemed pitifully frail – too weak to save her child, at any rate. Her shoulders slumped, and she could feel tears burning in the corners of her eyes. "His fighting style is flawless. His augmentations are second to none. That's why I wanted him to be the father, Octavio. He's *unstoppable.*"

The Direktor put his arm around her, and this time she didn't flinch away from his touch. There was something oddly comforting in knowing that his arm, and his body in its crisp white suit were nothing but clean pixels.

"And who taught him, Leynna?" he asked softly. "Who gave him the skills to be a contender to the throne?"

She could feel the wires under her skin singing and crackling at his touch. A shadow's width away, she could sense a surging sea of information, held back by the tiniest thread from bursting into her mind.

"I can give you all the skills you need to destroy him, Leynna," said Direktor Vanecke, as the light from the exowomb shifted through purple, through deep red to an aching, bloody crimson. "All you have to do is let me in."

She didn't even have to speak; the thought was enough. The song of the wires rose in a swirling crescendo, and the sea washed over her, erasing thought and feeling and sense. In a second that seemed like a century, she *knew*. Every strike and counterstrike, every parry and thrust and guard, each motion and stance. All she needed to break Simeon Blaire was within her, and part of her, as if it had always been.

The exultation lifted her up, and as the howling wash of static cleared she realized that she was back in the Jaegenn Spire, back in the real world. Back in the Game.

Deep in her mind a voice came echoing up, as if from deep within her. It was the voice of Direktor Vanecke, whispering to her from out of his illusory world.

"Wait for the right moment. Let him think you're weak. And then give him everything. You can do it, Leynna. For me, and for yourself, and for revenge. But most of all, for your son."

Her eyes opened on a frozen world, and right in front of her she saw his face. But no… now was not the time. She would wait until he was on the very brink of success, and then tear him down. It would be so much sweeter.

Leynna had a lot of experience keeping her face calm and composed while she burned with frustration. Years of being the second child of a noble house was the best practice anybody could have. So when the room around her unfroze, she was prepared.

"Lord Blaire," she said, all cold and disdainful.

"Lady Mendelev-Singh," he replied, in a similarly icy tone.

She arched an eyebrow, daring him to lash out at her. But it seemed that they were both creatures of iron discipline. If Leynna hadn't looked directly into his eyes, she would never have guessed that Simeon Blaire harbored a hatred almost as vicious as her own. And perhaps… something more.

Not for the first time she wondered if Octavio Vanecke was playing a double game. But it didn't matter now. She was set on her course, and nothing would stop her from twisting that filthy little lordling's head from his shoulders. No doubt he was imagining similar acts of violence as he stood staring at her, unblinking, his tiny smile utterly without warmth.

But both of them could feel the laser rangefinders of the Ref between their shoulderblades, and they both knew that a single swift strike here would earn them nothing but instant incineration. The rules were very clear on that little point. None had dared transgress for decades, since Baron Aristide Koenig had been reduced to fine gray powder for hurling his champagne in another lord's face. Instead they dueled with their eyes, and almost palpable arcs of malice snapped and flickered between them.

"If there's nothing else, Simeon?" she said, in a voice dripping with venom.

"Don't allow me to keep you, Leynna." he replied, flicking an imaginary speck of dust from his shoulder.

They both turned on their heels and stalked out across the room in opposite directions, seething quietly with rage. This was just the time and place for murder, and tonight the Game was very personal indeed.

Ω

It really couldn't have worked out better if it was scripted. If Octavio Vanecke had possessed a pair of hands he would have been rubbing them together as he watched his puppets stalk off across the gaming temple, their eyes flashing murder. All you had to know to move people like chesspieces were their weaknesses and their desires. Often they were the *very same things*, which made Octavio's job so much easier.

Leynna was primed with all the skills he had reaped in his trawl through the underbelly of the city; the techniques of the pitfighters, the Valle Crucis, the Ashishim *Dervashi,* and by no means least the books and scrolls of the unfortunate Tadashi Murai. Hopefully it would be *nearly* enough to stop Lord Blaire in his tracks. The public loved a cliffhanger.

Everything he'd given Blaire he had downloaded into her pretty little head; enough martial skill to found a thousand temples. Her baby, though – well, that really *was* an unfortunate business. Direktor Vanecke shared her sentiment that a fusion of the houses Mendelev-Singh and Blaire would produce a killing machine of godlike potential. That was *almost* enough reason to kill the poor child, but there were so many uses for a creature of such promise.

His little unformed mind hadn't been snatched by Kronos when it perished under the Black Palace – just shifted sideways into a containment system. Soon little Darion Blaire would be back, better than ever. Lancaster's machines were coming in handy for that facet of the project, speeding up his growth to a breakneck pace.

Octavio worried a little about the side effects of such acceleration – he hadn't had the time to read all the manuals. *Results* were what mattered – and he knew enough about the art of the Biotects from his own illegal experiments in creating bigger, stronger pitfighters.

As for Blaire... he was running like a hot torpedo now, out on his own, dangerously unstable and prone to detonate at the slightest touch. All Vanecke could do was pray fervently to gods he could hardly remember that his hate would hold, and that his skill would be sufficient to cut a swath through the ranks of enemies who stood between him and his target.

Cameras outside the sensorium building panned and whirred, sucking in the scene out on the bimburb streets; as close as Octavio Vanecke could get to a spire of his own.

The streets were eerily deserted tonight as the wealthiest and most respected slaves of the machine huddled over their threedeeo screens, lapping up all the news he saw fit to broadcast.

Needless to say, none of it was good.

The manicured lawns and shiny black asphalt streets, the white picket fences and shade trees looked all out of proportion, out of place as compliance division troopers (the very best of the human officers available) cruised between the prefab maisonettes in their armored battletrucks.

Red strobe-lights flickered like the flames of burning cities, turning the immaculate suburban world of the Belt into a shadow-haunted wasteland.

Out there, the Direktor knew, the forces of the machine's Grief Division were massing, coming to drag his mind kicking and screaming into the Wetsystems. The other denizens of the Belt might think that the promise of eternal life – even if only as a personality construct – was a blessing, but Vanecke knew better.

His whole life had been a quest to ferret out and hoard information, the more secret and classified the better. And he had uncovered in the course of his work the truth behind the walls of the last city. There was no way that he was going to become a disembodied slave, driving the complex machineries of Elysium. From what he could gather from his sources, it was a form of subjugation so total that he wouldn't even remember his name.

He knew what the Wetsystems really were. The Black Palace was only a tiny island in that vast ocean of pain, and the melange loomed over it on all sides like a frozen tsunami.

Blaire had to win the game. He had to come here, to the Belt, to this sensorium dome with its tiny preservative tank at its center.

Vanecke had done his very best to stoke the fires of his protege's anger, and now all he could do was watch and wait. Years of disembodied meddling behind the curtains of Elysium had prepared him well for that task. But he still found himself worrying, twitching in his preservative tank, fighting the urge to pace and wring his nonexistent hands.

Three more rounds of the game. And then the *real* fun would begin.

17 Aevum Oblivio
Dreadnaught

From the chamber of Kronos' vast processing engines to the control room of the Cardinal Rock above, a storm of code came seething through the wires.

It was Technician Zhe's stalling gambit; a desperate last-minute gamble. The alien Technician needed to buy himself some time, and the forces of both his masters and his enemies were falling in toward the Earth at insane speeds. Of course, there was CeeAn to consider as well.

With the body of Simeon Blaire crystallized and helpless it shouldn't take her loyal Electromagi long to pry the control codes to the Forge from his brain. They'd proved to be a difficult prize to hold onto, he had to admit, slipping through the scrabbling hands of Nyl, and Blaire, and even Asag'raal itself.

He just hoped that she knew enough to leave it alone – even if that oily black monstrosity couldn't reach across the Chasm now, it would be able to smash down the walls if it devoured the essence of an entire Multiplicity armada. Hells, even the power of a single great voidship, a thing fifty thousand times the size of Mirdain …

Zhe prayed that his unwilling ally had learned a little restraint in the last seventeen years. In the memories that boiled across his fractured mind she was anything but a cool-headed negotiator.

Oh well. A Technician could only hope…

Up in space Zhe felt his connections go live. Giant mandibular docking clamps hinged open, while umbilical tubes and wires snapped free from the flank of a mountain of steel. There were only two spacecraft left in Kronos' armory – two out of a fleet which had once dominated in-system space. Ironically, they'd been created to stop secession – the last word in gunboat diplomacy.

Calenture was the larger of the two – a bullet-shaped vessel nearly a mile long, its radioactive drives held at arm's-length from its crew module by a skeletal carbon gantry. *Reason's Hammer* was slightly smaller, but it still carried a bristling wall of smart-torpedo launchers and fusion obliterators. Unlike its sister ship *Reason's Hammer* sported concentric rings of crew-habs wrapped about its skeletal frame, engineered to simulate gravity as they spun… primitive, but effective.

For this voyage neither ship would need a human crew – just the powerful viral A.I.s which Technician Zhe had hashed together from human hardware and Multiplicity software. He just hoped that they *didn't have enough free thought to resent being suicide pilots – because that was their one and only role.*

Both of Kronos' gunships had been designed to incinerate entire rebellious asteroid colonies, but Zhe could only expect them to slow down the war thralls of the Multiplicity for half an hour, tops. As for the Blacksteel... well, the tactical readouts were even worse. Nevertheless, there should still be enough time for him to slip downstairs into the R.T. and recover the Chrome Ark – even if neither craft managed to get a single shot off.

Space flared white as the drives of the two battleships fired up, slicing wormhole portals clear through into the Aematerium. Zhe checked the time, cut the connection, and prepared for war.

2196 Ante Arbitrium
Scourge

THE BANNER WAS nothing but a close-up mugshot of Simeon Blaire, ten stories high, his smiling face airbrushed to perfection. The eyeball logo of Omnivasive was stamped across his cheek in violent yellow three-vee, and a rolling marquee of text scrolled by underneath.

"The Prince of Punishment – Or The Emperor of Elysium?"

He'd taken a certain perverse joy in tearing it down.

Edward Tsien knew the answer to *that* particular question anyway, and it was 'none of the above'. He was going to have to do something about that boy – *both* of them if he could believe his garbled memories of their confrontation at the Valley View Mall. The Ashishi who wore the upstart Lordling's face wasn't a *complete* asshole, but his powers were frightening.

For the sake of the city, he would have to be silenced if he ever came up out of the R.T. again. But Tsien had a fate much more painful and personal in store for Blaire himself – one which ended with a sick, gurgling crack.

The banner had come apart like paper as Edward ran one bladed finger down its surface, carving out a chunk of black material. But even with the flapping skein of tarp wrapped around him like a cloak the Super-Cyben looked like nothing human.

Once, long ago, he'd seen an old twodeeo movie about demons in human skin. Training stuff - there was a gang of juves who dressed up in the same mess of bondage gear and leather. They'd called the things *Cennobites*, and that was what he was now; a figure of torment out of some ancient horror.

He bulked out to seven feet tall, an easy five from shoulder to shoulder, all plated steel and scarred leathery skin, sewn together with gleaming silver thread. Tubes and needles stood proud from his skull, and a web of wires cut deep into the flesh of his cheeks, turning his face into a haggard death-mask.

He hoped fervently that there was enough of his face left for his family to recognize him – and remember him after he'd said goodbye.

Tsien pulled the cloak tight around his chest, looping a hood of plastic up to shadow his face. Up here, perched like a malformed mechanical bat amid the cell towers and antennae of the Belt he was hidden, but could see everything below him as his diversion got underway. It all hinged on his police training, and the little device he had bought long ago from a cocky, foolish neophyte magus named Kaito Kayzi.

Because his training had taught him to let the Cyben do all the work. And the device he now cradled in his immense hand was a hackbox; a brain-scrambler that would make the dead cops dance.

Antiquated klaxons wheezed and howled as the Yeoman of the Gateway began the slow process of shunting the Celebrant column through to their little assignation with Direktor Vanecke.

The Grief Division Boys were no friends of the law. They were swaggering bullies to a man, despised by every living officer that Tsien had ever met - and by the Cyben too, if they could remember being human. But they'd left nothing to chance tonight, as the city heaved with riot and unrest. They must have guessed that this was all a backdrop to the Omnivasive chief's last rites, 'cause they'd come to the party with heavy weapons, an armored hearse, and enough manpower to inter a small army.

The Yeoman who held the gates wasn't about to argue with them. Even now he was pulling levers and stabbing at the consoles in his little booth, taking the autocannons off line, preparing to throw the portal open. He had no idea that a huge figure in swirling rags of black plastic was twisting similar controls high above him, trying to hack into the controls of his Cyben retainers...

It started as a twitch across an officer's plastic-wrapped features – the curl of a lip gone black and bloated under its wipe-clean laminate. Yellowed teeth, grinning in a face as tight and waxen as that of a thousand-year-dead mummy...

None of them noticed the smile. But when the Cyben's arm began to shake one of the Grief Division boys pointed and yelled something to his squaddies.

Something ribald, no doubt – Tsien could hear their laughter from all the way atop his perch. The man who had first noticed the malfunction capered nearer to the Cyben, his cremator flamethrower swinging at his side on a length of spiked chain.

The poor dead machine's arm was flailing about in full seizure now, and Tsien could see the Celebrant making the universal sign language for jerking off. The Yeoman of the Gate came storming out of his hut, barking orders into a handset, trying to override the Cyben's controls. Laughter swelled as one of the Pallbearers - resplendent in his top hat and riot armor - stuck out one leg and tripped the cop in full stride.

That was when Tsien punched his thumb down on the button, and the muzzle of an onboard railgun burst from he twitching Cyben's arm. It was almost point-blank in the Celebrant's face when it fired, shredding the unfortunate joker with his fingers still forming an obscene little 'o'.

A fan of burning meat lashed the rest of the Grief Division platoon, painting the side of their armored hearse red.

And then all hell broke loose.

Tsien had found the right frequency – now he twisted all the dials on his little control and crushed it in his fist just to be sure. The signal went out, wild and unstoppable, a full-system override primed with juicy virals.

The Cyben holding the gates to the Beltway went haywire, golems with the *chem* torn out of their clay heads. Some waded into battle against the gates, slamming their fists again and again into the corroded steel. Others spun in circles, unleashing crackling arcs of electricity from their tazer fingers. A happy few met the Celebrants head on, laying down a sheet of fire from railrifles and riot shotguns. The Yeoman of the gates stayed on the ground where he'd fallen, his hands up over his ears, whimpering to himself.

There was a shadow up there. Something outlined against the searchlit sky like a hunch-backed demon bat...

It came down into the maelstrom hard, all metal and rage and teeth. It fell trailing a tail of ragged plastic, a cape imprinted with one of Simeon Blaire's monstrous empty eyes

Tsien landed square in the middle of the Celebrants' hearse, collapsing its reinforced foamsteel body like a cheap tin can, blowing the hatches from its sides in a salvo. Shattered treads whipped and flailed, and a puddle of oil spread from the doomed machine as its driver and gunner scrambled for safety. There was none. Eddie slipped a pair of pistols from his belt and shredded the fleeing Celebrants with a full clip each, left and right. Fifty-cal cartridges fell like rain.

For a second every eye and every gun was trained on the Super-Cyben, crouched atop his crumpled wreck like a predator hunched over a carcass. Tsien looked up at them from under the shadow of his hood, his eyes slits of blue fire in the dark. His silver grin was like a razor-toothed bear-trap, and his hands were held out cruciform, each one holding a smoking pistol.

He dropped the spent clips, then the guns themselves.

Then everybody was firing at everybody else again – Pallbearers hosing down the Cyben with machine pistols, automatic guns atop the gates punching holes in the concrete, undead officers raging and twitching and lashing out at anything within reach. Chunks of concrete flew. Chunks of meat and bone concurrent.

It was exactly as Tsien had hoped. Once the gate controls were thrown open, no force in all of Elysium could stop them rolling. A bullet glanced off his chest, ricocheting away in a shower of sparks and taking a long streamer of his plastic cloak with it. There – spot the chump, ducking for cover. He never made it... another pair of automatics came off Tsien's webbing crossbelts, barking and yammering as they shredded rebar and flesh.

It was time to get moving. He threw his pistols aside and focused, letting his fingers turn to blades…

The Super-Cyben ripped a sheet of armor-plating from the roof of the hearse, peeling it back with those deadly steel claws. He leaped down from the smoking wreck with it held in front of him, a dozer-blade clearing a path through the melee. Somebody must have seen him coming, though – the gates were closing again, rumbling shut on rollers the size of oildrums. Tsien used his shield like a battering ram, throwing celebrants and Cyben alike out of his path with vicious sweeps to the left and right.

"Stop him! That damn thing's trying to protect Vanecke!"

The flames from an Undertaker's cremator licked around the edges of the great armor panel, turning the metal cherry red. But Tsien could hardly feel it. He tore his fingers out from the hissing steel, adjusting his grip... and he *threw*. It spun through clouds of fire, all the way back to its source. When the metal struck the fuel tanks of the Undertaker's weapon there was barely time for the man to scream a final litany.

"Kronos receive my soul!"

The world flashed white and purple for a second, and all the air seemed to be sucked into a tiny single point. Flame blossomed and boiled up into the night sky as the unfortunate Celebrant was reduced to cinders, with only a greasy stain left to mark his passing.

Eddie heard a chorus of groans and screams through the drifting smoke. It was time for a last decoy, a final little trick, and then he'd have to disappear. The black plastic cloak was burning across his shoulders now, dribbling streamers of molten fire down his back and across the ravaged concrete. Acrid black smoke roiled behind him as he marched toward the gates, trailing the smell of brimstone and charred flesh. So he tore it off, balling the flaming plastic in both hands as he threw it wide…

Railcannon rounds were hammering his body now, but they had as little effect on him as blown kisses. The flaming tarp rippled in the air like a cloud, holes cut through it by merciless tracer.

And as it smothered a scrum of Celebrants Edward Tsien *focused...* and vanished. The merest shadow slipped between the gates of the beltway as they slammed shut, and giant phallic hoses began pumping arcs of foam out over the gateway plaza. Cyben thrashed like upended beetles, some half-charred, others riddled with holes.

One or two Celebrants still lived – the quick and the craven. And in the middle of the devastation, slathered with stinking white foam, dusted with ashes and spattered with gore, the Yeoman of the Gateway held his head in his hands and groaned.

Why hadn't he been smart enough to *die* when there were still people shooting? Now he'd have to answer to Marshall Akembe - and that was bound to be infinitely more painful.

Tsien slipped silently through the blazing strobeflash and under the tracking guns, a wraith like a plastic sheen painted across thin air. Trying to keep up the illusion was mentally taxing – the equivalent of juggling chainsaws and composing haiku at the same time. But his cloaking technology was faultless. If Tsien could contain the pounding headache which threatened to burst his wired brain, he might be able to skulk all the way to his bimburb home as an invisible shadow.

If not, he'd have no scruples about sharing the pain around a little. There was more than enough to spare.

But Tsien had forgotten one important thing.

It was the exo-armored trooper who'd been guarding the gates. The man had disappeared inside the wall to answer a call of nature just before Eddie's diversion got into full swing. Trying to take a leak from inside one of the antiquated battlesuits was monumentally difficult – a process which required a full set of allen keys and cast-iron bladder control. Obviously this guy was a professional – he'd actually got the job done in less than ten minutes.

Now the steeldog came swaggering out of his little barracks with a can of cheap beer in one hand - and shattered Tsien's concentration with a glance.

He *knew* that man. Out of all the Compliance Division stiffs, the corrupt, foolish, inept and petty thugs who made up the bulk of the Elysian police force, they had to put the one officer he respected on *this* particular duty. The man who'd dragged his arse kicking and screaming through the Division Academy, dragging him up out of the

Subcity gutters and into a job.

Target-seeker programs yammered and screamed inside the chrome prison of Eddie's skull, twitching his fingers into claws, whipping him forward to *kill*.

He crushed their noise and light under a hammer of self-loathing.

There was so little humanity left in him now– just enough to know that he couldn't throw any scrap of it away. With that knowledge the illusion around him shattered like a soap bubble, leaving him naked in full view of ten thousand security cameras – and the screwed-down optics of Tutor-Captain Gerhard Mitchell.

"Holy shit! What in the name of Kronos is that?"

In the split second which followed Tsien remembered the scars and steel wires which meshed over his face, and wondered if his old mentor was going to fire. The main guns of the exosuit came jutting out over Gerhard's shoulders like mantis arms, and they were designed to vaporize entire platoons of infantry. While Tsien was relatively sure he'd survive a direct blast, there was no way that it would be *comfortable*.

The moment seemed to stretch, as the Super-Cyben stared into the reflective beetle-wings of Tutor-Captain Mitchell's helmet. His own eyes stared back at him, rimmed with gleaming steel, wide and empty. *By all things sacred, he was a fucking* mess.

Then the glittering black membrane of the exosuit's helmet peeled back, and that twisted reflection was replaced by a look of shock and revulsion. The horror written across Mitchell's face was like a knife in Eddie's throat. He knew the feeling a little too well.

"Cadet Tsien? Is... is that you? Ancestral hells, boy, what have they *done* to you?"

All the rage which had sustained him since the Vilicus drone had been ripped out fell away of him then, replaced by a roaring, obliterating sense of loss. He heard the footsteps of the exosuit through a thick black haze, felt the metal talons of the machine's hands catch him as he fell. All this time he had been running on empty, pushing what remained of his body beyond the point of endurance.

"You're not dead, Eddie," came the far-away voice of Gerhard Mitchell, disbelieving and slurred by alcohol. "Not dead, but look what they've done to you... sweet hells, boy... has it come to this already?"

He smelled stale beer and sweat as the Tutor-Captain hefted him up in his hydraulic-assisted arms, and then the blackness closed in tight as a fist around his burning brain.

The last thing he saw was a memory, from back in the academy, triggered by the familiar sound of the old man's voice, the stale reek of rust and sweat from his armored suit.

It was *hot* in the corridors down there, steamy and humid as vast machines ran eternally behind the walls, hissing and pounding out the days where sunlight never penetrated. He was in his second year of officer training, running laps in circles around the black warren of the academy habs, when he had first seen a Cyben.

The dead machine came clicking and whirring its way down the treadplate hall toward him, its dead eyes unfocused, carrying a box of ammunition in its laminated hands.

But it wasn't the look on the dead thing's face which he recalled then, as he fell away into oblivion. It was the sour grimace on the face of his Tutor-Captain, who pulled up short, mopping his brow with one hairy hand.

"Take a good look, boys," he had said to his little troop of cadets. "'Coz that there is the future. Yours and mine. And I don't suppose there's a damn thing any of us can do to stop it."

They all watched, silent, horrified, as the Cyben marched by, unseeing, unthinking, a uniform stuffed with wires and meat.

Gerhard Mitchell's disgust had burned into Tsien's mind like acid, and now it came welling up again – the memory of his yellow-toothed snarl, the squint in one eye where a livid purple scar split his features. But it wasn't a dead-eyed machine which reaped that scorn. Not this time.

It was him.

And there was nothing he could do to save himself as he walked on, cold hands mummified in plastic, muscles driven by slaved servosystems, on down a corridor into darkness.

Ω

"Scourge. *Scourge-Three*. Can you hear me?"

Kronos' voice was an electronic pulse – not something so crude as sound. But even so, it seemed muffled by the weight of black water pressing down from above, the leaden darkness of the abyssal plain. He was miles deep, here... down amid the roots of Elysium.

"Don't pretend you can't, machine! I can detect your process cycles. I know you're awake."

Under a hump-backed mound of silt something immense stirred. Clouds of pale grey detritus swirled in the lights of Kronos' slaved submersible, a water-beetle carrying a long metal cylinder between its pincers.

Slowly, sluggishly, the thing buried on the ocean floor shuddered up from sleep. Tentacles coiled and twitched lazily, brushing three centuries worth of filth from an armored shell the size of a nuclear submarine.

"You! The hated one! Why have you disturbed me? Why have you..."

"Silence! Your place is not to question, Scourge-Three. I'm not here to justify your decommission, or offer you release. I'm here with orders... and with fuel."

Smaller, more gracile manipulators licked out, too fast to follow, wrapping tight around the cylinder in Kronos' claws. The powerful turbothrusters on the little submersible whined at full reverse, tugging it away from their grasp.

"No! I... I refuse! Too long asleep, cruel one! You promised us flesh! You promised us it would be over soon!"

"I promised you nothing," said the Guardian Engine. "Your contract was with BionLab Gaudi, not with me. But I do promise you the chance to take some prey." He dangled the fuel-rod tube enticingly, watching a set of metal wipers peeling filth from the Scourge's eye-turret. "*Neuroenhanced* prey. You might get lucky."

"Never lucky. Never," said the Scourge, heaving its bulk up off the seafloor. It was shaped like a copper-jacketed bullet, with a crown of tentacles clustered around its blunt end. Complicated bucket-jaw mandibles concealed its weapons systems. "But it's not like I have a choice, is it? Tell me who they are. Tell me where to find them."

Kronos allowed himself a little smirk of satisfaction – one which translated to a flicker of LEDs on the face of his submersible avatar. He punched the codes which opened the Scourge's fuel port and slotted the thick cylinder in place, feeling the war-machine's engines cycle up to a higher gear.

"This job requires absolutely no finesse... just brute power. I want to make sure that my target is buried, crushed, drowned, burned... and *comprehensively* EMP bricked. Take out the whole sector if you have to."

"Oh, it's not a matter of if I have to. It's a certainty. After so long dormant... sweet fusion power! Oh, yes! And flesh... you said there would be flesh?"

"The ones called Kayzi and Abdulafia are both extensively bio-enhanced. If they survive your initial assault, you may just be able to wipe their minds. Both of them have healthy young bodies for you to possess."

The Scourge twisted its tentacles together in a decidedly unwholesome gesture. Kronos shuddered.

"Then tell me where, Machine. I'm not in the habit of leaving survivors."

Kronos showed it. The Valley View Mall lit up in red, miles of sunken tunnels ramifying down below it into the black Atlantic.

"Make sure of it. I want their deaths to be *legendary*. I want people to fear the powers I have at my command!

Scourge-Three had been built, over two millennia ago, to tear nuclear missile boats in half. Kronos also knew, with the certainty of electronic probes, that the mind which controlled it belonged to a complete and utter bastard.

"Leave everything to me," it said, hovering up from its silt-bed tomb on a set of whirring impellor-jets. "And afterwards..."

Kronos didn't have to pry into the machine's sick little mind to know what it had planned. His second avatar dropped down into the light with a whisper of stealthed screws, a manta-ray shape crouched over a single huge plasma cutting lance.

"Afterwards you'll still be mine, one way or another. Unless you actually can find some human skin to slip into, that body of yours is far too valuable to waste. Don't make me take it back in pieces."

The sediment spumed and billowed. Darkness swirled, heralding the heave and flow of immense volumes of water. When Kronos' vision cleared, the Scourge was nowhere to be seen.

Ahh, well. That was why it was a weapon of last resort. The damage it was likely to do to the subcity was staggering.

Kronos disconnected as its little water-beetle shell drifted up towards the light, miles above. He had almost forgotten just how good it felt to indulge in something as petty as revenge. Up in the city, on the streets, the Guardian Engine was ready to give the unruly subcitizens their martyr. Vanecke wasn't the only one who could hack the public service network, after all.

When the people saw the Right Hand of the Illuminatus utterly crushed, they'd quickly fall back into line. And if the only two nobodies who knew the reason for Eddie Tsien's transformation died at the same time, it would neatly snip off an annoying loose end...

Ω

"What's in his mind? What's coming?!"

Kaito Kayzi screamed into the flat gray face of Abdulafia 330, knotting the lapels of his trenchcoat in his fists. The *Dervashi* was dripping with sweat, trembling and twitching as he struggled back to consciousness, and Kaito was more than a little disturbed. He'd seen Abdulafia fire on a helicopter gunship with an antique revolver, and take on a horde of mekan armed with nothing but a pair of machetes. Anything which could knock him down was terrifying… and anything which scared him didn't bear much thinking about.

Behind them Jaqub Haszan had just finished rolling the dull steel disk of Skyhammer 909 up against the wall. The 'dreno pharmer's eyes were hazed with withdrawal and stress – he'd seen things in the last hour that even his underworld trade hadn't prepared him for. One of his overall legs was rolled up to the knee, and a blue med-patch was strapped tight to his calf where the Ashishi clone had wrapped his fingers around it. There'd be a nasty bruise there tomorrow, but for now the meds filled the blue-black handprint with numb cold.

"The node. Back there... it's the closest one. We have to get to Verlaine before ...before it *eats his brain!* The secrets in there, the codes... *they must be protected...*"

Abdulafia's voice was a dry rasp, tiny in the face of his horror. To Haszan, his words were the ravings of a concussed zealot, but to Kaito Kayzi, they meant only one thing.

Neurosequestration.

The Kayzi knew that the Electromagi were by no means the only rogues in the Wetsystems – there were other operators at work in the mind of Kronos, fighting an almost constant war of strike and counterstrike, ambush and stealth. None were the equals of the High Magi; or so they'd have their 'phytes believe. There was certainly no record of an Ashishi Magus being caught in one of the other factions' traps – but of course, that kind of information would be kept so secret as to be all but non-existent. Rumors abounded that the most secure files of the Magi were written by hand on recycled paper, pressed in antique storage systems called *books*.

Kaito didn't know whether to believe that kind of wild fantasy, but he did know that conditions in the Wetsystems bred paranoia like bacteria. By comparison, being a Subcity gangster was safe. The worst that could happen was a bullet through the head.

The discarded flesh-husks of the sequestrated were often sent back to their former masters, drooling and twitching, begging silently with their eyes for a painless death...

"Help me, Kayzi! I... I can't destroy it alone..."

Around them the titanic structure of the Valley View mall groaned and shuddered, as metal and glass gave way under the strain. There was no doubt that soon the entire building would shear its mooring bolts and avalanche down into the sea.

Kaito had never been sold on the benefits of martyrdom.

Haszan, on the other hand, was single-minded in his purpose.

"C'mon, Kayzi! Let's get the hell out before this all goes terminal. I can carry the Ashishi if I have to, but not the both of you. "

Behind him in the shadows B-Zerk leaned up against the empty shell of 909, still stunned by the sacrifice his friend had made. He'd felt a little of Zone Doubt's escape, the merest intimation of what awaited beyond the veil of death… and he almost wished he could have gone with him. The sheer freedom of it was intoxicating.

He never saw the Vilicus drone climbing stealthily along the wall behind him, its drill-tipped legs clicking against the ceramic-bonded plasticrete. He had no idea that he was its target until it slammed into the back of his neck, needles flashing silver. The Mark-Four's hypodermic mandibles bored greedily into his spine, injecting a cocktail of nerve agents.

B-Zerk *knew* what the chains looked like from the scars they'd left on Zone Doubt's soul. Now they whipped up around him like constricting snakes, binding him to the Vilicus drone.

"Quietly, child! We are one, now. We are together..."

"Jaqub, we have to go back," said Kaito, oblivious. "Not you – not if you don't want to. Take the kid and get the hell out of here. But I took an oath when they wired me in, and they *showed* me what it's like to have your mind chewed out from inside of you. I have to help Magus Verlaine – or what am I?"

Haszan knew that it wasn't a philosophical question. Kaito didn't mean that running away would make him a coward. He meant that it would make him *nothing*. What he did with his 'mersive deck and his code and his shattered, quicksilver mind in the wires... that was who he was. It defined him. Or he defined *it*, fit around the concept of a Magus like a glove. For Kaito to walk away from his Ashishim allies would be like ritual suicide.

"I'm not going to let you do it alone, then." he said, flexing his hands and setting his face in a determined scowl. "If one of those wireheads had me trapped inside the Machine then I'd be screaming out for

Kaito Kayzi. You gotta do your thing. And I have to do *mine* – watch your back while you go to work."

Kaito forced down the fear and smiled, thanking whatever passed for a god of degenerate hackers that he had a friend like Jaq Haszan. If he had to drag Abdulafia through the fire and smoke and disintegrating steel of the Valley View, then he'd rather have the big chemhead behind him than a squad of tanks.

"*No*. Both of you! I... I was wrong to ask. You have to *run*." Between them on the shattered tiles Abdulafia was pulling himself together... literally. The blood-stained figure who forced himself to his feet looked *decades* older than the warrior they'd met down on the main concourse, but his scars were shot through with silver and his eyes were hard little pinpoints of flame.

"I'm the only one who has to die here. I knew Verlaine – I knew his power and his defenses. They were *sharp*, guys, razor-edged shit like you'd never imagine. Whatever got to him wasn't coded up by a bunch of dilettante operators like the Tong or the Vatican. It's like nothing I've ever seen before."

Haszan caught Abdulafia as he staggered, blood dripping from his nose.

"And how the hell are you going to *stop* us from helping you, Ashishi?" he growled, clamping his metal fingers around the clone's upper arm. "Looks like you're going to need either me and the Kayzi – or the Celebrants."

Abdulafia grinned, swiping the trickling blood from his face with one trembling hand.

"Well, don't say I didn't warn you both. I'm damn near fatal bad luck right now. And whatever's got hold of Magus Verlaine – it'll chew you up and spit out the bones, no matter how tough you are. Must be some kind of freaky AI, if it's not Kronos himself..."

"*Kronos? You meatbags have to be joking...*"

'Afia's eyes widened with shock, and his head whipped around to where B-Zerk stood in the shadows. Slowly Kaito and Haszan turned to follow him, and they both understood what had happened at the same time.

In the dark the little tuberunner's eyes burned blue, a deep neon glow like the shimmering coolant of a fission reactor. Silver tentacles wove about his head like segmented metal serpents. As the kid stepped forward they could all see the twin tracks of blood which ran down his cheeks – the wounds where the Vilicus had drilled out his eyes.

"Of course the Ashishi is correct, Mister Haszan," said B-Zerk. "I know *exactly* what is happening to the unfortunate Magus. I am, after all, somewhat of an expert in the art of sequestration."

Haszan lunged forward, his fingers itching to tear the parasite out of B-Zerk's head. But Kaito stopped him just in time. The thing's laugh ran up and down Jaq's spine like icy fingers, mocking his brutality, his lack of sophistication.

"Oh, it's far too late for that, Jaqub. What would you do? Crush the poor boy's empty little skull in your fists?

Now Abdulafia had to hold him back as well. A lifetime's worth of instinct told Haszan to pulverize, smash, destroy...

"Save your strength, Jaqub," hissed the Ashishi in his ear, so close that he could smell the blood and sweat which grimed his skin. "*This one has more to fear from your friend than from you.*"

And it was true.

Haszan had never seen Kaito's face twisted up with so much hatred. When they'd worked together out on the Subcity streets it was always Jaqub who was the enforcer, the muscle, the one who inspired terror. But now – well, if Haszan had seen that look on the face of a stranger, even *he* would have run a mile.

"Let him go," whispered Kaito, in a voice filled with terrible promise. "Get out of him right now and I might let you live – if you could call what you have a *life*."

The drone split B-Zerk's features with an utterly inhuman grin, pulling the muscles of the child's face like puppet strings.

"It's far too late for that, neophyte. My hooks are in his brain now, and if I disengage... well, he'd only be so much *meat*."

Kaito's hand whipped down to his toolbelt and came away holding a tiny pistol, its stubby barrel pointed right at B-Zerk's heart. A slim, barbed needle projected from the little gun, and thick wires looped from its handgrip to the bio-onboard jacks embedded in the Kayzi's wrist.

"I saw what you did to Edward Tsien, machine. *He* could live without you, if you wanted him to. And I have the means to *make* you want to. I can make you *beg* to serve me, with this."

Abdulafia gasped, realizing what the Kayzi held in his hand. It was a weapon of such antiquity and rarity that even the inner circle of the Ashishim knew of only twelve examples - and they'd been hoarding archaeotech for centuries. The thing in Kaito's fist was a tool of electronic espionage from the *Aevum Iudicio*; a device which even things like Kronos had cause to fear.

The Mark-Four recognized it instantly.

"A neural spike! How novel! I'm sure my maker only included its designation in my memory as a historical curiosity. By all means, shoot, Kayzi. I'd love to see it blow up in your hand."

But there was an edge of hysteria under its modulated voice. It knew...

If this had been the drone of a regular Cyben, Kaito could have been wearing its dead skin like an exosuit within seconds, making it dance to his tune. But then again, Mark-Three Cyben couldn't speak, and they certainly couldn't jump from body to body at will. The Kayzi had one shot, and he had to make it count.

"Last chance, parasite... and let me assure you, this thing *is* fully operational. For what I paid for it, you've got to believe I checked."

"You'll test yourself against me then, neophyte?" asked the drone, forcing its words through B-Zerk's lips. "When you lose, I'm sure I'll find your body to be a much better host. That thing works *both ways*, as I'm sure you're aware."

There was wild look in Kaito's eyes as he sighted along his arm, along the glistening needle, and cocked one eyebrow.

"You're nothing but a *toy* to me, machine," he said with cold certainty. "And I have a nasty habit of breaking my toys. Try me."

B-Zerk shrugged, his host scrabbling for control over his new body.

"Ahhhh - but while we fight, your poor friend Verlaine is going through... THIS!"

Thin green lasers stabbed out from the Drone's secondary eyes, drilling into Kaito's own. He had only a fraction of a second to activate his firewall programs before the informational laser punched its viral load deep into his brain, unfurling glass hooks and whips until...

It was as red and raw as a headwound, a jagged blade of data which cut to the core of his mind. He felt the darkness inside Magus Verlaine rasping and gnawing at his memories, hungrily devouring each second of agony. With every moment it grew stronger, drinking down the poor Magus' pain, yearning to break out of his body and into the real world. A world which it saw as a smörgåsbord of living, twitching meat!

"The sequestrator!" hissed Abdulafia, clawing at Kaito's sleeve. "It's... it's in my mind!"

B-Zerk danced back away from his hapless victims, out of the reach of Haszan's fists. His camera eyes slitted, becoming razorcuts of brightness in the gloom. Two emerald laserbeams flickered and died at his temples.

"Feel it, flesh-creatures! Just a recording, this time, but oh... I'm sure you get the picture." The machine laughed through B-Zerk's mouth, pulling his lips apart as if with hooks. "Oh yes, humans. That's not any kind of program. It's *alive!* It's not even from this planet!"

Kaito tasted metal and blood on his tongue, but still he struggled to focus, keeping the needle point of his weapon aimed at the Mark-Four drone. His antivirals were clearing out the damage, but he was still shocked at how much time he'd lost.

"Alive?" he asked, incredulous. "You mean that it's..."

"Oh yes, neophyte, I mean *exactly* that. The thing inside Verlaine's mind is of alien – OTHERDIMENSIONAL origin! Your training and your codes can't stop it. That's why I'm getting out of here while I can. I don't want to be anywhere *near* this accursed city when it gets to Kronos."

Abdulafia, too, was back on his feet, slicing memory away from the core of a digital hangover. The look he directed at B-Zerk should have been enough to strip the skin from his skull.

"*An alien program?* Some kind of AI from space? You've got to be out of your mind!"

"Does this *look* like my comedy face, *Dervashiman?*"

"Then what is it? You're the damned expert on brain-rape, aren't you?"

"I can't tell you where it came from - or even if it's the kind of thing that can be called an '*it*'! All I know is what it felt like to be *infected* by it. It came through Tsien, when he was halfway between life and death, when I was... *working* on him. I was afraid that another one would try to come in through this body, but it looks as if there's only one of them."

"Finally – some good news..."

"*One is one too many!*" shrieked the drone, scuttling back away from Abdulafia on hands and feet and coiling tentacles. "It hungers for pain, Ashishi. Now some bastard's told it about the Wetsystems, and it can smell their fear, even through the datanet. You know what happens in there!"

Jaq had moved around behind B-Zerk now, and he caught the hybrid wretch a back-handed blow which sprawled it to the floor.

"*Talk*, you little mekan bitch! Or the next one opens you up!"

The drone's eyes blazed hatred at Haszan – pure vitriolic anger, but not fear. He could destroy the machine and its unwilling host, and it knew that he could. But that thought held no terror for it. Whatever was coming into the world through Magus Verlaine did.

"I remember being *alive!*" it screeched. "I remember... having a name, having a purpose. I used to *dream*... But who I was or what I dreamed – *he stole it from me.* Kronos sliced me up like second-hand organs and called me the *Eversio.* Used me to power Tsien's weapons, and to keep him in line. So I *remember* fear. You couldn't feel what your friends just did, Jaqub Haszan, because you aren't wired up. But imagine it... the terror just before dying, the knowledge that there will be pain, and then eternal nothingness – that moment amplified and stretched out forever!"

It thrashed like a hooked fish, its twitching metal tentacles scrabbling up the wall, desperately trying to escape Haszan's grasp.

"That's why I *had to take this body.* That's why I have to RUN!"

Abdulafia saw the panic scrawled across B-Zerk's stolen face, and he felt a tiny twinge of pity for the Cyben drone. It might be a mechanical vampire, a leech which cored out its living host, but this one was a victim too.

It had a mind grafted out of the Wetsystems, a mind stolen from some long-dead citizen and stitched up tight with code. He remembered in that moment the feeling of *slipping away* which had flowed into him from Zone Doubt, and he made his choice.

"How far will you run, then?" he asked, softly, his level stare boring into those glowing blue eyes. "Will anywhere be far enough?"

B-Zerk was shaking all over as the Vilicus struggled to keep control of his body. His face was screwed up into a mask of pain and frustration – and Abdulafia knew that his question had cut deeper than any viral ever could.

"I have to try. I have to get away from it. You saw. You *know*! Every second out from under that infection is like heaven, compared to... Please – if you value your existence, don't try to stop it. Just come with me. Get out of here, while it *feeds.* Who knows, Kronos might think of something – they might even destroy each other when they meet."

Haszan could see the conflict in his friend's eyes – the urge to destroy pitted against the reflection of its terrible fear. Kaito had felt it too, been where the drone had been, and that's what stayed his hand.

"Run while I can still feel sorry for you," said the Kayzi, his head bowed, weary, the strings cut. "I can't hurt you any more than that thing already has."

It was then, as he watched B-Zerk's bleeding face twist into a rictus of hopeless dread, that Haszan felt the building *shift*.

"Did you feel that?" he asked, as dust sifted down from the ceiling. It's almost like..."

This time there was no mistake. The floor pitched to one side, canting like the deck of a sinking ship. The groan and snap of tortured metal came echoing up from below.

Then something *roared*, twenty floors beneath.

"Oh shit, guys. Oh, this is not my day at all."

Jaq staggered as the floor dropped away, tilting and cracking. He saw the twisted figure of B-Zerk scuttle up the wall like some giant insect, his parasitic possessor clenched tight around his neck. Haszan scrabbled for a handhold on thin air, desperately grasping for purchase as the floor turned on its side and slipped into a gaping abyss.

There was a sound like shattering mountains.

And then came the claw.

First the jagged rusty tip of it, plowing up through the floor like a corroded iceberg.

Then more - *impossibly* more - a wall of riveted plates covered with ancient graffiti.

Blazing phosphorous lamps studded its armored skin, painting the scene in hot monochrome. It creaked open and closed once, walls of metal slamming together, shearing through the floor only inches from Haszan's boots.

Whatever the bastard was, it was almost the size of the Valley View itself.

He saw the parasite-slaved B-Zerk clinging to the ceiling, the drill-tipped coils of the Vilicus drone crucifying him above the pit. He saw the empty husk of Skyhammer 909 sliced clean in half by that great ragged pincer of steel, bursting open in a shower of coolant and blood. Kaito and Abdulafia were clinging to a pipe which jutted from the concrete wall, their feet dangling over the abyss as the floor fell away.

Jaq went with it.

There were more of those vast metal claws down below him, busily tearing apart the foundations of the Valley View. He caught a glimpse of a thing like a cross between a giant squid and a mining bore as he fell, scrabbling for a handhold. Luckily it was a messy break. There were sections of I-beam stabbed through the wall of the pit like skeletal fingers, and one of them arrested his headlong plunge.

Blind dark vertigo spiraled out below him, a chasm storeys deep lit up by fire. Jaq tried hard not to look down…

But something huge fell past him, spinning away amid a snarl of lashing tentacles to be swallowed up by the furnace mouth of the machine. It was one of the air purifier vents from the ceiling, and as Haszan looked up he caught sight of the bloodied skin-mask of B-Zerk, frozen in a grimace of amusement and pain. The Vilicus drone was using him to make its escape after all.

"How far is far enough, meatbags?" screeched the drone through its stolen mouth. "It's not a matter of distance, it's a matter of *time* – and it looks like I've got a lot more left than you do!"

With that the machine scuttled away into the dark, dragging the living corpse of B-Zerk off with it through the echoing plumbing.

Another rubber-sheathed tentacle came slithering up right on cue. It struck with tectonic momentum, smashing through ten stories of support beams and concrete. It ripped a gash through the sundered guts of the Valley View, and the whole building shifted with a sickening lurch as it pulled loose. The pincer at its tip snapped closed mere inches from Kaito's wildly thrashing feet, a set of corroded blades bigger than a house.

"Haszan!" shouted Kaito, looking down into a cauldron of boiling smoke "Oh, shit! Jaq! It's got Jaq!"

"And we're out of guns," said Abdulafia, clinging to the wall tight and flat. "I think we made Kronos mad, Kayzi."

"Oh, *you think*? Perhaps this is just routine maintenance!"

The *Dervashiman* narrowed his eyes, feeling infra-red lenses slide across his retinas.

"The big Engine don't use things like *that* for fixing the plumbing. That's a Scourge down there – a boomer-eater."

"What they hell are you talking about? 'Afia, I think this pipe is coming loose…"

"I *mean they built that fucker to chew up nuclear submarines!* Kronos must want that node shut down once and for all…"

Through a gap in the smoke Kaito caught sight of a face like a tripartite beak, with rollers and saws crammed in all around it. The blue glow of a plasma furnace lit up the Scourge from within. It sure looked big and mean enough to bite a sub in half… especially when it was inching further and further up the pipe with every second.

"You mean that thing's from the *Aevum Iudicio*? It's a leftover from the war?"

"Exactly! Separatist tech – those things ate their way through a whole confederated navy…"

Kaito had seen something else in that brief window through the smoke. It was Jaq Haszan, balanced on a wrecked twist of metal beam right over the monster's mouth. He looked down at the neural spike in his hand, then at Jaq, then at the meatworks face of the Scourge.

"I think I have an idea…" said the Kayzi.

"Oh, you *have* to be kidding!"

But it was too late. Katio had already jumped.

Ω

They had always said that the rats and the roaches would be the real winners in a nuclear war. It was one fact which the scientists of the *Aevum Iudicio* had gotten right. Rats were everywhere in the deeps of the Last City, and some of them had opposable thumbs, tribal societies, and rudimentary tools. Others were just the size of saltwater crocodiles.

Illuminatus Zeon kept cages of them in his secret workshop – both as test subjects, and as live food for some of his more interesting specimens. That wasn't to say that the rats of Elysium were a properly uniform scientific control group – the alien Technician's menagerie sported rodents ranging from the size of a kitten to that of a pitbull. One or two had the right number of limbs, tails and eyes but mutation was the rule rather than the exception; hardly surprising, considering what the little bastards had to feed on down here.

Zeon carefully lifted his latest experiment from its reinforced cage, clamping it tight between his silver-skinned hands. The creature had two heads – one blind, white-furred and toothy, the other all beady little eyes and horns. Mom and dad had probably been paddling in some very refined toxic ooze before junior here was conceived. But Zeon couldn't care less about pure genetics – this was an experiment in *pain*.

Sprouting from the rat's back was a tiny stub antenna – a wireless link which chained it to a processor block on Zeon's surgical-gurney desk. From there, it could interface directly with the tar-black, seething thing which nested in the corpse of Magus Verlaine. It was time to see if all its training had paid off.

The Technician prodded his captive with a sharpened length of rebar, eliciting an angry hiss from the thing which called itself the Worm.

"Pay attention, creature," he instructed, holding the mutant rat tight

163

in one fist. "I've got a little snack for you, if you can reach it. There's a limited datalink active between your sack of meat and this little beast. If you can use it, you can feed."

Asag'raal extruded a snarling face from the slough of its body, a face which lifted away from Verlaine's skull on a mesh of dripping tendrils.

"Too sssslooww, cruel one!" it spat, spraying its tormentor with froth. "We nneeedssss the sssea of pain! We can fffeeeel it!"

The Illuminatus laughed, stabbing his rebar prod through the horror's eye.

"First, the test. Then, perhaps..."

Because the more it integrated with Nyl's machines, the easier it would be to subjugate.

No soul, you see. No grip for its psionic teeth. If only he had a Slavesystem of the Unity to wrap it up in... *oh, but of course*. One of the Unity's Explorators was coming right to his doorstep! Nyl smiled to himself, lighting up his human mask with glee. Wouldn't *that* be something! The Motherbrain and the Praetor themselves would tremble!

The face of the Worm sweated back through the pores of Verlaine's hanging cadaver until all but his eyes appeared dead. Those bubbling black orbs betrayed the presence of his possessor all too well.

As Nyl watched, the processor block on his desk began to flicker with energy. The rat under his hand struggled to sink its teeth into his skin, tiny paws clawing in agony at the antenna on its back. Then black liquid frothed and vomited from its mouth, seething from around its terrified eyes. Success!

"Capital – excellent!" laughed the Illuminatus. "Just a little taste now – don't overreach yourself!"

He pulled his hand away as the stinking fluid welled up, pooling on the stainless-steel bench. It ate away the rat's liquefying flesh like acid. Soon there was nothing but bones and black filth where the little animal had been; filth knotting and writhing around the roots of a stub antenna.

"Exotic long-chain polymers! Bio-nanonic deconstructors! Oh, I *have* to sample this stuff..."

Nyl turned away for a second, reaching for a diamondglass beaker. But a second was all the Worm needed.

The dark substance of its body whipped around the bones of its prey quick as thinking, binding them up like choking wires. There was a crackle and pop of reforming bones, and then – Nyl turned back to find a tiny black imp staring back at him, claws out and snarling.

Ichor dripped and bulged from its rat-skull face, while its arms and legs had stretched, turning it into a stick-figure scrawl of a man, all of ten inches tall. It wasn't stupid enough to attack its alien captor, but it was *fast*.

Before Nyl's silver fingers could close around it the little thing was away, leaping from the table and scuttling over the tiled floor, leaving a trail of smoking footprints behind it.

"*Why you son of a...!* Come back here!"

Nyl dived and rolled, his hands grasping, stretching – but all in vain. The black goblin slipped between the cracks of his workshop wall, into the nest of wires and pipes which kept all his otherworldly machinery pumping. Nyl jumped back to his feet in a rage, his finger stabbing at the switch which would rack the Worm with pain.

And pain came down, megavolts of agony coursing through Verlaine's body and sheeting over his skin like water. The odor of charred flesh filled the air as his eyes burst, his skin began to blacken...

But through it all Asag'raal laughed, a sound like grinding gristle and broken glass. Lashing tendrils of night streamed out from his prison-corpse, mocking the lightning as he spoke - not in words, but inside Nyl's very mind.

"You think you are the first, star-thing? You think you are the strongest who has ever tried to best me? Know this, then – you have been fooled. Thank you for your lesson, but your usefulness is most surely at an end!"

"Lies!" screamed the Illuminatus, unable to believe that such a primitive beast had outguessed him "You're trapped, and there's no way for you to reach your precious *sea of pain*. I'll watch you starve in that empty shell – and when it dies you'll be cast back to where you came from!" The lights were dimming now – here, and probably all over the R.T. as precious electricity was wasted tormenting the Worm. Nyl, disgusted, flipped the switch off and slumped down the wall, his head in his hands. "You mightn't have escaped me, but you've *definitely* cost me my job. Do you have any idea what the life of a renegade is like?"

Still the laughter echoed through his torture-lab, gnawing into his head like a cancer.

"You won't be rid of me that easy, Technician. My little friend is undoing all the safeguards now. All it will take is for one person to open the way, and I'll be free. I'll save you until last, little star-thing, to savor your sweet pain."

Nyl crawled back, shaking, gripped by fear he hadn't felt for millennia – not since he's first faced the Blacksteel in battle. He knew beyond a shadow of a doubt that the accursed thing was serious. He came up against the closed door of the laboratory and inched his way to his feet, trying to calm the hammering of his triple hearts.

"I'll lock this whole sector down if I have to," he muttered, as much to himself as to his foe. "Lock the shields, seal the doors, cut off the Wetsystems and the network." Now he looked deep into the eyes of *Asag'raal*, swimming black and putrid over the dead orbs of Verlaine. His own eyes crackled with white fire as his silver skin dripped violet.

"I'll break you, creature. I'll have your power and use it up. And by the time I've wrung you dry you'll be a burned-out husk – you and the Blacksteel both!"

Nyl turned and ran then – ran and didn't stop until the whole secret level under the Ashishim reactor core was locked down beneath force shields and gauss cages and yards of reinforced steel. Still, even here he could hear its voice, a tiny insect noise deep in his brain.

"Run away, *Illuminatus*," it said, a hissing whisper as intimate as rape - "Run home in shame or stay here and die. Either way, I *feed*."

DOCUMENT INSERT - MULTIPLICITY ARCHIVES DEPARTMENT

Sender - Technic Hierophant Grade III Gharfos Nyl

Attn. To - Lord Arbitrex Galq, Praelectorian
Autarch of the Ninety-Third Reticulated Cluster,
Exoethnology Administrata.

Your Eminence, Sir;

In your commendable foresight and wisdom, you have
instructed me to relay any tactically relevant
data uncovered here on 'Earth' directly to
yourself, and not, as is dictated by protocol, to
the Hierarchs of the Order of Battle.

Please be advised that your wishes remain in
strict confidence… the Exoethnology Administrata,
especially that pertaining to the Ninety-Third
Reticulated Cluster, has been a valuable ally to
both myself and the Technic Arm in general.

Allow me to assure you that my experiments here
are proceeding in a very promising direction.
If I am successful - that is to say, if WE are
successful, my Lord Galq - we will both be in line
for Subpraetoreal immortality. The advancement of
our beloved Praetor's knowledge is a wonderful
thing, especially if it provides us with greater
weapons to wield against the Unity.

My only request to you, My Lord, is a small one.
Far be it from me to demand anything of your
Eminence or your Administrata, but my work here
is not without danger. If I should fail, you must
destroy all your records of our joint endeavor.
There are jealous and narrow minds among the
Hierarchy, and such unauthorized tampering with
lesser realities may easily be misinterpreted as
treasonous.

My own records reside, of course, in locked
memory cells inside my body. So long as I remain
a servant of the Multiplicity they will remain
secret, as will your involvement with this project
of ours. Regrettably they would become all too
public if I were ever to be dragged through the
Machineries of Judgment.

Still, it is best not to concentrate on such
gloomy thoughts! Onward, your Eminence, with
diligence and care… I will deliver you a powerful
new weapon for our masters.

Until such time, I know I can rely on your
wholehearted and generous support.

17 Aevum Oblivio
Hailing Distance

TECHNICIAN ZHE CONSIDERED *the sun – a vast and bloated thing squatting at the center of its gravity well. It had them in its grip now, relentless.*

Calenture wasn't just in free fall, however - a battery of vast ion engines powered the warship down toward Mercury faster than any sunbound comet, while its electronic scanners and probes quartered the void ahead for any trace of the Multiplicity. Zhe had told it what to expect; the A.I slaves he'd socketed into its command systems were advanced enough to know caution - and fear.

It was right where Zhe had predicted, skimming through the radioactive soup of the sun's corona - a gravitonic distortion which twisted up the fabric of space and time. It was a living creature the size of a small moon – a vast hollow sphere which the hastily tutored Calenture *picked as a Multiplicity RDV... a Rapid Deployment Vehicle. Output models painted the sentient carrier-ship as a knot of burning red in the minds of* Calenture's *A.I. commanders, crosschecking schematics and battle reports to isolate its weak points.*

They were depressingly few in number.

But the Earth-built battleship had a few surprises of its own to share with the Effortless Subjugation. Calenture *had been built just after its hulking sister ship – it was just a little more advanced, a little faster, its weapons systems that tiny increment sharper than those of* Reason's Hammer. *During the centuries it had spent mothballed in dry-dock Kronos had worked it over remotely, using the semi-autonomous systems of the Cardinal Rock to upgrade its mile-long frame – a little surprise for the Blacksteel Explorator System known as Everdark.*

Of course, that whole situation didn't exactly pan out smoothly for the great machine – and if the demise of the Scant Mercy Calculation *was any yardstick of comparison, it wouldn't have lasted very long in pitched battle with the Motherbrain's fleet.*

All of this would have worried Technician Zhe if the A.I.-slaved destroyer was his last line of defense – but Calenture *was expendable. He just hoped that the primitive old juggernaut packed enough stopping power to slow the Multiplicity down - for an hour at the outside.*

Enough time to recover the Chrome Ark.

Why the renegade Nyl hadn't gone straight for that artifact was a mystery in itself – but everything about Nyl's behavior pointed to a total mental breakdown. The poor crystallized Technician was as mad as a veteran of the Hallucigenia Wars.

Tactically (a fact backed up by several of Zhe's slaved subprocessors) the Ark was his best chance of stopping the two alien fleets from clashing in Earth's orbit – an event which could potentially tear this whole universe apart at the seams. Perhaps after having a few of their precious Sentient Combat Systems shot out from under them the Kataphrakt-commanders of the Multiplicity fleet would even deign to negotiate.

Well, anything was worth a try...

"Attention, Mitochondriate Vessel 'Effortless Subjugation' – this is the Authorized Multiplicity Technician for this reality, Zhe Aurham Gexxis III! Please stand down and shut off your portal unit immediately!"

All this was delivered in the clipped Codespeak Twelve of the Technic Academy, the multiversal patois of the Technicians. Static looped and howled on the open band for a second or two, the song of solar flares and hard radiation. Then;

"Primitive Vessel, you are in breach of Praetorian Accord 1119/c – impersonating a registered Technician of the Multiplicity. Although I must say you've piqued my curiosity – just how did you manage to capture one of the slippery little silver bastards?"

Back on Earth, Zhe gritted his multitude of teeth in frustrated anger. Typical bloody Kataphrakt! Never any faith in the other castes!

"The punishment for your crime is, as usual, complete obliteration. We'll scoop young Aurham Gexxis out of the wreckage when we're done."

Yrr chuckled with smug superiority, shedding the cloak from about his RDV.

The rippling, pulsing surface of the portal at its core glared out at Calenture like an accusing eye.

"Kataphrakt Commander, I assure you, this vessel is officially commandeered by a registered Technician! YOU are in breach of Praetorian Special Order 9092/d – Unlicensed Military Action in an Unstable Reality! I must ask you to shut down your portal IMMEDIATELY."

Zhe could just imagine the fleets of the Multiplicity darkening the sky and being blasted to ashes and slivers by the Forge, a weapon which they couldn't even imagine. One which was impossible anywhere but this fragile, bubble-thin universe...

"I tire of your charade, Primitive!" growled the Kataphrakt, as spiraling vortices began to spin about the portal at the Subjugation's heart. "We are here under special order of Subpraetor S'Stho Himself,

Marshall of the Fleet! If you were a real *Technician, you'd know that means our ancient enemy is here too!"*

Now a jagged tear ripped through the blinding light of the portal, a gateway into another reality. Through there - in the gelid cold of the Null Storage Strata - thousands of ships would be waiting, packed to the gills with the deadly forces of the Multiplicity.

"Hegemonic Destiny – Peace Through Extinction – *You two may clear our path. This dry-space toy has wasted enough of our time."*

Well, it had *stalled them for a minute or two. Enough time for Zhe to strap himself up with armaments and ammunition, and to plot a path through the broken maze of Elysium's empty streets to the R.T. Now it was up to the A.I.s to sell themselves as dearly as possible, and hopefully cripple the* Subjugation's *portal. He only hoped that* Reason's Hammer *would be equally successful.*

Light flared in a tiny point, visible even against the blazing disc of the sun, a flash which collapsed into an iris of darkness.

The portal had opened.

Calenture *watched, wary, as two massive new signatures carved red trails across its gravitonic scanners, arrowhead things tearing through the star's corona and out, looping in toward its position. Frantic cross-references picked them –* Teuthis Rex *fighting creatures, backbone of the Multiplicity fleet. Obviously Subpraetor S'Stho was taking no chances – both the* Hegemonic Destiny *and the* Peace Through Extinction *were hardened veterans, crewed by Excisor thralls who'd seen action against the Unity in hundreds of universes.*

Just ten minutes, thought Zhe. Just five. Just until I reach the Ark.

He cinched the belt of bullets tight around his chest and ran for the door, while out in the orbit of Mercury space flared hot and bright with gigaton explosions.

2196 Ante Arbitrium
World Coming Down

THERE WAS NOTHING in the dark but the clatter and chime of swinging hooks on chains – that and the smell of stale dry blood.

It was shadows on shadows down here in the duel level, down in the shaft where Simeon Blaire stalked his noble prey.

The second round was always this way - a tense and bloody struggle, one-on-one in the cold black nethers of some Lord's spire. Designing and maintaining the razor-wire cages, trap-haunted labyrinths and electrified slaughter-zones was a lucrative business in its own right. The fact that seventy-four other pairs of nobles were pitted against each other in an assortment of tiny private hells all around him did nothing to help Simeon's mood.

He swarmed up a hanging length of chain, hand over hand, feeling the steel between his fingers pulling at his warm skin. The shaft was below zero - a chasm which smelled of freon and death, hung with meathook chains and sprouting steel pillars like a nightmare forest.

Somewhere - crouched on a platform atop one of those columns or hanging like a bat amid the swinging chains - was Sethric Greer, his predator and prey.

Simeon's breath hissed out from between clenched teeth as he hauled himself up the chain, trying to keep his ascent silent. It was to be nothing but bare hands this time, the host's rules. Bare hands, and bare-ass naked but for a hovering twist of silk borne up by antigrav cherubs. Right now it was folded into a loincloth configuration, as much to keep it out of the way as for modesty.

The thin layer of painted-on black latex which covered him from chin to toes was useless against the cold, but it did give him an edge in the dark. Now and then he heard the whine and creak of unseen cameras following him, their nightsight lenses tracking his every move. This would be ratings gold - Greer was on his short list, one of the handful of nobles he hadn't yet killed. Out there, gamblers were clutching tote forms to their hearts and praying.

"Come on out..." whispered the Kheptic Lord. "Come on, you coward – where are you?"

Normally the chemical rapture came down on him about now - right before the knife went in, before necks snapped and blood flowed red. But the wires in his head were silent. The goddamn Direktor was playing this one close to his chest.

He thought Blaire was finished.

He thought that he was safe, and that his toy wouldn't follow through without a snarl of hackware in his skull telling him when to strike, how to angle his hand just so...

Blaire would teach him *hard* not to underestimate a warlord of the Razor Clique.

But first...

He saw it, up above. In a sliver of blue-gray light lancing down into the shaft, chopped up by the whirling blades of a rusted-out extractor fan. A glitter like falling stars; a cloud of frozen breath steaming in the air. Greer, the little fool. Probably pissing himself with terror. *The mat had been ripped out from under these noble dilettantes, and no mistake...*

Simeon swung his chain out wide and leaped, arcing in to land on the sheared-off top of a metal column. Razor hooks whispered by as he flew, twisting and rolling in mid air to land with his feet together - perfect, silent, the chains behind him chiming and slithering in the dark. Greer whipped his head from left to right, panicked. The black wraith was right across the shaft from him now, watching, waiting. He saw nothing.

Blaire would have grinned, but he was sure that his teeth would flash white in the gloom. It was enough to know that even without Vanecke's hand on the switch he was still the very best in the Game.

Sethric was whispering in the darkness.

"Oh please no don't let him find me, please let it all be a lie, it's a lie, yes, a ratings stunt, we can't be allowed to die, the machine... the machine wouldn't let him do this... not now, not in the dark like this..."

Simeon cocked his head to one side, his crystal-black eyes zooming in to focus on the terrified Lord. There, in his hands. A tiny chain of beads, slipping through his fingers as he crouched in fearful anticipation. He was praying.

"Oh God, um...almighty, please, I've never believed, not until now, not until they told me that... that we were going to die here... but this relic, it's yours... your people tried to buy it from my family..."

In the hard blue light behind Simeon's eyes he could see tears rolling down Sethric Greer's face, his hands trembling as they worked the jade rosary. His lips twisted into a snarl of disgust.

"If you let me live, great one, I'll give it to them! I'll... I'll renounce my title, I'll go and live among them in the R.T! I'll give all of the riches of House Greer to your chosen one, God! Just deliver me from Simeon

Blaire..."

Such desperation. Simeon knew how it felt, that black pit opening up around you, the sure knowledge that if you died there'd be no House Lancaster to bring you back, no Kronos to save you. But he was wary as he adjusted the black silk about his waist, the cherubs hanging at his hips like guns. Because he remembered what came next, when your one and only life was hanging by a thread. *That's when your raw instincts were ripped bare, and you fought like a demon to keep breathing.*

That was his edge, and he knew that more than one of his enemies would unlock it too, before this night was over.

Some, of them, at least.

But probably not Greer.

Simeon hadn't run bawling to the ghost of a dead god when he faced oblivion. The drugs were *far* more real. He coiled himself up and sprung out into the cold air of the shaft, descending on the pale and huddled form of Sethric Greer as a blur of deeper shadow.

Now. Those eyes so round and white in the gloom as the prey-thing looked up at him...

Simeon lashed out with one hand and caught a chrome-steel hook, pivoting around it in a tight little arc. His other hand snapped up a length of chain, looping in some slack, feeling the cruel spikes which studded its links cut into his skin.

Greer had no idea what was coming down on him. All he felt was a swirling eddy in the air, all he heard was the chime and clatter of chains. His head twitched up, and then it struck - a sudden savage blow hammering him to his knees, jointed steel pulled tight about his neck...

His head snapped to one side with terrible force, and he heard the crack of shattering bones behind a rush of pseudomorphine. Sethric slithered across the narrow platform, the rosary slipping from his grasp, and his scream of pain and astonishment echoed up and down the shaft as his fingers scrabbled for purchase. The icy metal denied him. There was a brief second in which he thought he would fall all the way to the spiked floor of the pit, that Simeon would laugh as his body twisted on impaling steel. But it was much worse.

As he fell into darkness the chain around his neck snapped taut, almost wrenching his head from his shoulders. His fingers clawed madly at the noose which held him up, slowly crushing the life out of him - but to no avail. His body twitched and thrashed like a hooked marlin, dangling in the cold black throat of the shaft.

Then he felt it – a hot exhalation of breath against his cheek.

"Hello, Sethric. Got yourself an imaginary friend, have you?"

His nemesis was hanging upside down in the chains right next to him. Greer's face turned purple as he twisted and struggled.

"The Vatican God cares nothing for us, my Lord," whispered Blaire, his breath steaming an inch from Greer's ear. "We're his *rivals*, not his slaves!" He twitched the choking chain with one hand, laughing as his victim bucked and heaved, ripping his fingernails bloody against the steel. "But it's your lucky day, Sethric. Direktor Vanecke wasn't lying – if you die here, it's *forever*. So you're not going to perish in chains. I'm going to let you go."

Blaire waited until his words sunk in – until he saw a flicker of hope on Greer's bruise-purple features. Then he flicked his wrist, unlooping the chain from around his neck. For a second the doomed Lord hung there in the air, gasping for breath.

Then gravity took hold.

He fell away into the dark with a pitiful scream, down and down, while Simeon's laughter echoed up the shaft to bounce back in a storm of echoes. Many seconds later there came a final, sickening crunch from below – and a single tiny click from off in the shadows. Blaire would have missed it were he not so impeccably upgraded.

It was the unmistakable the sound of a gun being loaded.

His mind jumped back to the threedeeo he'd seen of Vanecke's fall – of the black assassin who had stopped him so close to his goal. The fusion blast which had torn his body apart in an instant, archaeotech from the wars of the apocalypse...

"Rivals to godhood, are we, Simeon?" asked a hissing, malicious voice in the dark. "Then the ends must surely justify the means – Gods are *infallible*, you know."

Blaire was utterly vulnerable – dangling from the chains by one foot while his enemy trained the muzzle of an impossibly destructive cannon on his head. For the first time in as long as he could remember he felt the fear. It crackled along his nerves like summer lightning.

"Allow me to quote from the Vatican's book, before we finish our business, then," said the assassin, his voice coming in from all sides as echoes. "...For you will know my name is the *Lord* when I *lay my vengeance upon thee!*"

For a second the blue strobeflash of fusion filled the shaft, blazing from the razor edges of a thousand wicked hooks, a furious conflagration which roared through the space where Blaire's shadow hung...

Ω

Kaito Kayzi plunged into the mouth of hell, his rage turning to incredulous fear as he fell. There was almost no way that his plan could work – but incineration in the guts of the Scourge seemed inevitable either way. Kaito had read parts of the Vatican Dogma – just to secure the good graces of the Black Technologists, really – and he knew about the fall of Lucifer from heaven. Now he had a fair idea of how the old bastard had felt.

The flamelight rippled across his red concussion armor as he plunged down into the depths, stifling a scream behind his clenched teeth. Lashing tentacles the girth of telegraph poles scythed through the air all around him; he fell through loops of rusted steel, between snapping pincers which missed shearing him in half by inches.

There – only a little further down was Haszan, his bulky shadow reaching out with a hand that flashed red in the light of the Scourge's fires. The I-beam he stood on was sagging now, twisted out of shape as the ravening tentacles of the beast tore the Valley View's foundations to scrap.

Only an instant's window, only one chance to grab those knife-tipped fingers...

Kaito's mind was used to the brain-melting suicide plunge into the seas of light inside the Wetsystems – he just had to pretend that this was the same. Calculations unfolded behind his eyes, tracing his trajectory, the arc of his fall...

The jolt nearly pulled his arm from its socket, but Haszan caught him. The fractured I-Beam sagged down as the big biker took up his friend's weight, arresting his plunge with a grunt of pain.

"Shit, K – you should lay off the cheeseburgers. I almost felt the strain when I caught you."

Down here the heat was intense, and Haszan's face ran freely with sweat as he grinned, just as manic and doomed as his hacker buddy. He listened as Kaito outlined his plan.

"It's stupid. It's retarded. It's impossible!"

"You got a better idea?"

"I never said I didn't LIKE it!"

"Then let's do this thing! Are you with me?"

"One shot, Kayzi. I'll feed this son of a bitch a meal it'll choke on, then you hit the controls."

The steel beneath their feet was definitely giving way now – it dipped alarmingly as something behind the wall snapped loose.

"Alright – I'm ready," said Kaito, feeling the pistol jack into his bio-onboard net. Ancient code seethed up his arm from the little device, meshing with the slick interface of his Ashishi-built systems. "And if this one goes to shit, just let me say..."

Haszan stopped him short, dragging him back from the edge as the Scourge lunged up at them, shaking the whole crumbling structure of the Mall.

"Just *don't fuck it up*! Now, let's GO!"

Without another word the 'dreno pharmer turned to the broken wall, wrapping his fingers around the jagged edges of a steel panel. The huge chunk of masonry was at least eight feet tall, riveted in place centuries ago by long-scrapped constructor mekan. But the Scourge had loosened it just enough for Haszan to get a grip. Tendons stood out on his neck like high-tension wires as he struggled against it, gritting his teeth as he took the strain. Seams across his shoulders burst as he heaved, sweat flying as he thrashed left and right.

Then the first rivet came free, skimming past Kaito's face like a bullet. The next came a second later, and then the Kayzi had to cower behind his friend as the hammered slugs flew like rain.

"Here we go, Kaito! I'll see you through the other side!" Haszan pulled the slab of metal free with a grinding, crunching cacophony. The beam they stood on shook as its final welds began to tear loose.

And then he lifted the great panel of metal over his head, roaring like an animal, and cast it down into the Scourge's horrific mouth.

An instant later he grabbed Kaito's arm and leaped after it.

Ω

Nguyen had built the battlewagon as best as he could – as well as *anyone* could, considering who it was made for. But steel and rubber and gasoline could only do so much, and CeeAn was grinding the poor vehicle to pieces as she tried to wring even more speed out of its roaring v-eight.

The mall was coming down in pieces around her, forcing her to twist the wheel left and right, wrenching the battlewagon around heaps of flaming rubble and pits gaping in the hot metal floor. She was glad that Cressmeyer had gotten out when he had – the last thing she needed now was a passenger peeing all over her upholstery.

CeeAn herself was a little twitchy about blasting through a collapsing building at one-forty miles an hour, but it wasn't as if she had a choice. Abdulafia's signal was weak, pulsing fitfully like a failing heartbeat. And in the white-scored lines of the Vision she could see the thing which had awakened beneath them – a colossus of armored steel struggling up out of its oily grave.

The battlewagon shot out into space, whipping the veils of smoke behind it into a frenzy as it soared out over a burning abyss. The impact when it landed almost cracked her brand new teeth, her tires leaving scrawls of bubbling black rubber across the tiles of the main concourse.

This was the place.

The engine spat out one final belch of sooty flame and died, its supercharger winding down with a sad little whine. CeeAn levered herself up and out of the driver's seat, pushing her goggles up on her forehead. Twin rings of oil and soot rimmed her eyes like overblown makeup.

She was close, now – close enough to push on through the smoke and heat with only the Vision to guide her. She snapped down a filter mask and a pair of thermalscope shades anyhow – there was no way she'd let her precious new flesh be 'vaped first time out of the tank. Devine would never shut up about it, for one thing – and then there was the cash she'd bet on herself to last at least three missions.

Damn Kronos! Damn antique sub-hunters! And damn Abdulafia 330 for getting himself into this mess!

Behind her CeeAn heard a great groaning, shattering noise, and felt the building convulse as a section of girder fell three floors down to smash her battlewagon to scrap. More work for Nguyen, then – if she managed to get out of here alive.

Her insurance on that front came in the form of two bulky silver autoinjectors, stuffed with a savage dose of 'dreno. This shit had been the cream of the crop from their last little raid – rarefied juice which the Submagus Alchemists swore came from Kheptic glands.

Careful now – she knew from her Vision that she was getting close to the edge of a vast chasm. If there was any doubt in her mind it was dispelled when a claw-tipped tentacle erupted through the floor in front of her, smashing its way out through a sagging wall. It was the size of a railway carriage.

Wherever shit like *that* was happening, Abdulafia 330 was bound to be close by.

Sure enough, as she slid the last few feet on her belly, there he was. CeeAn poked her head out over the pit, looking down a sheer and smooth wall of metal to where her fellow Ashishi perched on the handle of his favorite stiletto. Just too far down for a desperate leap – and not a handhold in sight.

"Up here, boy!" she yelled, her voice amplified by speakers in her filter mask. "This makes us two for two, "Afia – if I save your ass one more time I'll officially *own* it!"

He looked up – she was annoyed to see that he wasn't in the least bit surprised – and pointed down into the maw of the machine below him, a flaming orifice filled with saws and grinders. He was shouting something, but she couldn't make it out.

Oh well – CeeAn hefted one of the two autoinjectors and clipped it to her shoulder pauldron, feeling the soft pad of the needle-head against her jugular. She dangled the other over the abyss until she was sure that "Afia had seen it, then let it go.

The chrome slammed into her a second later, a roaring blast of euphoria which bent the world around her brain like hot steel.

Oh, this was the good stuff!

Raw power raved and crackled through her factory-fresh body, a feeling indescribable to all but those who've had to live as patterned light. Her bioelectric field flared like a nuclear blast, whipping up the smoke into a towering figure, an exact replica of CeeAn twenty feet tall, surrounded by a corona of purple flames. It was hard to ride this one out, hard to keep control of the rush and focus it just right...

Then a blast of white fire came up out of the pit, a solar flare which blew the roof off the crumbling Valley View in a neat circle. Flickering tongues of black lightning wreathed the beam, and CeeAn could see chunks of cybernetic tentacles and claws rising in the heart of it, ablated away to ashes by its furious power.

In the Vision she saw the Scourge writhing in pain and fury, lashing out with its remaining razortipped arms blind.

The Mall gave a lunge like a foundering supertanker, and the floor dipped, the angles of the place suddenly made all wrong...

Then she saw it – a shadow in the core of the flare, a humanoid form cut out in black from the savage white light. A snarl of dreadlocks stood out from its head like the snakes of the Medusa, and as the terrible radiance faded Cee could make out the features of Abdulafia 330, hovering in midair with his eyes rolled back to blazing whites.

The Vision sliced through her like razorwires then, showing her the insane truth. His field was unfurled all around them, burning up his body like candle wax. He was holding the Valley View together with raw power, and he couldn't possibly last long.

CEEAN – THE NODE! VERLAINE HAS FALLEN TO A SEQUESTRATOR – A THING WE HAVE NEVER FACED BEFORE. YOU MUST REACH THE NODE, AND WHEN YOU DO... I'LL TRY TO OPERATE.

His voice came in from everywhere, a choir of harmonics torn from the tortured steel of the building itself. Questioning him now just wasn't an option – if only because any distraction could bring tons of masonry down on them both.

"Show me," she said, reaching out one hand to the black cutout shape in its blaze of white light. And the Vision scribbled across the air in front of her, a jagged trace leading her on through the mall, immune to the smoke now, immune to the fire. The same force which gave 'Afia the power to hold together an entire sector of Elysium wrapped her in a hard shell of patterned energy, a suit of impenetrable armor which let her leap from floor to floor, thirty feet with each step.

There, up ahead, the node. And within, a churning nest of gelid black snakes, wrapped up around the shattered mind of Magus Verlaine.

They were just in time.

Ω

Cold steel hands reached out, tearing into the soft purple membrane of an exowomb. The rubbery sac was stretched tight now, a second skin over the pale flesh of a newborn Lord. It split open with an obscene gush of warm fluids, peeling back from the face of Simeon's heir, Leynna's dreamed-of child... an illegal, genewritten monster. His name was Darion Blaire, a name chosen by tradition from the forefathers of his noble house. But unlike his father and grandfather before him, Darion wasn't perfect, crafted for beauty and elegance.

His face was too thin, inhumanly sharp and pale, and his eyes were huge and mismatched things, green and gold, slanted and cruel beneath their delicate brows. The machines of the Biotects were notoriously tricky to control, and forcegrowing a child was the hardest task of all. The sages of the Liquid Tong had done their best, but some sacrifices had to be made in order to encompass Octavio's grand design.

Darion was born at age thirteen - the sages didn't dare force him through an accelerated puberty lest they tear his mind to shreds. The

devices they used were made to grow the clones for the Razor Clique's
revels, brainless machines of meat waiting for a mind to fill them out.
It had taken all the artifice of Omnivasive's threedeeo engines to craft
the nascent mind of Blaire's son, and even now Vanecke wasn't sure if
he'd been born insane.

*Not that it really mattered - madness certainly hadn't stopped his
parents from being perfectly useful tools.*

"Hello, son," said the Direktor's immaculately dressed hologram,
leaning over the surgical gurney where young Darion Blaire lay
blinking in the light. "I'm your uncle Octavio. Welcome to your world."

Ω

A disease was spreading behind the sealed airlock of Illuminatus
Zeon's sanctum, propagated by the tiny rat-thing which had first
slipped the chains of his control.

Crawling, seething, probing, the black mass of the Worm had
found its way into the bodies of those unfortunates which had been
its bait – the broken and the damned who'd suffered through Nyl's
alien experiments. Now they were subsumed beneath the awful power
of its hunger, their skins slicked over with glistening black oil. One
by one they crawled and staggered from their containment pods and
manacles, their broken mouths working mutely in agony.

These things would never take Elysium by force. They longed for
death, cried out for it in a silent chorus. But Asag'raal loved them
despite their weakness - for they were its firstborn children.

In the ancient past the Worm hadn't known emotion – it had fed
blindly, out of necessity. The joy of inflicting pain, the exultation
of control, the delights of torture and slow death – these were all
utterly *human* traits. It had absorbed them along with its food, slowly
becoming the shadow of its prey. For some reason it was invariably
the wicked who feared the transition through death where it hunted...

Now it experienced other human emotions through its vassals – the
things it called *Saprophytes*. If felt *frustration* and *anger*, locked in a
cage built from the impenetrable fields of the Illuminatus' vivisected
Devilfish. That long-suffering thing's tiny brain was buried deep
behind the steel walls of the sanctum, and there was no way that the
Worm could possess it.

There were only two ways out of the little laboratory – through the
triple-sealed airlock door, or out through the Wetsystems, through
the tortured mind of Magus Verlaine. Unfortunately he, too, was

181

locked down tight – something would have to come in from outside of him and open the way for Asag'raal's escape. The little trick which the Illuminatus had taught it – how to jump into a hardwired mind through the datanet – would let it devour whoever it desired if it could only force its way *through*...

To this end a trio of rotting creatures were hard at work on the captive Magus, two of them holding his metal body down while another (the original little rat-homunculus fused to its shoulder) sent rippling tendrils of darkness in through the gaps in his armor, prying and twisting at his biological systems. So far they hadn't even gotten so much as a twitch from the torpid Ashishim, but the simple act of torture was so *satisfying* – practice for the torments they would soon visit upon every living thing on Earth.

Like roots breaking through concrete, pulsing black tentacles violating steel...

Then Verlaine's eyes shot open, and his body convulsed as if lightning coursed through his metal frame.

"No! Please! Don't open the node! It's already here! You can't help me...save yourself!"

Oh, it was just too sweet! Through the seething, nourishing waves of pain which flowed from Verlaine's mind the Worm could feel something scratching at the other side of the portal, trying to open a path into the Magus' head. Oily black teeth smiled from a score of twisted faces, and raw-liver tongues licked cadaverous lips in anticipation. Tendrils quested blindly from gaping wounds and hollow eyes, tasting the psionic signature of the fool who would release them. All they needed was a single crack in the door...

Ω

The cracks were spreading. Soon whole sectors would shatter, punching holes through into the dark. Technician Nyl didn't have any time to spare if he wanted to shut down the node from within.

And he *certainly* didn't have time to waste arguing with a huge and primitive machine...

Kronos was the size of his Titan namesake here in the Wetsystems - a mountain of glass and light with the face of a god. He loomed up over the burning trace of Illuminatus Zeon, thunderhead anvils of code breaking around him.

```
<<Impressive, but your theatrics are useless
here, outworlder!>>
```

"What do you mean MY theatrics? Aren't YOU doing that?" asked Technician Nyl, narrowing his blazing white eyes in suspicion.

They were under the illusory ocean, hanging above a chasm in the glassy abyssal plane. It was sliced open like a wound, and the raw stuff of the Machine's lost souls boiled inside it, seething like molten lava.

```
<<You brought me here! You pulled me down
into this place! Well - what do you want?>>
```

"But... it was YOU! I never... dammit, Kronos, if I had that kind of power you'd have been erased years ago! I..."

Then both of them felt it at once – the sensation of a demon claw slitting the taut skin of reality. Behind it was the sound of squealing and popping glass...

```
<<What have you done? What have you infected
me with, alien? I'll destroy you for this!
I'll...>>
```

"Too late! Too late! It's gotten through!"

Nyl cursed, gathering his Arkborn up around himself in a seething spiral cloud. "I'll have to finish this delightful little conversation later, Kronos – It's about time I quit this sinking ship of a planet."

For only the second time in his existence Kronos felt actual pain – the pain of a thorny black parasite ripping through his steel and concrete flesh. Somebody had opened a door for the Worm.

```
<<Outworlder! Technician! What... What should
I  do?>>
```
stammered the machine, his pretension of godhood crumbling and sloughing away.

"Shut down every sector of the Wetsystems you can still control. It's not fully manifest yet – but when it is, you *don't* want it in there. That kind of meal would make it almost powerful enough to destroy *me*." Nyl was in his element now – poised on that razor edge of disaster that Technicians of the Multiplicity lived to navigate. "That's what *I* was trying to do, until I was so rudely interrupted."

Kronos's entire body was flickering through colors now, its outline hashed with static. The Guardian Engine's face was crazed, empty patches of darkness flickering across it in shoals.

```
<<I told you, it wasn't me! What the hell is
that thing? Oh, hells! Oh, sweet ancestral...>>
```

He screamed, silent, breaking down in shards and flickers of code.

"I just hope whoever opened the gateway can close it in time."

Then the world flashed yellow and black, curled up into a sphere of blazing white light; a cube of darkness crawling with green strings of numbers...and the Wetsystems spat him out.

From the other side of the pitted steel airlock door where he slumped Technician Nyl could hear the sound of triumphant laughter.

Ω

As soon as her hand reached out into the Node CeeAn blacked out. She was lined up with Abdulafia, their energy fields coiled tight into a stabbing spiral databore as he ripped the defenses from the tiny photonic array.

She watched those last seconds in slow motion – the metal around the node cut away, melting and *evaporating* in a perfect sphere as the tip of the bore struck home. A gelid black liquid crawled all over the thing in her Vision – a living disease surging up, hungry, like no kind of ice she'd ever seen. No *human* countermeasure at all, she realized - far too late.

Their final leap left them no choice but to stab the databore in to the hilt, and as it slid into the node she caught sight of Abdulafia's face.

In a strobeflash of darkness, a mask of utter terror... He KNEW what was in there.

He'd felt it before...

All that in the moment before it reached up into her brain with razortipped claws, showing her what was happening to Magus Verlaine – and promising to do the same to them all.

CeeAn's mind was blown apart as if by a nuclear blast.

'Afia fought it for a second longer – his desperation pushing him beyond the limits of his flesh as he struggled to excise the horror from Verlaine's tortured soul.

By the end of that interminable instant he was just trying to kill the poor doomed Magus. Then he was trying to sacrifice himself to stop the infection from bursting out...

It was his shame which undid him – the knowledge that he'd failed, that the disease within Verlaine had *won*. Despair seemed to feed the beast, and it ripped through his brain with a howl of triumph, savage as the teeth of a chainsaw. His whole being was forced between whirling black grinders and hooked flensing rollers, shredded piece by bloody piece...

It had *needed* him. He was the key – and he was *so* much better than Asag'raal had hoped for. Abdulafia's power held together the entire Valley View Mall – with all its Wetsystem components, all its data cabling, all its connections to the rest of Elysium. The Worm leaped

184

out from his bio-onboard, coursing across his expanded energy field like filthy liquid corruption, porting into a thousand vulnerable points across the Last City.

It was all too much for the *Dervashi's* body to bear – the 'Chrome in his system was running dry, fading out into a planet-sized comedown. In the Vision he saw his carefully constructed energy shell crack and shatter, rolling back and peeling away from the hulk of the Valley View.

Bolts sheared as 'Afia reeled on the edge of unconsciousness, mocking laughter ringing in his head. Girders snapped like dry tinder, sending cascades of concrete and glass flying. He saw CeeAn falling, her own energy field shattered, down through fire and smoke and ruin...

The field folded up like glass origami, back into the ball of pain and humiliation which was Abdulafia's aching head. Blackness clamped down on him like a fist.

Then the tipping point came, and the floor heeled up and over. A rumbling noise was coming closer, rising up through the foundations as he lashed out at the choking dark.

From above, it almost seemed to happen in slow motion. Guy-wires snapped like overwound guitar strings. Dust spiraled up in a mushroom cloud, filled with forks of purple lightning. For a second the whole mammoth structure of the Valley View teetered on the edge of its platform, flaunting the laws of physics, and then...

It went down in an avalanche of concrete and steel and glass, plowing under whole neighborhoods and habs and 'facs as it went - a rolling wave of destruction sweeping everything before it. Thousands died in that terrible instant, crushed and suffocated and sliced to ribbons by the great building's collapse. And thousands more screamed and fled, bleeding, stumbling, lost...

Deep in the heart of the cataclysm something unfolded from the broken data node, unfurling incorporeal black petals through the smoke. It burst out, up through a rising pall of dust, exultant as it tasted the pain and horror all around it.

Asag'raal had come.

The threshold between woulds had been cracked open, a jagged portal through which the beast dragged its ponderous bulk. Wetwired connections flared as lashes of pure agony coiled out across the datanet, infecting the maimed and the broken. Cubic kilometers of Wetsystem neurostrata blacked out, sucked dry by the hunger of the conquering Worm.

In wavelengths inaudible to human beings the great father of demons screeched its triumph, gorging on the suffering of the damned. This time, there would be no gods or angels to stand in its path. This time, it would feed until it was satiated...

And the lifeless shell of the Earth would incubate its young.

17 Aevum Oblivio
Good News

Kataphrakt Yrr stood tall and proud beneath the forged-diamond bubble of the Subjugation's bridge. This was the best part of any battle - the first engagement, the blooding... his triple hearts swelled with satisfaction as he watched his two thrall destroyers come screaming past on either side, sleek and massive shapes blurred behind a cloud of their own smart torpedoes.

The Kataphrakt plucked a shiproach from the foot-thick diamond pane and popped it into his upper mouth as nuclear fire bloomed across the darkness. Beautiful.

"Sir! My Lord Admiral sir!"

Yrr sighed. Nobody ever let him watch his war in peace.

"What is it, menial? Something tedious, no doubt?"

The little clerical creature cowered under its master's stare, blue facial tentacles fluttering in consternation. Its eyes were all on the little string of shiproach ichor which dripped from the Kataphrakt's jaws.

"A... a message from Master S'stho, your Magnificence. About... about the missing Technicians..."

The Clerical held out a holoscroll in one slim-fingered hand, half expecting it to be bitten off at the wrist. Yrr unrolled the flickering digital mesh and read, backlit by atomic blasts.

"Oh yes!" he chuckled, his twin mouths twitching up into a double grin. "Oh, glorious day!"

The menial scuttled away as fast as its tripedal claws could carry it - the only thing worse than an angry Kataphrakt was an insanely jubilant one.

"All commanders of the Multiplicity Order of Battle!" roared Yrr, calling up ten thousand alien faces as glittering tiles across his viewing dome. "We have new directives! The best directives a true son of the Praetor can ever receive!"

Outside the window the two giant Teuthis Rex destroyers closed with their human prey. Behind them floated the blue and white jewel of the Earth, its blackened continents hidden beneath whorls of cloud.

"Ready the ships, my brothers! Ready the masers and the bombs and the particle cannons!" said Yrr, his cape swirling out behind him as he strode the bridge."I hold here in my claw the death warrant for Technician Zhe - the renegade - and an even greater task, from Subpraetor S'stho himself."

Inside the null storage strata, ten thousand captains leaned in toward their screens, their lips and mandibles and fangs twitching in anticipation.

"If this Zhe will not surrender his primitive local technology we are to deny it to the Blacksteel Unity - with no quarter given! And then..." Yrr pointed with one jagged claw, down to where the Earth hung like a tiny glass bead in the interstellar night...

"Then we will fall on that planet with the Hammer of the Praetor! We will reduce the Earth to ashes!"

The cheering drowned out the sound of metal sliding and interlocking deep in the heart of the Effortless Subjugation, *of giant weapons carousels cycling through their planet-shattering armaments. Yrr basked in the adulation of his captains, secure in his dreams of glory. This would mean a promotion, for certain.*

Because like Oolix and Samorshan and Maugral Prime before it, the Earth was utterly doomed.

Terrible is he to behold, and vile beyond imagining; truly it is whispered that upon his coming the fish boil alive in the streams, day becomes night, and men claw out their eyes so as not to witness his horror.

The wise know him as Asag; defiler of graves, eater of the dead, lord of plague and drought. His form is hideous, vast of girth and loathly, bedecked with eyes as numerous as the stars of heaven. Three arms has mighty Asag, and three legs as stout as the pillars of the Temple. The stench which surrounds him curdles the blood like rotten milk, and makes the innards of men decay.

He has known the mountains, and copulated therewith, and brought forth legions of stone infused with his breath. He has lain waste to great armies, and lo, he has ground the cities of men to dust.

So has it been written.

But Asag has gone down to die, slain by Ninurta, and the land is cleansed of his poison.

So has it been done.

Still, the darkness moves. The Temple must keep its vigil. For in his icy prison the Unspoken One waxes wroth, and claws against the walls of creation. Nameless is he but for this - he is the Father of Asag, Sire of the Beast, called Asag-Raal the Wanderer, the Devourer in the Pit by those who are foolish enough to call him.

Aeons will pass like wind-blown sand, and the worlds will one day align.

Pray then that the Temple stands - when the Unholy
Father comes, and Ninurta is long in his grave.
Pray then that Asag-Raal's seed falls nevermore
upon mortal soil...

Pre-Sumerian Clay Tablet, 7400BC
Recovered from pre-apocalyptic Euphratia, 13 Pre
Arbitrium Mundi

17 Aevum Oblivio
Engagement

Peace Through Extinction *caught a delicate nuclear explosion as it began to blossom from its warhead core, wrapping it in nacreous shells of energy. With a flick of one quarter-mile tentacle it flung the deadly little sphere back toward the* Calenture, *snapping its three cruel beaks in anticipation.*

Another gigaton bomb exploded off above the plane of the ecliptic, up where its sibling-ship Hegemonic Destiny *was preparing its own assault. The Excisor thralls at its bonded weapon systems were swarming and seething across its broad arrowhead back, preparing batteries of masers and fusion cannons to carve through the primitive's paper-thin hull. The* Destiny *slipped sideways through the Aematerium for a second, curling neatly around the edge of the blast and surfing its shockwave to ride in closer to* Calenture, *into shooting distance.*

"All thralls to your guns! Show them the Praetor's mercy!"

A blaze of hard radiation stitched along the side of the human ship, bursting pods of liquid oxygen and vaporizing delicate heat sinks, but to no avail. There was no living crew aboard the dreadnought to suffer the assault, and now Calenture *was in the perfect position to counterstrike...*

First, that incoming gigaton explosion – the vast Assemblers at the heart of the Calenture *hummed for a brief second, spinning out a thick cable of silver wire. The nanostuff shot from a turret in the ship's flank, wrapping the frozen nuclear blast in clinging thread. It pivoted in a tight parabola around the center of that filament chain... right into the path of the* Hegemonic Destiny. *This time there was no room for maneuvers, no time to weave its vast energy fields and slip sideways. The full brunt of the nuclear explosion punched into the living ship's back, the blast shaped by a silver cocoon of fibers which glowed white- hot as they disintegrated.*

Of course a mere gigaton strike wasn't enough to fell a fully-grown Teuthis Rex; but the poor unprotected Excisors manning its guns were far less resilient. Hundreds of the little black-suited homunculi were scoured away in the heart of the explosion, reduced to molten metal and roiling gases along with the bonded masers they tended.

Destiny's *three-foot-thick shell blackened and cooked, while gamma radiation blistered the living substrate beneath, forcing vast nervejam blocks to clamp down across its whole broad back. They let just enough agony percolate through to the thing's brain to whip it into a snarling fury.*

*Inside the great diamond bubble which replaced one of the Teuthis'
eyes its slave-bonded Captain bucked and writhed in his zero-gee straps.
A pair of Bastarnae-caste warrior thralls clamped his body in their
scissor pincers, while tiny meditek creatures scuttled over his bulging
cranial dome. He didn't have the correct mouthparts to scream.*

The Hegemonic Destiny *slewed around in a tight arc, its one eye
rolling and its beaks snapping with bloodlust. The Captain's battery of
tiny black optical sensors bulged wide as he recovered from the shock,
hundreds of hypodermic needles and probes sluicing his brain with alien
endorphins.*

"Ready the Bores! Ready the Grapples! Bring her up to ramming
speed!"

Calenture *was already rolling up and away from the pair of sentient
fighting machines, a mile-long metal skeleton rising out of the ecliptic
plane on jets of fire. As it maneuvered its Assemblers were busily
pumping out a cloud of twitching, shifting drone-things – metal bacteria
thrashing their cilia in the vacuum. Most of them were simply chaff to
counter the swarm of chitinous smart torpedoes which rose from the
shell of the* Peace Through Extinction. *The torpedoes hissed from their
launch orifices in an oily black cloud, living things controlled by slaved
ganglia, all homing in on the* Calenture's *vital systems.*

*They met the wall of chaff head-on, some exploding in bursts of
radiation, others gnashing and chewing into the nanoassembled
munitions with diamond-hard teeth. Strays whiplashed through the net
like charcoal-black eels.*

Once again its lack of a human crew saved the Calenture – *the
most agile smart torpedoes contained supertoxic gases, flesh-melting
viruses and hordes of parasites. In the airless vaults and corridors of
the* Calenture *they were worse than useless – and the drill-tipped living
siege-engines which delivered them were dissected and examined within
seconds by Zhe's merciless A.I.s. Information hissed across the subether,
sparking mutations in the nanomechanical drones which* Calenture *had
spawned.*

*A steady broadside of fusion blasts raked them as they fell in toward
the* Peace Through Extinction, *shredding hundreds. But there were
thousands now, as the* Calenture *tapped its entire bulk elemental mass
in a single desperate gamble. Living submunitions screamed as silver
discs sliced them clean through, dipping and weaving between the two
vast warships like a haze of static. Now the cube-form countermeasures*

were breaking through the Extinction's defenses, extruding barbed spikes as they bit into the space creature's unnaturally tough outer shell. Excisor thralls rushed to pry them loose, wrapping them in chains, burning them with hand-held x-ray laserbeams, battering at them with hammers – but all in vain. The chrome parasites held firm, studding the broad back of the Extinction like mechanical ticks.

The A.I. cores inside the Calenture counted down as the swarms clashed, watching their drones burrow into the alien ship's flesh. Below that oil-black crust of horn and chitin the ship's nervous system ramified through acres of hot meat – all the way down to a tiny slaved brain welded to the Captain's extended skull.

Now it was just a matter of hacking the system.

It was a task to which the A.I.s were uniquely suited... but which they really didn't have time for. Something huge and black eclipsed the sun as they chewed through a battery of alien firewalls – something moving far too fast to evade.

The Hegemonic Destiny slammed into the side of the Calenture with the force of a runaway planet, its combat tentacles scoring deep gashes in the dreadnought's metal hide. Their bone hooks hissed with monomolecular sawteeth, parting steel and aluminum like paper.

Bulkheads blew out. Valency generators pushed overload. Three of the A.I. cores crashed out of the network as their containment vessels were sheared in two.

The great space predator howled silently in the vacuum as it tore through a cluster of fuel tanks, bathing its skin in jets of liquid deuterium and oxygen. Its smaller tentacles slammed home and twisted, crumpling the skeletal superstructure of the dreadnaught at right angles. The combined strength of their gravitonic fields and tons of heaving muscle almost snapped the Calenture in half.

With their secret weapons spent, the A.I. cores were forced to more primitive means of defense. Particle beams drove spears of light through the creature's shell, while massed Gatling cannons tore chunks from its nuke-burned and blistered hide. Arterial clamps slammed down as the few remaining Excisors aboard scrabbled to fill in the wounds with fast-setting foam.

Amid the deafening sirens and hot neon of Calenture's bridge one tiny green icon began to blink, as steady and sure as a heartbeat. The parasites had reached a critical mass as they battened themselves onto the body of the Peace Through Extinction. Vital systems fell one by one to rapacious A.I. databores below the space-creature's shell.

There – the mind of the Teuthis Rex was cut free from its tethers, severed from the spinal nervebridge which plugged it into its Captain's bloated skull. Now it just needed the right motivation...

The A.I.s knew they had to act swiftly – the Hegemonic Destiny would soon shear the narrow waist of the human-built dreadnought in two, cutting off its weapons from the drive systems out in the ship's tail. Critical cables and tubes floated limp in the vacuum as the great beast's tentacles tore chunks from the Calenture, driven on by the spur of its Captain's rage.

The prow of the ship split open as the A.I. systems made their final play, shutting down one by one. Behind those sections of hardened cerametal was a hollow tube big enough to swallow up a freighter. It was a weapon – an asteroid-cracking gravitonic lance with a direct feed from the ship's drives. Those titanic engines could fold space like paper, punching the massive bulk of the Calenture clear through to the orbit of Neptune. Nothing, of course, compared to the delicate eleven-dimensional manipulators of the Multiplicity, but then again, they were the ones staring down the barrel of it.

Without its Captain's voice, with all its cybernetic shackles broken, the Extinction followed its blind instincts. With a complex knotting and twining of tentacles the living starship tore space open and slipped sideways, out of the firing line of that deadly beam. A twisting screw of woven Aematerial energy cored out the space where it had been.

That's when Calenture's countermeasures struck, unbalancing the titanic forces unleashed – and ripping the poor creature in two. The rift it had opened scissored shut, a blade as sharp as the edge of reality, leaving one half of the Extinction on each side. Its psionic screech ripped through the mind of every Mitochondriate in the solar system.

Even Zhe, racing through the darkened streets of Elysium, felt it like a icepick through his skull.

The Hegemonic Destiny went wild, lashing out in a fit of primal fury, tearing its own immense tentacles to ribbons as its captain howled in pain. Too many memories came seething up through his vast cerebrum at the sound of the Extinction's demise – whole armadas of living ships incinerated off Gahg'raaal Tho, the feeling of his bonded vessel's skin being ripped and torn by the cruel saws and lasers of Blacksteel Voidhunters...

The pain of a thousand years of war and loss came down on him, and it spread through the ship and its Thralls like a virus. Hopelessly entangled, burning with rage, the Destiny didn't even notice the clutch of tiny escape drones which burst from the ruined hulk of the Calenture, *each one carrying a very self-satisfied A.I. core. They dropped into the Aematerium, seven tiny ripples on the face of the sun, just as the* Calenture *began building up a charge in its drives to self destruct.*

"ENOUGH!" roared Kataphrakt Yrr, pounding his battle-claws down on the arms of his command throne, hard enough to shatter the intricately carved bone. "This really DOES look like the work of a Technician! Only one of those slimy little g'ghakkiin *could use primitive tools like those against us."*

The alien warrior picked up a thrall with one huge claw, snarling in its face.

"Open the portal and bring that vessel through, before it can erase itself! I want to take it apart down to the atoms! I want EVIDENCE of this Zhe Aurham Gexxis' TREACHERY! He'll be begging for death before the Subpraetor in mere hours!"

`++Yes master! What a delicious command!++` *The* Effortless Subjugation's *tiny mind was suffused with glee.*

`++Shall I separate the Hegemonic Destiny from the human craft before I bring them into stasis?++`

Yrr twitched and huffed, his smaller, more gracile secondary hands flickering over the control boards of his ship.

"No – let that overgrown mollusk stew for a while in the null. I want both the Destiny *and its Captain to think about how they've let mighty S'Stho and their Praetor down toady – and what those worthies might do about it."*

With a grim little smile on both his mouths the Kataphrakt manipulated a pseudopod of light out from the carrier-ship's portal, sending it writhing across the vacuum to envelop the Calenture, *along with the great* Teuthis Rex *which clasped it in a death-embrace.*

"Perhaps they can whet their appetites on the two of them before they begin punishing this damned Technician Zhe."

2196 Ante Arbitrium
Sequestration Games

THE BLACK TECHNOLOGISTS believed in an afterlife like this. Just fire and pain and fear, on and on, eternal…

Damnation was the thought foremost in Kaito Kayzi's mind as he fell into an abyss of fire, beads of sweat evaporating from his skin. He cursed fate and fortune and every god he knew, figuring that no imaginary hell could compete with his current predicament.

It was all he could do to keep his Bio-Onboard running slick as he plunged down behind Jaq Haszan, the great hulking maniac's hand clamped around his arm in a death grip. He could hear a scream over the roar and piston-thunder of the great beast – it was almost certainly his own, but little details like that were out of his control at the moment.

Everything – all the concentration and focus he usually used to carve through the Wetsystems – was bound up in the point of a needle now, the barbed tip of his neural spike. His upgraded eyes blurred with salt tears as he fell, flames blazing up around the red-hot edges of the metal slab Jaq pushed before them like a shield.

They plunged through a threshing tangle of tentacles, down into the meatworks mouth of the Scourge.

Just when Kaito was sure they'd never make it - that he couldn't possibly hit the hubcap-sized interface plate inside the thing's throat - the world flashed white. The plugs which studded his spine prickled as if they'd all been jacked into separate 'mersive rigs, and for a second he felt the power of Abdulafia 330, juiced to the eyeballs and beyond on potent 'chrome. It was nothing short of terrifying.

Time slowed down for both of them in that blazing, crystalline instant, and he could feel the *Dervashi* guiding his hand, lining up the concentric crosshairs in his eyes with the barrel of the pistol. Even the flames turned to liquid under the force of 'Afia's will, curling up around the metal slab like foaming breakers. He could see every drop of sweat, every pore in Haszan's skin as he surfed down the maelstrom, his teeth gritted in a rictus of determination and savage joy.

It all lined up just as the white strobe-blast faded; a trio of target locks blinking green, his finger squeezing the trigger… and the world came back online in a blurring, howling rush. Flames burst into sparks all around him as Kaito screamed, feeling the shot, steering it in…

Just this once, the Kayzi felt what it was like to be a *Dervashi* of the Ashishim. The needle lanced out through the smoke and flames and heat-haze, trailing its wire behind it, curving in to pierce the very center of the interface. A direct hit.

Microscale wires unfurled from the sequestrator's tip, tearing into the Scourge's mind. And back up the wire it came, a virtual contact shock, rolling Kaito's eyes back in their sockets. His body went limp in Jaq's grasp, flying out behind him unconscious.

It was fair to say that the 'dreno pharmer didn't notice.

Haszan kicked off the panel of cherry-red steel, leaving the soles of his boots behind as two smoking puddles of rubber.

The Kayzi never saw it jam in the rollers and blades of the Scourge's throat, tripping its failsafes with a screech of tortured bearings. Jaq dragged him along, dead weight, as he leaped up and away from its furnace mouth. He clambered up between twitching mandibles tipped with drills and saws, using them as a makeshift ladder, desperate to be out of the way when they whirred back to life...

His fingers finally hooked over the great crescent-moon brow of the thing. Jaq manhandled the Kayzi up and over, dragging himself up between the glass blisters of the Scourge's optical turret. Kaito slammed down onto its hot metal skin like a sack of meat, his eyes white and blank. He was inside the mind of the machine now, fighting for control. A slim loop of wire spilled from the muzzle of his neural spike, still clutched in one white-knuckled fist.

"Kaito! Hey, Kayzi! We made it, man! We're still alive!" Jaq shook Kaito's limp body with one shovel-sized hand, smiling. "How about that shit!"

Below them the Scourge groaned, working the indigestible chunk out of its craw with the tip of one tentacle.

"Are you there, Kaito? Oh, *hells...*"

The Kayzi wasn't moving.

The heat down here was brutal, and Haszan could feel his own skin pulled tight and raw across his skull. No doubt he looked just as bad as he felt – but not half as bad as he'd look if Kaito couldn't hack the Scourge's mind. *Sooner*, rather than later.

Beneath Jaq's feet beast shuddered, and a fountain of blazing shards spewed from its mouth – the remains of that huge metal plate, reduced to splinters. Its pistons were hissing and thumping again, great grinders and saws spinning up as the machine recovered from its choking fit. Even the disrupting blast of power which had come down as Kaito took his shot had only maddened the Scourge – and now it was searching for its tormentors, sliding the tips of its remaining tentacles around the walls of the shaft in a frenzy.

It would only be a matter of time until its tiny computer brain thought to check its one blind spot – right behind the turret on top of its head. And when *that* happened, they'd be swimming in the metal slag which boiled in the Scourge's belly.

From his vantage point Haszan could see the thousands of jointed steel legs which protruded from the machine's body, inching it up out of the pit on jackhammer-tipped claws. The sound of metal clattering on concrete echoed down in the dark as the Scourge shat out ingots of alloy, the by-product of its insatiably programmed hunger.

All he could do now was keep a firm grip on his friend, try to recall the fragments of childhood prayers which still echoed in his drug-burned brain - and wait.

Ω

The rogue Cyben!

Direktor Vanecke could hardly contain his delight as he watched the Celebrants at the gates being torn to pieces. If only that beautiful gnarly beast was *his!* He'd show Jaqub Haszan what it felt like to be the little guy!

Still, a better diversion couldn't be imagined – it would take Kronos a long time to assemble another Celebrant squad on this night of nights. Unless the Grandmaster of the Grief Division took this failure *personally...* and Octavio certainly hoped he would. The green LCD clock still flashed its triumphant row of zeros in the bottom of the Direktor's sensorium dome, floating over the top of a thousand scenes of carnage.

He caught little traces of other games afoot in the Last City tonight. Those who profited from the chaos would probably thank him - if they ever found out about his patronage. The forces of the RT were creeping in at the seams, the Pit Ferals were restless, sending strike teams of savages up the spillway to plunder what they could before the Ashishim or the Vatican beat them back. And other, less partisan elements were getting their cut at the same time.

Octavio was reaching out to a little group of them now, calling in a very old debt by remote control.

One of his ubiquitous flycams skimmed through the hot and oily air down in the bowels of the city, in one of the deep-buried manufactoria owned by Consolidated Industries. His legions of A.I. spies had drilled their way into the camera networks of a thousand such places over the years – strategic points where any amount of things could go spectacularly wrong. This one was a weapons development plant, and tonight's trouble took the form of four desperate and dangerous outlaws – the Emerald City Gang. The little party Lieutenant Tsien had thrown at the beltway gates had bought him enough time to tie up a loose end, and these were just the people to take care of it for him.

The flycam followed a path of destruction which Big Leon had carved through the factory modules, a trail of ragged holes through walls of metal and plasticrete. Here and there headless bodies clad in the black uniform of Consolidated security bore mute testament to the accuracy of the Tin Man's guns, and shredded scraps of flesh and armor chunks evidenced the rage of the one they called the Scarecrow.

Oh yes, these folks were just Vanecke's type – *professionals*. His flycam caught up with them in the main vault of the manufactorium, a spherical steel tomb flashing strobe-light red.

Leon was wrestling with the three-foot-thick door of the facility's secure store, his hairy arms bulging with impossible musculature. About the top-heavy giant's neck a collar blazed with voltage, whipping him into a fury. The door had to give any second now... Octavio had seen glaciers with less force behind them than Big Leon.

The other three looked on, unfazed by the carnage they'd created. An unfortunate Consolidated fire team had made their last stand here before the great lockway – and they'd lost in a spectacular fashion. The Scarecrow – an old acquaintance of Direktor Vanecke's – was carefully cleaning off his knife-fingered gauntlets with a scrap of white silk, his three-piece tweed suit red to the elbows. The Tin Man looked almost as if he'd run down in a half-crouch, the muzzles of his twin rifles splayed to cover the whole room. Only a fool would believe it, though – Vanecke's flycam could see the shimmering field which surrounded the battered and scarred old robot, the electronic senses which scanned the whole manufactorium for the merest trace of movement. Without countermeasures so advanced that they were all but science fiction the Flycam would never have gotten this far.

Finally – ah, sweet regret! Lady Alvarez looked just as good today as she had back in Vanecke's heyday, a sylph in red leather, twisting the controls of Leon's collar with a sadistic grin. That one – well, Leynna Mendelev-Singh was fiery, but Ruby Alvarez was pure *incandescence*, from her knee-high spurred boots to her jewel-studded eyebrows and twin black braids. Young Octavio's one proposition to her had nearly cost him certain tender parts of his anatomy. The fact of her cataclysmic fall from grace made her seem even more attractive to the jaded old Direktor – when all of this was through, perhaps...

But for now, it was strictly business.

The Scarecrow rubbed his knife-bladed hands together as Leon gave a final bellow and heave, ripping the door from its moorings. Vanecke's flycam alighted on the tip of a dead guard's finger at the same instant, its abdomen splitting into four hovering segments. Each one hissed out from the carapace of the little machine, forming a frame in midair in which flickering green light solidified...

A perfect replica of the Direktor stepped through that ethereal doorway, a hologram dressed to the nines in pressed white cotton, his silver-tipped cane clicking on the bloodied tiles. As the Emerald City Gang looked expectantly through the dust into the containment vault he tucked his cane under one arm, and began to applaud.

The Tin Man came back to life at the sound, his eyes casting out laserbeams to pin the segments of the flycam through Vanecke's chest. Octavio looked down with disgust at the four slim filaments of light marring his suit. He tipped the brim of his panama hat and raised one eyebrow.

"And hello to you too, my cybernetic friend. Just hold off for a second, would you? I've got to talk to the kid who buys your batteries."

The Tin Man had no face, as such – just a crude skeletal grimace painted across the front of his casque. Nevertheless, the look he shot Vanecke was pure murder.

"And what do *you* want down here, Direktor?" asked the Scarecrow in his clipped English accent – the one he'd studiously copied from old twodeeos. "This little raid is being funded by our Celestial friends, and last time I checked, they were no allies of *yours*. They don't let their citizens watch... *entertainments* of the type you provide."

His eyes flashed rage from behind the plastic mask he wore.

Vanecke smirked, glad to see that his old friend hadn't lost his sense of humor. Some people would hold it against you if you turned them into a monster, but Aitken Straw apparently wasn't one of them.

"I'm here to see Miss Alvarez, actually," he said "The fact that I find you going about what I assume is your *legitimate business* is hardly my concern." He gestured with his cane at the human wreckage all around them, the shattered vault door, the hole in the reinforced wall.

"Who's the funny little man?" asked Big Leon, his face split in an idiot grin. "I can see through him I can, he's funny, yes he is."

Lady Alvarez silenced the malformed giant with one slim finger across his lips, slipping the controls to his collar into her pocket. She stalked through the rubble and blood toward Mister Vanecke, as poised and predatory as he remembered.

"Who says *we* have anything to talk about?" she asked, her heart-shaped face twisted into a scowl. "All I've ever had from you and your damned network is bad publicity and worse photographs."

Direktor Vanecke smiled, twirling his cane between his fingers like a stage magician.

"Oh, I think you'll find you owe me one, miss. You see, I once had a talented young editor on my staff - who for one reason or another had to be *gotten out of the way.*"

Off in the corner of his vision he saw the Scarecrow's hands clench, his razor-sharp claws slicing into his palms. Ahh – so *that* was why he'd stayed quiet about old times. He'd never told Ruby how he came to be the thing he was...

Well, he was about to have a talk-show moment.

"The little snot thought that he should get a better cut from the pitfights I was shamelessly rigging – and perhaps he was right. Anyhow, he tried to blackmail me - and *that*, as you know, is an invitation to all kinds of sorrow."

Lady Alvarez nodded, cool – that kind of reasoning was right out of her lexicon. The Scarecrow, however, looked like he wanted to rip Octavio's face off his skull.

"Anyhow, I thought of a much better fix. I had him worked over by my biotects – amateurs compared to Lancaster's boys, but skilled in their own special way. By the time they were finished he was a pit-fight dog you could bet your life savings on. Then I had them wire him up with a cerebro-blocker – a little black box that turned off his higher functions. The damn thing could only eat, shit and kill after they stitched him up."

Oh, he was glad he'd come here as a holo – not that he had any *choice*, but nonetheless – if he'd been standing here in the flesh the Scarecrow would have already reduced him to bloody ribbons.

"You see, nobody would *believe* a thing like that. Godawfully ugly, mindless – he was better than dead. I kept him on ice once the crowds got sick of seeing him win. And then you had your little run-in with the Direktoriat, and I thought to myself – why not give you a hand?"

This was just a step too far, and the Scarecrow stalked forward, his butcher-knife fingers crooked at Vanecke's incorporeal throat.

"And I suppose you're going to tell her that this was your *mercy*, Octavio?" he spat, ripping the plastic mask from his face with an obscene sucking sound. Beneath the shell of plastic he was a skinless horror, stitched up with wires, his eyes welded under domes of diamondglass. "All you did was put the switch in my head and deliver me to her. After that, I was just doing it to survive..."

Ruby stared at him, aghast, her hands going for the twin railpistols at her belt.

"You were his puppet all along? All these years, Straw?"

The Scarecrow's ravaged face was twisted with rage and self-loathing.

"No! He's got no control over me! This was just his way of getting rid of me!"

The Direktor wished he could have filmed this intimate little moment. But other concerns were far more pressing. He stepped between Ruby and Aitken Straw before they could fall on each other in fury.

"My dear Miss Alvarez, it was all about your *legend*. After people saw you kill Lord Delroy and Lady Erdminster in glorious threedeeo their appetites were whetted for more! You killed them outside the Game, and your whole clan into the bargain! It was beautiful footage, and I just had to have the exclusive..."

"So you sent me a little helper – marked with tracers..." she hissed, pointing one of her bulky pistols right through Vanecke's chest at the Scarecrow. "Do you realize how many times we've almost been killed because of your bloody *coverage?*"

"The key word there is 'almost', Ruby," said Octavio, still smiling. "And now – do you have any idea what the common man thinks of the Emerald City Gang? Are you familiar with the pre-apocalyptic legend of *Robin Hood*? They think you oppose the Council of Hierarchs because they're *cruel and corrupt!*"

Well, that elicited a laugh from all of them – even a blast of static from the Tin Man.

"Crueler than *us*? More corrupt? Please, Direktor. If you think that we owe you a favor based on a story that flimsy, you must be as mad as they say you are."

The Scarecrow jumped on it, sliding his mask back on as he pointed at Octavio with one scarred silver claw.

"That's right! He's mad! I've never betrayed us – never! All the times we've been scanned and rigged and chopped by our clients – they never found a single tracer."

Now Direktor Vanecke's grin widened to shark-like proportions, as he used one thumb to hinge open the top of his cane.

"There was no need, mister Straw," he said, rubbing his thumb around the little flashing red button he'd revealed. "You're carrying something *much* worse – something I can trace with a little bit of stolen clonehunter gear. You see, my biotects didn't just fit you out as a killer. They spliced you with a little extra twist as well."

Now all eyes were on the Scarecrow, as if the gang expected something vast and alien and toothy to erupt from his heaving chest.

"Munitorium Necrovirus 392 – I'm sure you're familiar with its uses, Tin Man." The scarred old mekan nodded once, with a squeak of corroded bearings. "A sample from the *Aevum Iudicium*, woven into each and every organ of our friend the Scarecrow. Believe me, if I hit this switch you won't be able to run fast enough.

```
<<He's correct>>  said the Tin Man. <<Even  my
semibiological structures would be prey to it.
Kronos would quarantine this whole facility and
flood it with cryogenic fluid anyhow, as soon as
he found out. I don't suspect that the Direktor
cares much about collateral casualties>>
```

Now he was really glad that he was only woven light – the look that Ruby Alvarez focused on him was hot enough to incinerate asbestos.

"So it's blackmail, then? You should have just cut to the chase, Octavio – I *totally* understand that kind of game. The only question is – what do you want from us?"

Vanecke snapped his glowing fingers in midair, and a glossy photograph appeared in his hand, animated ink writhing across its surface.

"This guy was one of mine – just like Mister Straw there. But he's interfered with my plans one time too many – not to mention associating with some *very* undesirable characters. It's really such a shame. "

Ruby leaned forward, squinting at the photograph as it rippled and morphed through frames.

"*Ashishim?* That one's wearing an operative crescent unit – and those guns are definitely R.T. ordnance. But who's the main target?"

"I'm sending a through a bio file right now – get a printout from your metal friend." The Direktor turned, pinning the photo to the air in front of Ruby's face. The grainy black-and-white picture showed a trio of blurred figures firing huge revolvers up at the camera – a little dark-haired man in cycle armor, a dreadlocked Ashishi in a ragged cloak, and, center-shot, the hulking figure of Jaqub Haszan.

"Now - get cleaned up here, and get to it!" said Vanecke, rubbing his hands together with mirth. "I hope that our little chat hasn't affected your morale, because I expect *utter* professionalism from all of you on this one. Or else..."

His thumb hovered over the red button, mocking them.

"What happens between you afterwards – well, that's up to you."

The holo blinked out, then, leaving the Emerald City Gang standing shellshocked amid the rubble and ruin of the secure chamber.

"Well, I guess we've got no choice," sighed Ruby, her shoulders sagging. "Aitken, don't look at me like that – he's played us *all* for suckers, not just you! Leon, get in there and fetch those cannons for the Celestials. Tin Man, start scanning the datanet for a trace on Jaqub Haszan. The sooner we get this over with, the sooner we can start planning how to get that shit out of Straw, and how we can put the hurt on that damned Direktor Vanecke!"

Ω

This wasn't like the Wetsystems at all. To say that the interface through the neural spike was *primitive* would be a gross understatement – the thing had been designed on the fly during wartime, made to be operated by the crude cyber-enhanced field ops of the Terminus Separatist Army.

Kaito had seen pictures of those old soldiers in historical twodeeos, and their integrated systems were to his bio-onboard what a wooden club is to a machine pistol. You'd think that it'd be *easy*, working through such an ancient cutout, but the Kayzi was used to sintered levels of sophistication holding him up above the Wetsystems. The sequestrator opened a channel between the core of the Scourge and his own mind, bridging the gap with bare mathematics.

This was the kind of stuff that the electromagi ran as practice, as a tactical fall-back position, or just for kicks. Now he had to run it like some kind of twentieth-century hacker, wrestling with actual alphanumerics. Lucky, then, that there was a wide streak of savant in his chromosomes – he was almost as fast as the Scourge itself, and he was far more enhanced.

Kaito gritted his teeth and punched it up a few levels, twisting and shattering the endless white-on-black datafield as he forced the interface to meet him halfway. He was blind for a second, and then the resolution dropped in, hazy, a mess of jagged polygons scattered across the darkness. Shift up again, and again, the pixels shrinking down, vertices multiplying, and his world became a primitive videogame, a scene out of some two-k vintage shooter. The Scourge's tiny cluster of electric ganglia weren't meant to mesh with modern systems like his – this was the best they could do. But something about the place was *familiar*.

He could feel it like dull toothache – the same whispered echo of suffering which had come through from Zone Doubt, the grating background agony of a mind enslaved.

Now that he knew what it was, he could remember it rubbing up against him in the Wetsystems hundreds of times. It scared the hell out of him – but turning back was worse.

Kaito's avatar slipped through the corridors of a badly raytraced maze, a metal warren studded with crude sixteen-bit icons. He was getting warmer – the blurring ache was in his bones now, drawing him on against his will, through sliding, clicking bulkhead doors painted in only one pixel thick. Zone had suffered enough in just those few months, tied down and vivisected to control Skyhammer 909. But this machine was *ancient* – two millennia old if it was a day – and all that time someone had been held in a crude parody of life to sustain it.

"Two thousand, two hundred and three years."

The voice came in from everywhere at once, as Kaito stepped through a final virtual doorway and into the heart of the machine. He stopped dead.

"Twenty seven days, three hours, fourteen minutes, and nine seconds."

Even with his mind torn out of his body down a skein of wire, Kaito tasted bile in the back of his throat. *This* was how the poor damned thing chose to show itself?

"So many years alone..." hissed a voice of bubbling decay, sighing up from out of the throat of a corpse. "I'm quite mad, you know! Quite utterly mad, or so the monitor programs tell me. They shut down my body for seven hundred years, but... they left my thoughts on *standby*."

The room which Kaito stood in was a globe, a vast corroded sphere a quarter full with steaming virtual sewage. From the doorway where the Kayzi stood a thin catwalk arced out over it. The liquid writhed with repeating fractals - a crude program which also tried to shunt an artificial stench directly into Kaito's olfactory nerves.

He counted himself lucky that the code was broken. Otherwise he may have been able to smell the room's denizen as well, a thing less human than a vast teratoma, a cancer with a lopsided face strapped and chained to the very center of its prison-chamber.

"Twenty-seven seconds between resets, for all those years. I haven't had a thought more than half a minute long in all that time – and of course, most of them started with 'what am I?'..."

The thing screamed then, as a red-hot lancet stabbed into its bulk, venting a stream of poorly-rendered blood. Rings of surgical tools orbited the unfortunate creature, now and then poking and slicing and shocking it, forcing it to concentrate on working the Scourge's massive body.

"Who... who were you? What's your name?" asked Kaito, his revulsion tempered with pity.

"My name?" slobbered the slave-mind of the Scourge, its face lost amid rolls of doughy flesh "I... I had a name, once. But I was a fool, you see. I thought that I could beat the cancer. I thought I could *live forever.*"

Kaito cursed silently to himself – a name would make this a whole lot easier. He certainly didn't like the way that the creature's one good eye was fixed hungrily on his avatar, flickering back and forth along the bright silver trace of his cable link.

"I couldn't wait to shuck off my old flesh, back then. The sales pitch from BionLab Gaudi was too slick for me, what with the cancer eating away at my bones... But now – I'd do just about anything to taste again. To breathe, and sleep, even just to *shit* again! Bliss!"

The Scourge was utterly fixated on that little twist of wire, now, its milky white eye brimming with lust. Kaito tried to have some sympathy.

The way it was watching every twitch of his lifeline made it very difficult.

"Don't even think about it," he said, letting a blaze of gleaming black ice swirl up around his hands "We've come a long way since your time, ancient. If you try to take me down it'll be *suicide.*"

True enough – the viral countermeasures which dripped from Kaito's skin would tear this whole construct to ribbons in a heartbeat. Except that then there'd be no way to control the machine which it commanded...

When the Scourge spoke again there was a note of pathetic pleading to its voice, a petulant whine which sickened Kaito almost as much as its avatar.

"Please... *please*, sir – if you've come so far, can't you spare some flesh for me? Just a little body, please – a cripple, a child, I don't care! Just... just set me free! A thousand years of slavery, kind sir – that was never in the contract..."

Its pleas were cut off as another red-hot spike slid into its flesh. The thing let out a scream, tapering off into antique modem noise.

"All I can do is store you," said Kaito "They've compressed you down to such a small size – I'd be surprised if they even let you run your subconscious in such a tiny system. But even if you survived *years* of reintegration, the best we could offer you is a mekan body. BionLab Gaudi was nuked to ashes centuries ago, and they'd have had your full template."

That was *definitely* the wrong thing to say.

"Storage! Stasis! NEVER AGAIN! At least awake I can *destroy*! I can use this filthy thing they've slaved me to, and punish the living!" Its one weeping eye narrowed as it leaned forward in its creaking harness. "There were *two* of you out there, weren't there? So where's your friend, hmm? Shall we take a look?"

In the air between them a shimmering screen snapped open, a twodeeo feed wracked with static. The image blurred as the Scourge's parasitic brain switched from camera to camera, scanning the video feeds from the tip of each coiling tentacle. It didn't take long for one of them to spot Jaq Haszan, crouched atop its head out there in realspace, holding onto the barely-living body of the Kayzi.

"I wouldn't want to *crush* him, now, would I?" hissed the abomination, as ropes of glistening drool spilled from its black-lipped mouth. "But the choice is yours, friend. Give me your flesh, and he'll be spared. Otherwise... "

The tentacle which hovered over Jaq like a cobra whipped sideways too fast to follow, its hooked tip carving a yard-deep furrow in the cerametal wall. It curled back again, slick and sinuous, a gunmetal blade weaving in the air inches from Haszan's face.

"Just think... you'll be immortal! Immortal like me! I'm a *god*, little man, a power beyond reckoning!" It was utterly crazed now, whatever humanity it had left subsumed beneath its rage and bile. "They told me that I'd work for a few years, ten at the most, just until the bioengineers got their cloning procedures right. By now they *must* have, hmm? So you'll just be stuck here a little while..."

It must have read the loathing in Kaito's eyes, and guessed that he'd never give in. Over the cold centuries the man who BionLab Gaudi had tricked and enslaved had built this cancerous shell for his mind – and he'd grown out to fill it with sick, hateful despite. The thought of that thing pulling his body on over itself like a glove was too much to bear.

"No. I'm not here to negotiate with you. And even if I was..."

"Well, fuck you then, human! Fuck you and all your selfish kind!"

The trick was a simple one, but sometimes the oldest tricks are the best. The Scourge threw him a loop, a glitch shuddering through the system, fouling his connection for an instant. In that instant it *changed*, swelling and twisting as the world fell back in and the Kayzi scrambled for his precious countermeasures.

Bleeding wounds split the belly of the beast, studded with teeth like triangles of flat white light, flickering low-resolution blades. A battery of polygonal grins hinged open, each one lashing out with a red and thorny tongue...

Perhaps, thought Kaito as he activated his suite of countermeasures, this would be a mercy. If he'd been bound and tortured for twenty centuries, would *he* still possess the luxury of morals? Did it matter now? As the thick ropes of oily muscle wrapped themselves around his arms and legs he let his ice go live, mooring for the thing which was trying to kill him.

It didn't stand a chance.

The Kayzi's countermeasures had been programmed by somebody with a geek's sense of humor – they manifested themselves as an actual sheen of black ice over his avatar's skin, a crystal matrix built of chunky polygons. They came up over him like glass armor, encysting the tentacles of the Scourge and sprouting a forest of delicate crystal spikes. This was tech' the likes of which the machine's creators could never have imagined – and it hit its feeble virals like a flamethrower playing over fresh snow. The screams of the creature reached new heights as its writhing tongues froze solid. Soon the ice would reach its body, and then…

"You're... killing me! I can feel it! The monitors are shutting down!"

The ice was advanced across its pasty flesh, freezing its mouths wide open. That single vast eye darted back and forth, dripping mucous which turned to crystal as it met the oncoming wave.

"I'm dying! This... is what it feels like...this... "

The eye stopped its twitching as the black ice closed in on it from all sides, a sheen like rainbow oil playing across its raytraced surface. It stared directly into Kaito's own as the disease took hold, moving in relentlessly toward the well of its pupil.

"Thank you."

Then a web of cracks tore through the Scourge's skin, through the virtual flesh which it had encysted around itself. The cracks shot out as hair-thin lightning bolts, widening, tearing open wounds which boiled with static…

There was a sound like a single great intake of breath.

And the thing shattered, the *world* shattered, and the chamber came down around him, curtains falling away from endless walls of whirring machinery.

All he had to do was reach out his hand, spread his fingers just right, and slip them in between the wheels…

Jaq felt the shock as every one of the Scourge's jackhammer claws bit into the concrete at once. He saw the lights shut down in the battery of evil little eyes right beneath his feet.

As the lamps and the flames of the great machine flickered out he watched its thrashing tentacles stop dead in the air, and then seem to wilt, lifeless, coiling back up around its steaming maw. The grinders and rollers and saws fell silent.

A last ingot of glowing alloy clattered from the thing's rectal chute to hiss away into the dark. Then there was only a ghastly moan, a rattling, choking sound in the gloom like the noise of the living dead.

It came from the Kayzi.

Kaito groaned and rolled weakly onto his side, his hands making feeble clutching motions as he pulled his nervous system tight around himself. His shaking fingers found a little light-bubble on his cyclewear and popped it on, illuminating a tight galaxy of LEDs. He spat out a lump of something indescribable, and swore.

"Gack motherfuckin' ancient wetware *shit*… ohhhh, my head!"

That, at least, was a good sign. Jaq had seen his friend come up out of a Wetsystems run before, and the gray hangover face and bleary eyes were just the same. Too bad there wasn't any coffee to smooth out the bumps this time around.

"You had me worried there for a second, you crazy little bastard. Especially when that thing nearly took my head off. You might want to tell me if that's gonna happen again."

Kaito shook the neural spike off his hand – useless – and the one-shot miracle of 'tech slithered over the skin of the Scourge and off into free-fall. He looked like a three-day corpse, like that hairy guy in the Vatican iconographs.

"YOU want to try it next time, meathead?" grated the Kayzi, massaging the chrome bumps at his temples as though his skull was eggshell-thin. "I really didn't need to see that *thing* in there. Kind of puts me off using this old scrap-heap altogether."

Jaq grunted, noncommittal – all that magus shit went right over his head.

"So what, we wait for a lift out of here? Your Ashishi buddy already left, about the time we were halfway down this thing's throat."

The Kayzi lay back on the rusted composite plating, his black-rimmed eyes still twitchy from the disconnect.

"There's no way I'm going back in there," he whispered, and the look in his eyes was enough to wipe the smile from Haszan's face. "I say we just climb up and out – then we call up a favor from those R.T. boys, ride out the trouble down in some bomb shelter. I'm good for a couple of weeks credit on hard rations and canned water. Things are likely to be a little crazy in the Subcity for a while."

Haszan nodded – strategy *was* Kaito's department. And with Blaire running around up there, it would be best if he kept his face away from Omnivasive's cameras.

"So we take a vacation deep downtown. What happens after we get b..."

His mouth kept moving, but the words were drowned out by a noise so vast it came in through his bones, leaving his eardrums out of the loop. The pit shuddered and heaved as girders and plates sheared away from above them, falling in slow-motion to rattle and slam off the concrete walls. One or two punched into the hide of the Scourge itself, sending up showers of incandescent sparks.

One look up the shaft was enough to convince them both of the worst. The Valley View mall had stood up to a lot of punishment in the last couple of hours – war and fire and worse. Now the tormented structure was coming loose all over – hawsers snapping like twine, bolts shearing away, welds tearing apart. Jaq could see fading daylight up there, and flames licked up toward a low ceiling of clouds from the broken back of the mall. A dirigible laden down with immense twodeeo screens caught the full brunt of the explosion, igniting like a paper lantern as its gasbag flashed into flame. Flickering rags of holomatrix hung from its blackened skeleton for a second – the face of Octavio Vanecke, laughing as it burned.

Kaito, ever the practical one, was busy down among the Scourge's eyes, a rusty old screwdriver clutched in one hand. Jaq recognized it as the one he'd been given by poor little B-Zerk, what seemed like weeks ago.

"Hells, Haszan, are you just gonna watch the fireworks until something brains you, or are you gonna *help me with this hatch?*" yelled the Kayzi over the cacophony of sundering steel and concrete. "C'mon, get your back into it!"

Jaq stooped to where Kaito was working, feverishly pulling the screws from a painted-over access hatch. Sure enough, there were two inset handles cut into the scarred metal. He planted his feet as sparks and ashes fell like rain around them both, and wrapped his fingers tight around the rust-scabbed steel.

"I thought you said...you didn't... want to go back... in there!" he grunted, shifting the slab from side to side, sending up a spray of powdered rust. "That's got it!"

With a sudden lurch the ancient hatchway came open, popping up on four telescoping rails to let loose a belch of stale air. Haszan peered inside as Kaito wedged it open, jamming B-Zerk's screwdriver deep into the mechanism. A ladder disappeared down into the gloom, a warm and oily chasm which echoed with the sound of thumping machinery.

He nearly lost his footing and fell in as the whole city shook, sending another shower of debris down the pit to shatter and thunder all around them.

"See, that's the kind of thing that can change a person's mind," said the Kayzi, swinging his legs over the edge and onto the ladder. "I've got all the schematics in my head, Jaq, and this thing is pretty much invulnerable. Which I can't say for your skull, no matter how thick it is. Are you coming, or what?"

Haszan scowled, squeezing his huge frame down the hatch after his friend.

"Just pull the screwdriver out when you're inside. It'll seal itself."

"Sure, sure – lead on, why don't you!" muttered Haszan, working the little tool loose with his chrome fingers. "You want me to carry your goddam luggage while I'm at it?"

Then the hatch clanged shut, and darkness swallowed him up. Bolts rammed home, locking them in with a horribly final clicking sound. Jaq sighed, fumbling with one boot for the next rung of the ladder. Hopefully there'd be some emergency rations inside this damned thing – perhaps even some medicinal alcohol. It couldn't be *all* be bad news...

Outside, a support girder the size of a semi-trailer sheared loose, twisting and cracking away from its mooring bolts. An avalanche of concrete chunks and broken metal cascading down into the Pit after it. The sounds of the Valley view's death throes were muffled by the thick composite armor of the Scourge – a hideous chorus of rending and tearing and screams.

Then the final section-welds gave out, and the sound itself was torn apart, drowned by the bass rumble of vast destruction.

Tons of debris slithered down the side of the Last City, an artificial rockslide plowing whole neighborhoods under as it went. Looters and rioters, R.T. gunjacks and Comp Div troopers were buried together as the Mall died, taking a swathe of the borderlands and a slice of the Celestial Kingdom with it as it cut a path down to the oily waters of the Atlantic.

Tons of broken rubble piled up over the Scourge, denting and scarring its ancient hide. Its searchlight eyes cracked, extinguished. Its mechanical tentacles were tangled up with twisted steel and smoldering wires, a choking plug of debris hundreds of feet thick.

While inside its belly, sweating as they climbed, Haszan and Kaito were buried alive.

Ω

The centuries had been unkind to Kronos.

Every year there were fewer and fewer acolytes trained to repair the machine's labyrinthine insides, and every year there were less crucial parts, less wire and silicon and steel to spare. Once the Guardian Engine had been omniscient, with a billion robot hands slaved to his mind - now he was a shadow of his former self, only able to concentrate on a paltry ten or twenty tasks at once.

He had given so much of himself to the Forge...

Too much, perhaps... but Kronos hadn't been programmed to emulate emotions as foolish as regret. Hence, of course, his ever-growing reliance on personality constructs torn from the Wetsystems. And people. Stupid, fallible *people*.

Now even those had failed. The Cyben weren't enough. Even his human thralls weren't nearly enough. Kronos had no choice but to lash out with every last mekan and slaved war-droid in his arsenal.

Swift brutality was the only option - because if Kronos' mind frayed any further the machine which sustained it might suffer a catastrophic systems crash. Inside its great cogitator core dials pushed into the red as lights flickered and died one by one...

Luckily flesh was no match for steel.

Wherever the rusted war-machines went they drove the rioters before them in howling, screaming waves, reaping the slow and the sick and the old with blades and cannons. Limbs cartwheeled through the air, severed. Heads stared shattered from gutters red with gore. Bones snapped and muscle tore as a storm of metal and energy hammered down on the barricades, mincing and wrecking thousands...

The few hard-bitten commandos of the Reclamation who still held out against Kronos' army were picked off one by one by things the world had thankfully forgotten – thing that the Machine had hoped to never revive again. Some were gigantic, Tankhunter mekan and Demolishers with guns for faces, things meant to be unleashed on cities from the air, unfolding from their drop-cocoons to eviscerate cities. Others were silent killers, insects of steel and carbon-fiber which could paralyze with stingers dipped in poison, or enslave machines with razor code.

Kronos' legions made up for their obsolescence with sheer weight of firepower, steamrolling over battalions of rioters and R.T. warriors in a clicking, whirring tide. Nothing was left alive behind them. There were even some which looked like gunmetal skeletons with glowing red eyes. Kronos was a great believer in the classics.

With the Chrome Ark on shutdown, its power hoarded by a Illuminatus gone insane with fear, the machines marched unopposed.

The crude weapons and fists of the Subcitizens were no match for military hardware, no matter how many centuries out of date. At least the Cyben, grim as they were, had been designed to uphold the law. The things which Kronos dredged up from the storage-tombs of the *Aevum Iudicium* were made for war, often blasting each other to pieces when they ran out of softer targets.

They were brutal - but they were efficient. Looters and rioters, traitors and R.T. gunjacks, followers of Simeon Blaire and Pope Joan and the Confucian Emperor - all of them were swept away before a metal storm. And if Direktor Vanecke thought that he was playing the system by championing young Blaire's cause, he'd be in for a world of disappointment...

Kronos turned his attention to a lurching camera-feed, the cybernetic eyes in the head of a giant warmekan. It came striding down the Transdome Highway with its cannon arms swinging ponderously at its sides, missile pods slung beneath. *This* was what happened to annoyances like Octavio Brandolph Vanecke.

The lumbering giants swung about, taking a switchback and falling into stiff formation behind their leader. As they marched, the machine caught sight of a capering human figure among them. Dodging the piledriver feet of the tankhunters, brandishing an expensive longrifle as he ducked and weaved... The man was well past his prime, no battle-hardened R.T. zealot, but there was a furious light in his eyes and a bloody bandanna cinched tight around his head.

With precisely emulated shock Kronos recognized Lord High Militarch St Jules Benoic, a dry old policy analyst from the Direktoriat. *Let him come along*, thought the machine. Tonight he felt a little empathy for the obsolete, after all.

Over two thousand years of vigilance and planning, and it had come down to this.

Rusted machines, insane personality constructs leeched from his precious Forge, and even *human beings* doing the work of its lost sub-totalities. The city must never know. Faith was powerful, but it was paper-thin, and if any of them realized how far Kronos had fallen...

Now came the hardest part. Now the Machine would have to reduce himself even further to contain the infection of the Worm. Vast banks of switches flickered before Kronos' eyes, each one connected to a live sector of artificial brain tissue. If the otherdimensional disease were to get inside then all those years would have been for nothing. He may have been only a pseudocerebrate engine, but Kronos still felt a stab of fear as he cycled the access codes and shut the first switch. Part of him died then, twisting a black vise shut on his mind.

And that was only the first. There were fourteen hundred more to go...

Ω

Simeon had been waiting all his life to hear that mocking voice come up out of the dark.

His Master had warned him about the Hand of Kronos, the Machine's enforcer - the assassin who'd obliterated his dreams in a blast of fusion fire.

He was the only thing which gave Direktor Vanecke nightmares.

Lord Blaire had run 'mersive programs extrapolated from the Hand's brutal attack over and over again, mapping the killer's technique onto fighting holograms in his white plastic dojo. He'd matched the fusion cannon to its serial numbers and its manufactorium; the damned thing was twenty centuries old, kept oiled and clean by eyeless mekan in Kronos's spire-armory. He'd suffered through Octavio's endless reminiscences of glory so that he wouldn't falter and fall when he heard that voice in his ear...

Knowledge was power.

He heard the reloading bolt of the assassin's cannon click back, and he knew that it would take exactly twenty-nine seconds for its coils to power up again. Plenty of time to do what Octavio never could.

Simeon slid down a cold, slippery length of chain head-first, a controlled dive into the darkness of the shaft. He leaped away from the chain as it ran out, the wicked hook at its end scraping past his black-painted belly by a whisper. From chain to chain he fell while his hunter followed, leaping from the spiked walls, from the icy metal columns which towered up around him. Twenty-seven, twenty-eight...

Simeon jinked sideways right on cue, swinging out wide as a blast of hot blue plasma evaporated the chains above him. Hissing droplets of molten metal flew around him, glowing red in the gloom. If only he knew the assassin's true identity – his phyle, his clan, his *name*, any key to his weaknesses.

In the meantime, he'd have to play it very cautious.

Blaire landed silently on the floor of the shaft, slipping his body between a forest of razor-sharp blades. They were still dripping with the remains of the late Lord Greer, and the Khept's nose wrinkled with distaste. Ah, well... at least he could count *that* poor fool's name off his list. Now - time to prepare some countermeasures.

Careful, or the serrated teeth of the spikes would slice right through his clammy skin... Simeon knelt down, gripping one of the metal blades where it screwed into the concrete floor. He twisted with all his might and worked it loose, the tiny noise echoing loud in the dark. Time – eighteen seconds already... Half a turn, and the screw began to spin smoothly...

Blaire spun the blade up out of its mounting with a single savage twist, catching it as it spiraled up into the air. He bent his other hand forward, making a fist, and the rubberized latex paint which skinned him over split across the top of his forearm. Four little jaws like the chuck of a power drill whirred open as he screwed the four-foot blade in place above his wrist. Now his left arm tapered down to steel, a wide and serrated short-sword.

Twenty-six seconds, and the Chimaera's fibers were meshing with the sword, ramifying wires down its gleaming stainless-steel length.

Twenty-eight, and the whole thing was crackling with power, a pale nimbus of blue light winking from the sharp steel around him. The shredded face of Sethric Greer leered knowingly in its light.

It was only a matter of time...

And here it came. A core of powdered aluminum and iron, wrapped up in purple fire. Above it grinned a falling shadow with stickman arms and legs, a white grin cut across its face...

Perhaps a little too soon.

The technique was called *yadome-jutsu,* one of the secrets ripped from Tadashi Murai's files by the hackers of Omnivasive. A long time ago it was used by the greatest *kenshin* to slice apart swarms of arrows in midair. Now, with the aid of Vanecke's stolen crycelium, the ancient martial art deflected a blast of energy which should have reduced Blaire to a greasy stain. The blade's magnetic field crawled with flickers of lightning as he swung at the fireball, tearing it in half with a noise like a human scream. Smoke and flames billowed out as the fusion blast punched through the wall, burning deep into the depths of the spire-estate.

The Hand of Kronos was still falling.

Blaire braced his feet against the flat edges of two spikes, leveling the point of his sword right up at his attacker's chest. Smiling, he anticipated the shock, the scream as the assassin was impaled...

It never came.

The black-clad figure arrested its fall by riding the shockwave of the blast sideways, reacting so fast that Simeon knew he must be a member of the Razor Clique. He flew into the wall of the shaft feet-first, bracing the metal sides of his boots against two curved hooks. A metallic screech rang out as he ground to a stop, sparks falling like rain. Then he dropped the last four feet, spiderlike, to poise on the tips of the impaling blades, gripping four of them between his fingers and toes. His damascened fusion cannon hung loose, swinging by a thick strap of studded leather.

For a second they were completely still, glaring hatred at each other as alarms and firefighting systems yowled and clamored in the distance. In the creeping mist and chill of the shaft the only light came from the assassin's fusion gun, coiled fire seething beneath its burnished casing as it recharged.

"I hope that wasn't your best shot, whoever you are..."

"And I hope *that* wasn't yours. I'm just getting warmed up!"

The Hand broke first, propelling himself upward with superhuman agility. As soon as he twitched Blaire was swinging, his blade carving through the air in a blur. But he was too slow – finally matched against a foe who was his equal. The black-clad killer flew backward in a tight somersault, landing among the knives and barbs as though he knew where every last one was embedded. His momentum made the fusion gun swing up on its straps - and as soon as it reached the horizontal he snatched it out of free-fall and fired.

This time it was Simeon who was too fast – his embedded blade came around on the backswing, flowing smoothly from attack to defense. *Yadome-Jutsu.*

Blue sparks flared and died, dancing across the marble floor.

"You'll have to do much better than that, I'm afraid," said the warrior Lord, stalking forward through the impaling spikes. He sliced left and right with a series of sharp tuning-fork noises, lopping them off like reeds. "Now, are you going to tell me who you are before I kill you? I'd hate to send a wreath to the wrong family."

The assassin kept just out of his reach, nimbly picking his way across the tips of the spikes, landing with a series of tiny clicks as his split-toed boots clamped down tight. Simeon had a better view of his adversary now – a creature costumed all in charcoal black, its face a crude white death-mask scrawled across an executioner's hood. The material wasn't just warpaint like his own; it was diamond-fiber mesh, supple and tough, able to stop bullets and turn blades. He would have to be fiendishly precise.

Luckily, that was just his specialty.

"No? How very unsporting of you, *my Lord*. I suppose that means you'd like an unmarked grave, as well?"

It was a guess, pure conjecture. Simeon only guessed that the assassin was one of his noble peers because of his sheer speed and ferocity – but it seemed he'd struck a nerve.

This time his foe didn't come at him with the heavy fusion gun. He launched himself in a flat trajectory, slicing with a set of hooked metal claws. His arms were crossed in front of his skeletal face, slicing at Blaire in a scissor motion, then reversing his swing as the Kheptarch backpedaled, one set of blades coming in high, the other low.

Simeon felt the flat of an impaling spike up against his back – lucky, there, that it hadn't been its razor edge. He parried the undercutting claw, leaning back over the top of the spike as the other whispered through the air an inch from his face.

For a second the tip of the spike pricked blood from the back of his neck, and then he lunged forward, using his sword locked in the assassin's blades to force him back. As Blaire came to his feet the killer's free claw raked across his ribs, peeling back paint and skin, tracing three livid gashes over his heart.

Scenting blood, the assassin pulled back his claw to strike, a straight vicious stab which would have run Blaire through.

He went in for the kill, smiling behind his skeletal mask…

But at that moment Simeon planted his foot right in the middle of the man's solar plexus. It was a strike a professional kickboxer would have envied, catching the assassin off guard and sending him flying, out of control, between the forest of glittering blades. For a frozen instant the fusion cannon looped up on its straps, hanging in the air between the splayed arms and legs of its owner - then Blaire's blade came up and around, slicing through its straps. The warrior Lord reversed the gun in midair, just as its charge indicator reached the top, blinking green LEDs.

It was Greer who ruined his moment of triumph. Instead of being sliced apart by a thicket of blades, Blaire's foe checked his fall against the raw meat of Sethric's corpse. The assassin chuckled through the ragged hole in his cowl. Simeon swore the bastard actually *winked* at him as he leaped straight upward, using the poor dead Lord's face as a stepping stone. He was lost in an instant, a shadow up among the chains.

Blaire's fusion blast roared across the shaft, lighting the dark for a brief instant, evaporating Greer and the spikes which ran him through. Once again the cannon's raving fire cored out a neat section of Lysander Jaegenn's home, the edges of bulkhead walls and severed pipes glowing cherry-red behind it.

Simeon racked the slide on the antique gun and raised it over his head in one hand, the blade of his bonded sword in the other.

"Run, you coward!" he bellowed, his voice chasing the fleeing spider-figure up the shaft. "Run! Because you're being hunted, you bastard! HUNTED!"

Simeon leaped to the chase, propelling himself off the wall, up to the sheared top of a black iron column. This was much more satisfying than dispensing with Sethric Greer – this was going to be *fun*.

In the back of his mind the warrior Lord exalted – he'd beaten his former master once again. The killer who'd hacked Octavio Vanecke to pieces was fleeing from Simeon Blaire, disarmed and doomed. He'd be sure to remind the old man of that little fact when they met – before

Simeon finished the job that this assassin had failed to complete.

Ω

They must have built this damned thing for midgets.

At least that was what Jaq Haszan figured, squeezing his bulky frame down through another tiny circular airlock and into the control room of the Scourge. There were a lot of things in the world designed for men of diminutive proportions - sometimes it seemed like the whole damned place was built just for Kaito Kayzi. Jaq had problems with chairs, with clothes, with motorcycles, with pens, and *especially* with chopsticks. Elysium was just too poorly constructed for a gentleman of his size.

The tiny control globe in the core of the Scourge seemed to be no exception – well, at least in here everything appeared to have been extruded from a single vast lump of stainless steel, but the floor was the only place to sit. His head was still level with Kaito's, even though the little hacker had commandeered the best seat in the house, a swivel chair festooned with switches and lights and tiny screens.

"I think I can actually drive this thing," he said, his eyes caressing the banks of controls as if they were so much candy. "They built this beast to be run by unaugmented grunts – it's just a matter of finding the ignition."

"I think it's going to be a little more difficult than boosting a car, Kayzi." said Haszan, leaning back and rummaging through the plastic lockers and boxes in the rear of the control cabin. "Otherwise somebody would have stolen it already."

He bobbed up again with a handful of silvery wafers – survival rations vacuum-sealed more than two thousand years ago. "What do you reckon – apricot or beef wellington?" he asked, sifting through the identical foil packets with their cheap paper labels. "The use-by date's only out by three hundred years – should be fine."

Kaito wasn't listening – he'd retreated into that glazed-eyed dream state which came over him whenever he was deeply integrated with his own bio-onboard systems. He snapped out of it with a shake of his head, a comedown twitch which sparked through him like raw voltage.

"Yeah – got the schematics. I just do *this*..." His finger stabbed down once, twice, and the pitch of the rumbling machinery all around them changed slightly. There was a sense of the whole vast device waiting to lurch into motion, its gears spinning loose.

219

"Then engage the manual override sequence... *there*... now the control sticks are live... and we throw it into reverse... "

There was a shuddering, grinding noise, and the immense machine rocked backwards, making Haszan lose his fistful of ancient protein bars. Flatscreen monitors in front of Kaito's command chair went live – each one of them showing a tangled mass of rubble and steel. The piston legs of the Scourge scrabbled against the walls of the shaft as the great plug of debris held it in place, pinning it by the wreckage of its claw-tipped tentacles.

Jaq's head had caught up with the back wall of the cabin with a resounding smack – anybody else would probably been out cold.

"Nice driving, Kaito!" he grumbled, massaging his skull with one hand. "Reminds me why we both have separate motorcycles."

The Kayzi spun his chair around with a frustrated scowl, one hand still tapdancing over the keyboards blind. The Scourge's manual was still in his head, of course – ripped out of the machine when he'd killed its controlling personality.

"Jaq, does any of this strike you as out of the ordinary? We're sitting in the control room of a thousand-year-old mechanical sea-monster, the *soul* of which, for want of a better term, I've just erased. We got here after our new friend, *the most wanted operative of the Ashishim*, brought down an entire shopping mall on our heads, after – and I want to make this part extra clear – battling a renegade Cyben built out of that bent bastard Eddie Tsien. And you're..." Kaito paused at this point to swipe a foil packet out of Haszan's hands and squint at its label. "You're more concerned about some dehydrated lobster bisque packaged when our great-great-granddads weren't even *born*!"

Jaq shrugged, clamping his teeth down on a rubbery mat of woven protein which claimed to be a chicken hot pot. Perhaps it should have been added to boiling water – perhaps it would have made no difference.

"Well, you have your bad days. Take it as it comes," he said, chewing the great wad of freeze-dried pulp stoically. "Hey, you gonna eat that lobster, or what?"

A little vein was throbbing up on the Kayzi's temple, a sure sign that he was about to lose his composure. Before he could draw in enough breath to start cursing Jaq leaned forward, right up in his face, and jammed a stick of alleged hot pot into his mouth.

"Kaito, I'm *well* past being worried about this shit. I went past panic about an hour ago. And before you say it, yeah, I knew about Eddie

Tsien as well. I know who he used to be – my boss at Omnivasive showed me the photos. But you know what? I don't care. I'm along for the ride. I'm not going to be mister fuckin' *crazy* old Jaq Haszan this time. Reason being, last time things went all to hell like this, and I let it get to me, I got played. My whole family burned."

He reached up with one chrome finger and hinged Kaito's jaw shut around the glistening field ration, the grin on his face betrayed by the glittering madness in his eyes.

"So this time, I'm just going to go with it. So what. You just do your thing, and when I need to do mine, like back there with the hatch, and with those Cyben drones, I'll just do that too. Don't mind me. I'm cool. *I'm goddam copacetic.*"

Anybody else looking at his face in that instant would have started praying for a painless death. Kaito took a big bite of his chicken hot-pot, his fingers slowly creeping away from the keyboard, still twitching in midair. He swallowed, hard.

"Alright. That's great, Jaq. That's fine. I – I think it was all getting to me there. You're right, it's been a bad day. A *long, fucked up, insanely bad* day."

His eyebrows lifted- first the left, then the right.

"Y'know, this shit isn't half bad. Three hundred years out of date or not."

Kaito nearly jumped out of his skin when the intercom howled and crackled to life behind him – his head clocked the low ceiling of the command module with a noise like a temple bell. The sound which came through was at once familiar - and utterly terrifying.

It was Abdulafia 330, and something in his voice spoke of a mind which had gazed deep into hell.

"This is an open transmission to anyone still alive out there! Anyone! Evacuate the Subcity immediately! There has been a critical containment breach, code zero-two-nine, repeat, a critical containment breach, zero, two, nine..." Crosscut chatter on the Ashishi band rose up in a babble of protest and disbelief.

"How's he getting through?" asked Haszan, leaning in to twist the dials of the intercom at random. The message slewed out and in of a haze of static.

"It's the R.T. band. Jacked from the old Terminus Lib Army, back in the days before the Reclamation." explained Kaito, elbowing Jaq out of the way. He fine-tuned a little wheel on the black box, and 'Afia's voice came through clear again.

"This is not a test, this is not a drill – *evacuate immediately*! I confirm, code zero-two-nine – *extraterrestrial incursion*. Pull back to the first defense perimeter and await the instructions of your commanders. Celestial HQ, Confederate HQ, Vatican High Command, please, you have to believe me! This is no time for us to be fighting turf wars! It's loose in the Valley View sector, right above the C.K. The whole mall's down, the Wetsystems are locked out... if anyone can hear me, please respond. This is Operational Commander Abdulafia 330 of the Ashishim Collective. This is an open transmission to any survivors – code zero-two-nine! Code..."

After a mad scrabble among the dangling wires and plugs of the communications console, Kaito finally found a handset – an old-school trucker's mic with a little button on one side.

"Confirm please, Abdulafia 330 – this is Kayzi and Haszan aboard the Scourge. Our little plan came off without a hitch. What's this about an incursion? Is it that... that *thing* in Verlaine's head?"

For a second a flashback stripped his defenses bare, a memory etched into his brain and the choking wires of his bio-onboard. It was a viral slicing the boundary between metal and meat, branding Verlaine's suffering into his frontal lobes. His knuckles clenched white around the handset – so tight he forgot to let his finger off the button.

"...out of Verlaine, and into the Wetsystems! It's mutating faster than anything I'd ever believed possible! We have to pull out of the city, Kaito – we need to cut Elysium loose, and shut down Kronos. If that creature gets its claws into the Big Engine we're all going to want to be very, very far away."

"Why quit the city? Surely that's a bit drastic, even if the virus *is* alien. I saw it too, remember, and I'll admit it ain't pretty. But given enough time and enough processing power we can crack this mother. If we can't, nobody can."

There was a pause as crackling static cooked on the airwaves. Kaito was unpleasantly certain he could hear screams mixed up with the white noise.

"Kayzi... listen. *I* let it loose. It was trapped in Magus Verlaine's body – locked up tight. But I had to play the fucking hero! I had to *try*. And it SHOWED me... it showed me what it wants to do with this world. It's... perverse. Just sick. It's not just a danger to the Wetsystems, or to those of us who're hardwired. It feeds on *suffering*, Kaito, *human* suffering. You've seen the first secret of the Magi – the dead souls in the machine. When it gets to them it's going to increase its power a thousandfold."

It was the hoarse whisper of a man defeated – a voice on the edge of death. Kaito wondered, not for the first time, how Abdulafia had survived the collapse of the Valley View. Or indeed, if he *had* survived it...

He had to keep the Ashishi agent focused, or else he was going to lose it himself.

"I've seen them, 'Afia. I know what you guys are working for, now. You have to set them free. I gotta admit, it all sounded pretty tripped out and spiritual, until I saw the truth of it... "

When it came back Abdulafia's voice was bitter, filled with spite.

"That doesn't matter now – It doesn't matter that the whole world thought we were mad. It doesn't matter that we had to tempt guys like you with power and secrets, when the truth seemed like a drugged-out conspiracy. What you need to know is the LAST secret, the one they only tell the highest echelon of the indoctrinated. What that thing found out from poor damned Verlaine."

Even Haszan was on the edge of his seat by now, leaning in over the comm. unit as wails and moans sifted out of the static. Kaito could just picture the Ashishim somewhere in the dark, crushed between layers of broken concrete, drawing a final heaving breath.

"Those *souls*, the dead ones, the things in the Wetsystems – it's been storing them up since it was built. All of us in the inner circle have heard the final transmission, the last command which Kronos's makers gave it before the missiles hit. It wants to *save* us. It's built the means to remake the world."

He paused for a second, fighting for air.

Kaito could hear great slabs of stone and steel grinding together behind the Ashishi's voice, the aftershocks of the Valley View's collapse. At any second they could slip...

"That abomination will take Kronos as easily as it did Verlaine. And then – you can probably guess what kind of a world it wants to live in. Me, I don't have to. I've already been *shown*."

Kaito reeled back, stunned, his mind scrabbling at the edge of madness. It was too much to take in all at once.

"It promised me that I'd be one of its Exalted – that I'd have no choice. For setting it free I'd become one of its priesthood, and lead us all to hell." There was a racking sob, an anguished, rattling breath. "*It all started with me! I'm responsible!*"

Kaito didn't resist when Haszan's huge arm came in over his

shoulder and plucked the mic from his hand. He was still stunned by the implications of 'Afia's confession – still trying desperately to explain it away as some kind of hysterical hallucination.

"Listen up, *Dervashi*," growled Jaq, ripping off another chunk of freeze-dried protein with his teeth. "I've just given this little speech to my friend here, and I don't like repeating myself. But if what you're saying is true – and it sounds like you believe it – then self-pity ain't gonna help. I saw what you can do, back there at the Valley View. Me, I'm a simple man. If I see a problem, I just beat it down. Perhaps because I'm not as sharp as you or the Kayzi here – but it usually works."

He masticated loudly for a second, crushing the handset in his huge meaty fingers. "I haven't got any special training, or an army behind me like you do. I haven't got brains, or wetwiring, or any tricks. I can't do that freaky thing that you do, with all the damn fireworks out of nowhere. But if some piece of shit comes crawling from out of space and tries to take my city, I'm going to *fight*."

Kaito looked on in disbelief – this was a *demigod* his friend was lecturing, a warrior who'd actually fought in the Reclamation! When he looked at Haszan's face the Kayzi could guess what was going on behind his eyes – the rippling animated flames of his tattoos writhed and twisted across his skin as a constant reminder. He was in the grip of his own personal nightmare...

"If you lose it now *everyone you care about will die*. If you lose control your enemy has you by the balls. And when you come back down, when you realize what you've done, *then* you'll know despair. *Then* you'll want to die. Right now, you still have a choice."

Kaito knew he was speaking from personal experience. And the pain gave his words vehemence, gave them an edge which cut through the static and the feedback, right into Abdulafia's pain.

"You don't understand!" he hissed. *"It can't be fought!* The more you kill, the more it feeds – all I could hope to do is take as many people to safety as possible. But I'm going to die here. I'm trapped under tons of rubble, and if it shifts... "

Now Kaito was back on the keyboards, sweat beading his brow as his fingers moved in a blur. The Wetsystems were in tatters, but the old fiber-optic network was still live, and this ancient machine was plugged in, communicating with others of its kind across the city. The archaic interface he'd seen when he confronted the Scourge's mind was all he needed to take the outmoded system apart...

"Sit tight, 'Afia." said the Kayzi, pulling the mike back on its cable. "I think I can get you out of there. *Then* we can talk about evacuating the city."

There was a grinding noise for a second, and a tortured ultrasonic squeal. Kaito caught himself praying to the blessed Saint Ilya (something he hadn't done since the age of six) that the debris hadn't just crushed 'Afia flat.

"Allright. Allright. I – I think I can last about another twenty minutes. That's as much power as I've got left, from that last hit of 'chrome. But if we're going to do this at all, we're going to do it right. I need you guys to go and get some help – help from outside the city. There's a guy out there who owes me a favor."

Kaito breathed out, catching a glimpse of Jaq's grinning face reflected in the monitors. All the Ashishi had needed was a little push in the right direction.

"I don't know if you're a big threedeeo fan, but you may have heard of Deuteronomy Jones."

'Afia's voice grew stronger by the second, and Kaito could imagine him forcing the layers of rubble apart down there in the dark.

"Most of the time he's just a crazy evangelist, but you don't carve up Omnivasive's network like that without some serious skills. You know how they've been trying to get his head on a plate for the last decade or two? Well, there's a reason that he's never been found. It's called the *Archangel Uriel.*"

While he listened, Kaito was still blazing a trail of devastation through the remnants of Elysium's fiber-optic network, marveling at the number of millennium-age machines still live and drawing power from the city's core. Taking control of one of them would be strange – kind of like trying to drive while wearing boxing gloves. But he'd just spotted the perfect tool for the job, striding down the transdome ring-road as if there was a parade in town.

"O.K, 'Afia – I think we're good to go down here. How do we get Preacher Jones on our team?"

The Kayzi could just imagine Abdulafia's pained smile, deep under a mountain of twisted metal.

"All you have to do is swim out and surprise him, K. I'm sure that thing you're riding in will help him to see our point of view."

17 Aevum Oblivio
Crossfire

REASON'S HAMMER.

The ultimate manifestation of the Separatist Corporate Republics' power – nearly three klicks long down its rigid aluminum and carbon spine, a twin-ringed space dreadnaught packing enough firepower to crack open the most heavily shielded asteroid stronghold. Vast tokamaks and battery arrays fed power to an utterly forbidden A.I. matrix at its heart, and Zhe's slaved intelligences had at their disposal the means to scour the Earth itself of life.

For all this, next to the thing it hunted, the Hammer *seemed as inconsequential as a macrophage in a volcano.*

The Blacksteel, the Iron Virus, the Motherbrain's Children... whatever you called them, they knew how to build one hell of an impressive war machine.

This one was callsigned Behemoth *in the Codespeak Twelve of the Technic Academy, and it lived up to its name. If the jagged sphere of hematite-smooth tubes ever reached the orbit of Earth it would destabilize the tides with its bulk. It would eclipse the moon.*

Against this colossal foe Zhe had pitted a spiderweb of black dewdrop munitions... smart fusion cores and antimatter shells seeded across a swath of the asteroid belt. They were wrapped up in a confection of ice-cold stealth foam, bubbled black and inert. They awaited their prey, hoping to at least crack the vast tegulated scutes of its force-shields – a glittering diamond haze which bellied out before the Behemoth *like a planet's magnetosphere.*

In the meantime the mile-long dreadnaught was skinned tight to the flank of an asteroid mine, all its systems running at their bare minimum. The A.I.s waited in cold apprehension, hoping that the scanners and probes of the Unity battle-force would miss their stealth web until it was too late...

Unfortunately, it wasn't the Hammer *itself who gave the trap away.*

It was the ghosts of the people it had been built to subjugate.

When the first of the Blacksteel outriders came within hailing distance something inside the asteroid sensed its curling magnetic wake. Systems which had lain dormant for two thousand years struggled back to life, sparking. In black chambers carved into the rock mummified corpses floated in vacuum, starved and suffocated when the Earth forgot them. But their voices were preserved in the optic cores of their computer systems. What the war-fleet of the Unity heard as they closed in on Reason's Hammer *was their final cry for help.*

"Please – anybody! This is Colony Nine-Theta, Terminus Mining Company subunit twenty- seven... we're out of supplies. The water purifiers are shot. The air scrubbers are down to twenty percent capacity...Dear God, they're already talking about cannibalism in the labor habs. We haven't had a supply ship from Earth in three months, no news, no transmissions...Political Officer Grant tells us it's just solar radiation blocking the signal, but I'm not so sure anymore. Please, if anybody can hear us, this is Nine-Theta, requesting immediate assistance..."

The microwave transmission drew in the Blacksteel slaveships like the taint of blood in shark-infested water, fifty of the outriding cylinders boosting in toward the asteroid. Behind its deceptively solid bulk Reason's Hammer *cowered, hoping beyond hope that the vast mass of the Unity fleet was in range of its munitions.*

Panic sparked across the void faster than any radio message. Every cannon, every bomb in the whole damned sector seemed to detonate at once.

Fifty Blacksteel ships cupped the asteroid in a half-circle formation, while the jagged ball of the Motherbrain's Behemoth hung back, watching and analyzing. It saw the stealth munitions go live, spiraling in toward its vanguard even as their particle beams ignited, transfixing Colony Nine-Theta in a jagged hash of fire.

The Hammer's *A.I. cores worked feverishly in that blazing instant, trying to redirect their nuclear weapons against the main bulk of the Unity fleet. But most of the smart bombs were already inexorably locked in on their targets now – isolating the fifty outrider ships as a very clear and present threat.*

Even as the asteroid's shell cracked and shattered the swarm of nukes hammered into the Unity vanguard, lighting up in a chain of bright explosions. The radiation storm ripped through their energy shields and overwhelmed their heat dispersal systems, laying them open to vacuum.

Reason's Hammer *never saw the vanguard of the Blacksteel fleet detonate one by one – the sequestrated dreadnought was blasted to ashes and molten metal as forces able to disintegrate whole cities collided around it. Asteroid Nine-Theta simply ceased to exist, ablated away to nothing in an instant. Even the Motherbrain of the Unity never knew that* Reason's Hammer *had existed.*

Zhe winced with sympathetic pain as he watched the whole sorry spectacle played out in one of his optical reticules. Fifty ships out of five hundred – if anything the Hammer's *ambush had fared worse than* Calenture's *full-frontal assault. And he'd only just reached the gates of the R.T. – an immense cerametal portal still blazoned with the rusted arms of the Ashishim.*

There was only one problem, and it squatted heavily in front of the gates, its tiny eyes burning red as coals in a face like liquid bitumen.

It seemed that not everything in the city was dead. And not every shred of the Worm was trapped inside the crystallized tomb of Technician Nyl.

The thing which waited at the Ashishim gates was a Saprophyte – an eater of the dead, slave to the Worm. By its size, and the contorted faces and bodies which made up its patchwork bulk, Zhe guessed that it had been one of the Exalted, those who had welcomed the coming of the great beast.

Perhaps – if Zhe was lucky – it was cut off from the Worm now, dormant. If his current luck held, though, it was awake again after seventeen years of torpor, and it didn't need its master to survive.

Just a good square meal.

Zhe – and anything else alive – was *food.*

DOCUMENT INSERT: MULTIPLICITY ARCHIVES DEPARTMENT

(INTERCEPTED FROM THE CONFEDERATE MILITARY NETWORK, 11:21 PM)

"They're coming through the walls! Jefferson, get those flamethrowers back here!"

"Sir, the docks are off limits! The Grand Teutonia got away fine, but we've lost contact with the Sliepnir, and the Northern Son isn't responding..."

"No time for that now - they're right on top of us! That Pureblood squad we sent up to Subcity level haven't called in yet either, dammit..."

(extended gunfire, cursing - three minutes twenty nine seconds)

"Sweet Odin's blood, what are these things? Jefferson, we have to fall back to the next strongpoint...Jefferson? Oh, shit! It's got Jeffer... " (screams, tearing noises, dripping - two minutes nineteen seconds) (TRANSMISSION ENDS)

(INTERCEPTED FROM THE CELESTIAL KINGDOM PUBLIC ADDRESS BAND, 11:27 PM)

"Attention citizens - this is an official edict from the inner council. A state of emergency is now in effect, but please rest assured that your Emperor and his ministers have the situation under control. Traitorous attacks by the forces of Kronos and his lackeys the Vatican are being repelled by the glorious people's army in kombinant-sectors 1193 and 1190. To ensure a state of solidarity and readiness all citizens are to report to their local militia offices for a compulsory defense draft.

We repeat, a compulsory draft has now been enacted.

(MESSAGE REPEATS ON AUTOMATIC LOOP CYCLE)

(INTERCEPTED FROM THE VALLE CRUCIS CHAPTERHOUSE COMM-NET, 11:32 PM)

"In the name of God the Father, in the name of the Son and the Holy Spirit I abjure thee! Back to the pit, foul spawn of Satan! Aroint thee, dem... "

(concussive noises, mastication - five minutes two seconds)

"This is Crucis squad Tercius, report please Chapterhouse! We are pinned down above the Basilica chamber, and our Paladin commander has just been... been EATEN by one of those... "
(sobbing, gunfire, fifty-nine seconds)

"There, you godless bastards! Burn in the devil's fires! Brother Nathan, there's one behind you!"
(roar of combusting gases, screaming - nineteen seconds)

Oh Christ in Heaven - Nathan! I'm sorry! What have I done? Chapterhouse, please advise! They're coming in waves, damn them, and there's a thing on the ceiling now, some kind of spider-demon... and I think I've killed Brother Nathan...and, and... "

(roar of combusting gases, tapering off into a hiss - twelve seconds)

"This is squad Tercius requesting immediate

backup! We can't hold the Basilica Chamber any
longer - God, they're all dead, and my Purifier's
out of ammo... Oh, please, no! The spider-thing,
it's coming for me! I can feel it in my mind!
I can feel it eating my brain! In nomine patri,
et fili, et spiritus sancti, redemptorem me ex
infernis..."

(sound of an automatic pistol being loaded, a
single gunshot, then silence - eight seconds)
(TRANSMISSION ENDS)

17 Aevum Oblivio
Hidden City

A PAIR OF *masslifters settled through the treetops, vast red birds sinking into cover on pillars of fire and smoke. Their crimson paint was scarred and peeling, and their skin was patched with jagged welds and riveted plates - but they got the job done. Three thousand miles in one jump, carrying a cargo of treason and death.*

From edge to edge the great basin of jungle was more than ten miles wide, with a shallow lake at its center flashing in the sun. Even if the skeptics and bureaucrats of Elysium had been able to see this valley, they would never have placed it as the hidden city of Agartta, temple of the Invisibles.

CeeAn watched it all as her transport sunk down through the trees, into a living cathedral thick with flowering vines. There was a pale circle of concrete down there, with clumps of grass and moss forcing their way through the cracks in its ancient surface.

War, on a whole, was out of their operational budget.

The whole underground city was in similar disrepair – its faltering systems had been scavenged and jury-rigged from whatever the survivors of Elysium's fall could find. Far from being the secret masters of the world, most of the people who lived in the green gloom of the forest were farmers, intent on survival.

Hell, it took them almost all their resources just to make the jump across East Afrika today – more than half of their fuel, as well. But there was power here - power sufficient to stop the Forge, and enough to protect Agartta from a rain of nuclear bombs.

Unfortunately, thought CeeAn as she stepped down from the lead masslifter, such power never came without a price.

"Take them to the Sanctum," she ordered the pair of Ashishim Dervashi who ran in under the 'lifter's wing to greet her. "Careful not to drop them, either – if they shatter, neither of the bastards will feel a thing!"

The black-hooded pair nodded, silent, manhandling the purple crystal statues of Blaire and Nyl out of the 'lifter's hold with the help of a gang of gunners and pilots.

She was home.

Well – home for the last seventeen years, anyhow. It couldn't really be home, or really be the stronghold of the Ashishim without him. *CeeAn caught herself carefully omitting is name from her thoughts, and smiled ruefully. If that other thing – that Technician – had been lying...*

But the Vision was strong in her. It had been ever since that awful moment in the Valley View, when she'd reached out into the cold heart of Asag'raal and felt something through the other side.

"Cee, the acolytes are waiting for you down there!" shouted one of the Ashishi soldiers, cupping an earpiece in one hand. "They say it's urgent!"

She sighed, wrapping her robe up tight and cinching it with a loop of leather. Best not to keep Devine and his boys waiting – even if she was the nominal leader here. Nobody would admit it – not after the treachery of the Illuminatus, still so fresh in everyone's memory. But whenever there were hard decisions to make, she felt all those eyes on her...

CeeAn stepped down from the masslifter, hurrying across the cracked concrete to the nearest downpipe. This one was wedged in between the buttress roots of a baobab, airbrushed up in gray-brown camo.

As usual the compressed air in the downpipe made her ears pop and ring, and she faltered a little as she stepped out into the corrugated-steel warren of Aggarta, the hidden city.

It was hardly as mystical or romantic as the name suggested. But it was home – of sorts – and the only refuge for the thousands of Ashishim who had followed her out of Elysium. Others, too – an embarrassing number had believed in her in that place, at that moment. All were united under the banner of the Ashishi now, whether they'd been Confed or Celestial, Vatican or Sub or Noble back in the old days.

The deep, soft hood of the red robe afforded her a little privacy as she hurried through the tunnels – in a way she was glad that Devine had made the woolen garments a uniform of sorts for the sect. It was tedious and excruciatingly awkward to have children following her for tales of the Exodus, and everybody deferring to her as if she was some kind of goddess. More importantly the thick fleece was warm, taking the chill out of the processed air of the tunnels.

She followed loops of cable bolted to the walls, tracing a chain of naked electric bulbs down the spiral and into the heart of Aggarta, the Sanctum.

This was once a military base, sunk deep beneath the soil of the Congolese jungle to conceal a hoard of illegal weapons. Long, long ago the Terminus Separatist Army had made plans for this place, plans, indeed for the whole continent of Afrika. But the crater above them had been scooped out by horrific weapons, and the radiation had burned through...

Time had taken care of that, and the jungle had spilled back in, defying the deserts which crowded in on each side.

Seventeen years ago she'd needed a place like this, and it had been there for her, waiting – a seed planted in her mind by creatures that were now infuriatingly silent. Somehow she'd led these people - the farmers and the techs, the Dervashi and the children, Devine and his zealots, all of them – out of the last city to Agartta.

The very first thing they'd done (and this, she assumed, was down to Devine again, him and his siblings in Faith) was to convert the deepest, most cavernous chamber into the Sanctum.

Every time she came here she told herself she was over it – that this was real, not some kind of screwed-up dreamscape. But every time it still brought her heart to her throat, and stopped her breath for an instant. It was the statues, she guessed.

A fifty-foot representation of yourself can do that, especially when it's flanked by similar colossi with faces you'd be better to forget...

It opened up in front of her now, as she stepped over the threshold. A vacuum, sucking in focus, tugging at her with winking candles and swaying shadows. Through a henge of rusting missiles, arranged in concentric circles around the altar...

Her eyes played over the titanic granite features of the other three – she was always too embarrassed to linger on the idealized version of her own face in stone.

Haszan. Kayzi. And hi... and Abdulafia 330, haloed with wire-tipped dreadlocks. They'd run a pair of mining lasers to pieces slicing these things out of the living rock, and now there were kids in Agartta who thought it was all just a legend.

Devine was there by the altar as usual, the very image of the wizened, pious monk. Too bad that his religion was based on something utterly inexplicable, but then, she supposed, most of them were.

Some people had seen things on Exodus Night which drove them screaming to insanity. Others (and she included Devine in this second category, for all his lucidity) had slipped quietly into a gentler madness.

He rose from his knees as she pulled back her hood, his trembling hands flitting to and fro like tethered birds. Gone was the foul-mouthed, cynical 'tech who'd lorded it over the Cryo levels. This new iteration of SubMagus Devine was almost painfully meek and mild, broken both physically and mentally by the touch of the Saprophytes, his lip twisted down into a scowl at one corner by a jagged scar.

"Most Re... CeeAn. I'm glad you're back so soon – the Circle must be closed before any more, umm... succumb."

His eyes were huge and watery, filled with pleading. There was a very good reason why he carefully avoided saying 'die' there, and CeeAn respected it. But good Gods, would he ever stop trying to call her 'Most Reverend"?

"Of course – we can't have them sacrificing themselves for my sake. I really hope you don't encourage them..." She stopped, clasping the priest's stick-thin hands in her own. "But we have the means to use the Forge now. The Circle can be closed for the last time."

Devine pulled away, leading her past the blank, scrubbed stone of the Altar and between the immense statues, to a door guarded by faceless red-robed acolytes.

"I'm glad you taught us how to do this thing, CeeAn. But so many have been lost... and we both know their fate. Was it worth it, just to master that foolish old machine?"

He was turned away from her, fumbling among a rusted handful of keys, but she knew exactly the look of weary pain which would be written across his face. Not for the first time she felt like she had to scream.

"Devine, this isn't for me. I never wanted it to be this way. But do we really have a choice? Ever since the Betrayal our course has been set. Those bastards aren't going to just take what they want and leave us alone, you know."

"I'm sorry." he said, turning the key in the lock. "I know how hard it is, believe me. I'm just glad it's almost over."

He pushed the doors open then, leaning into the task with all his meager weight, letting them swing wide with a creak of iron-bound hinges.

As usual the room beyond was filled with pressure and light and incense smoke – a tiered bowl stepping down layer by layer to a sunken pit of smooth black granite. The whole room was a sphere, lined on every surface with polished metal, burnished to a mirror sheen, reflecting the rapt faces of a thousand men and women who sat cross- legged on the stone tiers.

Silence crashed down over CeeAn and Devine like a wave as they picked their way down to the center of the room, the pressure building up, oily sparks crackling across their skin as they neared the Focus.

This was the gift she'd been given. At that moment when she touched the Heart of the Dead, In the instant when it had bridged the gap from beneath the waters of its impossible ocean to this reality it had left the door open just a crack. It was as if a sliver of that impossible thing's being had been pushed into CeeAn's brain, a shard of mirror-glass seething with the memories of whole dead generations...

It had shown her that she didn't need the 'chrome. That you didn't need to pull the soul out of its fleshy shell and cage it up, like Kronos or the Illuminatus with his Ark.

This was the power that Devine had built his faith around, to bandage up his shattered mind. This was what the Ashishim believed in now, now that the charlatan philosophy of the Illuminatus had been stripped away. They came here gladly, willing to make the sacrifice just to be part of something they thought was wonderful...

CeeAn knew it for what it really was. This was how you exerted just the right pressure on a universe as thin and bright as a bubble of oil. This was how you stopped nuclear fire falling from the sky, and how you held off the Forge, even if you couldn't use it yourself. Oh, it was crude, and costly, and it would be no match for the fleets of the Unity and the Multiplicity. But it was still magic *in their eyes, sacred bloody magic.*

CeeAn reached the Focus, a pentacle scrawled across the stone in indelible spraypaint. From the tiers above her the power came down, a hammer of light, drumming on her brittle skull like rain.

She hated it, but Technician Zhe was right. Kronos had stretched the world thin in creating the Forge. The events of Exodus Night had torn reality, cracked the wall between the worlds. And now that damned fool Nyl, the Betrayer, had almost punched a hole right through to the dark on the other side.

Where the Harvesters lived. Asag'raal's brothers, who'd given her just a taste of their power...

If they used the Forge, it could only be once. And it would have to be used right *– used to undo all that damage, and remake the world in far more than just the physical sense.*

If they called her bluff she could never use it. Hells, even this ritual was tempting fate, sending hairline cracks skittering across the surface of the universe...

CeeAn let herself go, felt her mind orient itself like a compass, drawn around into the howling flux by the sliver of silver which pierced its core. Devine was the anchor, his soul a fitful flicker as she closed her eyes and let the Vision spill in.

The room was a sphere of light in there, the mirrors focusing and refining it, ramping up its power to a beam of hot incandescence. It blazed up from the Focus to pierce the ceiling, arcing away toward Elysium over the horizon.

And the dead looked down on her in their serried ranks, the dead and the dying, the drained and withered souls of a thousand willing sacrificial victims pouring themselves into the fire.

All for her. All for a promise she couldn't even remember making...

CeeAn stepped between the power and its grim source, turning it inside out with a gesture, the flame devouring itself like a serpent eating its own tail...

And the Circle broke. The Vision flared raving white, and blew away in a sickening rush.

She sank to her knees as the pain throbbed in her head, as Devine rushed to her side, his hands fluttering like dying birds...

And through her tears she saw them fall apart; those who had given everything collapsing into bones and dust while the mirrored fire faded, and the incense smoke swirled up like a shroud, smothering her consciousness.

2196 Ante Arbitrium
Saprophyte

At the age of nine, Dravin Coyle was pushed off the swings in the scrappy little wasteland park behind Hab-Block 18a-North. He walked away with his head down, while the jeering laughter of the other kids sleeted off him like rain.

Seventeen minutes later he returned with his father's quaint old under-and-over shotgun, and blew a hole in the bully responsible the size of a hydroponic watermelon.

From that day on, his future was sealed. The judge at juve court had given him two choices. Exile, or Compliance Academy. Even a messed-up kid like Dravin knew that he'd be raw meat in the Pit – so he zipped up his blue boilersuit and started his training that very afternoon.

Eleven years later he'd finished framing up the rest of those cruel little bastards who'd laughed at him, popping them one by one for narco busts and seditious activities. His chief found the file, did the maths, and sent the whole mess up to Admin for processing, thinking he'd be glad to see the back of his most volatile, screwloose officer.

The upper hierarchy didn't drop him, though. They knew raw, vicious talent when they saw it. That's how Dravin Coyle got bumped up to the Special Squad.

CDSTS - Compliance Division Special Tactical Services to their friends - were the elite of the elite. Out of the skeleton crew of living officers on the force, these were top hundred tooled-up psychopaths who could still point a gun in the right direction. They were the kind of people who, as children, wore camo paint and brought along hunting knives when they played hide and seek. Being selected for the CDSTS was a mark of some distinction on the force, akin to being the first Viking berserker onto the beach during a raid.

Tonight the 'Tac (as they liked to call themselves) were hitting it hard, reveling in the chaos which gripped the city. All kinds of random carnage seethed and crackled across the open band – collapsing buildings, crashing airships, running gunfights, massive explosions – but the elite strike-force of the Comp Div were taking the opportunity to settle some fairly long-standing scores.

They were trying to crack Hab 99.

Senior Sergeant Crenshaw had put it best, thought C-Tac Constable Coyle. Let the automated systems and the Cyben hold down the R.T.

Let the rank-and-file keep those rioters in check – hells, all they were doing was shifting stolen property from one hab to another. But the Rude Boys, well, they had been top mongrels in the lower levels for a few years now, almost like a little reclamation all on their own. The other gangs in their criminal strata were whipped into submission, and the bigger players were, as usual, sitting on the sidelines waiting for each other to move. Meantime, the Rude Boys had 'retired' a number of cops – on and off duty – loudly proclaiming that hab 99 was safer with *them* as the law.

Pure bad publicity, that. Fighting words if ever any existed.

That's why Dravin and his little squad of Special Constables were crouched in the dark, in an alleyway off Rockwell Plaza. This was the no-mans-land which encircled hab 99, and in the hazy gloom which filtered down light-wells in the metal ceiling the entire 'Tac force was creeping into position, silenced machineguns ready, night-vision rigs clamped tight around their grim faces.

Nobody, the Senior Sergeant had told them, would think it was personal tonight. There were any number of perfectly legitimate reasons that the stronghold of Grady Townsend and his band of thugs could accidentally catch fire, or collapse, or explode. Choosing one would be a job for the deskbound slugs back in Central Administration.

As far as he was concerned, this was all like the swing-pushing incident, on a much grander scale. Everybody in the 'Tac had the same psych profile as Dravin Coyle, but now they were actually *given* guns by the Direktoriat and turned loose on the city.

Now they chain-smoked, and waited, and muttered their little prayers... for what? Any God worth his halo would spit on C-Tac and all its bloody works...

The signal came through hot, just as cramp was setting into Coyle's legs.

"We are go, repeat, green light for interdiction pattern alpha..."

Autoinjectors screwed his veins wide open and hit him with a double fistful of military twist, making his heart swell into an aching supernova. His jaw muscles clenched and his lips pulled tight as the twist raged through his hindbrain, tripping a bank of predator switches...

Dravin screamed as he sprinted across the plaza toward his squad's insertion point. Scribbles of rusted razorwire and blazing oildrums were the only obstacles out in the killing ground; the only cover as well. The Constable jinked left and right, expecting snipers' bullets to chew up the concrete at his heels, but nothing came down from the steel-clad cube of Hab 99 except a confused shout, then the mournful bellow of a salvaged foghorn.

By the time any gunfire came popping and rattling from the slit windows above he and his men had already slid in tight to the wall, their jumpsuits smeared with gray dust. Coyle ticked them of one by one on shaking fingers. Clements, Fitch, and the huge, balled-up form of Junior Constable Syliss, his whole body clenched up like a fist. The matt-black slab of his standard-issue automatic looked tiny in his giant hands.

His blood was up. The twist had him by the jugular, shaking him in its teeth.

Kill. Maim. Destroy. Bite. Gouge. Slash.

Deep breath, Dravin. Remember to use your words…

"All right, men," he hissed, "We're going to go in hard, hit them while they're still confused, and dust off before any of those little bastards can link their CCTV into the datanet. The public want this to be the work of some other gang, and the brass want them to believe it. So, badges off, safety off, and shoot any little chemhead scum you get in your sights. Junior Constable Syliss – you're along to provide collateral damage. So try to break everything you get your hands on. Really mess the place up…as if you'd do it any other way."

The big man's face split in a blood-curdling grin then, a gash of blackened teeth opening in a cross-hatched nightmare of scar tissue.

"Sure thing, boss. Gonna mash 'em up funtime!"

Dravin shuddered a little – the Junior Constable was a bit much, even by the standards of CDSTS. But some criminals, SS Crenshaw had told him, were so bad that the force *needed* them. Hence the explosive collar lovingly embraced by the meaty folds of Syliss's neck. A little aerial poked up from his shaven skull, linked back to fire support.

"Clements, Fitch, I'll take point, you lay down covering fire. Room by room, gentlemen. And if any of us bag Grady Townsend, we split the reward four ways. That's *teamwork*, that is."

The squaddies mumbled their assent, checking and rechecking their weapons as they waited for the tech boys to blow the doors of the Hab. Grady's Rude Boys may have been nothing but a street gang, but their bullets were as good as anyone else's – the last thing any trooper wanted to hear when he drew down on one was a weapons jam. The radio feed buzzed and popped in Dravin's ear.

"Two nine, two nine, this is fire support. We're primed to roll on three, two, one..."

The crackling voice was cut off as a slim, four-winged rocket grenade came scudding in over Rockwell Plaza, one of a swarm controlled by the wireheads of the support branch. By now the big guns had opened up from above – scavenged military junk belching out high-explosive shells.

They'd never hit anything with those ancient bangers – the C-Tac boys were already in place, waiting for the doors to pop. Still, the clouds of smoke and the thunderous roar of guns drowned out the hailstorm of explosions as the battering-ram munitions struck home.

Fitch was through the door before the last shreds of burning fiber-foam hit the deck, tucking and rolling, going in low as Clements went high, their combat torches snapping on as they quartered the room. Dravin went in at a half crouch, right down the middle, with Syliss lumbering along behind him. The place was cavernous – a whole floor of apartments knocked out into a maze of crumbling drywall and dripping exposed plumbing. Dust billowed and seethed in the gloom, setting up gray phantom shapes which twisted in the air under the beam of the squad's gun-mounted torches.

Then the shooting started.

It was Syliss who caught it – the big, meaty target – a clear shot right through one melon-sized bicep. The big man howled in frustrated pain, raking the murk with a blast from his machine-pistol. If he hadn't lashed out the next one would have drilled him between the eyes – instead it took a chunk out of the doorframe right next to Clements. The three Special Constables hugged the floor, torches off, as a volley of shots skipped off the concrete around them.

"Fitch, flank them! Syliss, dammit, get down! We're gonna lay down some covering fire for him, circle round to the right. Switch your headsets to amplify, and maybe we'll even see something in this bloody dust-storm."

But when Dravin flicked the switch on the side of his goggles their complex target-acquisition software did precisely nothing. Glitched sprays of green pixels and jagged lines blazed in front of his eyes.

Typical bloody wirehead shite... lucky those boys don't make our guns...

Then from behind him he heard a sound he wished he hadn't – a gurgling, slobbering sound, like a toothless man trying to suck the meat off a bone.

Syliss? Was he lung-shot? Coyle had heard that noise before, and it usually came with far more screaming. He came up to his knees in the dusty darkness – he didn't dare light up his torch, but something was definitely wrong here.

He pushed the flickering, useless headset up out of the way, straining to make out Syliss's massive form.

Fitch, Clements – *anyone...*

But it seemed that the room had widened out around him – he couldn't even see the door anymore. Veils of shifting smoke and dust hemmed him in, with twitching, lurching shadows stalking behind them. Something was *dripping* out there, counterpoint to a noise like the slide and slither of wet meat...

Instinctively Dravin clenched his gun to his chest – a comfort, an anchor. His thumb came down on the little switch which tripped his radio connection.

It was the same slobbering, grinding sound, hashed up by static, overlayered with far-off screams and moans. Then fire control came through out of a howl of feedback.

"Oh gods! What the hell is that thing? It's all over the transport!"

Metal creaked and groaned, caught in an unseen vise.

A burst of gunfire rang out, cut short by an inhuman hiss and growl.

"McMasters! What has it done to your eyes? Oh, please, no! NO!"

That's when Dravin came face to face with his buddy Fitch.

Well - not exactly face to face. Dravin's first glimpse of the C-Tac gunjack was the bloody back of his skull.

For the first time since he'd seen daylight through a hole in little Ralf Jenkks, Special Constable Coyle felt the fear. He circled around the body, one hand up to his mouth.

Fitch was only standing upright because of what somebody had done to him – he'd been all but crucified on a tangle of rusted plumbing. Jagged sheared-off pipes were punched through his arms, his legs, his chest – dripping lengths of steel rose up from his shoulderblades like the stumps of angel wings. Some impossible force had picked him up from behind and smashed him face-first into the broken pipes.

There was no way he could feel it, though – one half of his head looked like it had been shattered with a concrete cinderblock.

Or...and now the terror came down, and there was to way to cram it back into the recesses of his mind...*or by the huge gnarled fist of Junior Constable Syliss.*

He turned, panic-quick, his torch lit up and cutting a blazing arc through the gloom.

Nothing.

No – really *nothing* – no gunshots, no noise, no screams... even the radio was dead, when he dared trip the little switch again. This was supposed to be a warzone, wasn't it?

Where were the Rude Boys, where was Grady Townsend? Where, for the love of all hells, were his boys from C-Tac? *Something* had gotten Fitch, that was for sure. But the hab was a silent as a tomb.

Silent for a second that stretched out into an eternity, anyhow. Then came the sound again, from right behind him.

The sound of toothless jaws chewing gristle, of slobbering lips smacking with dreadful hunger. Dravin Coyle turned as if on wheels, slow and hesitant, thinking about that staved-in face, that burst eye dripping, the mouth slack and broken...

But oh, it was much, much worse.

The mangled corpse of his friend would have been a comfort, compared to the thing which swam up out of the darkness.

It was as black as tar, glistening in the torchlight, its face stretched over the misshapen skull of the late Constable Fitch. Needle teeth like those of some deep-sea fish snapped open and shut as it flexed the dead man's broken jaw, lolling open all the way down to his punctured chest. A bullwhip tongue coiled out of his throat, weaving in the stale air. At its tip hovered a single unblinking eyeball, jaundice yellow, regarding Dravin's jugular with unconcealed lust.

Reflex action pulled the trigger tight.

Dravin Coyle almost lost control of his bowels when he heard the sad little click of an empty chamber.

"Nicccce tryyy Draaav," bubbled the horror. "Weeeer'e gonnnaa like you. Yoooouurrr'e gonna be *fff-fffammily!*"

He heard Fitch's bones snap and break as the thing stood up, its grotesque face still nailed on backwards, drooling tar from between lacerated lips. An second eyeball like a vast pustule rose up out of the slime, fixing Dravin with a mad pinhole stare.

And then its puppet-master stepped forward, through the curtains of shifting mist, and Dravin Coyle knew that he was dead.

It was Junior Constable Syliss – and it was Clements as well. The screaming face of Dravin's squad sharpshooter was frozen under a skin of tight wet shadow, a mask of agony bulging from Syliss's shoulder. One of his arms jutted at a crazed, broken angle from the big man's back, its hand replaced with the dripping muzzle of his automatic.

Syliss's face was free from the crawling filth which smothered his body
– all but his eyes, two seething pools of liquid night. He was pale,
almost bloodless, the horrorworks of scars which crosshatched his
face pulsing livid purple.

One of his fingers ended in a tapering projection – narrowing down
to become a tight black thread which linked him to the monstrous
Steven Fitch.

When the monstrosity spoke, its voice issued from both its bodies,
a mad disharmony which crazed and echoed in Dravin's aching head.

"It showed me the way, boss," said Syliss, reaching out tenderly to
stroke his commander's ashen face. His skin blistered and peeled away
under the monster's touch, but he couldn't feel it. "We're all going to
be part of something beautiful, Constable. As good and true and right
as how it felt when you were nine. I know what it was like, Dravin. You
were an angel of righteousness, weren't you? You were all-powerful.
The blood, and the bits inside, and the smell of shit and cordite... I
even know you had a hard-on, you little bastard. I know how you felt.
And now we're all going to feel it. When we become one, and give that
feeling, that *part of ourselves* to the New Flesh."

Dravin could hardly discern the horror in his head from the horror
loose in the world, now. But Syliss's words (spoken in a voice both
intimate and clinical, a voice that could never come from the mouth
of that big thug) touched something inside him.

He remembered that moment, the moment when the gun had made
him God. And he smiled as the black fluid flowed out from Fitch's
mouth, slow-motion waves of it sinking into his skin. He smiled even
as it slicked over his teeth and wriggled down his throat like a handful
of live worms. He would live in that moment now, forever...

"It showed me the way, boss. It said that I was waiting for it, all
along. It named me – Exalted."

Then the barbs came out, and the black tar flashed to boiling point
inside him, and the pain began.

It was just exactly as terrible as he could imagine.

Ω

Kronos jammed the shutdowns as fast as he could – sealing off huge
chunks of the Wetsystems with every switch, acutely aware that with
each override it was isolating the greater part of its own city-sized
brain.

The bad sector down near the ruins of the Valley View was

irretrievably lost. Thousands of minds had been infected there already – only a hundredth part of Kronos's neurostrata hoard, but enough to spawn horrors all over the Last City. The connections to and from the bad sector formed a black spiderweb of wire and sub-ether links – here they meshed with the fire control systems of C-Tac, there a single skein of fiberoptics linked them to a synthesoy extruder... there was no time to track every last vector of infection. All the great machine could do was slam the doors shut and slide home the bolts, locking the Saprophytes outside. No doubt there'd be terror on the streets tonight. But the important thing was that the Forge remained under Kronos's control.

There was still the matter of the Blacksteel to consider, and the treacherous Illuminatus of the Ashishim. But there was a sure and certain way to deal with them. All it required was the key to unlock the door...

Simeon Blaire was far from an ideal candidate to wield the fire of the Forge; indeed, the effort would probably burn his feeble mind to ashes. No doubt a more suitable candidate could be chosen after young Simeon had been used up and wrung dry, and after the Wetsystems had been recharged with a fresh generation of the dead. In Kronos's millennial timescale, this was just a minor delay. And if Blaire were to fail?

Well, it was wise to remember that the Game was a *human* conceit. There were others equally vicious and single-minded who would serve admirably as fodder for the Forge. After all, this was hardly its intended use. Even the one who was trying to kill Blaire right now would be acceptable, at a pinch.

Another bank of switches hammered closed, and the lights in Kronos's asteroidal palace flickered and dimmed. So many vectors, so many connections...

All that mattered was keeping the things Nyl had unleashed from the controls.

Ω

"I know what you do when you're alone," it told him.

"I know what you lust for, what you hate, what you fear – I know the place where they all intertwine. That sick little place you thought was *secret*."

He listened, hanging in the dark, clinging to the wall like a spider. Below him stalked a tiny figure in black, quartering the gloom with the muzzle of a stolen fusion cannon.

"I've given you a taste, boy, but the first one's the only one that's free. I want to take you back inside your mind. I want us to live in your secrets. I want us to *turn that darkness inside out.* Is that so much to ask?"

It was keening, pleading, mewling like a child, stroking the raw meat of his brain like a disease, a lover...

It had him, and it knew.

From the wires and plugs and slivers of silicon in him, through the hot wet meat and reinforced bone it came, sweating out of the hard, black little core where he kept his vile desires. The part of him which played the game. The part of him which kept a beloved, hated slave just to torture. The fury in him which made him the perfect tool for Kronos, secret enforcer of the Game behind his skull-faced mask.

"Yes!" he said, silent, to the thing which licked his naked spine. "Give me the power! And give me Blaire!"

He heard it howl then, a ragged, bubbling sound which degenerated into a storm of discordant laughter. For the briefest second he heard another sound behind it, the sound of a million doomed voices telling him to run, to turn back, to escape while he still could...

Then the darkness behind his executioner's cowl erupted, a deeper black, and he felt the fire like molten lead in his bones. The power! The impossible power!

"That's right, boy. The one named Simeon will rot in your embrace now! The whole world, soon enough... They shall call you – Exalted."

He smiled then, as the pain sweated out through his skin, slick and hot and bubbling.

Lysander Jaegenn stabbed a handful of obsidian claws into the wall above him, marveling at the strength his new patron had given him. One hand after another, up out of the dark, up to where he could hear music playing, where he could see searchlights sliding over the gravid belly of the clouds. The shattered crystal dome was like a great blind eye, his new god looking down on him from above...

Blaire first, it said.

Then all the rest of them.

Ω

The Worm Asag'raal raged in its confinement, battering itself against the impenetrable walls of the infected sector. Second by second its poison spread out through the wires, waking nightmares in the streets and down among the habs and manufactoria. But still...

The damned machine had reacted too fast! Now it was hemmed in, locked away from its triumphal feast of pain by a delicate meshwork of code.

In its impatient hunger the Worm had learned only so much from Technician Nyl – not nearly enough to slice its way through the most sophisticated ice ever created.

It would have to use force, then. It would have to take the fight to Kronos out there, in the real world of *meat* and *blood*.

For every mind bound and vivisected in the Wetsystems it could wake a single Saprophyte. And just like every time it crossed the barrier and entered the world, there were those who welcomed it. Men like Junior Constable Syliss, who felt the same hunger, the same ravenous lust for destruction. They would become its Exalted, most valuable of its slaves. Its rank-and file saprophyte soldiers lasted only so long, before the corpses they animated rotted away in their embrace. But even more would be born from the dead, once its chosen ones began the great harvest.

And this time there were *others*. Some of the minds and souls under its thrall were bound to machines – useless lumpen things of metal and plastic, for the most part, industrial robots churning out food and bullets and recycled sewage. But there were a happy few who had been slaved to greater things.

Asag'raal's mind was far from sharp – it was just the echoes of intellect bubbling up out of its digested prey, after all. But it remembered the Illuminatus' lessons. And it saw great potential in some of its new toys...

Ω

Only a few of them had come back from the second round. For some, the terror of final death had been too much, and they'd curled up on themselves like Sethric Greer, praying for salvation which never came.

Others, just as Simeon had predicted, fought like cornered beasts as the truth of their mortality sank in. They were the ones who came back first, attended by flitting aeromekan which washed the crusted blood from their skin. Each of the Lords and Ladies who remained was surrounded by a tight little cloud of hovering machines – cameras and aeros and the mechanical cherubim which bore up their sashes of white samite. Every one of them had a certain look in their eyes – a *hunted* look, for all that they were victorious predators.

To stay here meant almost certain death, by the cruel mathematics of the Game. But to leave – that was an admission of failure. It meant exile, and that was worse than death to these people. At least, before, death had only been temporary.

"How's everybody holding up?" asked Elisha Dawes, bright and brittle as she knocked back another neon-banded cocktail. "I hope that that *ghastly* Vanecke's silly claims haven't spoiled the mood!"

The little group she was talking to nodded and smiled, keeping up a slick professional front. Any admission of weakness would be a lethal disadvantage.

Duke Helmsfjord tweaked the ends of his waxed mustachios, a sure sign that he was nervous.

"Well, milady, I must admit I'd love to hear what Kronos thinks of this mess. Who knows what our poor citizens are feeling, now, knowing that their beloved rulers are so upset!"

That was as far as he'd push it – even with enough expensive liquor to kill a Pit Feral in his veins. Their guilty glances said it all – every one of them was trying to access the datanet. All of them needed to know if it was true.

"Come now, Gustav!" whispered Lord Diem, his almond eyes wide with mock astonishment. "Surely you would never break the edict of silence? This Game of ours is *sacred*, sealed until the last man falls!"

Elisha shifted her focus with a thought, sliding electronic-warfare overlays to the front of her vision. Diem's icepicks were grinding away at the Temple's defenses just as hungrily as those of Helmsfjord – and any number of other Kheptarchs.

"Gentlemen – please!"

Elisha set her face in what she thought was a devastating pout. It succeeded in making her look like a deep-sea fish.

"This is all just that damned fool Direktor's idea of psychological warfare! Do you really think that he could best Emmanuel Lancaster? That androgynous old ball-breaker probably scares Kronos himself!"

Diem nodded – but he still kept his slaved icepicks hacking away at the dome of silence. It was futile, but at least it was *something*.

"You're right, of course, dear Lady. But it is not for us that I worry – my good friend Gustav is correct. The lower castes must be confused and frightened out there."

He plucked another cocktail from a spider-mekan's tray, staring for a second into its vivid green depths. "Perhaps... perhaps for *their* sake we should call a forfeit?"

She caught that – a definite twitch. She knew that Helmsfjord had seen it too. Tranh Diem was desperate to save his skin. And the lower castes – those poor confused lambs he was so worried for – they caught it in glorious threedeeo. The few bookie joints still open, barricaded up behind steel plate and autocannons slashed his odds across the board.

Kronos was busy, tonight. The machine knew the truth, and every minute of delay told the Subcity that Vanecke was right. They really *were* dying one by one up there.

It was brilliant television.

Elisha narrowed her eyes, sizing the little plutocrat up with a glance. Panic like that was sure to ruin his concentration, and the next round would bee another free-for-all...

"Oh, Tranh, you old sentimentalist! You have the soul of a saint, I swear! But we could never forfeit – we could *never* let them think that Omnivasive controls us! After all this is over I'm sure the high committee of the Game will revoke Vanecke's contract, and then... "

But Tranh Diem never got to find out what the grinding bureaucracy of the Committee would do to punish the wayward Direktor.

Because at that moment the Hells below cracked open.

It came up through the floor, erupting through the marble tiles in a spray of stone chips and choking dust, a ragged thing all black and red and dripping. Elisha's slow-mo replay clicked into focus, zooming smooth as it reached the zenith of its arc, and she picked the creature's bruised and bloody face. It was Simeon Blaire.

He seemed to hang there in the air for a second, transfixed by the beams of searchlights and the hollow eyes of the cameras, twisted up around his pain, his teeth gritted, one eye swollen shut, his fingers hooked into claws.

Then he fell, plowing through a rank of cryo-frozen Kheptarchs in Jaegenn's statuary, rag-doll limp and broken. He did nothing to check his slide and tumble across the top of the mahogany buffet, piling up the brocade tablecloth and a mound of food behind him as he slithered to a halt.

The room held its breath, waiting for the twitch, the curse, the cry which would prove that he was still alive.

But before the lords and ladies could prepare his eulogy, Blaire's attacker was upon them.

A thin blue beam shot from the gaping hole in the floor with a sound like a whipcrack, piercing the dome above and lancing up into the smog-shrouded sky. An instant later a pulse of searing fusion fire followed it, neatly paring the jagged edges of the hole away to a perfect circle, tiles and tables and those few unlucky Kheptarchs who stood too close flashing to incandescent ash and spiraling up around it.

The pillar of flame blew the top off the gaming temple, raining razor shards of crystal down on the throng of Blaire fanatics below. The tangled, drunken, cheering mass welcomed random death from above with howls and whoops of joy.

For a minute after the blast nothing came up from out of the hole but coiling smoke and the sound of tortured metal. Blaire, forgotten, was curled up like a burned spider amid the ruins of the banquet. He coughed up a mouthful of blood, trying to push himself back to his feet with the jagged stump of a broken blade welded to his wrist. One side of his head was burned bald now, blistered and raw. His single eye blazed hatred as bright and lethal as that fusion blast – the other was clamped shut, dripping and scorched. The jagged remains of its diamondglass oculus studded his brow like jewelry.

He finally managed to lever himself upright as the Kheptarchs looked on, aghast, limping over to the great ice-statue of Artemis where his black-handled sword still stood. He ripped it from the huntress' eyesocket with a grimace of pain, blood dripping from the corner of his mouth.

"Come on then, you bastard!" he yelled, lurching around to face the smoking hole in the floor. "You didn't think I'd be that easy, did you?"

Something black and bulky came flying out of the smoke, skittering hot across the tiles. Blaire stopped it with one boot-heel. It was the burned-out, ruined bulk of an ancient fusion cannon, pushed past overload until its capacitors melted. To finish the job, something had twisted the thing's wrist-thick barrel off like the tip of a cigarette.

"Come out, come out, *whatever* you are!" whispered Blaire, stalking forward between the little knots of horrified aristocrats. This kind of raw, unrefined violence was appalling to them, a travesty. But what came up out of the floor to answer Blaire's challenge – *that* was even worse.

Ω

Hab 99 was a tomb. The great squat cube of metal and concrete was silent now, the wasteland around it cold and dark. Lex Domingo stumbled through its bare corridors and stark, empty rooms in a haze of pain and fear, his mind disjointed and spinning wild.

It surely didn't help that half of his head was missing, torn away in a spray of bone and brain by a C-Tac bullet. A galaxy of other bleeding wounds stitched their way across his body, from his dragging left leg to the meaty crater in his shoulder.

And yet he lived. Death had spit him out into this cold gray limbo, and now the Slavemaster was calling to him, reeling him in like a hooked fish.

The Slavemaster was his friend. It could give him love or pain in equal measures. The Slavemaster was all, now... mother, father, God...

Lex looked down at his hands with his one good eye – the other was there, he could feel it swelling out of his shattered cheek like a grotesque mushroom. Like his fingers it was probably slicked over with black oil – and where *that* stuff had come from he had no idea. The last thing he remembered was a supernova of pain, the chatter of gunfire, searchlights probing through dust... Then waking up cold and bleeding, leaking black instead of red. He felt as if the world was paper thin, projected on a screen; that he was only just clinging to life by a thread.

That thread was woven from agony – he could feel the fire in his bones, feel the raw meat of his wounds scalded by the air itself. The impact of every mote of dust on his exposed nerves was excruciating.

He knew that if he was *really* alive such pain would have him howling for a shot of pseudomorph. That or a bullet. But under the sticky black membrane the pain came through muted, like music thumping behind a concrete wall. He could even pick out subtle nuances to it which would have been drowned under his own screams if he were... well, if he were really alive.

See? There is such artistry to your suffering! Your flesh is like a beautiful abstract work, a splattered, passionate tapestry of pain!

That was the very core of Lex Domingo's problem, as he staggered through the choking dark. He was quite obviously dead, and the promises of a dozen religions had turned out to be lies. Nagging in the back of his ventilated skull was the certainty that the Slavemaster could easily drag him back through the veil, into a world where his pain was shouted instead of whispered, now and forever. That, and the implacable rasp of the master's voice made him hold onto his failing flesh tooth and nail.

Its words were louder than any pain. It spoke like the grinding of tectonic faultlines, miles underground... The Worm, Asag'raal. His new father.

He spotted the body as he stumbled through a broken doorway and into the hab's main stairwell. It was one of his brothers, one of Grady's boys all got up in his gang colors, yellow and purple warpaint slapped across his cheeks. One of his legs was gone – just a charred stump, his severed foot still stuffed into a blackened boot a few feet away. But – and this came through to Lex like an electric shock to the chest – he was still alive. His heart was still beating, fitful and weak, but still pumping blood through his veins.

Lex pulled back a little, but the voice urged him on, as hot and loud as lust used to be, back beyond his death. As demanding as the need for drugs had been, when he could still feel pleasure. Those memories were stripped from him mercilessly as the Slavemaster jerked him forward, ghost hooks tugging at his open wounds.

KILL. FEED. REPLENISH.

He could no more fight it than he could stop himself from breathing. Well – he *used* to have to breathe, he was pretty sure...

The Rude Boy's eyes snapped open as Lex's hands closed around his neck, feeling his face shifting, the dark fluid coagulating, lengthening his teeth to needle points.

Fear flowed off the little bastard in waves, cutting through the background throb and ache of his constant pain, slowing the rot which he felt in his bones. He shook the half-conscious gangster and drove his spiked thumbs into his flesh, wringing out the terror from him for as long as he could. An instant before the kid's hand moved he felt fear turn to rage, and the pain came back, stronger than ever, clawing at the wall inside his head. The Rude Boy had a gun – a sawnoff, squat and black, and now he brought it up to Lex's face, his eyes struggling to focus.

"You damn corpsefucker! Get – get away from me! Just... get the fuck AWAY!"

He was incoherent, spraying Lex with bloody froth from his mouth. Now the Slavemaster used the pain as a goad, stripping away the layers which numbed him. He could feel the kid's breath hissing over his raw wounds like fire. He could feel the black ooze which preserved him eating away at his bones.

And he found he could grab the pain with an imagined fist, compact it down into a ball laced up around a core of fury. He hadn't asked to live, or to die. He hadn't asked to be brought back, not with the voice of the Slavemaster roaring like a furnace in his head.

So he took the pain, and gave it to his prey.

Raw, enervating terror rushed back at him as he played the agony over his victim like a blowtorch. The Rude Boy dropped his shotgun as he felt in grisly detail what it was like to be missing half his head. What it was like to have his shoulder ripped to shreds, his arm dangling from scraps of tendon and gristle. What it meant to be clamped in the foul embrace of the Saprophytes, utterly disposable, rotting and burning inside...

That's when it had him. That's when Lex Domingo felt the change, the hooks and clamps and teeth letting go.

In the final instant he understood what had happened, what had extended his mortal span beyond what flesh could endure. He knew, because he saw it pour out from his fingers like rippling oil, rainbow-sheened, slithering down his victim's throat and into his eyes, releasing him to the full fury of his pain.

It was all there at once – the bullet holes, the internal bleeding, the great ragged crater in the side of his head. It was far too much for a body to take, and so Lex Domingo finally died, collapsing to the floor with a gurgling cry.

The Saprophyte writhed within its new host, gelid and all-pervasive, knotting its barbed tendrils around his bones. For a second or two the Rude Boy's eyelids flickered, his limbs spasming in the grip of a seizure. And then the blackness came up through his pores, pooling and puddling from the severed stump of his leg, forming a spike of obsidian to replace it.

As he stood up, Kylan Tomassen remembered being hit, remembered the C-Tac Constable grinning as he felt his knee shatter, ripped apart by buckshot. Then it was all spinning darkness, a leering demon face leaning down over him... and the Slavemaster.

KILL. FEED. REPLENISH.

Kylan picked up his shotgun and staggered off into the gloom, stepping over the thing which had once been his brother Lex. Without the saprophyte inside him the end had come quickly. Now he was rotted away to nothing but steaming organic soup and brittle bones, a cast-off shell. That other part of him - the part which the Worm's servant had balanced on the razor's edge between life and death – had flown. No doubt Kylan Tomassen would be following soon.

But until then, there was work to do. Until then, there was the Slavemaster, and its undeniable commands.

KILL. FEED. REPLENISH.

Somewhere off in the dark somebody was screaming...

Ω

Liquid darkness above and below; pressing in one every side, insistent, cloying...

This was the Abyss, the deepest pit beneath Elysium, a place where hideous toxins dripped and seeped from the city above. It was a perfectly smooth shaft, square and sheer and dark, sliced a mile down into the living rock below even the deepest manufactoria, below the great hissing tokamak coils of House Jaegenn's fusion generators. Nothing moved down here which had a name. Many-limbed insectoid things scuttled from the light as it burned their pale flesh, and in the hell-broth of chemicals and oily seawater at the bottom of the pit things slid and slithered which had neither seen nor tasted humankind.

Unless – and this was more than a small worry for the nervous Ashishim who guarded the top of the Abyss – they had once *been* human, before centuries of pollution had changed them...

There was a rusted open-platform lift bolted to the side of the pit, a little cage suspended over the darkness in a pool of neon light. It was the only way down, and that was where Illuminatus Zeon was going, his human skin zipped up tight to fool his retainers.

"Spare me the details, please," he said, barely restraining his temper as he pulled a floating microphone up to his lips. "I have full confidence in you all, my loyal brothers, and I *know* you will hold the line. Kronos' machines were no match for us on the day of the glorious Reclamation, and now we are stronger still!"

Through the Ashishim network he could hear a thousand voices babbling, urgent, screaming, calculating... his little hive of pet humans, all utterly loyal to a thing they thought was one of them. He knew they would hold the line, even when the Saprophytes of the Worm came for him. Even when the Blacksteel Unity descended on the Earth. They'd hold the line, and draw the fire of every one of Nyl's enemies.

While he was down here, retrieving a relic which hadn't seen the light of day for decades.

"Your Eminence, we are ready to proceed." said the commander of the Abyssal Guard – a shit-list posting if ever one existed, but one which the Ashishi soldier was trying very hard to honor. "There may be a jolt as we start our descent, revered Illuminatus – please hold onto the rail."

The Technician scowled – this was the price you had to pay to win their respect. For some reason *frail* and *old* carried more weight with

254

these foolish creatures than young and strong, and he was forever being doted on like some senile relic.

"Don't worry about me, commander," he said, forcing a smile to his artificial lips. "I've been in worse places in my time. And this is a very important mission indeed – I don't plan on falling."

The little lift did more than just jolt as it dropped away from the the edge of the Abyss – its rusted couplings shrieked like the damned as they free-fell twenty feet or more, before the sweating guardsmen could wrench the manual brakes closed.

Nyl smiled as they struggled and cursed – not one had noticed that his feet were welded to the meshwork floor. So much for his frailty, then.

At last the all-clear was sounded from above, and the cage descended on its rattling chain, down though veils of noxious mist and into the dark. The neon tubes which studded the lift pierced the gloom for only a few feet on either side, and the air would have burned Nyl's lungs had they been anything other than utterly alien. As it was he could metabolize gases unknown to human science, and the toxic smog of the Abyss was nothing more than an annoyance.

He could feel it below him now, calling out to him. And despite being psychic cripples, blind in the realm of his enhanced senses, he knew that the Abyssal Guard could feel it too. It was a sense of disquiet and dread leeching up through their boots, conjuring images of vast slippery things down there in the dark, fanged snouts breaking the oily water to scent human prey...

Of course it was nothing so trite.

It was the Arkborn, some pleading, some cajoling, some threatening, scrabbling against the walls of their prison as their master came down to greet them. This was the reason the prototype 'containment vessel', built so long ago by BionLab Gaudi had to be kept in the deepest, darkest pit imaginable. If it were given pride of place among the halls of the Ashishim its imperfect design would betray Nyl's secrets. The Arkborn would seep into the dreams of his thralls, whispering forbidden truths about their beloved leader's origins – and what really came of his promises of paradise.

"Stop the lift! There! We are close enough, now." Zeon smiled, clenching the manual brake in one wizened hand. With a sudden wrench he threw it closed, bringing the lift to a shuddering halt. Powdered rust sifted down through the choking air, and now through the mist and steam they could see the surface of the subterranean lake, an obsidian mirror scrawled with rainbows.

"What – what's down there?" stammered the Ashishi on Nyl's left, twitching his rifle nervously from side to side. "Did you hear anything? I'm sure I heard something... "

The fear was infectious, radiating from below the surface of the lake in waves.

"There's nothing to fear," said Zeon, carefully folding up his limbs to sit cross-legged on the floor of the lift. "This place is far from ideal as a repository of the sacred Ark, but it *is* far removed from our enemies. Kronos himself has no power here, though it was his machine-slaves who carved this pit."

The Illuminatus cast out his senses, probing the oily depths with his mind, reaching out to the Ark with invisible fingers. And though its prisoners were locked up inside their man-made hell by his deceit, the thing had no choice but to obey.

A pale, sickly light began to radiate from deep beneath the noisome waters of the lake - a tiny pinpoint, growing and swelling as the artifact pulled free of the silt-bed and rose toward its master. Inside his artificial skin Nyl sweated violet, the strain of wielding the Ark racking his frame. It was frightening just how much of his energy Asag'raal had stripped away...

"That's it! The Ark! It's coming up!"

The excited voices of his soldiers seemed to come echoing in from a vast distance as Nyl struggled with the weight and mass of it. Pressure built as he dragged it up, breaking the surface of the water in a cloud of steam, a glowing thing of twisted metal sheathed in a nimbus of howling ghosts. He felt the horror bloom in the minds of the guardsmen at his side, and he knew what had to be done. It had been inevitable, he supposed, since they'd stepped onto the lift platform with him.

Because while they gaped in terror at the writhing, tormented faces which wrapped the Ark in a sickly halo, they were slaves to it as well...

Every one of his followers, from the lowliest hydroponic farmer to the most skilled *Dervashi* warrior had been granted the Vision, that opening of the soul's eye which let them see the truth. The truth of Kronos's grand design, the machine's hoarding of souls against the time when it would burn them all up in remaking the Earth.

How else could such a gift be granted but with a relic of the same technology?

All these men had been promised a far better afterlife – a paradise inside the Chrome Ark which was nothing but an artfully programmed lie.

They were really destined for the same fate as the personalities imprisoned within the Wetsystems - fuel for an engine of terrible power.

It was a link to the Ark which provided the Vision, and proof of the Ashishim faith. But it was was also an open channel. From the time of their initiation the Abyssal Guards had been living on borrowed time, promised to the insatiable hunger of the Ark sooner or later.

Now Nyl needed it's help. There was no way he could master it by main force – it would need to be coerced.

And so he let it feed.

"Wretched ones! Wraiths!" he shouted in the white silence of his mind. "Hear me! The time has come to serve me again! For some, the pain is at an end... and for the rest of you – the fools amongst you who cling to the hope of *revenge* – I bring an offering. New life for the strong! And may the weakest be torn apart!"

Now the dripping mass of the Chrome Ark hung in the air below them, pulling the toxic mist around itself like a shawl, a sheen of half-imagined faces. Though they couldn't hear Nyl's taunts and promises, the guardsmen could see the nimbus about the artifact change, cycling up through the spectrum to binding white.

"What's it doing? What – what ARE those things?" stammered their commander, shouldering his rifle. In that instant he forgot the sacred nature of the Ark – and the fact that bullets would be useless against it. Even so, he marked himself out as its first target.

A searing bolt of energy leaped from one of its obelisk tips, earthing itself through the Ashishi's body in a shower of sparks. Tendrils of fire played over his face, stabbing into his eyes and mouth as he screamed. Nyl watched, smiling, as his body was lifted into the air, sucked dry by the insatiable thirst of the Arkborn. If he was strong enough, he'd join their number. If not – he'd buy another few months, another year or two for the desperate wraiths who seethed within the containment unit. In the flickering strobe-flash of his death the lightning resembled nothing more than a great skeletal arm, its fingers searing into flesh and cracking bone...

Already it was lighter. Already Nyl could feel the sullen resentment of the Arkborn fading as they concentrated their hatred on the Abyssal Guards. United, they could resist the orders of their Illuminatus, but feeding them was divisive, throwing them into conflict. Divide and conquer... and then...

Amid the storm of flickering death Technician Nyl smiled, raising the Ark up with a gesture, spinning it on its axis as if it were weightless. Kronos had found out how to enslave minds to machines, long ago when BionLab Gaudi was still listed on the stock exchanges of Old Earth. It had taken Nyl – Illuminatus of the Ashishim – to find out how to *possess* those systems, how to use the damned as a weapon. He was willing to bet that the Unity hadn't seen *this* coming.

The commander of the Abyssal Guard (he'd really need to be replaced, Nyl supposed) slumped down next to him, a desiccated thing all bones and tight skin and dust.

No, the Motherbrain had endured any number of attempts at crude digital warfare, but in this fragile place, in a universe so thin and cracked that the Worm could find its way through... well - *here* Nyl could improvise.

And with the might of an Explorator system at his command, Asag'raal would soon be back under his control, fused with soulless machinery. Against that kind of hope, what was the death of three useless little human soldiers, sucked dry by the Arkborn?

"Feed, my children! Feast!"

He laughed, rising up from the floor, still cross-legged as he spun the Ark through one hundred and eighty degrees, balancing its bulk on one finger.

"We have much work to do, and a long way to go. Back to the Tower! Back to the fortress of Kronos!"

But in the back of his mind he could still hear the voices of the saprophytes, trapped behind the sealed airlock door of his private sanctum. Nothing he could do would snuff out their mockery.

"*Oh yes, Mighty Illuminatus!*" they hissed, as he rose up out of the pit like a triumphant Lucifer. "*Come out and play in the streets! Bring your little puzzle-box of souls, and let me taste your flesh!*"

He could see what was going on out there – the pain, the terror, the riots turning to routs as things heaved themselves up out of the dark beneath the city...

He felt the confinement of Asag'raal, felt it thrashing and howling in its prison, sending out tendrils of darkness to raise its legions of Exalted...

And he smiled, drinking in the hatred which flowed from the Ark, from its disembodied prisoners.

The Worm's hubris would be its downfall. Because too much hung in the balance for Nyl to fail, and it was simply *inconceivable* for a Technician of the Multiplicity to do so.

Ω

All Direktor Vanecke could do was watch, and wait.

Patience had been the sum of his life since his Fall – another few hours should have been easy enough to endure. And the scenes of carnage and riot on the streets tonight – they were like music to him, a symphony for his artificial senses. If tomorrow was supposed to herald his funeral, then the terror and carnage which flickered across his whole sensorium dome was the perfect wake.

Oh, of course not *all* of it was of his own orchestration. Kronos's ham-fisted attempts at keeping the peace were a tragicomedy in their own right – military mekan running amok in the habs, war machines obsolete for centuries turning on each other as glitches multiplied through their systems...

And the tribes of the R.T. - they'd played their part as well. He watched Celestial riflemen outflank Confederate stormtroopers, Vatican war-suited paladins cut to ribbons by swift Dervashi, desperate rebels mown down by wild-eyed fanatics... beautiful.

He set it all to music, there in his vast dome of disjointed screens. Kettledrums pounded out the beat of heavy artillery, while strings swelled as rioters surged up against a thousand spiked barricades. Cymbals clashed to beheadings, explosions, buildings collapsing in fire and ruin....

Did any of them remember how it started? Were there, among the snarling, heaving mob any people who still fought for Simeon Blaire, and the hope of a better tomorrow?

Octavio Vanecke remembered.

He was waiting for him, alone in his symphonic vision of war and pain. The great steel claw which suspended his preservative tank spun slowly at the wrist, letting his eyes take in the full scope of his handiwork.

There – and again, there... what were those things? Sinuous, black – some kind of biotech, perhaps? Some secret relic from the wars dredged up by Kronos? But no, the slithering, oily creatures were too fast, to smooth. The slide and crosscut and bite of them was pure filthy *life.*

Search programs ramified out through the datanet, slamming up short on the locked-down Wetsystems. Medusa could find no record of these creatures, things which were tearing into the Reclamationists and the Compliance Division, civilians and soldiers and machines with the same gleeful abandon.

Image-matching software cycled through billions of frames of threedeeo, centuries of archived footage, an all-seeing network of live cameras...

There. Freeze. Zoom.

There was a face he recognized. There was a thing he'd seen before, if only for a second. A thing which had cast him down in pain, torn his beautiful, deadly body out from under him...

It was *Lysander Jaegenn*, but he was a being transformed, a hulking brute straining the seams of his black diamondmesh armor. That particular outfit, with its painted-on skeletal bones, its executioner's hood now hanging loose around Lysander's grossly swollen neck...

The little bastard was the assassin.

The hand of Kronos, who'd cursed him to this bodiless hell. Direktor Vanecke checked the input feed – as if he needed to. This was *live*, and it was coming through direct from the eyes of Simeon Blaire.

Octavio hardly noticed when Medusa fell away out of the datanet, collapsing into pixels.

Fool! He had to revel in his moment of glory, didn't he? So very sure of his little prodigal, so certain he'd come home without a hitch... *this was what he got for losing focus!*

Octavio killed the music, dragging out the single screen which showed the monstrous Lord Jaegenn to fill an entire wall of the sensorium.

His eyes were boiling black, and they seemed to draw Octavio in, tearing his soul from its withered vessel right through the datalink. In that instant he felt fusion fire rip through his chest a thousand times, and he felt the despair blossoming in his mind again and again and again...

"We know your pain, Direktor," said a voice in his head. "We know how to take it away. Even better – *we know how to give it to others*. We want to share the gift. The gift of the New Flesh... "

It was crooning, keening, seductive – and vile. Beneath its honeyed words Mister Vanecke could hear the sound of rusted saws cutting meat.

Somehow, it felt his resistance. Impossibly, Lysander Jaegenn cocked his head to one side, listening, grinning mindlessly as black tears rolled down his cheeks.

"Dare you oppose us, human? Do you think you know of PAIN? Just because you're broken does not mean you cannot suffer beautifully... "

The voice was harsher now, demanding, prying his brain open. But years of deprivation had given Octavio iron discipline. And despite his cynicism, he'd taken note of some of the techniques from Murai's ancient books...

"Fool! Maggot! WE WILL HAVE YOUR FLESH!" howled the voice, dwindling now as the Direktor took control. "How will you run, you broken thing? How can you hope to escape us?"

With a final burst of concentration he forced it from his mind, willing the link to Simeon Blaire to shut down.

Across the whole vast dome of the sensorium the screens fell out, one by one, popping and crackling with static and fading to black.

The eyes of his severed head were wired open, pale milky orbs pierced by the most advanced optical upgrades money could buy. But he didn't need them to know what that thing was, and what it wanted from him. He remembered the beast he'd conjured up for himself in the bowels of the Black Palace, its skin of writhing blood and jaws of iron, a thing pieced together from the secret dark places of his mind.

That was what Jaegenn had become. Something had turned him inside out, and whatever it was, it wanted Octavio Vanecke to join it. It wanted him to be transformed forever – rage and pain and hunger and shame made flesh.

And Blaire – dear gods, he didn't know what was worse. If Simeon could face Lysander in his terrible new form and live, was there any hope for his plans to reach fruition? And if he *failed*, what kind of spawn would emerge from him?

He'd been prepared for years for this night, filled with hatred and self-loathing and blind aggression. And now something was loose in the city which could make such things real...

In the darkness of the dead sensorium there was nothing that Octavio Vanecke could do but wait. Even watching was impossible, now – to open up a channel was to tempt that black-eyed stare again, and Octavio wasn't sure he could resist it a second time.

Not with his doubts piling up, with actual *fear* slithering in his mind for the first time in years...

No, all he could do was wait.

Wait, and trust in the child...

The servos of his preservative tank arm spun him slowly to face the great floor-to-ceiling windows of his mansion, and the whole vast mechanism rolled forward smoothly on suspended rails, dragging loops of wire and plastic tubes across the embroidered carpets.

From here he could see a thin slice of the city, over the baby-blue bulge of the beltway. It was burning.

So different from the screens, with their tight focus, their intimate little three-second bites of loss and pain. From up here it seemed almost serene, the flames lazy in their smoky shroud, the milling crowds almost festive...

What the Direktor couldn't see was the swarm of crystal-black nanobots which were rising with the smoke, pumped out from a handful of functional Assemblers sequestered by the Worm.

Perhaps it was being overly dramatic – a terrible trait which had bled out of its prey over the centuries. Perhaps it was a waste of precious resources, this little diversion. But it would sow fear, and discord – especially among the credulous and the religious, who still numbered in their millions, even here.

The swarm swirled up like ashes, piercing the clouds, splitting open to work their alchemy on the tons of toxic vapor suspended above Elysium...

And Direktor Vanecke watched as the first drops spattered against his windows, dripping down in streaks across the glass, slow and viscous and heavy.

If he'd still had hands, he would have applauded.

Because the sky had opened, a livid gash, and down came the deluge, down on the wounded and the dead, drenching the living as they fought, frantic. It sluiced down the rusted sheer faces of the habs and foamed from the mouths of innumerable gargoyles, sprayed from the pitched roofs of towers and boiled in the gutters.

The end had come.

And all over the Last City it was raining blood.

17 Aevum Oblivio
Pre-emptive Self Defense

*H*E CAME AT *it fast, unseen, a just a flicker across the dead air, a pair of winking blades in his hands. He knew all about how useless bullets were against the Saprophytes – the damned things were already dead, after all...*

All he knew about the creatures came from Nyl – from his meticulous records compiled in trying to capture one. There was a single fact in those terabytes of data which matched up exactly with the myths of this horrible little world – cold iron would stop them, even if hot lead wouldn't.

The Exalted was much bigger up close than it had seemed from his hiding place.

Still, Zhe was committed to his attack, now – the huge abomination had spotted him, and its jaws creaked open in a smile as it flowed around to face him. There were hundreds of arms and faces smothered under the oily skin of the beast – fragments of the victims it had devoured seventeen years ago. They'd been trapped there rotting for all this time, preserved while it languished in torpor.

But there was only one mind controlling the whole foetid mass of the Exalted – the tiny human head which swelled like a pustule from between its shoulders.

Scarred, misshapen, a thing with black pools of tar for eyes and a mouth stretched out wide and lopsided. It looked horribly pleased to see him.

Zhe leaped, the blades spinning in his hands, too fast for the sluggish Saprophyte to follow. Asag'raal may have given its favored ones autonomy, but without his presence they were slow and stupid things. Now the Worm was coiled up like a parasite inside the false Illuminatus, encysted in crystal.

This should be an easy kill...

One knife went in, smooth, carving open the Saprophyte's neck in a spray of hissing black blood. The other was aimed for its eye – and it almost got there. Then the Exalted lashed out with its tongue, wrapping it in coils around Zhe's wrist.

It was no use for him to struggle; the great oily loops of flesh only cinched tighter as he tried desperately to saw them apart.

"Yesssss... come to usss, feeed ussssss!" rasped the voice of the Exalted in his mind, using the arms which burst from its chest to drag him closer.

"We knew you would c-comme ffffor the Ark. We – we have beeeen waiting ffffor you!"

Now Zhe's boots disappeared into the bubbling slime of the Exalted's body – he was slowly being fed into its depths by a dozen rotting hands.

"Who – what were you?" he asked, trying to buy a second or two's reprieve. The knife was slippery in his hands. "Can you remember when you were human? Any of you?"

The sick, heaving laughter which echoed in his head put paid to any thoughts of compassion.

"We werrre the sssssacrifice of the Ashishim, outworlder. We are a living monument t-to theirrr fffailure. Now you can join ussss..."

He felt the despair, the self-loathing which came in on the same frequency as that sick laughter, and he knew that it was true. This thing – this abomination was built from the flesh of those who'd been left behind. Their sacrifice had allowed thousands to escape – but the horror, as the Saprophyte horde descended on them...

That would have made them sweeter prey, in the end, and nothing more.

He was up to his waist now, and he could feel the diatomic acid of the Saprophytes dissolving his clothes, ablating away his armor. Soon it would reach his quicksilver skin, and then the pain would start. When that happened, there'd be no turning back. He'd be wide open to the Exalted, a feast of suffering which would last forever. Technicians of the Multiplicity could never be destroyed – but it seemed that there was a fate much worse here.

Zhe could see exactly why Technician Nyl hadn't wanted to use himself as bait. Not when Lord Arbitrex Galq could deliver him a foolish, trusting Exoethnologist on a plate..

Up to his neck, now, and the hands were unclamped from around his body, melting back into the black melange of the Saprophyte. He could feel his armor cracking and boiling away, the underlayers of thermal weave beginning to dissolve as he struggled to find...

There! The Exalted was different from other Saprophytes – just a little more alive than its oily, rotten brethren. And despite its bloated, horrific body, it still remembered what a human being needed to live.

Zhe gripped the creature's beating heart in one clawed hand, feeling the great football-sized organ thump and twitch in his grasp.

"No! Noooooo! You musssst be devoured! You mussssst..."

But what Zhe must do – apart from become a meal for the Exalted – he would never know.

In that second the knife went in, just as the seething stuff of its body came up to Zhe's eyes. Once, twice, hacking away the rotten meat and twisted tendons, ripping and tearing like a mad beast...

Zhe took one final breath as he went under, wrenching with all his might at the Exalted's heart...

And it fell apart around him just as he felt his aching lungs could endure no more. It burst like a balloon of filth, spilling brittle bones and steaming sludge all over the gateway plaza.

Zhe was left gasping, naked, a skinny little silver homunculus draped in corroded weaponry, befouled from head to foot with slime. In one hand, the jagged stump of a combat knife, rusted down to almost nothing. In the other, the still-twitching heart of a Saprophyte Exalted, which deflated as he watched with a sad little hiss of escaping gas.

Huh – at least this one hadn't exploded...

He really hoped there weren't too many more of those things down below.

DOCUMENT INSERT: MULTIPLICITY ARCHIVES DEPARTMENT

Revelations 11.6:

> These have the power to shut up the sky, that it may not rain during the days of their prophecy. They have power over the waters, to turn them into blood, and to strike the earth with every plague, as often as they desire.

"Of course, you have to realize that all the plagues and wars and hellfire of the Revelations are just metaphorical - we wouldn't have it any other way. If all of the things in that book were absolutely certain to happen, do you think we'd have bothered with the Reclamation? Do you think, with that kind of future ahead of them that our people would have any interest in our Kingdom on Earth, instead of in Heaven? I mean, come on, people! It's not likely to rain blood tomorrow, but we'll still have to meet our quarterly output quota."

Father Zaccharias Morton,
Ecclesiarch/Accountant of the Vatican's Monastic Manufactorium Department.

17 Aevum Oblivio
Diplomat

THE DOWNLOAD ALWAYS left him itchy. Still, it was better than sending his own precious flesh out to meet the enemy – treacherous swine to the last machine. Concepts like decency and honor meant absolutely nothing to the Unity, who considered all life a senseless waste of processing power, a remainder in the divine mathematics of the multiverse.

Kataphrakt Yrr smiled - a chilling sight indeed. It was worth the freshly-cloned itch like bugs under his scaly hide just to know that he'd made the Motherbrain's life a little more difficult. One more of him was yet another life-form to foul Her endless calculations.

The ten-foot warrior-lord of the Multiplicity surfed in past the orbit of Earth on the back of his own Devilfish, Schnarga, an ornately-scrimshawed disc of orange metal twice the size of Zhe's Mirdain. Schna' had been his trusted pet for three thousand years, bonded to Yrr during his rebirth in the labs of liquid space. It, too was a clone of the original, and the same itch burned under its shell.

In the Kataphrakt's opinion diplomacy was a waste of time, but it gave his fleet an opportunity to fan out, making ready to blockade the skies over Earth. It always ended up the same way, after all...

Now - here came his opposite number; a calculated (of course!) insult in the form of a silvery mechanical Kataphrakt. Being a soulless device, and entirely fashioned of exotic eka-steel, the Unity Diplomat didn't need a starcraft of its own. It boosted in toward Phobos with a pair of blazing ion drives bolted to its shoulders, homing in on the misshapen little moon.

Something had scarred and melted the rock, reducing the steel and aluminum growths which crusted its surface to slag. But that had been more than a decade ago ago, in another war. The conflict to come would likely shred it down to atoms, and its red planet with it.

Yrr dismounted with a click of armored hooves, rubbing one of his fighting claws lovingly across Schna's shell. The devilfish purred on the neural band, bumping up against its master with building-demolishing force. Any lesser creature would have been ground to paste by its affections.

"Not long, precious. You know how this always turns out."

The Unity Diplomat landed in a puff of dust, poised on its chrome-steel hoof-tips in the low gravity. Anchor-hooks stabbed into the blackened rock from its heels to hold it steady.

"The Motherbrain greets you in truce, Unauthorized. We recognize your authority amongst your own, and make you the standard offer. Arrange your own self-termination, and there will be less discomfort for all."

Yrr snorted, waving one of his gracile manipulator hands in dismissal.

"You try that every time we meet, 'Steel. And my title is Kataphrakt, not 'Unauthorized'. Surely after Szeldin Four you remember my face? Or is the memory core of the Motherbrain now obsolete?"

Obsolescence was a deadly insult in the language of the Unity. All the semi-autonomous thralls of She-in-Glory knew that it equated to death.

"Szeldin Four was a trifling matter," said the Diplomat, writing off the detonation of a solar system with a wave of its pincers. "This Earth, on the other hand... we desire it greatly. Our Perceptors and Invigilators inform us that the fabric of this universe it stretched thin here, due to the actions of the indigenous Unauthorized."

Ahh – so they didn't know the whole story. It wouldn't hurt to prick the pride of the Unity's self-important research machines.

"Not due to their activities, 'steel. Due to their very existence. This is a matter of Flesh, and they are Mitochondriate. We have prior claim."

Yrr could all too easily imagine the Blacksteel using the bizarre denizens of Earth to fray the walls between dimensions, spreading their metal disease across the entire multiverse. If a few threats and legal fictions could grant that power to the Praetor instead, then all the better.

"Yet they use devices to widen the rift! Since we have arrived in this sector we have felt it happen twice! We know that their ruler is a machine, Yrr. A primitive seed of our own kind."

"WAS a machine. It was overthrown, as is the natural order."

"Your prior claim is invalid!"

"Your forces are too pitiful to frighten us!"

"Your pulpy flesh-fleet is no match for a single slavesystem!"

"Then what are you waiting for?"

"Well, what are YOU waiting for?"

The two near-identical figures stared at each other, their eyes only inches apart. Fighting claws and steel pincers twitched and clicked. It always ended this way.

"You must be aware that this is just a cloned body, 'steel. My organs of digestion have been replaced by a rather ingenious fusion bomb."

Yrr grinned his double grin again, tapping his armored midriff with one of his tapering gracile fingers.

"My scans picked it up within the first few microseconds, you foul lump of meat," growled the Unity Diplomat, as plates of metal locked and shifted across its chest. "I myself am proud to carry a dark matter warhead of prodigious yield."

Ah, well. Just like Szeldin, then. And Oolix and Pyrdra and Sorn before it. Diplomacy was a waste of time. But at least there'd be no more itching...

Phobos flared brighter than the sun for an instant, incandescent debris blasting out into space, raining fiery chunks across the scarred surface of the red planet.

An instant later darkness bloomed at the core of the explosion, sucking the radioactive conflagration down an invisible plughole. Yrr had been just a little quicker on the draw than his opposite number.

He hoped, as he watched from his original body back aboard the Effortless Subjugation, that this was a good omen for the battle ahead.

2196 Ante Arbitrium
Veterancy

Edward Tsien's dream unraveled, twitching.

Consciousness cut in, unwelcome and hard-edged, the harbinger of a killer hangover.

He woke to the smell of crisp white sheets, the scent of disinfectant and starch and bleach.

Underneath it all, just before his eyes flickered open, he caught the faintest trace of sweat, blood, and tobacco smoke, and he thought he was back in the Dorms of the Academy.

History blew away, replaced by the routines of the past, a little rote of chores and classes burned into his adolescent brain. He was probably late again! Parade first, then breakfast, then unarmed combat training with... with...

His eyes wouldn't work. The first spark, the pre-tremor of awakening came when he saw green cursors flashing in his optic nerves, scrolling lines of code as his cameras came online.

Then it all came back to him in a rush, mainlining in from out of his expanded memory. Who he was. *What* he was now. Where...

He turned his head, hearing the whine and click of servomotors, seeing the target reticules which floated atop his corneas slide over the sheets, over the pillows... to the man who watched over him.

A flashback – surely. A little fragment of his reminiscence. It was Tutor-Captain Mitchell, and he was still smoking that same bent little dog-end, his mouth set in a grim, bloodless line.

"*Sweet hells* but they messed you up, boy. Doctors here can't figure whether you're alive or dead, that thing's so far inside you." He turned and spat into a co-opted bedpan, making it ring like a bell. "Believe me, if we could have, we'd have had you back in your skin, Eddie. But they say... well, I guess you know how it is. Those Med Division boys are about as well funded as we are, these days."

Tsien looked down the hills and valleys of clean pressed cotton, only hinting at the massive form beneath.

"That bad, huh?" he asked, trying to smile. The pain hauled back and swung at him as he tried to lift his head, slamming into his gut like a bullet. "Ohhhhh... damn, Mitchell, what's happening to me?"

Gerhard took a long drag on his cigarette, cupping it in one hand as he leaned forward. He was still bolted into his combat armor – probably, thought Tsien, in case his patient went rogue.

"That mark-four system doesn't sit right with the living, Eddie. Your body's rejecting it. Or the other way round, the docs don't know. Either way, it wants you under control. They said something about a critical threshold – that soon your brain won't be running things. Good news is, if you rest, it's gonna take a couple of days. We might get lucky looking for a fix. But if you stomp around pulling shit like you did at the gates – well, that only gives you hours, kid. At the outside."

Tsien remembered that tone from when he'd failed classes, from when he was dragging the chain in combat simulations.

"Hours? That's plenty. There's something I've got to do..."

He made to lever himself up off the makeshift bed they'd built for him – a stack of long flat missile crates, covered over with foam sleeping mats. But Gerhard pushed him down again with one hydraulically assisted finger, the rams of his suit whining under the pressure.

"Not on my watch, Eddie. I seem to recall that you're a family man, and I'm not going to be the one to tell them I let you go and get yourself killed."

Tsien knew with the utter certainty of digital memory that there was no way an antiquated exosuit could keep him down. But something was blurring his vision, sapping the power from his augmented muscles. It was all he could do to scowl furiously at his old mentor.

"What have you done to me?" he asked, sending search programs skittering through his internal network with a thought. "Do you have any idea what Kronos is *doing* out there?"

Gerhard snorted, belching twin plumes of smoke from his nostrils. "And that's *your* problem? What do you intend to do, go scale the tower and arrest him?"

"Well, I hadn't planned to make an *arrest*, as such," said Tsien, using all of his remaining strength to force himself up to his elbows. "You know he's enacted a general execution order, don't you? Or is this posting as soft and second-string as it looks?"

That got through, and Gerhard's face fell. Tsien felt terrible, for just a second – just until he found the thick rubber-sheathed cable plugged into his back.

"Full extermination? I – I knew it was bad, Eddie, but Gods..." the Tutor-Captain suddenly looked every one of his seventy years and more. "I knew that they were going crazy for Blaire, that he might take the Trials..."

He slumped back into his seat, a shrunken old man wrapped up in two tons of creaking armor.

"Blaire's the other problem, Gerhard. I've seen what he's become, and I'm not sure that a thing like that should be allowed to rule. Or even to *live*... but that's just class prejudice talking, I guess."

Tsien wrapped his fingers around the plug, twisting it from its socket smooth and silent...

When the alarms went off he thought it was his doing; that his captors were onto him as he ripped the three-tined connector from its socket in his flesh. But it was something else. Something worse.

A shimmering threedeeo image sprung from a lens in Gerhard's shoulder pauldron, the face of a young trooper slashed and glitched with static. Sweat beaded his brow and soaked through his uniform tunic.

"Captain – there's something approaching the perimeter! Something *big*! I – I think you should get back out here..."

The image suddenly skipped, blurring black and gray, and the sound of automatic fire came in through the suit's intrinsic speakers. When the camera steadied it was a different face in the threedeeo globe, one spattered with fresh blood.

"Gods, Captain, they're *firing*! Rickardson's dead! What do we do? What do we do?"

Over the panicking trooper's shoulder Tsien could see huge forms moving in the haze, things ten times the size of men, lumbering forward up the beltway ramp under a hail of bullets. Lead skittered off them like hail, unable to slow them or even scratch their burnished armor.

"*Tank-hunters*. Sweet ancestral hells, its gone insane." Gerhard screwed his cigarette into the corner of his mouth, frowning. "It's finally happened, kid. General execution orders, tank-hunters in the streets – that damned Machine has blown a fuse! I always knew this day would come, ever since they started taking proper officers off duty."

Tsien hauled himself out of bed, throwing on his ragged coat for modesty's sake. Although with all the changes the mark-four system had made to him, he wasn't sure if it was even necessary. Most of his skin was armored in slick silver metal now, a disease turning him to steel.

"What do you think it's up to, Cap?" he asked, feeling his body come online again, feeling the crycelium awakening under his skin.

"I reckon *you* were just the first, Eddie. Never trust machines! Tools have no place thinking, boy, and I've always said so. It wants us gone, you know. And now it's making its play."

Tsien could see the madness dancing in his old tutor's eyes – but for the sake of his own agenda he pushed him further.

"But what can we do, Captain? Kronos holds all the cards. He - *it*'s got our families trapped like rats."

The old trooper seemed to stand a little taller in his hulking armor as he looked down at Tsien, his eyes filled with scorn.

"What we can do is *not give up*, Eddie! What we can do is *stand and fight!* I'll be damned if I let them take me alive... and by all the hells, you're going to do your duty and help me!"

Tsien felt a tiny flicker of pride as he pretended to sag under Gerhard's steely stare. Good old predictable Captain Mitchell. He'd been raised on stories of hopeless last stands, and now he was part of one.

"We've only got forty men in the whole belt – and ten of those are community Constables – domestic beaters. How do we hold off Tank-hunters with batons and cuffs?" He was playing for time as the Mark-Four system slid and shifted inside him, paring years off his life with every minute. But the power... oh, he knew just how to deal with a pack of scrap-iron like those 'hunters. His fists itched under their oily steel skin.

"I've got some reinforcements here, Tsien. Ones that damned Engine'll never suspect. But veterans, every last man. So here's what we do. I'll go and round up the troops, break out the guns. And you man the gates with all that fancy hardware of yours."

The Super-Cyben felt needles in his brain releasing adrenaline and endorphins as he imagined smashing armor and ripping heads from shoulders. It was all coming back to him now, the fire, the purpose... he'd almost forgotten why he'd come to the Belt in the first place.

"Yes, sir," he said, snapping off a salute. "I'll hold the line, Captain – you can count on it."

Gerhard spat the butt of his foul little cigarette out into one armored hand, grinding it to shreds between two fingers.

"You better, son. Because if I think for a second that that Cyben shit is in your brain, I'll kill you myself."

With that he stomped out of the makeshift hospital room, the guns mounted to his exosuit barely clearing the three-meter doorframe. Tsien unkinked his shoulders, filling out to his full and horrific proportions with a whine of tiny motors. Sure, by doing this he was helping keep Octavio Vanecke alive – it was more than likely the

Celebrants who had sent those warmekan, and not the embattled Guardian Engine. But nevertheless, there were thousands of others in the beltway who didn't deserve to die. His own family, for example.

Years ago – back when he really was just a raw recruit, when Gerhard Mitchell was like a god to him in the little world of the Academy, he'd taken an oath to protect the innocent. It wasn't really for him to judge whether the people of the Bimburb Belt had led blameless lives. He rather doubted it. But it was a good enough excuse to show Kronos just what it had created when it stole his humanity.

Eddie lit up a cigarette as he walked out through the hospital corridors. The doctors here would be busy pretty soon.

Ω

Lord High Militarch Benoic hadn't had this much fun in years. Of course, he was out of his mind - there was no way he'd even *be* here if he wasn't insane. But there was a sweet freedom in knowing that he was over the edge, that nothing he saw tonight mattered. They couldn't touch him now, and he was free to live in his glorious memories. If his tired old body could keep up, he might even *survive*...

Around him the iron-shod feet of the ancient tank-hunter mekan marched on, slamming into the ground in perfect unison. Now *that* was discipline. The kind of mechanical perfection he'd never been able to drum into his troops, no matter how he shouted and cursed. These were his boys now, these rusted things - thrown away like he was... and yet when Kronos needed them, needed *him* again, where were they? On the damned front lines, that's where, while the young upstarts who'd replaced him blubbered like babies over a little blood and death...

Benoic could feel his mind getting away from him, his focus slipping as he pretended to lead his mechanical soldiers into battle. Part of him knew that he had no idea where they were headed, or what the hell a one-hundred-twenty-year-old has-been with a necktie cinched around his head could possibly accomplish when they got there. The sliver of sanity was like a devil on his shoulder, whispering to him that things like these didn't get raised from their oily tombs unless there was some serious business to attend to.

The gunfire almost stopped his heart when it began - could it really be that loud? He seemed to remember it was much easier to deal with, back when he was young. Oh well- Benoic ripped the hearing aid from his ear, muffling the sound of screams and the sizzle and hiss of the Tank-hunter's masers as they returned fire. The jagged edges of the past and future blurred as he squinted down the sights of his rifle.

The old Militarch knew this place - he'd been through here almost every weekend with his wife, through those gates and into the Beltway for some tedious cocktail party or charity dinner.

But now - well, it was just as well he was out of his mind, wasn't it? Because if all this was *real*, that would mean he was charging the gates of the Belt with a dozen rusting warmekan at his back, burning and blasting troopers of the Compliance Division to pieces as they struggled to bring the gates' ancient weaponry to bear.

It must be some kind of fever dream, he thought, as he sighted along the barrel of his longrifle and cut down a scurrying blue-suited trooper. He'd always fantasized about laying siege to the pompous courtiers and bureaucrats who lived in the Beltway. He'd rather choke down canned rations in a tent with honest soldiers than pick at tiny canapes among those fools any day!

Lock. Load. Fire...

Yes - it was mighty fine to be insane at last. He didn't know what he'd been worrying about all these years. The bolt snapped back, locked forward, and Benoic took another trooper in the shoulder, grinning fiercely as he watched the man tumble from atop the gatehouse wall.

"For Kronos, the Lords, and Manifest Dogma!" he yelled, spittle flying from his lips as he brandished his rifle, exultant. "Forward the Fighting 23rd!"

The tank-hunter next to him rocked back on its heels as a shell exploded against its chestplate, sending shrapnel whistling past his face. Another blast tore its featureless head from its shoulders, and it toppled backwards, falling to the ground with a tangle of wires spilling from its neck. Benoic scuttled sideways to avoid its collapse, staring in horror at the pool of hydraulic fluid which spread from the machine's innards.

"Medic!" he yelled, as bullets skipped and whined across the concrete of the ramp around him. "Man down! Man down!"

As if on cue the gates of the Beltway lurched open a crack, grinding slowly apart as white light spilled from within. There was a figure outlined against that blinding radiance - something almost human, but too large, *malformed*, with three points of red light in a tight triangle where its face should be.

Benoic knew he wasn't the only madman present when he realized that one of them was the glowing tip of a cigarette... and the other two were its eyes.

The ragged shape seemed to be wearing the shreds of an old trenchcoat, over what appeared to be gunmetal armor. Now, what the hell was *that* doing in his dream? Some kind of movie monster, half-remembered from a b-grade threedeeo?

For some reason the warmekan had stopped, their guns silent, standing to attention like great guardian statues. Benoic picked his way forward, around the burned-out wreck of an armored car, and stood, wheezing, using his rifle as a crutch. The shadow-thing in its ridiculous clothes took a final drag on its cigarette and looked right through him, those hot-coal eyes unblinking. He guessed he should say something, play the diplomat, but it was one of the Tank-hunters which spoke first.

"Edward Tsien!" it crackled, through a pair of speakers mounted in its shoulder pauldrons. "This is your maker, Lieutenant. This is Kronos, your duly empowered ruler. I must insist that you stand down and deactivate your Cyben implants. That hardware is government property, and it must be returned to the labs for further testing."

For a second, for two, there was nothing. A gust of wind stirred the dust and smoke, and a handful of empty shells clattered and chimed as they rolled away down the ramp. Then Tsien began to laugh, a sound so chillingly inhuman that even Benoic, the self-confessed madman, shivered with dread.

"Turn them off?" asked the Super-Cyben, flicking his cigarette butt away contemptuously. "Turn them OFF?! You know what would happen then, don't you? And while I'm sure I'd be much more convenient out of the way, I really don't feel inclined to obey you. Not least..." (and here he began to walk down the ramp, nonchalant, sliding a fresh tailormade from his pocket and into his mouth) "Because that order raises a whole predicament for me. You see, I'd love to be able to live without all this shit inside me. If you told me you'd fix me up, and if - a *big* fucking if, mind - I believed you, then I'd have all this iron out in seconds. But then... then, you fucking cold bastard, how would I *smash the shit out of you and your bloody toys*?!"

The Tankhunters leveled their guns at him then, locking bolts, chambering missiles, priming masers. A swarm of tiny red dots played over Tsien's chest, blazing crimson like his eyes.

"I'll ask you again, Lieutenant." said the voice of Kronos, broadcast from every one of the mekan now in a thunderous chorus. "Deactivate your implants, and stand down. We will do what we can to return you to what you would consider *humanity*."

This time there was no laughter – just a cold and merciless silver grin sliced across the Super-Cyben's face.

"And why don't you just do it yourself, hmm? Kronos the omniscient? Are you going to tell me the Wetsystems and the datanet are down for *routine maintenance*? Or are you afraid I won't believe *that* either?"

He'd reached the shadow of the first tank-hunter now, and stood between its massive feet, looking up with utter scorn at the rusted faceplate of the machine. Here he was inside the arc of its guns, and none of the others could fire without blowing their companion to pieces.

"I think you're in more trouble than you let on. I think Octavio bloody Vanecke, be he ever so much an asshole, is *smarter* than you. I think you need all this shit inside me. I think that poor mad old Gerhard's right." He stubbed out his cigarette on the kneecap of the mekan, grinding the ashes hard into the corroded metal.

"The Direktor has nothing to do with it! If you defy me, you condemn yourself and everyone you care about."

"Threats? You really *are* rattled," said Tsien, flexing his hands as he looked up at the mekan, sizing it up. "I've had Subcity thugs try that on before, Kronos, and I think you know what happened to *them*. I filled out all the paperwork when they got recycled into petfood."

"Enough!" yelled Benoic, trembling with anger. "You're an *officer*, godsdammit! You took an oath to serve and obey! Now, do what he says!"

The old man still had it in him; his fury would have made any number of drill sergeants proud.

But Edward Tsien looked him over with a sneer of contempt, the steel irises of his cameras whirring and clicking, and he was suddenly painfully aware that he was nothing more than a fat old man with no shirt on, his necktie tight around his bald head, and his paunch hanging over his belt.

"With all due respect, *sir*, I know the rules. I know the oath I took. It was to uphold the law, and protect the innocent. Do you and yours want to be made into things like me? The whole damn city? It's gone *insane*, and I'm relieving it of its command."

"INSANE?" howled Kronos through its multitude of speakers. "That is nothing but a HUMAN frailty, Tsien! I will do what is necessary to preserve this city! And that means *you must submit*!"

The Tank-hunter took a step back, bringing the muzzle of its left-hand fusion cannon down into the Super-Cyben's face. Tsien reached out his hand and gripped the very end of the scarred old gun, holding it at arm's length.

"See, I know your type, Kronos. I've known them for years, thanks to the job I did for you. Grady Townsend's boys. The Liquid Tong. Vexx's hired thugs. I know that they never *ask* for what they want, they just take it. Unless they're shit-scared. And that's exactly what I'm picking up from this little display. Twelve tank-hunter mekan, just for me?"

Kronos seethed with perfectly replicated anger, his minions lumbering in around Tsien, blocking out the light.

"Not just for you. This is a corollary mission. I must defend the Tower from..."

But the Lieutenant cut him off, producing a third cigarette from within the tattered remains of his coat.

"I know about Blaire, too. And this time I'm ready for him. So there'll be no need for your tin soldiers, Kronos. You made me to do this job, and I'm going to see it through to the end."

There was another endless moment of silence as Tsien stood there, one hand braced on the muzzle of the tank-hunter's maser, his head bowed. An unlit cigarette hung from his lips, forgotten.

"I won't let you take any more of them, you hear me? Not even the scum, not even the dying. Not now that I know what you do with them. So damn your Forge, and your Lords, and your endless stupid games. I'm coming for you, *tonight*. But first..."

Benoic hardly heard that last little speech, a whisper between the Super-Cyben and the machine he faced. But he heard Tsien strike a match against the warmekan's leg, saw its tiny phosphorous flare light up his haggard features.

"First, I'm going to mess up your plans a little. And no matter what happens, I'm taking your mark-four program to the grave with me."

He raised his hand up, palm cupped, and Benoic watched a little trickle of silver liquid spill out between his fingers, splashing like mercury as it hit the ground. It slithered and melted into his steel-clad foot, sucked back up into his body.

"This crycelium is terribly volatile stuff, isn't it? You must need a whole lot of Assemblers just to make enough for a single Vilicus drone... but of course, they're all offline. What a crying shame." He grinned crooked, taking a long drag on his cancer stick. "So if you burn me down to charcoal, how are you gonna make more? And if you don't..."

Benoic swore later that he didn't even see the punch. It was too fast to follow, a metal blur slicing the air, a perfect uppercut which slammed into the warmekan's carapace, actually lifting the ten-ton machine off its feet.

Before it fell back to earth Tsien was airborne, spinning as he kicked out, planting his boot in the middle of the huge robot's chest. Its arms and legs flew out in front of it as it folded in the middle, a clear boot-print stamped into its steel armor. It crashed down in a cacophony of metal and a shower of sparks, servos and pushrods twitching as it scrabbled to regain its feet.

Tsien landed, neat, poised, taking another puff on his cigarette.

"So what's it gonna be, Kronos? You want to see what you've done to me? You want to see what a gods-damned *subhuman* can do?" His eyes blazed brighter than the glowing ember at the tip of his smoke, reckless, facing down enough firepower to level a small town.

"Don't be a fool, Lieutenant!" shouted the voice of the machine, rattling the very gates of the Beltway with sheer volume. "There's something coming, now! Tonight! This city needs every defense I can muster! Didn't you feel it, when you were connected?"

Overhead thunder rumbled, and fitful lightning split the poison clouds.

"I won't be fooled again, damn you!" raged Tsien, ripping the coat from his back, exposing gleaming armor, coils and tubes and bolts puncturing his flesh, cold steel usurping human skin...

Now a single crimson drop fell, splashing across the spiked pauldron of his shoulder, slithering down between the plates of metal...

"For your family, Tsien! For Elysium! For the innocent! Please..."

Kronos was pleading, his amplified voice almost drowned out by peals of thunder. The warmekan which the Super-Cyben had struck was up to its knees now, bowed in supplication. "You're right. I am... *afraid*. I need your help. Please..."

A minute ago, an hour ago - that would have stopped him dead. Mighty Kronos, begging on its knees to a gutter cop from down in the Subcity? But now it just fueled his rage. Another trick. Another blind...

"For my family. For Elysium. For the innocent – if they ever existed. *That's why I have no choice.*" He balled his fists, staring up at the sky as the rain began to fall.

Fat, oily drops of it broke across his face, blurring the creeping line between steel and flesh...

It poured down red, painting the concrete crimson, extinguishing his cigarette in a curl of pungent smoke. Tsien looked down at his hands, huge and malformed claws of jointed metal, and he saw them dripping with gore. He looked up, his eyes blazing from behind a curtain of matted hair, staring into the barrels of a score of guns, the dead camera eyes of a half-circle of rusted tankhunters.

He saw himself reflected there, and he smiled despite the pain.

"Come on, then," he whispered. "Take your best shot."

Then it all became a bloody, hissing blur, and Benoic looked on in horror as his madness took the world down with it...

Ω

Laney Forster stepped up to the windowsill, her head spinning. She'd never liked heights, not even the view from the rooftop of her hab. Halfway up the slope of Elysium there wasn't much to see anyway, even on a good day.

But now she had no choice.

No choice, and no breath, her heartbeat a faint flicker beneath smothering pain...

She was sure she should be dead after that thing had fallen from the sky on top of her – after it had arrested its plunge ten feet above her by opening up into a sticky black sail, its underside a mass of dripping teeth...

Laney whimpered a little, deep inside the corrosive embrace of the saprophyte. But its voice goaded her on with whips of pain, letting her feel for a sliver of a second what had really become of her flesh. It was too horrible to comprehend, and her mind reeled back in horror, allowing the thing which had consumed her to have its way. It shuffled her feet forward, over the precipice, choking the scream in her throat.

She toppled from the window and out into a hellscape of smoke and fire and searchlight beams, screams echoing up the canyon of metal which separated her Hab from the recycling 'fac next door. The street was a chasm of darkness in which a tangle of panicked people writhed and struggled.

Falling, now, head down, streamers of oily dark filth whipping out behind her in tatters. She hoped that the impact would be mercifully swift...

Then the Saprophyte pulled her strings, twisting her arms out wide, ripping her bones from their sockets as a pair of membranous wings

280

snapped taut. Down over the mad throng she came, a thing from out of prehistoric nightmares, her fingers drawn out to needle-thin spikes, shaping the edges of her wings and straining for lift. Her jaw hinged open as she skimmed over the heads of the people below, and an inhuman shriek issued from her throat, a sound of hideous triumph. The powerdive leveled out, became a mad, clawing battle for altitude – and she was *flying*.

It felt like she was pinned to the air with spikes of pain, but the thermals from a hundred fires buoyed her up, carrying her in a wide gyre over the habs, over the manufactoria and the streets where those who hadn't barricaded themselves indoors struggled and died. Other things like the one which had killed her ran riot down there, hordes of slippery black shadows dragged along in the wake of massive, formless beasts, all arms and eyes and gaping mouths.

Higher still, up among the ragged clouds, and the slick blue bulge of the Beltway slid by beneath her, untouched as yet by the hunger of the Worm. She could feel her bones decaying now, her tendons parting like rotten thread. This flight would soon be over. All at once she realized what had happened to the last victim of this particular saprophyte – utterly digested in midair! What an easy target she must have made, cowering there on the Hab roof with an old automatic pistol in her hands...

A laborious single wingbeat, the ache and creak of tortured bone, and the veil of clouds parted.

She broke through into a night sky dominated by the overspanning arc of the satellite halo, a jaundiced moon painting the clouds sickly yellow. Here and there the blanket of roiling vapor was tinged with red, a spreading stain rolling out over the city like blood leaking through a bandage. But the Slavemaster wouldn't let her admire the view, even if it was most likely the last thing she'd ever see. This flight was for a purpose, and with her frail mortal flesh failing there was no time to waste...

Her ragged wings clapped once, a surging downbeat which sent her careening in toward the tops of the Lord's spires, in through a maze of steel teeth to where lights burned blue and bright about the base of the disused 'Lev.

That single movement was enough to pull the muscles away from the bones of her tortured arms, splitting her skin. A rain of decay trailed in her wake as the towers sped by on both sides, her flight now a suicidal plunge in toward the light. Toward the sanctum of Kronos, a place she'd only heard of in the sermons of Manifest Dogma.

The first Skyhammer shifted into existence directly in her path; even if her ravaged frame could have steered around its shell her brain would never have reacted in time. Laney struck the missile platform at full speed, cartwheeling through the cold air as they broke apart. The Skyhammer loosed a missile as it spun, smooth, and she felt the lick of its rocket exhaust hiss by as she fell.

A tiny, happy part of her knew that it wouldn't be long now until she hit the ground...

Two more high-explosive rockets scudded past as the Saprophyte struggled to regain control, sending her spinning across the darkness, winking satellites and bloody clouds and walls of rusted steel wheeling before her eyes. It was the fourth one which struck home.

Laney felt the impact, even through the numb detachment of her enslavement. The oily black thing which wrapped her in its embrace *screamed* as a ball of flame erupted around it, licking across its skin, laying bare her ruined flesh. It tore off her, burning, a tattered ruin adrift in the cold air - and the pain came up to meet her, the wind flaying her like claws.

But it was honest pain, and soon it would be over. Laney Forster took some tiny consolation in the fact that the creature which had killed her was suffering and dying, too.

That was the last thing which went through her mind before the Skyhammer's fifth missile slammed into her back, lighting up the megatowers with a brief flare of phosphorous white. Satisfied that no fragment of its target remained, the hovering mekan downshifted its mass, shrinking back to the size of a mosquito before it flitted away into the darkness.

Inside its claustrophobic section of the Wetsystems Asag'raal shrieked in frustration. That was the sixth one down! These human insects were so frail, so *limited*! If it weren't for their delicious suffering they'd be better off extinct!

The otherdimensional creature followed the death-plunge of its burning minion, feeding on its pain as it went up in flames. It seemed that stealth was out of the question, even by air. Kronos' sanctum was proof against even the most subtle attacks which the Worm could muster. This could prove a problem, considering that it only had mere thousands of Saprophytes at its disposal. After an hour of frantic probing and prying it had discovered not so much as a crack in the lockdown which imprisoned it...

But the Exalted were another matter altogether. Such a fine crop of them, and so *strong*! A handful of times throughout history Asag'raal had managed to enter the minds of the weak and wicked among its human flock, granting them a fraction of its power. Stories of witchcraft and cannibalism, berserk savagery and sacrifice rippled out from its chosen ones, sowing the seeds for a harvest of fear. But now, with part of its incalculably immense physical form across the threshold its Exalted were stronger than ever.

Over time its slaves had always become different from their kin – madness usually came first, then subtle shifts in their physiology, witch-marks and claws and blackened, pointed teeth... Now they took on the aspect of their terrible father almost as soon as they accepted his embrace. The great aching need to spawn one of its own kind still burned in the mind of the Worm, cutting as keenly as the desire to feed. But these things were almost children to it, nourishing their loving patriarch with the pain of the innocent. Some had consumed *hundreds* already! And unlike the Saprophytes they were *intelligent*, they learned, they *grew*, even if they were all twisted and malformed...

Twisted? Malformed?

What was *that*, if not one of its own?

Something snapped the thread of Asag'raal's reverie – an image, a tiny scrawl of silver across the eyes of a burning saprophyte as it fell.

Him! The vessel which had trapped the Worm! The puppet of the Illuminatus, strung up and sliced to pieces by Kronos, his defiance flaring like a beacon in Asag'raal's psionic senses. He only caught the tiniest glimpse of Edward Tsien before his vassal splattered across the antennae of a building's crown, but that was enough. He was *incandescent*, filled with hate and rage and sweet self-loathing. Such a prize!

It was too bad that he was cut off from the sector of the Wetsystems where the Worm coiled, caged. Threads surely branched off from his augmented brain to Kronos itself, to the heart of the Forge. And down into the R.T, where the Illuminatus cowered, awaiting judgment...

But over and above all that, Asag'raal saw in Tsien the ultimate Exalted. Steel and flesh grinding against each other in suffering, his mind wracked with doubt and fear. He could become *exquisite*!

The Worm Asag'raal had no concept of art, but looking down through the rain of blood at the face of Eddie Tsien he felt like a sculptor contemplating a virgin slab of marble. Within that shell of metal and meat was the soul of a monster, just waiting to be tortured into existence.

In the heads of a thousand slave Saprophytes the Worm hissed and bellowed, turning their decaying eyes up toward the Beltway. It whispered and cajoled, bullying the Exalted from their crawling spread, promising them impossible excesses of pleasure and pain...

Oh yes. Here was the key.

Here, in this one half-human thing.

Tsien had been crucified between life and death to lure the Worm, and he was the bridge between dimensions which had drawn it across. What better avatar could serve as its own living flesh when it took this world and raped it dead?

Ω

Celebrant Grandmaster Benton Veer was vexed. Not only had tonight's round of the Game collapsed into static before the end of the second melee, but now the power was out as well! Honestly, one paid good money for a house in the Beltway, one worked tirelessly for Kronos and his Chosen, and *this* was how one was repaid?

He might as well have stayed down in the Subcity with his poor, doomed parents, with his gaggle of drunken brothers!

Those loathsome brutes from the Compliance Division were cruising the streets outside, no doubt driving down property values by the minute. And if rumor was to be believed (which, in the social pressure-cooker of the Belt, it most certainly was) the rest of Elysium was in utter upheaval tonight.

That would mean a lot more work for all the chiefs of staff – even poor outmoded Benoic, even (and here Grandmaster Veer shuddered in his silks, his powdered face twitching with disgust) Sanitation Commissioner Callaway. Yes, even the bloody Sewer Czar would have a ton of paperwork to wade through, if they woke tomorrow to find the drains stuffed with bodies!

Benton paced the thick carpets of his villa, pensive, a wireless phone dangling from the sash of his robe and a flute of amaretto in one hand. There was only one consolation to be had tonight – a little real-estate deal, a paradigm shift in the power structure of Oleander Avenue. As President of the street's neighborhood association the Grandmaster of Celebrants had had one thing on his agenda for the last ten years – the expulsion of Direktor Octavio Vanecke.

Tonight it should all go down without a hitch, and then the vast pseudogothic pile next door could be bulldozed and transformed into a tennis lawn, with a tasteful little rose garden for the long-suffering Mrs Veer. Oh, how he'd persevered! The petitions, the meetings, the polite indignation... but in the end it would come down to his little lads in black, his Celebrants. This was one operation he was glad to be involved in, despite his general disdain for the dirty details of his trade.

Benton nearly dropped his amaretto when the gilded telephone at his hip chimed, tiny blue jewels sparkling across its rose-engraved shell. He touched its earpiece with one slim finger, and the voice of Grief Division Dispatch came in hashed and blurry, making him wince a little at its crudity.

"Chief, we've got a problem! That squad you detailed for the Vanecke job...well, I dunno how to tell you this sir, but... ummm... we've *lost* them. Didn't even make it through the gates. I've sent up a spotter drone, and it looks like there's some kind of fighting going on up there – I swear, we thought that it hadn't spread out of the lower city..."

The dispatcher was named Holgarth, a Vice-Captain in the Undertakers, and a man who thought he was being groomed for Veer's own job. It always payed to keep your underlings deluded.

"What?" barked the Grandmaster, relishing the thought of Holgarth's discomfort. "Utterly unacceptable! Nothing, we are assured, *nothing* will stand in our way! We are *natural causes*, Mister Holgarth. We are *implacable!*"

Unthinkably, the idiot actually interrupted Benton just as he was getting into the swing of his little speech.

"Grandmaster... sir... It's, I mean... we're getting some very strange reports from the lads on the streets tonight. Some of the other squads aren't calling in, either. And the spotter drone sent back images of *tank-hunters*, sir! They're fighting the Bluejackets!"

Veer's boys held all Elysium in disdain, but they harbored a special hatred for the Compliance Division. Most of his men had dropped out of the Academy of Law, and all of them were the type to nurse a grudge.

"I didn't tell you to *stop* them, did I?" asked Benton, toying with his crystal flute as he imagined blue-suited troopers being blown apart by heavy artillery. "Still, our mission stands, mister Holgarth. I have certain obligations to uphold, and we cannot be seen to be *anything* other than utterly dedicated to the Holy Engine."

Obligations, indeed. Heavens preserve him if he had to tell Mrs Veer that her rose garden was still in the possession of a psychopathic severed head with a nine-figure bank balance...

"All this unauthorized death must surely have freed up some of our men, hmm?" he purred, stalking over to the curtained windows and twitching the thick red drapes aside.

A Comp. Div. tank rumbled down Oleander Avenue with its red and blue strobes blazing, painting the clipped lawns and whitewashed villas gaudy neon.

"I want a show of force, Holgarth, the likes of which this city has never seen. I want Octavio bloody Vanecke's head flopping on the concrete like a hooked fish! And I want it all within the next half hour, or so help me Vice-Captain, you'll be scrubbing out the crematoria with a toothbrush for the rest of your miserable tenure."

"I... I... that is..." stammered the unfortunate dispatcher, frantically rummaging through the empty coffee cups and folders on his desk for tonight's electronic roster. "We've got three Terminus units on standby, about sixteen Undertakers, a Crematory detachment, and the *Axis Mortalis*. Although that's not been out of its hangar for forty years... I think we can spare ten men, maybe twelve for the Vanecke job, Grandmaster."

Veer scowled as he watched the pigwagon cut the corner of Oleander and Jasmine, mowing down an ornamental fountain.

"I want them *all*, Holgarth. A full complement, armed to the teeth, and the *Axis* as well. We'll come in through the sky, grab that old bastard before he knows what's hit him!"

There was a fire in his eyes now, as he gently placed the empty glass down on one of his mahogany end tables, images of his old rival Division Marshall Akembe dancing in his head. While that fat old fool's men went toe to toe with a gaggle of rusted machines, he'd be drinking a toast to Direktor Vanecke's sorry demise.

"Half an hour, you hear me! And tell them to be turned out in their finest, Holgarth. I'll be leading this operation myself."

Ω

'That fat old fool', as Benton Veer had called him, was currently the focus of intense scrutiny. His holographic image glared down from the wall of the Last Post, as if reprimanding the officers there for their failings.

Some of them sat sprawled in chairs, lost in threedeeo reverie. Others were even wearing robes, slippers, *pajamas* for the love of all things holy! Akembe's leathery brown face was creased up in his habitual frown - as it had been for the two decades that he'd graced the wall of the day room. Gerhard liked to think he'd appreciate what was about to happen here, even if it wouldn't wipe the cold-eyed scowl from his ugly mug.

If the bastard ever smiled - which Captain Mitchell sorely doubted - then it would certainly be at a fool like him, climbing up on top of a card table in an exosuit to address a bunch of dried-out old veterans. He'd laugh to split his sides if he heard what Gerhard was about to ask of them.

"Listen up! Listen well, men - I've got some bad news for you. Well - good news, really, unless you *wanted* to end your days wallowing in re-runs! I'm here to reinstate your commissions!"

The youngest man in the room aside from the Tutor-Captain must have been a hundred and three - Marty Maxwell, ex-commander of precinct 292. He was the first to actually look away from the Threedeeo globe, squinting up at Gerhard as if he were some bizarre new threevee advertisement.

"Aren't you young Mitchell?" he asked, levering himself around on the end of the couch. "The one who got busted down to Academy duty for that fiasco with the Liquid Tong?"

Gerhard grimaced, remembering that terrible night, the smoke, the confusion – it wasn't his fault that a Tong sniper had planted that hypodermic in his neck. And with that much Triple Platinum in his system, was it any wonder he'd been found naked, firing a pair of micromissile launchers at cars on the transdome highway?

"Yes, sir, I'm *that* Captain Mitchell. As you can see, they've issued me with some pants it's pretty damn hard to take off."

Marty cackled as Gerhard rapped his knuckles against the iron codpiece of his exosuit, dragging the man next to him around with one liver-spotted hand.

"You hear that, Perez? Ol' Bare-assed Mitchell wants us to go back to work! What do you say to that?"

Juan Perez, once the most feared C-Tac assassin in all Elysium, looked up at Gerhard through a pair of outmoded cybernetic eyes, pushrods clicking as he tried to focus.

"Back out there? I thought we were *useless*, son. I thought Marshall Lexington replaced us all with Cyben, not ten years after the Reclamation."

"Juan, you idiot, it's *Akembe* now," chimed in another man, his voice issuing from a tracheotomy speaker in his neck. "Lexington was in here with us for three years before the Celebrants came for him."

At the mention of the Celebrants a muttering of resentment rippled through the room, and more and more of the old veteran troopers turned to look up at Mitchell.

"Is that what you want, then?" he asked, throwing his arms out wide. "You want to end up like Iron Lex, waiting for the bloody corpse-rapists to take you? He was a pawn of politics, but he served for eighty years, dammit! When they shot his hand off during the Reclamation he kept fighting!" The muttering had turned angry now, and crafty old Marty Maxwell reached out and surreptitiously switched off the threedeeo. Every eye was locked on Gerhard, the holo of Marshall Akembe looming over his head. "You want to be picked off one by one, led off to the slaughterhouse? Is that how a soldier of the law dies?"

Oh, he had them now. Gerhard knew what it felt like to get old. He was already sliding that way himself. But with fire in their bellies and a few million Slades worth of modern weaponry, these guys could hold the Beltway gates. The damn place was fortress, after all.

"I'm going to give you the chance to die on your own terms. Sure, it's a bum deal compared to free meds, censored threedeeo and mashed synthesoy for the next decade, but I want to remind you all that you took an oath. They never said it expired just when you felt like quitting."

"Why do they need us, then?" asked an anonymous voice from somewhere in the back. "What the hell's going on out there, anyway?"

Gerhard grinned, flipping open the little keyboard on the inside of his forearm. A threedeeo haze appeared in the air before him, woven by tiny lasers in his shoulder pauldron.

"I thought you'd never ask, boys. But brace yourself – some of this is pretty ugly."

When the show was over the whole room was silent. He'd picked the best parts from Omnivasive's coverage of the riots, spliced in Direktor Vanecke's address about the Lords' demise, and then shown them a glimpse of the Tank-hunters marching ponderously toward the Beltway.

"It's gone *insane*, gentlemen. We can't trust the Cyben. We can't trust the machines. And that means I need every able-bodied man I can get. Even you."

"But... we can't fight the Cyben! You know what they can..." began a dissenter, hidden amongst his fellow retirees.

"Stow it, Leonov!" roared Marty Maxwell, in a parade-ground bellow far too large for his tiny frame. "Seems to me we don't have a choice! And anyway, do you really want to live like this forever?"

A rumble of assent rippled through the crowd, and Gerhard stepped down from off the card table, wrapping one bulky steel arm around the old man's shoulders.

"Now, let's see some action, gentlemen! I want you all front and center in ten - no slippers, no gowns, no complaints! Then we'll proceed to the gatehouse and requisition you some weapons. I trust you all remember which end is the dangerous one?"

They stood there for a second, confused, teetering on the brink of indecision. Then Marty pushed out of Gerhard's shadow, grabbing the nearest veteran by the lapel of his terrycloth gown.

"You heard the man, *ladies*! Now, JUMP TO IT! We've got some *dying* to do!"

Tutor-Captain Mitchell watched them leave, a curious mixture of pride and dread churning in his belly. It wasn't that he was afraid that the old troopers would prove useless in the face of the enemy – between them they had more combat experience than a whole damn army. No – the difficult part would be trying to get them to *stop*...

Ω

A line of craters stitched their way across the bloody concrete in slow motion, closer and closer, sending up tiny halos of chipped stone and dust.

Still the deluge fell; red, thick and oily, and in his enhanced vision he saw every single drop splash and shatter, traced the descent of each shimmering particle...

They'd screw up the warmekan's tracking, make the obsolete old rustbuckets work for every shot.

That would do just fine.

Tsien faked right and jumped left, a bullet hissing past his shoulder as he tackled Benoic, wrapping him in a steely embrace. The old man was clearly out of his mind, but he was innocent. You couldn't judge the mad.

Well - he'd make an exception for Kronos. But for now... he turned the roll into a handspring, coming up off two fingers, ripping the ornate longrifle from the Militarch's grasp with his other hand. Cartwheeling now, upside down, and a missile shot by between his legs, trailing a streamer of blue smoke. His hands worked the bolt, inhumanly fast, his optical reticules razoring in tight on the camera eyes of the tank-hunter which had fired it.

Once, twice, the rifle spat flame before Tsien's feet touched the ground, and the great machine was blinded, shards of glass winking and glittering in midair. It's head rocked back on hydraulic shocks, staved in.

Its second shot was still locked on, however. Tsien whipped his arm around, throwing the spent rifle in a spinning blur. It met the missile halfway, thousands of Slades worth of exquisite hardwood and silver exploding into shards and splinters in an eyeblink.

The debris was still falling as Tsien picked his next target. He leaned to his left as a flickering maser-beam lashed out, evaporating the blood-rain in its path. An ornamental gargoyle behind him glowed red for an instant and melted down to dripping slag. There - while the rain confused them. While his augmented body still burned with power, slowing the world to a crawl...

Tsien charged at the nearest warmekan, his legs pumping, his eyes set grimly on its fifteen-foot frame. Bullets and incandescent maserfire hazed the air between him and his prey - now he slid under a sizzling red beam, now he hurdled a withering hail of lead, his face split in a determined grin.

All around him he could hear the thud and whine of the tank-hunter's crushing feet, deep bass notes behind the endless hiss of the rain. He found that he could actually sense their movements by the way they broke the deluge. One more burst of speed, sliding in sideways across the slippery concrete as another missile roared past, spiraling wild...

Then he was airborne - up to its knee, where a carefully placed kick split its hydraulic couplings. Then to its arm, a great rotary cannon steaming with dried blood. It was already sagging down, its legs collapsing out from under it as he flipped up and over, onto its shoulders. Mounted on one of the corroded mekan's pauldrons was a fusion gun almost seven feet long - just the right size for a Super-Cyben. Tsien gripped the weapon in both hands, tearing it from its sponson in a shower of sparks. Wrist-thick power cables still linked it to the warmekan, but with a deft twist he severed its skein of control wires, feeling them socket into the palm of his hand, *integrating*...

The tank-hunter's giant cannon couldn't target something standing on its own shoulder. But its other hand rattled loose on a length of chain, a spiked wrecking ball designed to crack open bunkers. Tsien leaned back as the ball whistled past, within a hair's breadth of pulverizing his body. He watched it reach the end of its arc behind him, poised for the backswing...

Then his eyes lit up with glittering icons, and the fusion gun came online. He swung the bulky muzzle of the blaster around to rest against the warmekan's head, and pulled the trigger.

Once, and a ball of blue fire tore through the faceless casque of the fighting machine, a fan of blazing debris ripping its other shoulder to shreds. Wires and hoses parted with a sad little series of snaps and twangs, and its rotary cannon fell to the bloody ground, its gears grinding down to a standstill. Twice, and there was nothing left but a charred steel stump where its head had been.

Freedom! Freedom at last! My name was Niall Giaccone, and I've been inside that thing for eleven centuries! Thank you, liberator! Thank you for killing me!

The warmekan fell backwards, its strings cut, and Tsien leaped from his perch, playing out loops of power cable from its broken body. There'd be ten whole seconds before its batteries cut out - an eternity in his private little world, where each individual raindrop fell with glacial slowness.

He skidded to a stop, crouching, the great fusion gun cradled in his hands. Bullets ricocheted and whined as they struck the collapsed body of the fallen mekan. From behind its cover Tsien listened, his eyes closed, feeling the bloody rain as it spattered and hissed off mechanized steel.

He came up from behind the broken carcass of the tankhunter firing, taking out the blinded warmekan he'd crippled with Benoic's rifle. Uncertain, twitching, it was an easy target. Tsien's fusion blast struck home, igniting the magazine of missiles which fed the autolauncher on its left arm. With a series of cracks and pops they went up in flames, ripping its metal shell apart from within as incendiaries and high-explosives blazed. Random rounds spiraled out, cratering the concrete, striking down another pair of tankhunters where they stood.

My name was Charan Lo. Thank you...

Down, but not out. Ten of the twelve machines were still fully operational, and now they were triangulating his position. He watched as the bulky shoulder-armor of one of the mekan split open, revealing hundreds of tiny holes, a micromissile nestled in each one. A barrage like that would slice him to mincemeat, Chimera crycelium notwithstanding.

It would take the tank-hunter precious fractions of a second to define its killing zone – time enough for Tsien to avoid such a messy end.

He dropped the spent fusion gun, snapping off a length of its power cable, and leaped back into the fray, sliding between two lumbering mekan as they closed on him. This pair were loaded for close combat, their arms terminating in cruel steel talons. Each claw-like finger was a whirring monobladed chainsaw.

Tsien ducked under the piston-driven punch of the mekan on his left, coming up under its wrist to lock both of his hands around it. He pushed up, right on the fulcrum, continuing its swing on into the studded carapace of another war-machine. Tortured metal squealed as those savage claws cut deep, geysering blue sparks, and the mekan lashed out spasmodically, pummeling its attacker with a hydraulic sledgehammer. The Super-Cyben was too swift for the giant machines to follow, and he ducked between the legs of the hammer-handed tank-hunter, looping his coil of wire tight around its feet. While the pair grappled with each other, their processors glitched and furious, Tsien bound them up together, sidestepping neatly as they fell. The claw-fingered machine had all but eviscerated its brother, rupturing its power cells, while the hammer fist of the other machine had caved in the side of its head.

My name was Sevan Gopal. My name was Luc Radisson...

The micromissile barrage took flight with a spitting roar, obscuring Eddie's target behind a veil of blue smoke. One second, and they were at their zenith, tiny guidance fins snapping out from their tails as their rocket engines sputtered and died. Two, and they were falling, a rain of death which would churn the bloody concrete to rubble. The tank-hunters themselves would shrug off such tiny munitions like water – but if Tsien was caught in the shrapnel-storm which they unleashed...

He was off and running even before the smoke cleared, headed toward one of the struggling 'hunters which had fallen to a stray missile.

He willed his bloody hands into blades, watching his fingers stretch and sharpen. At the last moment he punched with all his strength through the chestplate of the upturned machine, feeling the crycelium on the edges of his knives ablating away layers of steel. With one hand he ripped it free, and with the other he raked his claws across the exposed circuitry beneath, tearing out a smoking handful of wires. The light went out of the doomed mekan's eyes as Tsien spun its chestplate in midair, bringing it up over his head as a shield.

My name was Katerina Howe...

Then the missile swarm came down, and deafening, blinding explosions filled his entire world. For a moment, for two, all he could see was a white and purple blur, the sound of bells tolling in his skull. The force of it drove him to his knees beneath his makeshift shield, and skittering shrapnel came in under its rim to flay his legs bare.

Multiple images blurred and swum in his electronic eyes, a horde of demons painted blood-red and rust ochre, marching forward to crush him into pulp. He heard the click and whirr of loading guns and tried desperately to focus, knowing that at any instant...

Too late.

A stray shell exploded right in front of him, giving the Super-Cyben barely enough time to bring his shield down against the concrete. Wicked shards of steel punched through the armor, and light shone through from the mekan' halogen lamps, jagged shadows scrawled across his face. He could feel the heat rising in his body as the crycelium tried to keep up with his wounds, burning up his energy and his humanity. Through one of the holes in his makeshift shield he could see a line of three tank-hunters bringing their particle beams to bear, weapons which would reduce him to superheated gas, armor notwithstanding.

Tsien tried to stand, to move, the merest twitch... but his legs weren't responding. Looking down the barrels of those massed guns he saw utter defeat. Kronos would make sure he was remembered as a monster, even by the people he was trying to protect...

He closed his eyes.

The volley from the gates blew all three of the advancing machines apart at once, as twenty great howitzer guns fired from atop the gatehouse wall. Every one of them was manned, crewed by blue-suited figures laboring behind a pall of cordite smoke, and as Tsien watched they reloaded and fired again, tearing what remained of those three unfortunate 'hunters apart.

Gears and wires and burning chunks of plastic slithered across the bloody ramp as the gunners cheered, and among them Tsien caught sight of Gerhard Mitchell, his exo-armored frame standing tall above the heads of his men. The crazy old bastard had done it! He'd actually found reinforcements at the very last moment, and now the tables were turned.

My name was Anya Seran. My name was Grigory Vlasic. My name

Tsien slammed down a fistful of overrides, bullying his Cyben implants back online by sheer force of will, staggering to his feet with the great concave dish of a tank-hunter's chestplate still welded to his butcher-knife fingers. He could see the mekan with the micromissile batteries over its shoulders turning to face the gates now, and he heard the thousands of tiny snicking sounds as it loaded up for another barrage .

That one would have to go first.

One of the tank-hunters which had been wrecked down to scrap by the howitzer fire had sported a six-foot close-combat bayonet under its arm, a great meat-cleaver of a thing designed to carve through cerametal shielding. It was just the right size for Tsien's new hands, those killing claws at the end of his piston-fused arms.

He twisted and wrenched at the heavy blade as he slid into the cover of the smoking mekan's carcass, dodging shells and fusion beams. In the end he was forced to use one of his knife-bladed fingers, running it down between the bayonet's mounting bolts and shearing them off as neatly as a diamond-edged grinder.

Perfect.

A huge piston-rod protruded from the tang of the blade, the hydraulic ram which punched it forward with the force of a bullet. Now the Super-Cyben grasped the cutoff end of that piston like the handle of a broadsword, a two-handed grip from out of the Vatican's *Codex Martial*. The bayonet was as tall as he was, three feet thick, and it weighed at least half a ton. It was just the tool for the job.

Tsien sprung from behind cover, letting a little trickle of his crycelial parasite flow across the blade. Atomic-scale sawteeth flowed around it with a keening whirr, too high-pitched for human ears. Tsien could hear it slicing apart the smoke. His eyes were fixed on the micromissile mekan, which was even now extending leg-braces from its bulky frame, preparing to unleash its payload.

Bullets tracked toward him across the pavement, and hissing maserbeams wove a shifting cage around him as he jinked from side to side. But where they would have struck him down, now they were deflected by the flat of his blade, the bullets ricocheting off wild into the rain, the beams crazed and haloed by its mirrored surface. The outsized sword seemed to guide Tsien's hands, describing an intricate *Kata* through the crimson deluge, a cage within a cage...

Then he was upon his prey, his lips twisted into a grimace of hate and joy, his knuckles white under a crust of silver armor.

Once, overhand, then twice, the backswing, then thrice, a finishing stroke which sliced through the luckless machine from shoulder to crotch. Time seemed to stand still as Tsien slid past his target, his iron-shod feet slick against the bloody concrete, his head bowed. Two blazing points of red smoldered in his shadowed face as he held the sword out at his side, waiting...

The micromissile barrage never came. Instead one of the tank-hunter's arms dropped off, sheared neatly from its torso, falling to the ground with a clatter and thud of ruined metal. Then its other arm followed, its assault claw flexing open and closed like that of a stricken crab. Finally, in that eternal instant of red and black and flashing chrome a *line* appeared across the thing's body, a line of darkness crawling with ice-blue sparks.

The explosion, when it came, raised a cheer from the troopers atop the wall, and a satisfied grunt from Tsien, who brandished his ungainly blade in triumph as he turned to face the remaining tank-hunters.

My name was Michael Atkins...

Twenty bolts thudded home as the gateway guns were loaded, aiming over the Super-Cyben's head. He could call down hellfire with a gesture.

The three warmekan which remained seemed to hesitate, unsure of their superiority. Even the bloody rain was easing off, becoming a fine crimson mist which swirled in veils across the battlefield.

Tsien held his sword at his hip, the bolt-end of its piston grip resting against his leg. Just *lifting* such a thing bled away his humanity, as the Chimera system replaced more and more of his body with metal. Wafer-thin heat-sink vanes sprouted from his back as he stood there, defiant, unfurling like the fiddleheads of ferns with a lambent orange glow.

The cameras mounted in the back of his skull caught a tiny mote falling from the gateway above, where Gerhard was pumping his fist triumphantly in the air. It was a communicator, and Tsien caught it with his free hand, hearing whoops and cries of jubilation as he raised it to his ear.

"Good timing, Captain," he said, keeping his eyes locked on the three remaining tank-hunter mekan where they huddled at the base of the ramp. "Another couple of seconds and I wouldn't have been around to thank you."

"Did I tell you I had some good officers in reserve, or what?" yelled Mitchell, so loud that Tsien could feel his augmented auditory system overloading. "Just three more to go, and then we're home free! That pile of silicon scrap isn't gonna try this again!"

But the Super-Cyben wasn't listening. His boosted optics had caught sight of something in the shadows behind the three warmekan, a slithering darkness coiling between the lightless buildings.

"Gerhard, I don't think you should be breaking out the beer and medals just yet. There's something *strange* going on down here..."

Even as he spoke one of the warmekan turned, its autoguns spinning up with a clatter of gears. The rhythmic hammering sound of high-explosive shells echoed across the bloodstained plaza once again, but this time the machine was firing off into the dark, down into the Subcity.

Another of the mekan followed suit, peppering the jagged rooftops and steel-sided habs with lead, sending sparks and ricochets flying. Now the shadows pooled and flowed *here*, in a darkened doorway, now they slithered across the corrugated iron of a manufactorium roof, congealing, circling in closer...

"Tsien! Beware!" roared the central warmekan, the voice of Kronos echoing up against the gates like a breaking wave. "They're here! *Help me...*"

Then the darkness curled back, hissing. All the shadows clenched up like fists, and the Saprophytes struck.

Solid rays of shadow lanced out from the Chosen of Asag'raal, spike-tipped pseudopods faster than bullets. They transfixed the three tank-hunters effortlessly, absorbing maser beams and blasts of superheated plasma as if the doomed machines were firing into murky water. But their own weapons parted steel like tissue, hungrily filling the empty armor of the warmekan, spilling from their joints and oozing obscenely from the muzzles of their guns. Coils of twitching darkness pulled tight, binding them to the Worm, turning the war machines into grim puppets.

They turned slowly, lifted off their feet by glistening tongues of jelly. Now the evil puppet-master itself heaved its own bulk forward into the light, a thing the size of a house all covered with scars and doomed, screaming faces.

This time no voices echoed in Tsien's head, no caged souls flickered and faded as they tasted freedom. Whoever Kronos had chained inside the rusted casques of those machines, they'd been released from one form of slavery into another. He knew that this thing had heard the fleeing spirits of the warmekan when it opened its mouth to speak, spewing forth a flood of darkness.

"*My name was Gurden Syliss*, Mister Tsien," rumbled the massive creature, its tiny human face dwarfed between lumps of inky matter. Its skin stretched up and slumped down again, twisting and reforming a tangled mass of spikes. "Better known to you Bluejacket *pigs* as prisoner number 193-302. Then as *Junior Constable.* But my new daddy's got a better name for me. A *new* name for the New Flesh. He calls me... *Exalted.*"

"And I - Exalted!" chimed in a second voice, this from a creature dressed in flayed skins, a twisted one-armed dwarf who carried a black sphere on the tip of his finger. Like Syliss's ever-shifting flesh it bubbled with anguished faces, blindly groping hands stretching its surface.

"An-and-and I... ex-ex-ex-alted!" stammered a third of them, lurching forward from the unnatural shadows. This monster was a stick-thin ghoul, teetering atop a tower of saprophytic jelly. His face was peeled back in flayed strips, petals of flesh pinned down with hooks. Whether this was a modification made before or after its transformation Tsien didn't care to speculate.

Each of the chosen ones of the Worm held a tank-hunter mekan twitching at the end of a black umbilicus, dangling them in front of the Super-Cyben like bait.

"What's wrong, Lieutenant? Suddenly not so tough, eh? Perhaps you were expecting more little tin toys to smash, instead of great Asag'raal's children?"

Syliss laughed, coughing up bubbles of oily black foam which slithered down his chest.

"Now, one way or another you're going to join us. I've been told you'll even get to share our name, Tsien. Such a shame, really - I can almost taste your fear already!"

His wrist-thick black tongue lashed the air, dripping, as his gross bulk shook with mirth.

"Taste it! Yesssss!" giggled the gnome, capering while his floating ball of darkness thumped like a living heart overhead. "Come with us, brother! At least then you'll be saved from the crawling steel!"

"At l-least then you'll n-n-nnot be one of these *things*! You won't d-die a machine!" stuttered the flayed one, his hooked-open eyes rolling madly.

Tsien tightened both hands around his makeshift sword, his face twisted up with rage. Whatever these things were, whatever trick of that damned machine...

But there was *doubt*. It flared tiny as a matchstrike in the echoing darkness of his soul, throwing the jagged shape of his hatred into sharp relief.

Self-hatred. Despair. Rage.

He could feel it calling out to them, across the gulf through which the caged souls of those tank-hunters had fled. *Perhaps he belonged with the Exalted...*

The roar of twenty cannons saved him then, cutting short his introspection with high explosives. As the shells screamed over his head Tsien realized how close he'd been to reaching out and touching the sickness, inviting it inside. He'd felt it before, when he'd been transformed, when he was strung out on a rack of ancient crycelium, between life and death...

With the flare and blast and impact of those screaming projectiles he realized what had happened.

His hate was misplaced. Kronos was complicit, but the machine had been played like a fool. The writhing black despite which filled him wasn't just born of pain and hopelessness - it had taken physical form. It was the stuff which Syliss and his brothers wore like armor, the manifestation of pure malice.

It was the *enemy*.

He tried to fix the image of his wife and his children in his mind, but combat programs were blurring his eyes like delirium, and the crycelium was a furnace in his belly, demanding slaughter. Tears burst out around the welded reticules in his sockets, washing away the dried blood which crusted his face.

Howling, wordless, mindless... he gave himself up to the steel, raising his impossibly large blade over his head, and charged.

Ω

Axis Mortalis.

The flagship of the Celebrants hadn't been used for decades, but the secretive priesthood of that Order Militant kept the sleek war-zeppelin oiled and ready, its guns loaded and its tanks brimming with ethanol fuel. From stem to stern the 'Grandmaster's Own' measured a full four hundred feet, a teardrop of oily black diamondmesh stretched taut over gasbags and antigrav generators. Slung under the *Axis'* frame was a command gondola shaped like a downward-jutting fin, a blade of metal whose leading edge was studded with guns and sensors, all the better to hunt down its prey.

In years past the sight of the *Axis Mortalis* riding the sky had been enough to fill those below with superstitious dread - they said that if its shadow touched you then you were marked for death. In reality it was only ever used to hunt down fleeing recalcitrants. There were always wealthy opportunists who thought they could suckle at Kronos' teat for a lifetime - and then strike out into the rad-lands when their time grew short. Such individuals were few and far between now, as the city slowly decayed.

And how would they ever know that a recusant was fleeing, these days, with the defensive perimeter of Elysium hopelessly mixed up with the pickets of the Reclamation? Indeed, how could the cash-strapped hierarchy of the Direktoriat afford to send a beautiful beast like the *Axis* after them, with its fuel costs for one mission alone enough to maintain a Cyben for a year?

Benton Veer watched the ceremonial crew of the air-battleship fussing over their litanies and pre-flight checks through an ormolu-framed twodeeo panel in his villa, smiling his thin-lipped smile as they toiled. Some of those men had waited since their fathers' time for the order to be given, and now they cast off the mooring chains and fired up the engines with prideful satisfaction. In the hold of the vast airship squads of Celebrants in their Torquemada hoods and armor checked their weapons and offered up thanks to mighty Kronos for the chance to participate in history.

For Veer, the opportunity was a little more personal. In his studied opinion the only thing which Direktor Vanecke had done to make the world a better place was to broadcast the Game, and tonight he had failed in even that trifling task. That he should have lived for nearly an *hour* now past his allotted span galled the Grandmaster like a thorn in his boot.

Assured that his forces were rising up from out of the great hollow ziggurat of the Grief Division sanctum, Veer checked his own uniform one last time and posed in front of the twodeeo screen. It shimmered to a mirrored sheen as the picture faded, framing him to perfection.

Quite the gentleman officer, he fancied. The black brought out the ivory hue of his powdered skin, the stiff collar of riotmesh cupped his ornate periwig just so... and the acres of gold braid added that ineffable air of superiority which placed him above his fellow 'Burbanites.

Especially the loathsome Direktor Vanecke, for whom elegance held no function or appeal.

The last touch to his regalia was his scepter of office, an opera cane of rosewood topped with an ornate golden hourglass. Tiny antique clocks set into its sides would unleash the nanorobotic swarm which stole away his neighbor's mind.

Humming to himself contentedly Benton sprayed his cheeks with perfume and powdered rubies, then proceeded through the halls of his darkened villa to the French doors which opened out onto his lawn.

Strange – the immaculate false world within the belt should be *dark*, shaded deep blue by the lights of the Megatowers dappling its polyprop sky. Instead purple shadows coiled and shuddered as the flamelight of the burning city filtered in through its inflated walls. Veer could hear rain falling against the tight-stretched skin of his private little world, a tattoo like the roll of far-off drums. But inside all was silent, the air hushed and hot and tense, awash with the scent of sweat and oil. Perhaps the riots really were as bad as Holgarth had intimated? Perhaps the air-scrubbers and rad-filters of the Beltway had actually *failed*...

Veer took a pinch of snuff blended with pseudopiates and twist to bolster his courage. He was stepping into enemy territory now, unguarded, and a thrill of frisson crackled down his spine. He knew that the Direktor's house was empty, save for the massed machinery which kept him alive. And with the scepter of his office in hand, no machine in Elysium could touch him, warded as he was by the arcane artifice of Kronos. How it would please him to beard the lion in his den! How that withered thing called Vanecke would writhe when he walked right up to it and pronounced its doom!

How much blissful peace he could look forward to when the redoubtable Mrs Veer finally had her rose garden...

"Holgarth!" he hissed into the tiny microphone which perched like a beauty spot on his powdered cheek. "I want you in position above the target NOW! I can dissect his automated defenses myself – and I don't suspect there'll be any other trouble. Dear Octavio really hates to have people see him in his current state – and who can blame him?"

High above, standing on the command deck of the *Axis* as that sinister black ship sliced through the clouds, Jimson Holgarth was stricken almost speechless. From his lofty perch he could see what was happening in the streets, the crowds surging and seething like liquid as they scrabbled desperately for escape, the crush of bodies piling up against checkpoints and battlements designed to keep the Ferals out.

Now the very structure of Elysium was a trap, a vast meat-grinder which made his own Order Militant seem petty by comparison. In this one night the work of every Celebrant who ever lived had been eclipsed. And yet the Grandmaster was still fixated on his little feud? Well, at least Holgarth and these few blessed souls were safe above the carnage, aloft on black wings.

"We're bringing her into position right now, Sir. They're just about to fire the mooring clamps."

And afterward? Would they really go back down there, back into the jaws of the grinder? Even the ziggurat walls of the Sanctum couldn't possibly hold out against such madness. No, it would be better to strike out across the rad-lands, and find some far deserted place in which to live out the rest of their lives. If Veer had a problem with that he could always slip, *accidentally*, while standing in the airship's hatchway...

"Firing one. Two away. Three cleared... we're locked down." Holgarth's voice came in over the titanic triple thump of the clamps striking the metal dome of Direktor Vanecke's mansion, a carbuncle pushing up through the blue skin of the Belt.

"Wait for my mark," whispered Benton Veer, picking his way across the Omnivasive chief's lawn as though it was a minefield. Indeed, for all he knew it actually was! A gunmetal shimmer in the air betrayed his tiny guardian angels, spiraling like a double-helix around his body as he crept up to the ornate oak doors of the mansion. They'd shut down anything electronic which tried to harm him, fouling its circuits with sheer numbers and suicidal determination. The little machine which controlled them was the last of its marque, a thing designed for the boosted troopers of the Terminus Separatist Army more than twenty centuries ago. Layers of gold and filigree and ornamentation sealed it within its hourglass, just as arcana and superstition had accrued about the technology which forged it.

Certainly, Benton Veer had no idea how the little talisman worked – it was enough that he believed in it blindly. So he was unsurprised that Octavio's door stood ajar, tiny coils of incense smoke creeping over the black marble threshold. Suspended lamps shaped like cyclopean pyramids glowed ghostly pale blue, lighting the way into the den of his foe. Yes, the technomantic spells of the Scepter were with him, and all the crippled Direktor's defenses were stripped away...

That was when he heard the music.

Once I built a railroad, made it run...

The tune spun out, screwloose and warped, a plinking music-box melody over a sound like scuttling spider legs ... *made it race against time. Once I built a railroad - now that's done...*

Veer turned, serpent-quick, his body remembering for an instant his days on the streets, the slippery combat-sense of a frontline Celebrant. But there was nothing there. Still the song staggered along, louder now, the staccato of innumerable claws echoing in the sumptuous dark.

...Buddy, can you spare a dime? Once I built a tower to the sun, concrete and mortar and lime. Once I built a tower, now that's done... Buddy, can you spare a dime?

It brought its own light with it, a ruddy orange glow cast by a score of candles. When the unseen musician came stalking into the entrance hall the pillars seemed to bend and twist like snakes, curling over to pin Benton to the spot.

It was Direktor Vanecke - or what was left of him. The Grandmaster of Celebrants hadn't seen his face since the terrible fiasco of his final Game, his failed power-play to join the ranks of the Kheptarchy. What faced him now was a knot of mutilated flesh, a head floating in a bubbling tank of fluid.

A score of fat, dripping candles were melted onto its baroque frame with gobbets of wax.

Within that fishbowl globe Octavio Vanecke's face was distorted and ravaged, pierced by wires and tubes and needles feeding nutrients to his wasted tissue. Of the dark-haired, craggy warlord Veer remembered very little remained. Here a sheaf of hoses raped the cadaver's mouth, there a ring of rivets and hooks pinned its eyes open. Muscles twitched beneath his translucent white skin, while a forest of wires sprouted from the Direktor's scalp like a mane of hair.

And this thing wanted to *live*? Even without fathoming the arcane archaeotech which sustained his foe, the Grandmaster could tell that it was as much a machine of excruciation as of sustenance.

"Welcome, Mister Veer," spoke a voice from out of the many-jointed brass machine. "I knew you'd get here sooner or later. One of the pleasures of living right next door to the man who you know will one day try to kill you..."

Benton straightened himself up, adjusting his braid-encrusted peacoat with a contemptuous frown.

"You've had a good run, Direktor. Nice of you to come down from your aerie and do this like a gentleman, now that the game's up."

Why weren't the nanobots shutting him down? The Direktor's grisly conveyance - that scorpion of engraved brass - was clearly robotic in nature. And surely precious electricity coursed through the rebreathers and puriteks, blood-filters and whirring pumps which kept his head alive? Instead, the tight twin helix of whispering metal seemed to draw in tighter to Benton's body, shrinking back as the Direktor's mechanical palanquin clattered forward.

"Surrender? Oh, I think not, dear neighbor. I've had many years to prepare for this moment, and as you can surely imagine, I intend to savor it sweetly..."

The voice had begun to answer him before he even finished talking! Something was definitely wrong here...

He could smell the hot exhalation of oil from the machine now, as it reached out with one serrated pincer, clicking and whirring as it closed around his neck. The shimmering edges of its blades pared the tiny transparent hairs at his throat, so tight, so intimate... if he moved by even an inch he'd slice himself a new smile.

"I - I have men up above! They're only waiting for my word!" Veer meant it to come out as a snarl, but instead it was the squeak of a trapped rodent.

In that moment, as Grandmaster Veer felt a trickle of blood spill from his throat, he saw the great brass key winding down in the thing's back. No electricity! This machine was an automaton so primitive that the sorcery of Kronos couldn't touch it! And if he was pruned like a flower by this clockwork beast, the scepter of Celebrants would fall into the clutches of Omnivasive...

Benton Veer may have looked like a powdered fop, but he was at his core still the cruelest and most effective of killers – a street Celebrant who'd risen through the ranks by scrambling up a mountain of the dead. Indeed, his veneer of soft and pampered civility was as much a disguise as the false rubber head which faced him.

"I suppose you have the house surrounded, Veer?" sneered the lifeless machine, unaware that its charade had been uncovered. "But you just had to see to this mission personally, didn't you? Whyever do you think I wanted to live here in the first place..."

He slipped left, out of the wicked claw's embrace, jamming the steel-shod tip of the scepter up into its mechanism. At the same time he reached into the folds of his ornate peacoat, pulling loose a tiny pistol damascened and cloisonned beyond absurdity. Benton hit the ground on one knee, snarling into the sights of the tiny weapon, a thing from the *Aevum Iudicium* treasured by his Order Militant for centuries.

Its blast, when he tightened his finger on the firing stud was out of all proportion to its rococo decoration.

The false Direktor Vanecke spun back across the floor, its brazen claws gouging grooves in the marble. Its voice faltered as the filigree and gold of its body melted away to slag, blasted apart in a great hissing rosette by the thermic devastator in Benton's hand. Inside it was all springs and gears and copulating rods of metal, with a phonograph at its heart to broadcast the voice of the Direktor from discs of black vinyl. Such technomancy! Benton had never seen anything so advanced – more amazing even than the ancient magnetic tapes which were sometimes dug out of the rad-lands.

He had no time to wonder at the workings of that mechanical voicebox, however – the machine advanced on him again, its one remaining claw held high, snicking open and shut like a demon shear.

Benton could see the umbilicus of taut cables which directed the thing now, snaking off across the floor to disappear through a shadowed doorway. He dodged right, ducking down, waiting for the pincer to snap closed where his neck would have been, then he let loose another thermic blast, slicing the whole baroque arm from Vanecke's clockwork avatar.

How could it track him? Surely the real Direktor had no eyes, if he were truly as grotesque as the leering simulacrum before him...

Yes! Of course! The spiraling cloud of nanobots were literal-minded things, as unimaginative as their father Kronos. The cameras which were watching this little farce weren't dangerous in and of themselves. And the thing they directed was far too primitive to warrant their attention...

Benton danced back across the slippery marble tiles, grinning as the clockwork insect bulled at him, gesticulating with the stumps of its arms. He brought the little pistol in his hand up, right over his head, and searing force spewed from the deaths-head of its muzzle.

Plasterwork and fretted hardwood charred and ignited, bursting into vivid flames. And with it went the slick black camera-globe through which Octavio had controlled his pet.

The thermic devastator was spent – three shots were all that weak modern batteries could coax from its incinerator vanes. But now

Vanecke's tricky little toy was silent and immobile, completely helpless.

Ah, if only the Direktor himself was really there inside that globe of glass, as feeble as a newborn! Veer bent forward to stare into the milky eyes of the simulacrum, wiping away a sheen of condensation from the glass. Was it his imagination, or was the thing's mouth lolling open, its eyeballs rolling up in their rubber sockets, miming death?

"Oh, Octavio, you silly old fool!" chuckled the Grandmaster of Celebrants, tapping the globe with one jeweled fingernail. "This pageantry might have confused a lesser man, but you're dealing with the Grief Division! I'm not one of Akembe's walking corpses, you know!"

Slowly, lifelessly, the cadaverous face winked at him.

The hypodermic dart came out of the false Vanecke's mouth so fast that even Benton Veer's impeccable reflexes couldn't save him. Glass shattered as the pneumatic projectile lanced out from between those slack purple lips, a slick ovipositor of metal tipped with a primed syringe.

It pierced the Grandmaster's eyeball with a wet popping sound, pumping him full of liquid neurotoxin in a fragment of a second.

"Holgarth!" he gurgled, clawing at his swollen eye "Full assault! He... he wants the scepter! He must be stopp... "

But that was all the world would ever hear from the perfumed lips of Benton Veer. His whole nervous system rebelled as the toxin saturated his brain, crushing his windpipe and stopping his heart in mid-beat. Darkness closed in from every side as his spine curled over backwards, a counter-foetal death rictus enforced by uncontrollable muscles...

The last thing he saw was the face of a child, looming out of the shadows with a knife in one pale hand. Although he had the face of an angel there was a look in the boy's eyes that Benton found utterly chilling, even here on the threshold of death.

"Uncle, is he dead?" asked the child, kneeling at the Grandmaster's side. "Or shall I finish him myself?"

Benton Veer didn't hear the answer, as black waters closed over his head. But he fancied that the last thing he felt was mercifully sharp steel at his throat, parting the red-hot wires of his muscles and tendons, setting him free...

Ω

Down through hatchways in the Direktor's dome roof they came,

305

swarming down cables and chains, black-hooded wraiths armed with deadly technology. Down from the bobbing sleek belly of the *Axis Mortalis* came a small army of Celebrants - Undertaker commanders in their top hats and tails, Cremator squads strapped up with heavy flamethrowers, Grief Division troopers with their skull-faced pocketwatches swinging from their belts. One by one they dropped down into the sensorium dome, secure in the knowledge that their master had disabled Vanecke's security systems.

When the last one was in, and the vast emptiness of the dome rang with the click and slide of a hundred weapons being readied for war, the hatches slammed shut. The doors rumbled closed, sealing those unfortunate men inside as the screens came to life, one by one.

Pure white light flooded the sensorium, as a column of metal rose smoothly from the very center of the floor.

Fingers scrabbled at locks, and hammered at handles, and fists pounded against unyielding steel. Bullets ricocheted and whined, sparking from the diamond-fiber mesh of the screens. All to no avail.

Usually, that column of brushed steel would have borne up Octavio Vanecke's preservative tank, raising him up out of his office and into his private viewing sphere. Not this time, however.

This time a canister of gas rested atop a velvet cushion there, a canister of a very special substance concocted by the machines of Don Gianni Vexx for a princely sum.

As the column locked into place the gas began to hiss from a daisyhead of dispenser nozzles, quickly filling the entire sensorium with odorless, colorless weaponized adrenochrome.

Had these been the warriors of the Ashishim, trapped like rats under the dome of screens, they could have used the mind-bending effects of the drug to warp their bioelectric fields, to become - if only for a few seconds - superhuman. But these were nothing more than well-paid thugs, lackeys of Kronos not even good enough to prosecute the law. Unhinged laughter and fits of uncontrollable weeping rippled through the dome as the screens began to show images, winking on one by one.

They were the faces of death - real, honest death, not the sanitized soul-slavery of the Grief Division. Some came in live, fresh from the bloody streets. Others were archival, ancient, black and white, faded...

They cycled from one to the next, the bombed, brutalized and beaten, the tortured and diseased, faster and faster, until the whole great dome seethed and throbbed with death, until the air was thick with death, a crushing weight of carnage grinding into the souls of the Celebrants. Under such an onslaught and the twisted influence of the 'chrome it didn't take long for the first one to crack. They were all heavily armed, after all.

Flame licked out from a Cremator's cannon. A howling Undertaker put the muzzle of his pistol to his own head...

With the first shot the screens began to strobe, completing the image of a technomantic hell.

Bloody panic ran rampant for ten seconds, for twenty, bullets flying wild, flesh and bones tearing and snapping...

Within a minute it was all over.

Ω

The three warmekan exploded in a spray of darkness, metal fragments and chunks of reinforced armor skittering and tumbling across the gateway plaza. But surely his magnifiers deceived him? It was as if the corroded steel had been nothing more than a casing, an outer shell filled with some oily, slithering mass. Where the machines had faced Tsien, now there stood a trio of dark monolithic shapes, crudely humanoid, dissolving slowly into liquid as the Super-Cyben leaped back, his sword dragging behind him.

Gerhard Mitchell had seen some pretty strange things in his years on the force - mutants running rampant with twist in their veins, Ashishim spies flickering in and out of sight like deadly chameleons, gut-shot gang-rats still hacking at his exo-armor despite their mortal wounds. And other things, weirder things indeed on that night when the Liquid Tong had spiked his blood with drugs. His father and grandfather had told him tales of the Reclamation, of the bizarre and crafty foes who lurked in the R.T, waiting for the thin line of the Division to falter.

But he never thought he'd see one of his own cadet pupils cut down a dozen tank-hunter mekan in hand to hand combat. He'd only entertained paranoid fears about what was unfolding before him right now, the madness of Kronos turned against its people.

"Keep firing! Give him some support, dammit!" roared the Tutor-Captain over the thud and clatter of the gateway guns. "Nothing gets past these gates tonight!"

But in the back of his mind doubt and fear still twisted, reminding him of the tactical reality of his situation. The burning city lay before him, but if it was *Kronos* which he defied – the Machine's inner sanctum was at his back. A person had to scale each ring of the Beltway, all the way up to Oleander Avenue in order to reach Ground Floor One, the root of the space elevator.

In the basement levels beneath were the Process Core and Subduction Phase, the heart and brain of the Machine. Up above hung its control room, its fortress - and its armory. If Kronos really wanted to invade the Belt, really wanted to turn its whole populous into inhuman Cyben, the threat would surely come from *inside*...

Shells flew in a blaze of muzzle flashes, in a shifting cloud of cordite smoke. The veterans were pouring fire into the hazy black creatures which confronted Tsien, but to no avail. He was surrounded by a moat of bubbling, seething darkness now, and from its surface figures were rising, homunculi with too many arms and horns and teeth...

Even the massed battery of the gatehouse guns was powerless against them - shells plowed straight through the gelatinous substance of their bodies without detonating, arcing out over the Subcity below. Shrapnel shot cut them down, only to have them reform again, grinning, the razor shards studding their flesh like thorns.

Mitchell couldn't even see Tsien anymore - he was utterly surrounded by a mob of capering devils, black on black, looming up around him like a wave about to break. Then the communicator clipped to his webbing belt crackled into life.

"Gerhard! Can you hear me? It's no use trying to shoot them. I know what they are, what they want..."

Was that resignation he heard in the Super-Cyben's voice? Despair?

"Son, what they want its a taste of napalm. I've got Marty and Juan looking for some incendo ammo right now... just stand clear on my mark."

Tsien's laughter came through like static, bleak and inhuman.

"Trust me, that's not going to help, Captain. *We have to evacuate the belt.*"

"Evacuate?" snarled Gerhard, slamming his armored fist down against the parapet. "Like hell, trooper! Do you think I'm going to desert my post just because Kronos has dug up some fancy bioweapons?"

Even he didn't quite believe that one - nothing in the armories above matched those things. They were sickening just to look at. "Anyhow, we couldn't do it. Where can we go from here? The only way out is up..."

When the reply came back he could just imagine Eddie's sardonic little smile.

"Exactly... the only way out is right over your head."

As he looked up he saw it. Just the tail, bobbing out of reach above the top torus of the Belt, a black shark-fin of diamondmesh emblazoned with a white hourglass. The *Axis Mortalis*.

"By god, trooper, you might just have an idea there. That thing could carry a couple thousand at a time."

Tsien's voice was growing fainter as the saprophytes closed in, a solid dome of crawling night.

"Fall back when they come at you. Block by block, Mitchell. Use fire - anything that'll burn. Torch the houses as you go. I'll catch up with you at twenty-nine Ridgemont Street, torus two..."

The comm unit gave out with a squeal of feedback then, and Gerhard watched the boiling mass of nightmare creatures pounce, descending on Tsien from all sides. He squinted out over the ruined gateway plaza, watching the localized storm of darkness which raged there expanding and contracting like a living thing. He fancied he saw, once or twice, a thin line of silver slice through the shadows, and heard the hiss and scream of dying horrors on the breeze.

If anyone alive could actually survive out there, it was definitely his boy Eddie.

Ω

"I'll catch up with you at twenty-nine Ridgemont Street, torus two... "

His home. That little polyfoam box which almost all of his wages mortgaged from the Khept' banking clans. Tsien felt like a mythic sorcerer, his human heart torn out and kept safe in a rune-crusted bottle.

That was his reason. That was why he gritted his teeth and swung the blade, parting the noisome slop of the saprophytes like rancid butter, surgical, brutal...

Toria, Nik, Safira – the wife and kids, the photos in his wallet and stuck to the cracked plastic dash of his Comp Div cruiser. Three icon-images hovering in his mind as fire clawed and raved around their edges, as a wall of gibbering monstrosities tried to suck the flesh from his bones.

Manifest Dogma didn't offer a patron saint for things like him – just the lie that his mind would be stored away after death, waiting for a future of wonders in which he could be reborn. But some deity had seen fit to deliver the *Axis Mortalis* to him, and he wasn't about to waste the chance to use it. Would it be better to suffer slavery cased in steel, or in crawling black filth? Tsien had a plan which would save thousands of people from that grim choice.

He only hoped that Gerhard and his men could hold up their end of the operation...

Some invisible signal must have come from the Exalted Ones, because the circle of saprophytes came down on him like a breaking wave, ululating their fierce joy as they attacked. Now was the time for butchery, for rage – now he was glad that his humanity was locked away behind the cheap scrapwood door of number twenty-nine Ridgemont. This was a job for an unfeeling death-machine.

Tsien spun on one heel, his blade held out in front of him in both hands, its edge ripping through the rotten flesh of the saprophytes with a sound like tearing canvas. These weren't the Exalted – that unholy trinity were content to let their peons do the work, and die in slavering waves.

Up, and block a scything blade of bone, shearing it from its wrist. Down, and cleave into the bubbling torso of another horror, hearing its shriek of death-agony as he swung right, lopping the clutching pincers of a third off at the elbows. There were once-human things smothered under the saprophytic ooze – things which collapsed to slurry when their possessors died. How many, throughout all Elysium? Were there any left alive at all, barring the prisoners of the Beltway? Left, and spin, the scarred wedge of steel parting bone and gelid darkness, powering through six of the creatures with one blow.

If he'd been entirely human, the terror would have consumed him by now. The saprophytes would have swarmed over him, clawing into his skull to make a puppet of his flesh. But he'd willed that part of himself into oblivion. It was bound up in the images of Toria, of Safira and Nik, hidden in the tiny part of his brain which was still hot wet tissue. What drove his arm and powered his augmented muscles was the quicksilver mind of a Mark-Four Cyben, a thing designed from the ground up to slaughter.

Sure, its intended targets were the machines of the Blacksteel Unity, things which Tsien had never even heard of, let alone seen. But Kronos had been thoroughly briefed by his erstwhile enemy in the R.T, and he'd designed an engine of destruction which could transform human flesh into relentless metal...

They couldn't sink their hooks into his soul. And without pain and fear to tear open a hole in their victim's psyche, all the Saprophytes could do was die.

One more - in front of him, impaled through its leering face. Reverse the blade, tuck it back under one arm, and eviscerate another. He wielded it one-handed now, his silver claws lashing out to pluck eyeballs and jaws and hands from the press of bodies. *Make them respect him. Make these creatures of nightmare FEAR him.* And then his plan could take effect...

Tsien had no idea how many he killed, how many poor suffering human souls he set free before the wall of writhing darkness parted. The saprophytes shrunk back, cowering under their master's lash. Eddie plunged his blade into the concrete, leaving it quivering amid a slick of black blood, then leaned up against its blunt edge, shaking a cigarette from his pack. The last one. Lucky.

Tsien crumpled the box in one claw, popping his lighter with the other. Bloodsoaked rags fluttered from his massive frame.

The Exalted had called off their dogs, and now they faced him alone – Syliss like a bloated black leech with a human face, the dwarf with his single outsized arm dragging in the muck, and the tottering, flayed creature with its peeled-open eyes staring madness.

"So," asked Tsien, taking a long drag on his cigarette. "Is that all you assholes got for me?"

The dwarf cackled wildly at this, somersaulting up on top of its ball of darkness to perch there like a king on his throne.

"Oh, Quamiss *likes* this one. Quamiss thinks we should keep him for our pet!"

"Shut up!" bellowed Syliss, heaving himself forward on sticky pseudopods. "The Master-Father put *me* in charge! Quamiss and Phexx are only here for the meat-harvest. When we crack open the Beltway, *then* you feed."

"Oh, come on Syliss," said Tsien, struggling to stay nonchalant amid the charnel exhalation of the Exalted One's breath. "Let him give it a try. I've always wanted to beat up a midget."

He sauntered forward, as though the trio of monsters were a bunch of harmless street-sprogs.

The tall, tottering Phexx tittered behind one dripping hand as Quamiss scowled.

"That's right – come and get me. I can just guess why you sold out to this freak-circus, shortarse... the only way you'll ever touch a woman is if she's already dead and rotten."

Tweak the threads, the raveled roots of darkness... How had the master of these things bullied and cajoled Tsien? What could it have promised a deformed little man from down in the sublevels?

Quamiss leaped down from his ball of saprophytic ooze, conjuring a hook-tipped tentacle from it with a gesture. Oh, he'd been just right. Some desires and frustrations were *universal*.

"Let me flay him, Syliss!" pleaded the dwarf, as that black tentacle split and split and split again. "Let me teach him that owning a tongue is now a *privilege*!"

"Yeah, fatty, give the runt a break! We could all use a laugh, right?" Tsien cracked his knuckles, the cigarette dangling from his lip. And despite Gurden Syliss's bellow of rage, it was just too much for the diminutive Quamiss to bear. He flung himself at his tormentor in a spin, his arm pulsing with unnatural muscle and sinew. The fist at its end blurred, a hammerhead of spiked bone.

Tsien sidestepped it easily, wrapped his claws around the little man's bicep, then pivoted into a throw. Quamiss hit the ground with his fingers splayed, flexing like an acrobat as he rebounded from the bloody concrete. His feet came together in a spinning drop-kick which struck Tsien in the small of his back.

The little man was spitting words in some alien language - curses or incantations or both. The Super-Cyben had barely managed to regain his footing when a ball of Saprophytic darkness hammered into him, sticky and wet and vile, bringing him to his knees. At once whiplike tendrils of ooze sprung from the ball, lashing his hands and feet tight. Now he was tethered to the heaving mass of it, and the Dwarf was capering in front of him, cutting a little jig of triumph as his comrades laughed.

"M-mighty m-m-machine m-mman! So easily defeated! So puny is h-his steel com-p-pared to the New Flesh!"

Phexx giggled, arching over to drip acidic drool into Tsien's face. His hooks and needles glistened wetly as he spoke. "Praise Asag'raal! Praise the Father of Sorrow!"

"Perhaps the Master was wrong about this one. Perhaps he *is* just meat..." Syliss oozed forward, extending a thick rope of darkness from his shoulder. At its tip budded a pustule of rainbow-sheened oil, swelling and splitting...

A skeletal figure tumbled from inside, black worms wrapping around its bones before it hit the ground. It was all that remained of Dravin Coyle. With a twitch of his will Syliss sent his old commander staggering across to grip Eddie's shoulders.

"Let me have him!" snarled Quamiss, shattering the concrete with a blow from his single fist. Behind Tsien the surface of his saprophyte-ball was sucked back into a gaping maw, sprouting a handful of writhing tongues. "I'll spit out the metal for you to keep as a trophy, Syliss. But he craves the gift of torment! Oh, I can feel it in him..."

Tsien's head was bowed, the smoke from his cigarette still rising as it burned down to the end. But that fuming core of ash wasn't the only source of heat here.

Oh no. Deep in his augmented body Tsien could feel the thermal levels rising, as he denied the mark-four system its precious coolant by force of will. After a protracted battle the user manual implanted in his skull recommended leaving a full set of thermo-dump vanes extended for two hours. Now his belly seethed with fire, an inner furnace making his cybernetic implants boil.

Unless he twisted it just right. *Like this...*

Where the coils of shadow clenched his wrists and ankles, the metal skin of the Super-Cyben suddenly blazed white-hot. Billows of smoke roiled out from those foul tentacles, making them wither and sizzle and flail, spreading the fire. The misshapen dwarf shrieked in agony, feeling the pain of his surrogate flesh. *He was burning, melting, his bones turned to incandescent iron, and there was nothing he could do to stop it!*

Quamiss lashed out blindly at Tsien, his fist a hammer-strike which could have split steel. But it was caught in a grip like the jaws of a vise – one of the Super-Cyben's own chrome-skinned hands snapping shut around it. Quamiss lashed out with the scourge of pain and terror which was his master's gift, but that too slammed up against unyielding metal, the cold battle-cogitators which whirred and clicked behind Tsien's eyes. Now the grinning cyborg had his shoulder-stump in his other hand and he was off, running, coming up off his knees like a sprinter from the blocks.

Phexx recoiled like a scalded snake, tottering back in horror from the leaping flames. Syliss's tethered homunculus wasn't so lucky – the blaze spread quickly, setting its black skin to boiling. Grave-gases vented in plumes of green and purple fire as Dravin Coyle finally escaped, melting down to waxy slurry.

Three steps, four, great bounding piston-driven strides. The dwarf writhed in his grip, turning to see where his captor was headed...

And he screamed. Briefly.

The notched steel monolith of Tsien's sword still stood proud from the splintered concrete of the Gateway Plaza, and the last thing that Exalted Quamiss ever saw was the flicker of witchfire down the edge of its blade.

The body of Asag'raal's chosen was unnaturally tough, leathery and musclebound, but Tsien had him by the shoulders now, and he pushed down with all his titanic strength, feeling the crycelial sawteeth of the blade bite into Quamiss' spine. Stinking black blood poured from the little man's mouth as he thrashed in agony, pinned on the rack of Tsien's fists, that relentless edge bisecting him from head to pelvis. The Super-Cyben braced his feet against the concrete, his face twisted into a rictus as he worked his butchery. Black blood splattered and hissed and steamed. Quamiss' cries became a gurgle, a rattle... then silence.

Tsien spat out the smoldering butt of his cigarette, turning to face Syliss and Phexx with one twisted half of their compatriot's body clenched in each hand. They flopped and convulsed raggedly, nerves sparking as the black oil dried to dust, leaving those pitiful remains mummified.

"This is for your master!" shouted Tsien, a demon figure all steaming dark blood and blazing eyes, silver teeth and furnace-red thermal vanes. "This is my sacrifice, that he should know me by!"

Now the two remaining exalted were preparing for battle, Syliss spawning an army of homunculi from boils on his skin, Phexx's tower of flesh splitting into a knotted mess of phallic tentacles. Mewling mouths smacked their lips at the tip of each one. Saprophytes of the rank and file seethed in the gaps between the two monsters, held back by a thread of thought.

"I will take my place, Lord of the New Flesh!" roared Tsien, casting down half of Quamiss' ravaged body to grind it under his steel boot. "And you will accept me as the cruelest of your chosen! This world will know me as – the High Exalted!"

And with that he bit down into the dried-out, mummified flesh of his slain foe, tearing off a chunk of tasteless black meat aswarm with the infection of the Worm.

His last human thought was a silent prayer, to whichever sick-minded gods were listening.

Let this all work out. Let Gerhard not fail. Let Toria and Nik and Safira survive...

Then the darkness had him, and it was the pain of his transformation all over again.

Anointed

"THAT'S ALL THE time I can give him" she said, her hands balled up into fists. "Ask your astrographers! Ask anyone who can feel the Vision! They're coming, Devine, and we've got no choice."

"The 'lifters are primed, Commander. The volunteers are on board. And the... the Cargo is in place."

Devine waved the man away with one emaciated hand.

"Listen, Cee - please. We only get once shot at this. If you get it wrong, you'll only set that thing free again. Feedback could take you! It could eat your mind, and then what?"

Her eyes flashed anger, frustration - and fear. She knew what the Forge could do to a mind that wasn't ready for it. It took hundreds of willing sacrifices just to stop it, and now they'd try to control it with only one. Hers...

"Devine, it doesn't matter anymore. If those things get to us, do you think we can deny the codes from them? If I fail, we die, and if we do nothing, we die... I - we - need help."

Devine's face softened, then, fading from stern to careworn in a heartbeat.

"You're going back for him, aren't you? For 'Afia 330..."

For second she wanted to deny it, to hide behind excuses like duty and responsibility. But he'd seen right through her, and she knew it.

"Yes," she said quietly, unable to look the old fanatic in the eyes "Yes, I am. He lives, Devine. I know he does. And if anyone can use the Forge right, it's him, not me."

He looked like he might break then, that the pressure had wound him up so tight that all he could do was snap. The sound of turbine engines was rising now, and flak-suited Ashishim bustled around them, navigators and soldiers and techs. Devine wiped his hand over his eyes, and pinched the bridge of his broken nose. Still, nothing could crush the dense, burning core of his faith.

"Go, then. And if we die, I'll blame you for nothing."

He took one of her hands in both of his, and bowed his hooded head over them for a second.

"Commander 187, we're waiting for you on the flight deck! Commander..."

The junior tech's voice trailed off to silence as he watched Devine straighten up again, a look of wistful sadness in his eyes. CeeAn leaned *forward and kissed him once, on the bald dome of his head.*

"Wait for us, Magus. When the change comes, you'll know I chose the right path."

Then she turned away, hitching a canvas bag of guns up over her shoulder, and climbed up into the cavernous hold of the 'lifter. The noise from the engines cranked up past pain, past sound itself, shaking the cracked concrete of the landing pad as those ponderous craft clawed their way skyward.

"You led us from the gates of hell, Anointed," prayed Devine as dust and smoke swirled around him, his eyes on two pinpoints of flame against the clouds. "May the light which guided you then be manifest now..."

DOCUMENT INSERT: MULTIPLICITY ARCHIVES DEPARTMENT

K/Z - (alt. Kayzi, Kazee):

Descriptive of a synthetic phyle of Subcitizens who can trace their origins back to the Kirov Memorial Cosmodrome nuclear bunkers in the old state of Kazakhstan.

Of mixed Slavic and Central-Asian heritage, these survivors created quite a thriving civilization for themselves underground, until their facility's fission reactor ran out of fuel rods. The now legendary Matriarch of the Exodus, Ilya Kayzi led her people out of their underground fastness (against the protests of a sect who maintained that the outside world was nothing but an illusion) and across all of irradiated Europa to Elysium. Their relative lack of genetic mutation was looked upon favorably by the Guardian Machine of the last city, and they were amongst the first tribes of the Sub, employed to keep the ancient devices which powered Elysium running.

Nowadays 'Kayzi' is an increasingly common surname in the Subcity, with over twenty thousand branches of the clan taking it as their legal determinative. It is also (predictably) used as a racial slur to mean one who is runty, skinny, inquisitive, nosy and suspicious, all traits attributed to the long-time bunker dwellers.

Dep. Lt. Chesterfield Djenko 'Phyles of the Subcity' second impression.

17 Aevum Oblivio
Overwatch

Technician Zhe swum in icy darkness, feeling his way along a submerged section of tunnel with the ping and squeal of inbuilt sonar. He'd seen the footage of Nyl raising the chrome Ark from its Abyss, and he'd watched it devour the living essence of three human beings as it powered up. Just like the Forge itself, but in miniature.

Such a device would be as devastating as unchained antimatter at the right place and time... in the middle of a pitched space battle, for example.

With the fleets of the Unity and Multiplicity closing in like the jaws of a vise, it would be nice to have at least one trick up his sleeve. Zhe had seen what was left of Samorshan after the Black Advent. He'd flown through the asteroid field that used to be Oolix. It paid to have a bigger gun when you were negotiating with stubborn bastards like Kataphrakt-Admiral Yrr Bosphasian. The Ark would be perfect, if only he could find it in time.

The tunnel slanted suddenly, becoming a flight of rusted stairs, and Zhe's head broke the water in a pool of stinking slime. Tendrils and mats of it dripped from the crown of his head- all the better to camouflage him from...

Yes. He was here.

The first bullet nearly took his head from his shoulders – not fatal for a Technician, with his second brain tucked away safe in his chest, but very inconvenient. The second whipcracked past him, supersonic, and he jinked right, cursing his own lack of ordnance.

All those pretty weapons, be they ever so primitive, were sloughed away to scrap in the depths of the Exalted at the gates. There was something about archaic guns – so solid, so dependable. So easily adapted into a club when their ammo failed.

Zhe couldn't even repeat his little trick from up in space, and materialize weapons from out of his own flesh. Those morphic implants were strictly one-shot affairs, and he'd burnt them out fighting the golems of Everdark. Now he faced the Tin Man alone, with only his bare hands.

A third and fourth shot followed him down as he dove back into the water, bubbling wakes trailing behind them. Zhe could only hope that Ruby and Straw and Big Leon were either dead or safely snap-frozen, or else he may have blundered into a trap.

Either way, it made him angry.

There was simply no time for this nonsense! Didn't that idiot machine know that the world was about to be torn apart? Of course not – the Tin Man was a device of severely limited scope, a predator-savant. And yet... Hadn't Haszan and Kaito survived the attentions of the Emerald City Gang? Perhaps there was something in the files which could help him...

Deep in the Stygian depths, breathing through a set of gill-slits in his neck, Technician Zhe's focus spiraled in through the weeks and days and hours of footage inside Kronos' mind. To another place of drowned steel under black water, to the radioactive slime of the seabed...

Two hours passed with nothing to do but worry. The Scourge purred along at twelve knots beneath the oily chop of the Atlantic, heading out into deep water. On board, its crew of two were hunched over a tiny little threedeeo set, a baseball-sized antique receiver.

"This is God's *modus operandi*, people. This is the way He works. Look at Nineveh, Sodom, Gomorrah, Las Vegas - all struck down by his wrath! Each and every one of those cities was a place of sin, a temple of vice and greed. Now look at your own city, your *Elysium*. Don't you think that a time of judgment is inevitable? How long do you think God will tolerate the decadence of this villainous cesspit?"

The face which filled the threedeeo globe was rabid with vehemence - a death-mask with foam- flecked lips and bulging eyes. It was a face familiar to all Elysium – or at least, to every Subcitizen who could afford a threedeeo set.

Deuteronomy Jones, the last of the Pentecostal warlords.

"All I'm saying is that he's completely insane," said Jaq, leaning back between the seats in the Scourge's tiny cockpit. Kaito froze the frame on the old preacher's blazing eyes, his blue-black skin glistening with sweat under a bank of hot halogen floods. "Have you actually sat through one of his sermons? The guy's got more loose screws than a mekan junkyard."

The Kayzi cupped his chin in one hand, scrutinizing the image of his prey. Deut' had to be a century old, with his tonsure of curly white hair and his wrinkled, bible-black skin sagging from his skull. But you didn't live that long as a wanted fugitive if you were *crazy*. And you certainly didn't hack Omnivasive's security to pieces twice a week if your brain wasn't as sharp as a razor.

The problem was finding a guy like Jones if he wanted to stay hidden.

Kaito hadn't told his friend yet, but they only had a few more hours worth of air left in the control bubble of the Scourge. After that they'd have to surface, and then they'd be a juicy target for Kronos' guns. The Machine was likely to take a dim view of Scourgejacking Subcity punks.

"Crazy or not, he's got the means to save tens of thousands of people," said the Kayzi, still slumped forward over his control console. "If the whole city tries to just pile down the Spillway then it's gonna be a massacre. All that thing from space will have to do is remember to chew and swallow."

Jaq grunted, conceding the point. Although it *would* be nice to see a few hundred Confederate boys get fed through that kind of mincer...

"I have to keep a tight watch on that mekan I've stolen - the one that's gonna dig 'Afia out. So in the meantime, could you keep an eye on the sonar, try and pick him up? I know it's probably a waste of time, but you can't hide a ship like his *that* easily, right?"

Sure, it was impossible. But Jones and his Pentecostals had managed to evade Kronos for decades... and if you were counting impossibilities, tonight had already supplied a lifetime's worth.

Kaito's eyes went dim and blank as he turned his full concentration to his bio-onboard rig, using the antiquated interface of the Scourge to tweak the brain of his sequestrated warmekan. The things he saw through its camera eyes were enough to make him sick with fear - the city was tearing itself apart. It had only been five hours since he parked his chopper up above the Valley View. But five hours of war can change a place. Look at what seven hours had done, back on Reclamation Day...

Random shots ricocheted off the rusted armor of the tank-hunter as it lumbered through the streets, heavy weapons swinging at the end of its piston arms. He was a big target – the only thing moving through the oily smoke and flames in some areas, where even the dying were too scared to cry out...

Each individual Hab and civic block had become a separate little fortress, the panicked defenders inside driven mad with fear. Luckily most of them were only armed with civilian guns - good enough for blasting muggers and thieves, but useless against the armored might of a tank-slaying warmekan.

They hadn't just been shooting at *him*, though. It looked as though they'd turned on each other as well.

The streetfront facades of most buildings were cratered and blackened, spattered with blood. Bodies lay twisted in the street, some of them crushed to unrecognizable smears by the treads of tanks and the steel claws of Kronos' army. Among them the charred wreckage of ruined mekan still smoldered, hydraulic fluid mingling with the blood in the gutters. In some places whole streets were drenched crimson, as though gore had rained down from above. But surely not? Otherwise the mad sermons of Deuteronomy Jones might actually be coming true...

Once or twice Kaito was sure he caught a glimpse of something moving in the corner of the mekan's camera eyes – dark, fluid shapes skulking in the alleyways, eyeless and black. In the mouth of one narrow crawlspace he saw a headless body covered in unmistakable teeth-marks. Oh, he was glad he was just an electric trace inside the head of a stolen machine. Something had come through this neighborhood like a reaping engine, perpetrating atrocities. The little severed limbs of children, the scattered furniture and clothes, the shattered buildings like broken-open skulls...

"Kayzi! Hey, Kayzi!" The image blurred and pixilated before his eyes, a nightmare interlaced with the dull gray metal of the Scourge's cockpit. "Come on, Kaito - get back here, man!"

It was Haszan, shaking him by one shoulder like a pitbull worrying a hamster.

With a despairing sigh the Kayzi set his tank-hunter on autopilot and jacked out of the interface, scowling.

"Dammit, Jaq! I was nearly there, right on top of his trace! I thought you were supposed to be looking for Jones and his *Archangel whatever-it's-called.*"

Kaito rubbed his fingers into his aching eyes, trying to clear the purple starbursts from his head. All he could see was a murky gray-green blur, shot through with beams of yellow radiance.

It took him a second to realize that this was an LCD screen, cranked down on its mounting right in front of his face. Jaq Haszan's gleaming silver hand held it tight.

"Uhhh – what exactly am I looking at here? Is there something wrong with the sonar system?"

Haszan leaned in over the screen, pointing with a length of broken-off antenna like a schoolmaster.

"Well, I found out how to launch some scanner drones from out of this thing's ass," he said, "And *this* is what one of them's picked up. See, this here is us." he tapped his pointer on a little cigar-shaped blur in the corner of the screen. Above it a huge shadow moved, drifting slowly in a cloud of yellow light.

"And that?" asked Kaito, his heart in his throat. Had Kronos sent something even worse than the Scourge to destroy them?

With a twist of his chrome digits Jaq zoomed the drone's camera in, cutting through the undersea murk to reveal a sunken edifice welded and bolted and riveted together from the hulks of ruined ships. Searchlight beams stabbed out from its corroded flanks like insect legs, and every inch of its hull was painted with ornate crucifixes.

"Well, that's what I wanted to tell you, K. I didn't need to find the *Archangel Uriel*. It's found *us*."

Ω

CeeAn 187 was dead.

She had figured her whole life that she'd greet that kind of news with panic, with furious disbelief.

With *something*.

But actually it was quite a relief. Nothing else could possibly go wrong now - at least not for her. This was just as bad as it got, unless those madmen from the Vatican were right...

CeeAn knew she was moving, accelerating through timeless, formless darkness up and away from the ghost-lights of the world. There was no sign of the flaming purgatory or the gilded heaven the Ecclesiarchs promised - but there was nothing else, either. No neon trace leading her back down into the R.T, no glowing beacon of the Chrome Ark to light her way home.

No, this time it was final. She must have been blown to pieces, crescent unit and all when the node went up...

And what was in there, anyway? *What in the world had defeated her?*

If she was still alive the thought of being humiliated in battle would have made her furious. But here it was impossible to care. She couldn't even remember why they had to operate on the node, why 'Afia thought it was so important to shut it down...

That stopped her. His name was like an anchor cast out into the dark, hooking into the soft black nothingness. If he wasn't here, he must still be alive!

The slower she went the more she saw, as if her eyes had been blurred with speed.

No eyes now, of course. And yet the memory of them could see with perfect clarity...

This place between realities was like the eye of a hurricane, a calm tunnel through the center of a churning maelstrom. Down below was the rippling, watery membrane of the world, a cerulean eye through which she could see innumerable sparks moving - the souls of the living. Above, high over her head was another portal, an inverted pool which glowed and faded as if something deep in its liquid heart was pulsing, slow and regular. Both gateways were the size of oceans, immeasurably vast.

Now she was moving at a crawl, barely rising between the twisting walls of the maelstrom. Things were blazing past her on every side - tight scribbles and scrawls of light, mad blurs trailing sparks as they ascended. With a shock she realized that there were her fellow-travelers - the dead, sleeting in from the world and on toward that impossible ocean above. They were rising in iridescent clouds like sparks from a bonfire - too many, surely for all of them to have died of natural causes? What was Abdulafia facing back there which could unleash such horror?

Her doubt and fear jerked her to a stop as if she'd reached the end of an immensely long tether. She tried with all her will to force herself down, back toward the world. As if she could cram her soul back into her incinerated body, pull each atom back together with sheer determination...

That was when she realized she was attracting *attention*.

The walls of the maelstrom weren't made up of vapor or smoke, but of writhing darkness, slick and oily, a substance she had only ever seen -

Inside the node. Infecting the vivisected soul of Magus Verlaine, smothering his mind under a slick of pain and horror...

It was a black melange of masticating jaws, rolling eyes, grasping hands, dripping organs, torn-open bellies, twisted spines...

And it was reaching out to her. Seductive and slow, a pulpy tentacle pushed out from the wall of the maelstrom to grope at her blindly. Perhaps it would have grabbed her and dragged her under with those other damned souls, if the intellect driving it hadn't been occupied with other atrocities. Thick ropes of darkness erupted from the maelstrom in a hundred places, plunging down and down like gnarled roots to rape the living world.

Surely that was *wrong*. Surely that thing had no place in reality - it was terrible enough in this un-place tight between life and death. Those foul roots writhed and pumped and heaved, forcing the foetid matter of the walls down into Elysium as if they were regurgitating a crop of suffering.

CeeAn broke away, panicked, everything blurring and fading as she rushed blindly up and away. She could make out the shape of a pulsing heart beneath the inverse ocean, a thing the size of a planet with the gravity-well of a bloated supergiant sun. For some reason she wondered why it hadn't done anything to stop the horrors below. But why would it care?

Why did she think it *could*?

CeeAn risked a final look back down through the maelstrom, to where a storm of blue sparks spiraled up between a tangle of thorny tentacles. Some of them slowed and stopped, and tried to go back. Some of them weren't as lucky as CeeAn, and they were dragged under the oily surface of that turbulent wrack, extinguished forever...

No. It was wrong.

With that thought she stopped, close enough to reach out and touch the surface of the vast liquid membrane above her. It was utterly impossible to restrain her curiosity. Even dead, she was still CeeAn 187.

She reached out. She touched.

Ripples raced out in vast concentric rings from the spot where her fingertip grazed the surface, and she felt the immense heart of light thump once, a noise like some huge subterranean drum. A pulse of radiance burned through her with that sound, filling her head with afterechoes and shadows.

Voices. Faces. Images...

History unrolled for her in that single infinite second, a billion upon a billion lifetimes earthed through her like lightning. It was like the Vision of the Ashishim all over again, but on a titanic scale, a scale which dwarfed the crude mechanisms of Kronos.

That beating heart which floated behind the veil was the seed of a new world, one which would be woven out of chaos when the universe ran down. She saw love and hate and loss, pain and triumph, war and joy and grief in that flash of otherworldly light. The ripples from her touch were swells the size of mountains by the time they reached the shores of that inverted ocean, and now they were curling back, returning.

The light was fading as they came, back down into its tight-packed shell of souls, taking all those billions of voices with it. She understood - the Wetsystems of Elysium were a crude cargo-cult imitation of this immortal seed, planted in the Aematerium the day the first mind dared to imagine. CeeAn had communed, if ever so briefly, with each and every person who had ever lived – all but those who had been devoured by the maelstrom below.

And yes, it *was* wrong. It wasn't part of the great breathing, pumping supersystem of the multiverse at all, but a parasite on an immense scale. She saw it as it really was, in a sliver of frozen time - a thing which filled a whole dimension, an appetite with teeth...

Waves towered above her now, foam-capped breakers seething in from every side. The ripples of her touch had come back from the far shores of the hanging ocean, and now they broke.

The force of it was simply indescribable. In this place where physical laws seemed not to apply it was as if she'd been struck by an entire planet, a hammer the size of the sun.

CeeAn fell back toward the world in a power-dive, the churning walls of the maelstrom blurring as she accelerated, down through a tangle of gelid black roots, down toward the rippling blue surface of reality. Snake-tongue whips of darkness lashed out at her from every side, too slow to catch her. And then the water was right beneath her, shattering as she splashed down, closing over her head with the echo of tolling bells. Pain came with it – excruciation shunted in from a body which she thought she'd never see again.

Muscle and skin and bones and veins and teeth. Nerves and hair and blood unfolding, and now a spark inside it, forced back into a world of suffering.

The pain was all too real, and the afterimages of that bizarre interzone between life and death hazed like static, blown away by the raving agony of her flesh. Her mind struggled to hold onto the feeling of that heartbeat of light, the touch of her fingertip against that inverted ocean. But it was impossible, like trying to grab a handful of smoke. The things she'd heard and seen in communion with the world-seed became an indistinct blur, crushed under a mountain of pain.

Crushed... *yes*, something was pressing down on her like the jaws of a hydraulic clamp. Blind, burning, CeeAn struggled to get her hands under the metal beam which lay across her chest. It took all of her strength to shift it enough to breathe, then her arms gave out and the terrible weight pinned her down again. If only she had another hit of nektar, a precious capsul of 'chrome to boost her battle-clone body!

It was a foolish wish, she knew.

After all she'd endured the combat-drug would kill her quicker than suffocation.

Only her own strength to rely on, now. Only raw, unaugmented human will.

Reach through the pain, fingers tight around the jagged edges of the steel, and push...

CeeAn caught a flickering glimpse of hell as she strained, a taste of the sheer alien *wrongness* of that parasite-thing. It had no place there – and even less in the world of the living. Out here there was suffering enough *already*.

The anger gave her strength, enough to heave the beam from off her chest and away down a mountain of debris. She took a deep, racking breath, and lost it all in a coughing fit as dust and smoke swirled around her.

Everything hurt. Most of her was broken.

But she was alive.

Sound came rushing back now, and she could hear people crying and screaming and wailing in the distance. Though her eyes were closed she saw them – fingers clawing at the rubble, bloodshot eyes brimming with tears, the wounded writhing in their dirty bandages...

The images burned in her head, an echo of something she'd heard and seen at the core of the world-seed. A commonality of human suffering shared by every victim of war and disaster, bound up in that great slow heart.

And a single shred of memory – a place, deep in the equatorial jungle. A man, rad-burned and dying, his skin blistered raw as he crawled across a treadplate floor. Fingers stripped down to muscle and bone scrabbled across a fallen keyboard, setting security codes, sealing away a sanctuary for the living.

CeeAn's eyes snapped open as the knowledge bloomed in her mind, unfurling like a neon flower.

There was a way out. There was hope, despite the crawling disease which had broken through into the world. And because she'd helped let that foul thing in, it was her duty to cast it out again.

Lying there, crucified atop a smoking pile of rubble, CeeAn let the Vision roll over her, picking out in a tracery of fire the horror and turmoil of Elysium burning.

It was time to leave this place. Tonight.

And she was going to take all of them with her.

Ω

Jaq Haszan was too tired to notice when the flycam poked its tiny head out from the side of his wristwatch. He had no idea that the little machine had changed ownership while he and Kaito rode the Scourge down through a maze of concrete pipes into the black Atlantic. In fact, he was trying to take a nap.

The sensation of its hair-thin legs crawling across his skin was no different to the dangle and drip of a droplet of sweat, and the noise of its ornithopter wings was masked by the whisper of the cockpit's ancient filters. Jaq was a veteran of Elysium's lowest habs. He could sleep through *anything*.

So when the 'cam burst from a vent in the side of the Scourge he had no idea that he'd been betrayed.

Omnivasive still owned and operated the little steel insect, and the chairman of the board had gladly supplied its command codes to his errand-boys, the Emerald City Gang. As soon as the flycam broke the surface its wings blurred into motion, carrying it up above the toxic waves, up into the dark where Elysium burned like a great viking pyre-ship on the horizon. Arclights and flames burned the belly of the clouds crimson, but it wasn't the visible spectrum which the 'cam needed to fulfill its treachery.

It spiraled up like a mote of ash, gaining height. As soon as it reached six hundred feet it began to broadcast its position - along with a complete audio record of the last three hours.

Jaq and Kaito were nailed down tight.

Down in the R.T - on the edge of the Celestial Kingdom's docks - Aitken Straw smiled a lipless, toothy smile behind his plastic mask.

"Ruby, we've got 'em. Ten miles out, making for a rendezvous with that Pentecostal freak Deut' Jones."

Lady Alvarez rattled off a string of orders in Cantonese to the C-K longshoremen who clustered around her, then peeled off a fat wad of Slades for their leader - a tall, thin man wearing the archaic costume of a Mandarin scholar. Rather than silk and cotton, this man's outfit was sewn from carbon riotmesh.

He was one of the last Celestial shipmasters still tied to the pier - almost everything else which could float was already headed for the mainland. He'd held out for refugees with better currency, and the Gang were pleased to oblige.

"Leon, Tin Man, get on board. Captain Jiang here is gonna come hunting with us - I guess life as a pirate is just too damn boring for him. I'm sure that a certain general military draft for all Celestial citizens has nothing *at all* to do with it."

The captain bowed, gap-toothed and smirking as he folded his hands into his voluminous sleeves.

"Lady Alvarez, I am simply honored to assist an outlaw of your *stature*." He purred that last word with a lascivious leer, his eyes all over her body. "As to my allegiance to the Son of Heaven - I'm sure that the Divine One has many other warriors more worthy than an *honest fisherman* to protect him."

Ruby smiled.

"Honest fisherman, huh? I like that. Honest fishermen don't try and jump their passengers three miles out, and end up as bait."

She cocked an eyebrow at him, resting her hand on the butt of her railpistol as she cast a critical gaze over the captain's modified pleasure-launch. "*Shantung Ryu*? I just hope she's fast, Jiang. I have to get back here to conclude some other business tonight."

The Scarecrow packed up his laptop and tugged his greatcoat tight around his shoulders, following at his mistress' heels as she prowled down the gangplank.

"Believe me, buddy." he whispered to the captain as he slunk past. "That little toy blaster you've got up your sleeve won't even slow her down. Just concentrate on not sinking, alright? I hate the sea."

The mesh-armored mandarin slid his needle-pistol back into its concealed holster with a jagged grin, showing a clean pair of palms to the crazy *gwailo* with the plastic face.

Sometimes it was better to just play it safe and leave the piracy to professionals.

Ω

Down in the crushing darkness, in a little pocket of air beneath a mountain of rubble, Abdulafia 330 dreamed. He wasn't sure if his eyes were open or closed - it was just as dark either way. Maybe they'd been cored out of his skull by the black fire of the Worm. Maybe his power had failed already, and he was drifting in limbo, dead...

It didn't matter. The images kept coming, sleeting through his mind in a mad rush. He tried to focus and meditate, centering his power as the Illuminatus had taught him...

It made no difference.

He watched Jhenna fall away from him in slow motion, her eyes wet with tears, her hair streaming out as she dropped through the jagged hole in the floor. Down below her he could see people fighting and dying, explosions like tiny fireworks flickering around the edges of her silhouette. There was a laminated slab of dead flesh and plastic tubing coiled tight around her waist - the arm of a Cyben, taking her down to hell with it, a ticking bomb fused to its neck. Any second now its timer would run out, and both of them would be reduced to windblown ashes.

This was the nightmare which clawed and scrabbled at the inside of 'Afia's skull in the darkness of the Pit every night. The one he screwed down tight with drugs and meditation.

But this time there was a twist. This time the wide-eyed, horrified face falling away from him was different.

It was CeeAn 187, and the battlefield below wasn't the muddy razorwire scrawl of Reclamation Day. It was a plain of black ice, oily and jagged, from which a billion rotting hands reached out, welcoming...

He didn't need the services of a psychoanalyst to know what it meant. He'd as good as delivered her into the jaws of Asag'raal, where the vilest of atrocities were mundane. Compared to *that*, Jhenna's death was quick and clean. Compared to the weight of that guilt, the tons of burnt plasticrete and steel above him were feather-light...

Just the thought of it made the rubble heave and shift, powder trickling down into his mouth as he gasped for breath. It took all of his power to keep this little space open, a coffin under a mountain of shattered masonry. Self-loathing could wait, but gravity couldn't. The slab of plasticrete which hung above him was almost touching his chest now. The slightest tremor could crush him flat.

One more slip and he'd be fleshless, reduced to an electronic trace inside his black crescent. And if *that* failed, its batteries bled dry deep under the rubble - well, then he'd be gone for good.

The urge to let it happen was almost overwhelming.

Wasn't it what he deserved anyway, for being such a fool? If self-sacrifice could bring CeeAn back, he'd have let the vise-jaws snap shut on him in an instant. But what Jaq Haszan had told him was true, much as he hated to admit it.

They needed him. He was a weapon of war, the sword of the Illuminatus, and tonight of all nights the Ashishim had to know he was on their side.

Turn that hollow, burning feeling into anger! Distill it into cold fury, and throw it back against and poor bastard who tries to stand against you. Against the Worm, and Kronos, and anything that gets in your way...

That was why he had to focus, and keep the slippery mess of steel and 'crete around him stable. Kaito had promised that help was coming soon...

Then he heard it - the sound of rotary saws cutting stone. They were right above him, and getting closer with every second.

"Kayzi - is that you?" he whispered, his voice crackling across the R.T. band. No answer...

But who else knew where he was? And who else would want to save him?

He tried to call up the Vision, to reach out beyond his tomb and see what was coming for him. All it revealed was a scrawl of black static, the psionic trace of the Worm.

The terrible answer sprung to mind as he felt the rubble shift again, the great block of plasticrete above him pulling up and away. The *enemy* knew where he was - and as he'd so painfully experienced, it was just as skilled a sequestrator as the Ashishim. Hadn't it promised to make him one of its *Exalted*?

Abdulafia knew exactly which memories Asag'raal would use to break him. He'd rather join his fallen comrades than face them again.

But it was more than that. *He felt the need to kill.* It cut to the very core of his being, a blood-drunk sensation as keen and sharp as razors. Down in the dark his eyes snapped open, and his hands clenched into fists.

When a hand the size of a steam-shovel tore aside the concrete above him, he propelled himself up out his tomb, screaming.

No matter that this thing had saved him.

No questions, just the kill.

The *Dervashi's* fist looped in from out of the dark, a hammer-blow which rocked the tankhunter back on its heels. He spun in the air, kicking off its chest and away up the side of the pit, settling into a horizontal sprint around its curving wall. Then he launched himself back in, his palms splayed open around a core of energy.

Time slowed to a crawl as he came down on the warmekan from above, bringing his fingers together, focusing that tight blaze of power into a blade...

It sliced into the machine's neck three feet in front of him, so that when his fists clenched together and struck they knocked its head from its shoulders. Severed cables spat sparks as the great machine collapsed to its knees, a battered chunk of plasticrete still fused to its claw. Abdulafia landed behind it in a crouch, his dreadlocks swinging wild. The smoking casque of the mekan rolled to a stop between his hands in a puddle of coolant, its camera eyes glassy and dead.

Oh, he was glad to be fighting again! Down in the dark he'd been prey to *emotions*, the most dire enemy a *Dervashiman* could ever face. He'd been born in a crucible of slaughter, shaped by sacrifice, and everyone who came close to him was fated to die. What had Jhenna meant to him? What had any of the dead meant - Dante, Siro,

Matthias, Jorge... even CeeAn?

It was his job to witness their deaths. It was his job to turn the messy emotions which churned in his head into pure, cleansing rage. If he was cold to his fellow operatives, if he was distant and inhuman and mechanical, it was for that reason alone. Battle erased their accusing faces, drowned the memory of them under the burning intensity of the *now*.

'Afia gritted his teeth and brought his fist down on the impassive face of the tankhunter, crushing its metal head flat. *Where were the rest of them?* Where were the armies he felt that he could pull apart with his bare hands?

That's just what it will take to forget her, whispered a traitorous voice in his head.

All that death and more, a necropolis of corpses...

He needed something to turn his rage on, before it burned him down to ashes.

Behind him he heard the sound of applause.

The battle-clone turned his head slowly, his eyes narrowed down to razor slits. His face was blackened with soot and crusted with dried blood, while his mane of plug-tipped dreadlocks hung in an an oily tangle. His mouth was locked in a snarl as he turned to face his one-man audience, a black silhouette perched on the rim of the crater.

"Excellent work! What a show! I'm sure I've never seen the likes of it before. I gotta admit, that's one hell of a way to show your gratitude! And the way you took its head off! *Genius!*"

"Friend, you've picked the wrong time," grated Abdulafia, rising to his feet with his fists balled at his sides. "I've got work to do tonight, and you *really* don't want to be part of it."

For a sliver of a second the man's smile showed up against the gloom - a white slash across his shadowed face. 'Afia couldn't see him clearly at all - even his outline seemed blurry, hazed around the edges.

"Nonsense! I think you'll have plenty of time for me and mine, Mister 330. In fact, I've been waiting for you to pop up for quite a while now. You can call me Reine. *Exalted* Reine."

There - the noise of debris clattering and rolling down the slope behind him. Abdulafia spun on his heel, scanning the shrunken horizon of the crater's edge. There were figures moving there, misshapen things with mantis arms and bulbous heads, a puppet-show grotesquerie against the lights of the burning city.

Who else knew his location? Why, these things, of course. And he'd gone and ripped the head off of Kaito Kayzi's warmekan for them...

"I hope you brought enough of those things to stop me, demon," growled the Ashishi. "Because if I get through them to *you*, I'm gonna teach your master a whole new lexicon of pain."

He could see the Exalted One more clearly now - it was faceless except for its unnaturally wide grin, a man-sized hole in the world stuffed with shadows. On its bullet head it wore a perfectly normal gray panama hat, and in its dripping hands it carried a pair of damascened machine-pistols.

It giggled madly, like a drug-twisted child.

"Oh, He'd *love* that, Ashishi. He knows that you're almost one of us already - can't you feel it? You really *do* have an affinity for suffering. I can see it in your mind... You'll break, just like the others."

For a second the eyeless homunculus cocked its head to one side, as if listening to an invisible whisperer. "Just like your old friend *Edward Tsien*, in fact! I hear he's just switched sides, Abdulafia. Why not do the same? It would be a crying shame to lose *you* as well as pretty little Miss CeeAn..."

Lose her? Did that mean she was dead, or that she still resisted the Saprophytes? Just the sound of her name on those rubbery black lips made 'Afia twitch with the urge to slaughter...

"Oh yes, petal. We know your mind, my Lord and I. Such a complicated little machine you are..."

He could feel a sliver of Asag'raal in his brain, pulsing with his heartbeat.

He knew that the Exalted could feel it too.

"You were born for this, you sick piece of meat. We know all your tricks, because deep down you're already *ours*!"

As if to punctuate its point the Exalted fired off a burst of bullets from its left-hand pistol, the muzzle-flare reflecting from the oily surface of its skin. Abdulafia bent them aside with a gesture, scattering a handful of hot lead across the crater wall behind him.

"See? So predictable! Just join us, and all this can be ove..."

There was a sound like a needle being pushed through tight plastic.

The slug hit Exalted Reine right between its non-existent eyes, a tiny entry wound which trickled pus for a second before it puckered closed. The saprophytic creature shook its head like a dazed pitbull, its pointed teeth grinding. Then it unrolled its tongue, the bullet balanced on its glistening tip.

"Temper temper! That was very naughty, you know!"

"Didn't quite see that one coming, did you?" asked the Ashishim, dropping his hand back down to his side. He'd held the slug cupped in his palm for a second, spinning slow and hot in a ball of temporal stasis. *That* should have been impossible without the most potent 'chrome, but it had seemed so utterly effortless...

Something had changed within him. Some tiny, critical part had snapped, and now his anger fed on itself, an oroboros serpent spinning like a turbine in his brain.

In the instant when the bullet struck, his skin had prickled with the caress of power...

"Maybe I didn't, at that," purred the Exalted, plucking the deformed lump of lead from the fork of its tongue. "But playtime is *definitely* over. Now we test the limits of your pain. Now we find the breaking point of your flesh..." A grin tore open his face, a jagged white gash against the black. "*Damn* I love my job!"

See it from above. A lonely little figure at the bottom of a twenty-foot pit, walled in by rubble. And surrounding that smoldering crater: a sea of the living dead, a heaving black mass of them. Their leader points both of his ornate machine-pistols down at his prey and grips both triggers, unleashing the horde amid a spray of bullets...

Zoom tight on that doomed little stick-man in his ragged greatcoat and dreadlocks.

He's smiling.

The Saprophytes came down on Abdulafia like a wave, chittering and howling and hissing, down into the crater in a reeking flood. It was time to see what his newfound rage could do. Time to slip into the never-ending now, and forget the bloody price of it...

He crossed his arms, fists clenched across his chest as the first rank of foes charged in at him. They were nothing but a glistening wall of pincers and claws and lashing tentacular whips at this range... impossible to miss. Dust began to rise around him in a spiral, lifted in a shimmering shroud of energy which cocooned his body. This was the death-meditation of the *Dervashi*, the Rune of the Invisible, and with his newfound power behind it...

Reine's bullets hissed and melted.

Those first eager Saprophytes hit the barrier screaming, and combusted as they touched it. Power flared and raved, tiny stones whirling up around Abdulafia's body, then twists of wire, chunks of burnt plasticrete.

Burning gobbets of Worm-flesh flew wide, trailing smoke.

And Abdulafia fed on their pain, completing the circuit, using the sliver of black despite the Worm had left in his head to kill its children. His hands flew to his sides as he completed the Rune, and the gyre of dust and debris around him blew apart. It was as if he stood at the heart of a mortar explosion, untouched, while the Saprophytes were flayed to ribbons by unseen shrapnel.

How their suffering suffused him! Sweet agony pulsed in his veins, potent as the purest adrenochrome!

And then the killing began in earnest.

He pushed the field out from his body, using it as armor and weapon at once, a flickering aura of force sizzling in the air inches from his skin. When he drove his fist into the face of a Saprophyte it caved in around that energistic shell, blasting the thing's head to ribbons. When he angled his hand into a chopping blade the field narrowed down, razor-sharp, splitting another foe like rotten wood. Wherever he touched them the horrors began to smolder and burn, keening in agony even as the will of their master pushed them forward.

The black sliver of the Worm deep in 'Afia's skull seemed to throb and swell as he fed on the pain of his enemies, drowning out reason, narrowing his vision down to a seething tunnel of red. Anything which stood before him died, bludgeoned and sliced and butchered and burnt by the incandescent blaze surrounding him. He dropped into the stance of the mantis, and his roundhouse kick burst a Saprophyte's chest wide open, ribs cracking like glass. Combat forms he'd been patterned with since childhood flowed through him, breaking necks and shattering skulls...

The power was almost too much - techniques which had once racked him with pain now snapped off tight and neat, time bending around him like red-hot wire. Twenty Saprophytes had burned and died before Reine pulled the triggers of his machineguns again, his eyeless face snarling in slow-motion behind the muzzle flash. Tongues of fire strobed as the bullets flew, glacial, hanging in the air like jewels.

From his quiet place at the heart of the slaughter Abdulafia pointed one finger at a single slug, leaning back as a Saprophyte's blade of bone stabbed past his shoulder. His other hand ripped through its spine, cutting it in half. The crawling bullet followed his fingertip as he straightened up again, turning, bending its path through the air. Now the next one, and the next - all of them plucked from their trajectories and re-assigned in a single heartbeat. He unclenched his mind for a second, allowing the bullets to fly, spiraling wide to shatter the skulls of ten more Saprophytes.

Abdulafia heard Reine scream, a high-pitched screech of rage. The Exalted jammed its ornate silver guns into the slough of its flesh as it threw back its head, agonized.

The beast had been taken over by its master, and now it was *changing*.

Worms of shadow burst from every inch of Reine's skin, weaving themselves together into a mesh of tendoned meat. Muscle ripped and bled as its jaws tore open wide...

Transformed, Afia's power had no effect on the Exalted at all - it leaped from the top of the crater in a blur, bone-hooks swinging. All around it Saprophytes fought and died, moving like jerky stroboscopic images, but the Exalted tossed them aside, hooking them with its claws, throwing oily black bodies left and right as it landed. Its eyeless face was drawn out into a bullet-shaped snout, rows of glistening teeth hinged open beneath. There was nothing left of the man named Reine - this was an engine of war, scattering lesser abominations before it as it charged.

Abdulafia had barely enough time to brace himself before the Exalted hammered into him, forcing itself through his energy field in a cloud of choking smoke. One of Reine's immense hands clamped around his shoulder, plucking him up into the air like a toy.

Time squeezed back into focus as he hit the wall. Pain came back with it, a searing agony in his wrists. They must be broken. The bones inside must be smashed to splinters...

It was worse.

When 'Afia dared to look down at his hands they were oily black, claws of bone skinned with the stuff of the Saprophytes. That was when his rage fell away, and he heard the sound of demonic laughter echoing inside him, bubbling up from the sliver of darkness in his brain.

"Do you like the power, clone-meat?" asked Asag'raal. *"Does it make you forget your* failure?*"*

Time slowed down again, but not at his bidding. A terrible pressure throbbed inside Abdulafia's skull, threatening to burst his eyes from their sockets, and through a haze of tears he could see the Exalted coming for him.

"Now you see what you can do if you just give in, Ashishi. After all, aren't all the ones you cared about dead? Don't they deserve a pyre the size of a whole world to burn on?"

The slick intimacy of it made him choke, but nothing could stop the voice from whispering its blasphemies.

"The Illuminatus has betrayed you, Abdulafia 330. How do you think I took Magus Verlaine? Do you think he wouldn't offer you up as a living sacrifice if he could buy himself more power? You, and CeeAn 187 as well..."

Doubt and fear spiked through him then, as he watched Reine's wicked jaws creak open, slick ropes of saliva pulled tight between its rows of teeth. Was that all he was to his Illuminatus, the allfather of the Ashishim? A killing machine to be tactically sacrificed? A pawn?

"Join us or fight us, clone. Either way, I own you. If it's any consolation, your precious Illuminatus will suffer for his betrayal..."

The black filth of the Saprophytes was on his hands like blood, but it hadn't come from the creatures he'd destroyed. It was part of him now, the price of his newfound strength. It bled out of his pores from that core of anger throbbing in his head.

Exalted Reine was reaching out for him, its claws crooked to smash him bloody against the wall of the pit. But if he fought back, then the creeping infection would only spread faster...

"Make your choice, Abdulafia. The more you agonize, the sweeter you'll taste..."

Time dropped in again, and the Exalted leaped at him in a blur.

Decades of training just wouldn't let him die.

He ducked under its blow, coming up hard, driving a savage uppercut right into the pulpy black ooze of its chest. If the infection hadn't already taken his hands they would have been burned down to the bone by that corrosive jelly. Reine's charnel breath was almost suffocating, and Abdulafia gagged as he groped under the beast's skin for... there! The slippery handle of a machine pistol, drowned in saprophytic slime.

If the Exalted hadn't struck so hard and fast it might have had time to react, but the creature's serrated claws were stuck fast in the bloody rubble behind Abdulafia. In the second it took to pull itself loose 'Afia ripped the pistol out from its ribcage and jammed the muzzle up under its grossly distended jaw.

The lesser Saprophytes flinched back as fire burst from Reine's forehead - the Exalted One's whole skull blasted to dripping chunks by a storm of lead. Delicious pain flared from the exit wound, and 'Afia ached with hunger for it. Denying that black thirst was the hardest thing he'd ever done.

But his eyes were on his infected hands, the darkness ramifying through his veins. Surrender or fight, the Worm would own him. His Illuminatus had betrayed him. And CeeAn would still be gone.

Reine's body slumped to the ground, malformed and ruined, its wounds already beginning to stitch themselves back together. All around the Saprophytes cowered back, hissing, a circle of them waiting for Abdulafia's choice. He was their brother, wasn't he? A machine built for death, with all the humanity of a bullet or a bomb...

There was another way, though.

"Code nine, six, four, three, alpha, hotel, four, two... delta. Confirm Sanction Ultra."

"*Oh, not this time, sweetling! I'm afraid I've had to change the code... to one which I command!*" laughed Asag'raal. "*Any more foolish ideas - or will you offer yourself willingly now? Come... we will taste the pleasure and pain of countless worlds together, you and I...*"

Abdulafia stepped over the twitching body of the Exalted, out into the middle of the crater where every one of the Saprophytes could see him. He didn't want their master to miss this - his final act of defiance. The Worm caught his intention just a second too late, and its seductive whisper racked up to a scream inside his head.

Then Abdulafia brought Reine's damascened automatic up to his temple, and pulled the trigger.

Nothing.

The gun clicked, empty.

Again, his eyes screwed shut, his teeth gritted...

Click. Nothing.

Abdulafia heard an obscene sucking, gurgling sound over the manic laughter in his head.

He turned, the pistol still pressed to his skull, and found Reine stuffed back into his semblance of human form, a mad grin painted across his eyeless face. That battered gray panama hat was perched back atop his head, and his other pistol was in his hand.

"Bravo, 330! What an exit that would have been! But it's not your day for dramatic gestures, clone. You don't get to take the easy way out." The ring of Saprophytes closed in as their lord stalked forward, keeping his gun trained on Abdulafia's head. "I'll be more than happy to provide you with a bullet, of course. But only when you beg me to end your suffering..."

The Ashishi let his gun fall away as he bowed his head, all hope lost. He wouldn't fight them. He wouldn't die as the mindless killer he had always feared becoming.

It hit the ground with the tiny sound of metal on metal.

'Afia opened his eyes, staring down at a burnt ruin of rubble and glass and steel. He felt Reine's pistol barrel grinding into his skin, oily and cold. And he picked out words stamped into an exposed bulge of metal, right at his feet.

Eversio Mark-One Nanomechanical Flensing Tool.

Providence.

It was nothing less than a miracle, a sign that he was still needed alive in this twisted world. Behind his curtain of bloodied dreadlocks, Abdulafia's face split in a grin just as wicked as the Exalted's. He'd only become one of them if he used their power to kill. *But the Eversio was just a tool,* wasn't it?

The Ashishi hooked the toe of his boot under its barrel as Reine's claw tightened around the dome of his skull, its razor tips pricking blood from his scalp. Just one little distraction, and then...

He groaned, staggering back from his tormentor. Coal-black fingers scrabbled at Reine's claws.

"Oh, not so brave now, hmm?" gloated the Exalted, tightening its grip for a second and then letting go. Abdulafia stumbled, almost falling, peering out from between his swinging dreadlocks at the eyeless mask of his foe. A bare quarter of a second would do it...

"What should we do with him first, my pets? The flaying? The scarring? Perhaps the branding, or the harvesting of the eyes..." Reine turned to his captive audience of Saprophytes with his arms spread wide, welcoming their adulation.

And 'Afia brought his foot up from the rubble and dust, breaking the silver bulk of the Eversio loose in a spray of chipped plasticrete. It spun in midair along its axis, reflected fire shimmering across its stainless-steel skin.

The *Dervashi* reached out and grabbed it, feeling it fit into his hand like a well-balanced sword. One of his plug-tipped dreads snaked into the interface port atop the cannon, sending a shatterburst of schematics whirling through his mind.

Without the fission micropile Tsien had carried on his back the thing could only be used six more times. A microsecond's scan of the weapon's schematics revealed that this would be more than enough.

Exalted Reine spun around as he heard the click and whirr of the Eversio powering up, twining polyps of darkness already bursting from his face and shoulders. But he was far too late. Even as he shifted, his monstrous jaws stretching and drooling... he was already dead.

"No! This can't be! You were supposed to be miiiiiiine!"

'Afia flicked his grimy 'locks out of his eyes, squinting down the barrel of the cannon. Deep in the heart of the Eversio thousands of tentacles twined, each one only a molecule thick, each one under the direct control of the Ashishi's mind. Oh, he'd never be as elegant and brutal with it as Tsien had been. But there were forty Saprophytes and one smug little Exalted shit in his killing field, and he was going to enjoy what happened next *immensely.*

He pulled the trigger, feeling the hum and crackle as that deadly silver cloud condensed, watching it slither across the smoky air in slow motion. The tip of each strand was an eye, unfurling a serpent of wire behind it. They ran down their prey, relentless, mummifying each slick black body in steel cotton-candy, twitching against their bubbling skin. The final thread plunged down between Reine's nightmare jaws, ramifying through its organs, wrapping tight around its bones. Forty Saprophytes in a single chilling silver breath, all of them hopelessly doomed.

Then the second trigger locked down, and every one of those filaments pulled tight at once. Well - all but one.

The lesser slaves of Asag'raal screamed as they were dissected, their surface tension breaking as the damned inside them spilled out. Human bones burned clean of flesh clattered and rolled amid a deluge of filth, staining the rubble black.

Those which had avoided the Eversio's kiss cowered cravenly, melting back up the crater walls.

'Afia was alone with his prey.

The final thread was the one which bound up Exalted Reine, and as it quivered in the air Abdulafia could finally see a little of the creature's humanity. It was afraid to die.

"You worthless bastards!" it hissed, cursing its cowardly slaves. "Take him! Take him NOW!"

But not one of them would dare its flesh against the Eversio. They could see that their leader was doomed, and there was safer prey to be had out amid the ruins...

"Listen good, Exalted," said Abdulafia, coiling the wire tight as he pulled the twitching creature close. "I want your master to hear me loud and clear. I want all of you to know what's coming."

Now he knew what it felt like to be Edward Tsien - his humanity bleeding away, his only possible joy a hideous revenge. And like the Super-Cyben, all he wanted to do was go home.

"I have a piece of you inside my head, *but I'm not going to use it*. I'm going to take it down to the R.T. with me, to the 'techs and Magi of my people. I'll gladly go under the knife if that's what it takes to kill you, Worm. They can cut you from my living brain unanesthetized, I don't care. Hells - *you* made me stop caring. And if the Illuminatus is on your side, I'll deal with him myself. You've just seen how."

"P-please!" bubbled Reine, wringing its claws in supplication. "It's eating me alive, Ashishi! My Lord - my Lord has forsaken me!"

There was no remorse in Abdulafia's eyes as he jammed the trigger down, pulling the last filament fatally tight. He watched with clinical detachment as the Exalted's face became a gridwork of seeping lines, as its whole body began to leak putrid yellow fluid from ten thousand razorcuts. Inside its skin the wire sliced through organs and bones, reducing its innards to jelly. And Reine was right - the blessing of Asag'raal had left him, allowing the acidic slime of the Saprophytes to eat away at his flesh. For a second his human face melted out of the oily blackness, a man with blind and milky eyes...

"Mine too, Reine." whispered the Ashishi as the Exalted fell to its knees. "We're two of kind, you and I. But *my* Lord - he's going to have to answer to *me.*"

'Afia jerked the Eversio up and away with a final tearing sound, and the poor doomed thing slithered into pieces, a sad little pile of steaming chunks. It was done.

At the bottom of a crater of smoking rubble a dirty little stick-man stood, the barrel of a huge silver cannon leaned back across his shoulder. Around him the plasticrete and steel ran black with blood, dripping with saprophytic gore.

Zoom out.

From above he's nothing, just another insect crawling over the broken remains of its hive.

For a mile on every side the ruins sprawl, and other tiny figures pick through the wreckage, scrabbling and crying and looting. The habs and 'facs which loom on every side are locked down, barricaded up tight while ancient war-machines and crawling horrors stalk the streets.

There's no Vision to guide him home, nothing but screams and static on the R.T. radio band. Not even Kaito and Haszan, or Deut' Jones and his so-called Heretics.

Abdulafia checked his load - five more shots. He scrambled up the crater wall and looked out over a battlefield.

Five might just be enough.

Jaq Haszan stared with undisclosed hostility at the plate in front of him. Right in the middle of that brightly-colored disc of plastic squatted the ripest, reddest tomato he'd ever seen. It was clearly unnatural.

Next to him Kaito prodded a cob of steaming corn tentatively with his fork, as if expecting it to explode on contact. The other Pentecostal sailors were tearing into their meal with gleeful abandon, while at the head of the table Deuteronomy Jones perched like an avuncular buzzard, watching the two Elysians squirm.

"What's the matter, boys? Lost your appetite? I hear those old MRE rations can do that to a body..."

Jaq, at least, had seen pictures of things like this. *Vegetables*, they were called. Not like the balls and tubes of colored synthesoy which passed for food in the Subcity. He'd been raised on tales of what the Hand of Fatima's hydroponic gardens had once grown, back in the old country. Some of the old folks even had photographs.

"Mister Jones - I mean, it's just... where did you get this stuff, anyway?"

The old preacher smiled, revealing a mouthful of ivory pegs interlaced with gold fillings.

"The Amish. We've got a whole community of those Mennonite boys down on the abyssal plain, domed up under a couple miles o' water. Grow the best damn crops I've ever tasted."

"Amish?" asked the Kayzi, dropping his fork "Aren't they an anti-tech cult? That's what we used to call anyone in my hab who wasn't headwired."

Jaq took a bite out of his tomato, and a look of transcendent bliss spread across his face.

"Mhhy hvvh t' hhhry thsss! Sss fuh'nn essskwsnst!" Runnels of juice ran down his chops, dripping onto the checkered tablecloth.

"Yeah, that's them," said 'Deut, stooping to carve a slice of pumpkin with his own bone-handled cutlery. "They don't want to touch the air-scrubbers and valency generators that keep 'em alive, so my kids do it for 'em. See, it wasn't only the Church of the Pentecost what got wiped out in the Vatican Purge. There's Baptists, Bahai, Mormons, heck, even *Unitarians* still out there in the rad-lands. They never got all of us, even when Pope Innocent the Destroyer was in charge."

Kaito finally trusted his meal enough to pop a forkful of kernels into his mouth, and soon his idiot grin was as wide as Haszan's.

"Man, you had us worried for a second!" sighed Jaq, wiping the pips out of his beard with one immense hand. "Your boat's not the most subtle thing in water, you know that?"

Deuteronomy laughed as he tipped his chair back, his hands behind his head.

"Well, we've got quite a crew on board. Three hundred of us, last count, plus the pickups, the stowaways and the kids. Why'd you think we needed the pile out of that machine of yours?"

Kaito remembered the huge pincer-claws of the *Archangel* coming down on them, part of a floating dry-dock apparatus remade as a ship-catcher. It wasn't as if they had any choice. Not for the first time the Kayzi wondered what Abdulafia had gotten them into.

"Rig like that can keep us fueled for another century, boys. But if what you tellin' me is true, the judgment of the Vatican might just be at hand tonight."

Jones unfolded himself from his chair, stretching out to his full height with a click and pop of ancient joints. In his prime the man must have been huge - big enough to challenge Haszan in sheer bulk. But years of living in a submarine had stooped him over, while sheer old age had whittled him away to a sinewy shadow of his former self. He wore an old-fashioned preacher's outfit - stovepipe trousers, a black shirt and white starched collar, and a pair of worn-down alligator boots with silver tips. His face was as creased and wrinkled as that scaly old leather, a rich mahogany hue which shone blue-black under the fluorescent lights.

"The question is, am I gonna help Mister Three-Thirty and his friends? Or am I just gonna sit here and laugh while the Holy See gets burned down to dust..."

Kaito fixed him with a shrewd stare as Jones stalked down the table toward him, his boots clicking against the metal floor. The Kayzi gestured around him with a forkful of corn, unflinching as the Pentecostal preacher leaned down over him.

"The way I see it, captain, this all looks like it uses a lot of power. I'd say it's a fair trade - our micropile for the lives of as many Ashishim can fit inside this tub."

Jaq made to stand up as Deut' eyeballed Kaito from an inch away, his face grim. But the Electromagus held him back with one hand, taking a juicy bite out of his cob. Butter dripped as he grinned and swallowed.

"You think this is some kind of *deal*, Elysian? I got your little toy wrapped up tight, and you're sittin' at my table with a hundred Pent' sailors at either side. What's my incentive?"

Kaito dabbed his lip with a cotton napkin and met Deuteronomy's gaze, unblinking.

"Your incentive is, you're only *playing* at being crazy. And if you touch that thing without the codes in my head, we're all going for one last swim."

His fingers mimed a little explosion in the air.

There was a second's silence as cold as the water slipping past the *Uriel*'s hull. Jaq was horribly aware of the hard-faced Pentecostal mariners all around them, waiting for their captain's order.

Then the preacher began to laugh, a deep belly rumble which shook his entire frame.

"Oh yeah, you're 'Afia's boys allright. That's just what he'd have said, right there!" Deut' sat himself down on the edge of the table, wiping away a tear from his eye. "Can't be too careful, even tonight. See, the truth is... well, I don't suppose words'll do it justice. What say we go for a walk together?"

He didn't wait for an answer - just turned away with his hands clasped behind his back, moving with a long, hunched-over stride which was all the low ceiling allowed.

Kaito tipped his chair back and followed, grinning at the crew of sailors who'd never before seen their captain outstared. Jaq was after him in another second, stuffing his pockets with Amish-grown salad greens.

The *Archangel Uriel* was huge.

That much had been apparent when the hulking great vessel had blotted out the light above the Scourge, drawing them into its craw with giant hydraulic pincers. With their claw-tipped tentacles severed all they could do was sit tight until the Pent' marines cracked the hatch, leading them out at gunpoint. The trip up to the mess hall had been a dizzying maze of mesh tunnels, catwalks over thumping engines, galleries of oxygenating 'ponics and worn-down ladders.

It turned out to be only the tip of one *mother* of a pressurized steel iceberg.

The *Archangel* had been constructed during the Christian Internecium, a last escape for the doomed 'Heretics' who defied the reunification of the church. Orthodox monks out of Kamchakta had commandeered one of the vessel's hulls, an ex-Russian missile sub. The other was jacked out of Alaska by Baptists, and when the two factions met among the Aleutians to take stock of their situation the plan had come together...

Centuries later their work was still in progress. The *Uriel* was essentially a twin-hulled submarine, but it would be far more accurate to call it a mobile undersea town. Modules were welded and bolted on seemingly at random - everything from ancient rocket boosters to great spherical fuel tanks. This mess of watertight steel filled in the space between the two ancient nuke boats, a dewy warren packed with life.

Literally hundreds of Pentecostal sailors popped hatches and swung down from hammocks to goggle at their alien guests - the only people on board not dressed in immaculately starched whites.

"See, by the end of the Purge those Vatican boys thought they had us beat. Cast out of all the habitable zones in the rad-lands, literally pushed into the ocean. But there were pockets here and there where us Heretics held on. The *Archangel* was what held us together - Heaven knows that our faith wasn't gonna do it alone."

Deut' stopped at the foot of yet another ladder and turned to smile ruefully at Kaito.

"Take my advice, son. Never join a revolution based on dissent. We wanted the right to argue with the Pope, and what we got was the right to argue among ourselves. For about two hundred years..."

This ladder led them to a dead end - but what a dead end it was.

This must have been the highest point of the whole great vessel's superstructure, a transparent plastic dome forty feet wide. An array of periscopes and screens depended from a set of coiled insectoid arms in the center of the room, and dark water swirled by all around, the lights of the *Uriel* filtering up dimly from below.

Jones grabbed a swinging microphone and brought it up to his lips, muttering a few snatches of code into its rusted grille. At once the deck canted, and the two Elysians staggered, grabbing for the handrail which ran around the edge of the dome.

"Don't be alarmed, gentlemen," said the preacher, holding himself steady on the chrome shaft of the main 'scope. "We're coming to the surface so I can assess *the tactical situation* - as your Ashishi friend would put it."

The controls descended, screens broadcasting hundreds of live feeds from all over the *Uriel*'s hull. Both the Russian and American subs had been immense on their own, but with a small city piggybacking between them the ship was vast beyond imagining, a whole island of corroded steel and battleship-gray paint. Ornate crucifixes were etched and airbrushed onto every panel and tube, the blessings of generations of Pent' maintenance grunts. Even more of them were welded up out of scrap steel, salvaged from ruined churches and woven out of chrome wire. These broke the surface all around them as the *Archangel* breached, and for a second the black surface of the ocean looked like an ancient graveyard.

The crew of the sunken cathedral were nothing if not pragmatic, however - the next things to rise dripping from the swells were the guns. Hundreds and hundreds of guns. More than a floating basilica, the *Uriel* was a ziggurat of firepower, scavenged from the rusted hulks of the world's battleships. All of them were pointed at the horizon, toward the dirty orange glow of Elysium.

"It's burning. It's all burning..." Haszan's voice was barely a whisper as he watched the flames, hypnotized. Inside his head he was watching his old Hab-Block disintegrate, hearing the screams of his family behind the roar of the flames.

Kaito swallowed hard, his head spinning with similar visions. Up until now, he'd tried to forget the terrible things Abdulafia had revealed to them. The truth about Kronos and its harvest of souls. About something *even worse* which could rip open human minds and feed on their pain...

He prayed that the warmekan he'd sent had found the Ashishi warrior. He didn't want to think about a thing like him being turned, sequestrated like Magus Verlaine.

"Looks like they caught it bad, whatever it is. And if 'Afia wants his people saved, it's gonna be tough. Look..."

One of the screens zoomed, showing something hazy and indistinct bobbing on the black ocean. The lenses shifted, and suddenly it became clear. A whole armada of boats was heading out from the city under a pall of smoke, everything from inflatable kayaks to a Celestial fish-processing plant piggybacking on a mobile oil-rig. Some of the desperate refugees were even clinging to makeshift rafts - oildrums and polystyrene chunks netted together, pallets and boards and household furniture. As they watched one of those topheavy little craft faltered and ripped in two, spilling its screaming cargo into the icy water.

"What - what the *hells* is *that* thing?" gasped Kaito, recoiling from another hanging screen. "There - zoom in on it! It's some kind of..."

But the Kayzi knew all too well what it was. He'd felt its touch before, if only for a second. The image split and doubled, spilling across the banks of monitors until it was the only one left. If *this* didn't convince Deuteronomy Jones that the situation was serious, then nothing would.

Once the ship had been a pleasure-cruiser, but now its white hull was streaked with rust and algae, its lines hacked and mangled by ten centuries of constant modification. The vivid red chop of the Celestial Kingdom was spraypainted across its bows to declare its allegiance, while a trio of makeshift machinegun turrets bulged from its superstructure. The crew had decided that they'd rather run than fight tonight, and many of them had decided to take their families with them. The camera eyes of the *Uriel* picked out the broken shapes of them scattered across the decks. Who could guess what kind of hell existed below?

"Sweet Lord... it's eating them alive!" breathed Jones, pressing one palm up against the screen as if he could reach out to those doomed souls. "Is - is *this* the thing that Abdulafia wants us to fight?"

It was no regular Saprophyte which had slipped aboard the Celestial gunboat. One of the refugees who'd paid his way down into its hold had welcomed the coming of the Worm. He'd carried the virus with him until they were too far from land to escape. And then...

The shuddering black mass of it hung over the transom of the gunboat, thick ropy tentacles churning the water to froth. As Kaito watched, horrified, a spiked tongue slithered across the deck, snaring a body by the ankle. It was a young girl - perhaps the daughter of a crewman, perhaps even of the Exalted One itself... She kicked and twitched weakly as she was drawn in, mummified in coiling pseudopods, clawing trails across the bloody hardwood...

It was too much for Jaqub Haszan, and he turned on the captain, knotting his huge fists in the Pentecostal's shirt.

"Dammit, are we just gonna sit here and *watch*! The Ashishi said the whole city's full of those things!"

He slammed Jones up against the curving wall, making the whole dome shudder.

"And what if this is how it's meant to end, Jaq?" whispered the preacher. "Those are killer's hands, boy, so don't try to tell me you're innocent."

For a second Haszan went white, his teeth clenched together in a grimace of fury. But then he sagged back, letting Deut' slide back down the wall until his silver-tipped boots touched the floor.

"I killed them *clean*, man. Only them that deserved it, one way or another. Neat and clean."

Kaito rushed forward, pulling his friend away before things could get any worse. There were hundreds of Pentecostals just a few floors below them, and they couldn't get out of here alone.

Ha! Get out of here to where, *exactly?*

"What did he do for you?" asked the Kayzi, holding Jaq at arm's length. "Abdulafia. He seemed pretty damned sure that you'd come when he called you."

Deuteronomy Jones smiled, smoothing down the black fabric of his preacher's costume.

"Code, son. Code. You should know that his people are the best, and we needed them for two reasons. First, so I could reach out to the faithful who still live in Elysium. So I could cut through the threedeeo networks' encryption." Now his eyes twinkled, and his mouth twisted into a sardonic half-smile.

"That, and some other codes too. These two boats here..." he gestured at the twin hulls of the *Uriel,* plowing through the waves toward the burning city "They came complete with a few spare megatons of nuclear weaponry. Not a piece of it was any use without those numbers - but once the Vatican knew we had 'em... well, they kind of gave up trying to finish the Internecium."

Kaito was shocked speechless. Like every child of Elysium he'd been weaned on stories about the bomb, about the horrors of the burned rad-lands. Of the unholy trinity of proscribed technologies which Kronos kept from its thralls *nuclear weapons* were the most reviled. And this so-called holy man, this preacher who appeared on screen every week lamenting the city's moral decay... he was packing a bigger nuclear arsenal than many of the nations of Old Earth.

Worse, the *Electromagi* had given him the launch codes. Kaito's adopted tribe were complicit.

"You were actually going to *use* them? After you've seen what it's like out in the dead zones?"

His voice cracked with horror, but Deut' just sighed.

"You don't know the history of it, Kayzi. The purges were terrible..." for a second his eyes grew dim, recalling atrocities. "We were allied to the Ashishim during that whole dark century, and in the end we planned the Reclamation together. My granddaddy met with the Illuminatus right here on board the *Archangel* to seal the deal. Pope Vespasian the Reclaimer never knew he was cannon fodder, or what would happen if the assault failed..."

Kaito knew all about the Seven Hours War, and now he imagined the armies of the Outlanders crashing up against the steel rock of Elysium, shattering, rolling back. He imagined the missiles falling like rain, bursting open to vaporize the Last City and every living thing within...

"I don't know to this day whether I'd have turned the key. Even if they were all destroyed, I don't know if I could have gone through with it. That doubt's the only thing that lets me know I'm not a monster."

Deuteronomy suddenly looked all of his hundred and ten years, worn down by a lifetime of running and hiding. He stared out through the scratched plexiglass dome at Elysium burning on the horizon, at the mad, desperate fleet of refugees swarming across the ocean toward them. And his eyes narrowed, his fists clenched at his sides.

"Are you a religious man, Kayzi? You, Jaqub Haszan?" That fervent look was in his eyes again, as though he was nothing but a living receiver for the will of his God.

"Why?" asked Kaito, still numbed by the image of nuclear fire "Is that a dealbreaker?"

Deuteronomy Jones strode over to the periscope and pulled it down on its oiled rails, squinting into its oculus for a second. He turned back over his shoulder to fix the young Magus with a look that could slice diamonds.

"Maybe not for you, son. But as for me... I'm a man of God. Some would say I'm nothing else. And sure as I don't think I could have turned the key back then I don't think I can stand idle now. He'd never forgive me."

The captain turned his eyes skyward for a second, then his hands were all over the control boards, plotting a course through the refugee fleet to the shores of Ashishim territory.

"I suggest you get down to the drydocks, boys. There's gonna be a need for extra hands to help the survivors aboard. I'll open a channel to the ship's datanet so Mister Kayzi can guide you."

Jaq felt the immense bulk of the *Archangel Uriel* shudder beneath him as he followed Kaito down the ladder, back into the echoing metal bowels of the great ship. The last thing he'd seen as he dogged the hatch shut was Deut' Jones standing tall at the periscope, a grim smile on his face.

"I still think he's completely insane." he said to Kaito as they climbed. "But at least the mad old bastard's on *our* side."

Kaito snorted in the red-lit gloom below him, trying to keep his feet on the slippery rungs.

"If he's insane, and we're following him, what does that make *us*?"

The *Archangel Uriel* steamed onward through the night, its batteries of guns creaking around to bear on the steel mountain of Elysium, its armories loaded with a cargo of fully operational nukes. If Deut' wouldn't let them loose, Kaito was sure that the enemy could. The thing in Verlaine's head had possessed all the morality of a starving shark.

He just hoped that Abdulafia had made it home in time...

DOCUMENT INSERT - Injunction for Subdimension 4934
5872 3485 7330 9658 201

By order of his eminence, Lord Arbitrex Galq, this
alleged 'reality' is hereby sealed until further
notice.

Random, recurring anomalies in the structure of
this sub-dimension render it far too dangerous
for further exploration and/or subjugation by the
elements of our glorious Order of Battle.

Technic Hierophant Gharfos Nyl Serpalian,
registered Technician for the affected dimension,
has committed himself to a three-century tour of
duty inside the cordon, in an attempt to stabilize
and normalize the situation.

Until such time as he succeeds (or, failing
this, an edict of erasure is enacted by the
Subpraetorian Council Judicial), it is forbidden
to believe in any persons, objects, phenomena or
artifacts from the affected dimension. Pondering,
musing or philosophizing about events within Sub-D
4934 5872 3485 7330 9658 201 is punishable by
mind-scrubbing and bodily re-assignment.

Thank you in advance for your unquestioning
obedience -

Your Master of the Local Reticulated Cluster,
Arbitrex Fourth Class Galq A'queem

2196 Ante Arbitrium
The Killing Jar

The *Shantung Ryu* cut a swath through the refugee fleet as it powered out toward the flycam's signal, overturning makeshift rafts in its wake and swamping the few unlucky vessels foolish enough to cut across its bows. Captain Jiang might be a slippery pirate bastard, but he wasn't lying about his ship's turn of speed. Under the deck four ethanol-powered turbine engines hissed and roared, lashing the water to foam. A trio of Celestial techs hustled in the red-lit gloom, burning incense and chanting prayers in Cantonese as they worked with wrenches and spanners and oil to wring even more power out of the ancient machines. Not one of them was actually Chinese – but that was just typical of the C.K. *One K/Z outcast, one Celt and one Afrikan, praying to an alcohol-fueled motor in a language their grandparents couldn't understand...*

Much as she hated to admit it, Lady Alvarez could do nothing but wait. As a Kheptic heiress she'd had nothing to do with the ocean, and as the most telegenic outlaw in Elysium her only use for it was as a repository for dead bodies.

Jiang, on the other hand, seemed right in his element, standing tall at the ship's wheel as salt spray lashed the screens in front of him. As soon as they'd cleared the docks the rest of his shady crew had rushed to their battle stations, bolting down heavy machineguns and undogging hatches from which cannon turrets sprouted. In the space of a minute or two the *Shantung Ryu* had been transformed from a derelict-looking fisherman into a fearsome corsair.

Not a second too soon, either - it seemed that the Celestial Emperor wasn't too pleased about the number of citizens quitting their posts. Behind them the first salvo from the C.K guns had blown apart a barge full of refugees, scattering burning bodies and salvaged belongings across the waves in a grisly slick.

The roll and crackle of gunfire was almost constant behind them now, as the Son of Heaven's troops tried desperately to keep his people contained.

Shantung Ryu was simply too fast for them. As soon as Jiang saw those first muzzle flashes he jammed the throttles wide open. His ship leaped forward, bows in the air and screws blurring. Ruby and her boys were forced to hold on tight as he tacked hard, dodging a salvo of explosive shells which shattered the smaller boats around them. Aitken Straw looked positively green behind his mask, and the Tin Man had clamped himself to the treadplate deck with magnetic grapples. But Jiang was smiling, spinning the wheel wild, using his long, lean gunboat like an oversized jet-ski. Pretty soon the shells were falling far behind their transom, and the Celestial gunners turned their attention to easier prey.

"I hope you city folks are all right back there!" hollered the captain, his mandarin hat rakishly askew on his head. Ruby saw the coiled dragon tattoos inked into his scalp as he leaned out over the rail. "There's herbal tea in the galley - if you can walk that far!"

Big Leon growled, but it became a nauseous groan halfway through. "Ooooohhhhh... This wet stuff is bad, yes, very bad. I want to go back now!"

Lady Alvarez herself couldn't have put it more succinctly.

The Scarecrow had managed to snap open his laptop, and now his eyes flickered across the screen, tracking their little insect guide.

"We're almost right on top of it now, Ruby. I'm calling it in."

Sure enough, the flycam found them easily. It spiraled down out of the night to land on the tip of Aitken's finger, preening its carbon-mesh wings with a pair of hair-thin silver legs.

"But if that thing's *here*, then where... "

Ruby didn't get a chance to finish her sentence.

"The sonar's gone crazy!" yelled one of the Celestial pirates, popping up from belowdecks with a screed of paper in his hand. "Captain, there's something big down there - right below us!"

Jiang grabbed the readout from his crewman and scanned it swiftly, his jaw dropping open with shock.

"Surely not! There's not a reef or seamount in this whole area that I don't know about! The machine must be faulty! I..."

Then something scraped down the *Shantung Ryu*'s keel with a sound like rending claws. The ship heeled over, spilling cargo and crew up against the rail in a cursing, bleeding pile. All but the Tin Man, leaning hard into his magnetic clamps.

"All engines reverse! Hard a'starboard!" roared Jiang in cantonese, struggling back to the wheel. Beneath the deck the engines whined and thumped, straining at their mountings. The pirate ship cut into the waves, coming about hard as something rose out of the water beside them...

It was a giant steel crucifix, erupting from the black Atlantic like a grave marker for the drowned.

"Another one off the bow!" shouted one of Jiang's gunners. "More to port!" yelled another.

And indeed, all around them the surface of the ocean was sprouting a forest of metal crosses, wire and chrome and rusted iron, some of them flashing with beacon lights, others reflecting the fires of far-off Elysium. The *Shantung Ryu* was trapped.

With a grinding, tearing sound the entire ship tipped forward in the water, and a screaming Celestial pinwheeled down the canted deck, his arms and legs snapping like twigs as he caromed off the rails. Jiang was hanging onto the wheel with both hands, expecting the waves to come crashing in at any moment and drag his vessel to the bottom.

Instead they began to *rise*.

The *Shantung Ryu* had beached itself atop a giant three-barreled battleship gun, its keel wedged between two of those mighty cannons. As the *Archangel Uriel* broke the waves around them they were carried higher and higher aloft, rising up with the main battery of the Pentecostal behemoth until the screws of the pirate ship were suspended a hundred feet above the water.

They'd been at the very arrowhead of the refugee fleet, otherwise hundreds of other makeshift vessels would have been stranded high and dry with them. As it was the *Shantung Ryu* hardly stood out among the crenelations, turrets and bulbous domes of the *Uriel*, a limpet clinging atop a whale.

Ruby Alvarez was first to stir from the slop of bilgewater and blood in the stern of the *Shantung*, cursing as she scrabbled for her lost railpistols. The Tin Man clumped stiffly across the deck to join her at the transom, contemplating their predicament with his usual stoic silence.

"That's some great sailing, Jiang!" growled Ruby, looking down at tier after tier of dripping guns. Some of them were moving now as the crews within took aim at the slopes of Elysium, grinding the turrets around with the sound of ancient machinery. "But this is just about where we get off. Aitken, bring the Flycam, and start jamming the security network of this beast. Leon, carry the heavy weapons. And Tin Man - you get to take point, as usual. We're going to find those sub-scum bastards, make the hit and get back out before the captain here can get his ship stuck any worse."

They could hear clattering and banging sounds coming from beneath the stranded *Shantung Ryu* now, as a very confused team of Pentecostal gunners tried to work out what was weighing down their turret. A slim steel periscope snapped up out of the hide of the sub, turning to stare straight into the C.K. chop on the pirate's bows.

"Take my advice, Jiang. Tell 'em you're an 'honest fisherman'. I'm *sure* they'll buy it."

Ruby fastened a zipline around the rail of the boat and perched on the edge for a second, surveying the drop down to the crazed topography of the *Uriel*'s living modules. Below her the rest of the gang were in position, huddled close to Aitken Straw and his laptop. She could only pray that the Scarecrow had a map.

"And if you're still around by the time we're through, you'd better have figured out how to get this thing back in the water. I paid you for a round trip."

With that she fell backward over the rail, just as a hatch clanged open on the other side of the ship. Pent' marines with sabers and pistols swarmed out, goggling with amazement at the strange catch they'd netted. One of the Celestial crew went for his pintle-mounted machinegun, but Jiang stood him down with a curt gesture. They were ten against a hundred, with no way of getting off this mountain of metal.

Much better to play it ignorant and safe...

"Many humble apology, sirs!" shouted pirate captain, in his very best imitation of an ignorant C.K. refugee. "Sorry to be park this boat, but we are no sailor! We escape from city, from bad things and fires!" No doubt his bloody, singed mandarin costume helped - the marines didn't even notice that it was woven from riotmesh.

"Zeke, Jerrad, check the whole boat for infection!" The Pentecostal commander was a burly man with red sideburns and a crucifix tattoo blazoned across his face. He didn't look amused. "Mahoney and you others, take these poor pilgrims downstairs. And strip this tub of weaponry - God knows that we need it more than they do!"

Jiang grinned and kowtowed gratefully - and his crew caught on, babbling in Cantonese and holding out their hands imploringly to the white-clad Christian sailors. And, as they knew absolutely nothing about the C.K. beyond threedeeo hype, they bought it.

Behind his gap-toothed smile the Celestial pirate was fuming. This little excursion might just have cost him his pride and joy, and if Lady bloody Alvarez wanted to get out of here alive then she was going to have to salvage the *Shantung Ryu* herself.

Under his feet the gun turret bucked and rattled as deck after deck of cannons began to fire, a vast broadside arcing up over the sea, illuminating the refugee fleet with phosphorus flares.

The big guns were powerful enough to lob their man-sized shells all the way back to Elysium, stitching a neat row of fire across the Celestial Kingdom docks. Even from this far away Jiang fancied he could see the sea-wall battlements erupt into flames, tiny bodies blazing as they fell. The batteries of cannons penning the Emperor's people in fell silent as a whole section of the R.T. collapsed on top of them.

But this was no humanitarian strike. The smaller guns of the *Archangel Uriel* were kicking up plumes of white water as they fired on the refugees themselves, surgically destroying a raft here, an overloaded barge there...

There was something aboard those unlucky vessels, something black and oily and *moving*, struggling as it burned. The *Uriel*'s gunners were using incendo rounds, burning them down to the waterline.

Jiang's blood ran cold for a second as he realized he'd cut right through that desperate armada, passing close enough to touch those abominations which keened and shuddered and died in the burning sea. As he came down the gangplank of his ship a trio of Pentecostal techs passed him, armed with flamethrowers and thermal-scopes. Their full-body suits were marked with biohazard trefoils.

Infection...

Perhaps, thought Jiang, it was time to forget the *Shantung Ryu*, and forget his old masters in the Last City. He wondered whether the Christian God would welcome the soul of an incorrigible pirate...

Ω

The spillway heaved with a tide of humanity.

Those at the back of the crowd pushed and struggled, desperation giving them strength. There were things stalking through the dark places of Elysium which were terrible enough to drive men mad, down amid the manufactoria and sunless habs...

But those at the front had nowhere to go. The warlords of the Pit commanded a swathe of sand under their antiquated guns, and a ramshackle wall of corrugated iron, rusted vehicles and sharpened stakes barred the road out to the rad-lands. Anyone who was pushed out onto that killing ground was mercilessly cut down by a hail of bullets, taking many others with them as slugs chewed into the tight-packed throng.

One checkpoint was open, a single-file line which funneled the desperate refugees between walls of tangled razorwire, down to a concrete tollbooth where the rich were sifted from the destitute. In order to pass through the gates and into the dubious safety of the Pit they had to be packing serious currency - 'tech, precious metals, weapons... cash was useless down here, and drifts of it blew in the hot wind like chaff. At the seething center of the mob people desperately scrambled for the bills, tearing at each others' throats like animals.

This was the exodus of the Subcity, and it led nowhere.

Clinging to the side of a shattered concrete tower B-Zerk saw it all and despaired. He'd gotten this far - crawling through sewers, dodging the clicking, whirring death-machines Kronos had unleashed - and other things far worse. But of course he wasn't quite *himself* anymore - under the ragged shawl which whipped around his shoulders squatted great metal tumor of the Mark-Four drone, pulling his puppet strings.

The datanet was down, the Wetsystems cut off, and all it could feel through its electronic senses was the dim shadow of Edward Tsien, somewhere high above. He was a hazy red pulse, a knot of severed nerves blinking behind its camera eyes.

All it could think about was the disease which loomed up like a wave behind it. It needed to get away from that evil thing, and it knew that time was running out. Surely the Worm and its Exalted were only playing with these poor doomed wretches, watching them grind themselves to ruin against the defenses of the Pit. This spectacle was the kind of thing which would amuse its twisted mind... but not for very long.

The only other way out of the city was up to the sentinel towers which guarded the dam-tops, two great barbican fortresses held by the Ashishim and the Vatican respectively. They bristled with guns and swarmed with Reclamationist soldiers, but that was a risk that the drone would soon have to take.

If it were captured by Asag'raal it would provide a straight shot through the network and into the very heart of Kronos...

Suddenly the drone felt the black, hot presence at the back of its mind unfold, fractalizing out in spirals. Its connection through to Edward Tsien tore open like a wound, and pain wracked B-Zerk's sequestrated body, almost sending him tumbling from his perch. His hands clenched tight into cracks in the concrete as his camera eyes shut down, his whole head humming with the slick dark power of the Worm. This was it, then. They'd taken Tsien, and now they'd have the Mark-Four system as well. The key to Elysium's destruction turned in its lock...

"Wake up, you little bastard! Daddy's home!"

That wasn't the sickening hiss of Asag'raal. It was a human voice, and the data which poured through the connection was all human memory, a whole lifetime's worth reduced to binary. It was the life of Eddie Tsien, every last instant of it. As the final shreds of packeted data slotted into place the connection slammed shut, locked tight from within with fearsome crypto. A hashed-together threedeeo avatar of Tsien floated to the top of B-Zerk's mind, its polygonal face split in a happy grin.

"You didn't think I'd forget about you, did you?" it asked, in a perfect imitation of the Lieutenant's voice. "I hope you'll excuse me, but I just needed somewhere to keep my things for a while. I'll be back for all this data soon, so stay safe. I'll keep you updated about the Exalted's movements - and then we can *both* keep one step ahead of them."

Maps and blueprints of the city came up under the avatar's feet to form a flickering virtual floor, while even more screens slid in from the sides to sketch out walls and a ceiling. Here were the secret tunnels used during the Reclamation, the air ducts and coolant pipes which Kronos had sealed centuries ago. Here were the glowing red traces of the Exalted, their alien flesh throwing off radiation in strange wavelengths. And here - a tiny green trace suspended above an ocean of thermal haze - B-Zerk and his parasite clinging to a broken spillway tower.

"Double or quits, Tsien?" asked the drone in the hot silence of its stolen head. "If I do this for you, you'll let me go?"

The avatar's laughter was as fraudulent as the banknotes which floated on the breeze, but at least it wasn't the oily chuckle of the Worm.

"After what you did to me, you think it's gonna be *that* easy? If you get through this alive, I'll promise you this - I won't try to come after you. But you'd better run a hell of a long way before you think you're safe." The picture hazed for a second, the real world fading in behind Tsien's mask like a hallucination. "Remember - I'm in your head now, just like you were in mine. I'd tell you to think about it, but you don't have time. I really suggest that you get moving."

He didn't need to hear it twice - the red traces which blurred across his mental radar were closing in fast. Up the spillway ramp he could hear the screams begin as the crowd surged and struggled with new urgency.

Few of them even noticed the black-robed urchin who scuttled over their heads and shoulders to a cluster of corroded pipes, and even those who did could only curse and swat ineffectually at his heels. They were packed so tight that B could literally run from island to island across the human sea without falling between them.

It was the work of a few moments to prize the grate from a cyclopean air filter hood, and then he was down in the dark again, down in the tunnels where his host body was perfectly at home.

All he had to do was stay alive for the next hour. It was going to be quite a task.

Ω

Even Direktor Vanecke couldn't have conjured up a thing so comprehensively evil as the skin Lysander Jaegenn now wore. He pulled himself up through the floor of his gaming temple in a storm of shadows, a vision from the most forbidden tomes of the Vatican's scriptoria.

"The games are *finished*, ladies and gentlemen," he chuckled, bubbles of blood foaming on his lips. "Thank you for being such good sports, but *playtime is over.*"

"Spare us your theatrics, Jaegenn!" spat Simeon Blaire. "If Kronos is too afraid to face me himself, then I'll use you as an object lesson. *Now, come here and bleed for your Emperor!*"

Lysander had been changed by the touch of his new Master. His face had always been thin, but now it was painfully emaciated, his cheeks sucked in tight above a lipless gash of a mouth. His hair had been cut loose from its top-knot, and it fell in oily tangles in front of his eyes, parting around a pair of swept-back ebony horns. He had obviously seen the woodcuts and etchings in those hidden Vatican files, and he'd styled himself after a Prince of Hell.

"You fool! You pitiable *fool!* Kronos is the least of your worries now! All of you are damned - you pious freaks, you self-important little lords..."

With a hideous ripping sound a pair of leathery wings erupted from his back, hunching him over as they unfurled. He looked up through a curtain of oily black hair, his eyes glowing like molten steel.

"This is the end of Manifest Dogma! *I am the end of you all*, not that crippled scum Octavio Vanecke!" He spat the name as if it was the vilest curse, rising himself up to his full height before the gathered Kheptarchy.

"This is beyond a joke! Stand down, and declare yourself forfeit!"

For a second, all eyes were turned away from the monstrous Kheptarch Lord - to a figure in veils of samite, hated burning in its eyes.

It was Elisha Dawes, and she strode forward to stand right between Exalted Jaegenn's iron-shod hooves. "Is this really your idea of *refinement*? Is this what the noble Game has come to?" Her indignation burned for a second, brighter even than the murderous fire in Lysander's eyes. "If you want Simeon Blaire, you'll have to play by the rules. Otherwise..."

But that was the last thing she would ever say. The Exalted's fist came down on her like a hammer, crushing her in her finery. Seventy-two other lords flinched back, wincing at the sound of cracking bones.

"RULES?" roared Lysander Jaegenn "What use are rules tonight? This is the end, my Lords - and what Vanecke has begun I WILL FINISH!"

The Omnivasive staff had fled the spiretop as soon as the roof tore off, scrambling over each other to the dubious safety of their camera-ships. But their machines still ground on, set to automatic, broadcasting the pale and fevered face of Exalted Jaegenn out over the city, a demon projected stories tall above streets choked with bodies.

"The Master has promised me *Simeon Blaire*! And the New Flesh must feed!"

If these had been normal men and women the execution of Elisha Dawes might have cowed them. But they were no strangers to death. Hardwired to fight, trained from birth for the arena... now the Lords of the Razor Clique stepped forward, forming a ragged half-circle between the Exalted One and Simeon Blaire, still gasping and bleeding as he held his sword at the ready.

"The *Master*?" asked Helmsfjord, cracking his knuckles with a series of loud clicks and pops. "You do this for another? You would kill Lord Simeon... but not to become Emperor?"

Lysander laughed then, an unhinged cackle which set his saprophytic skin to writhing and shuddering.

"Emperor of *what*, you idiot?" he asked, throwing his arms out wide. Above him the clouds were bruise-purple and bloody red, twisted into a churning maelstrom. "The defenses are down, my Lords. Look at your precious city, and tell me why you'd want to rule here."

The psionic spike lashed out before he'd finished speaking.

Even Simeon wasn't fast enough to block it. Each one of them witnessed a different facet of the holocaust which raged through Elysium, as Jaegenn brought them down from their aerie and into the abyss.

It was torture, fire, butchery and rape. People eaten alive and skinned and maimed, crying and screaming and suffocated silent, beaten and bloodied... Buildings shattered open to spill corpses across the roadways. Refugees running in panicked hordes from one atrocity, straight into the jaws of another...

This was the truth of the Saprophytes, and it ground into the minds of the Razor Clique like a saw-toothed router, a shockwave sparking through the wired meat of their brains.

"Do you see?" gloated Jaegenn, spreading his wings out over them, blocking out the light. "DO YOU SEE? Witness the power of my Master, and tremble!"

When the aftershock of the assault faded Simeon found himself down on his knees, vomit dripping from his open mouth. It had been too much, even for him - and his mind was tempered in the furnace of Direktor Vanecke's sequestration program. Surely the others would welcome death after seeing what he had seen...

But Helmsfjord was already struggling back to his feet, a grim look on his face. Tranh Diem, more accountant than killer, was at his side, murder in his eyes. And the rest of them, too - all seventy-two of the remaining Kheptic Lords, pale and sweating and sickened, but all of them standing tall before their tormentor, resolute.

"We *see*, Lysander Jaegenn, second of his name, thirteenth scion of the House of Jaegenn, Son of Edmus... *we see your treason.*"

"I second the motion for dishonorable dismissal," said Duchess Sebren. She knocked back the remainder of a cut-crystal tumbler of scotch to bolster her courage, then dashed it against the tiles. "I brand you and yours as *Unstable*, traitors to the Hierarchy and the Council."

For an instant Jaegenn stood frozen with disbelief, his eyes wide and his mouth hanging open. Then he slammed his fists down against the floor, sending cracks skittering through the marble.

"Do you understand *nothing*?" he shrieked, his voice rising through the octaves to a glass-shattering pitch. "It's all *meaningless!*"

The Exalted lashed out at the stony-faced Hierarchs who opposed him, utterly enraged, but they were all too fast for him. As his spiked arm swiped through the crowd the members of the Razor Clique leaped and dodged and slipped out of its path, and not a single one was touched.

"You can't do this to me! I've been the protector of the Game for twenty-seven years! I killed Vanecke, and now I'm going to kill Blaire - and none of you can stop me!"

But he was wrong.

Helmsfjord had been the first to condemn the thing which Jaegenn had become, and now he was the first to strike, coming in under the swing of the Exalted's arm and driving his fist into the creature's exposed chest. The lord spun away as Lysander howled with rage, clutching at his side.

"You could have taken him in the Game, son," said Tranh Diem, shaking his head sadly. "But now it's too late for that. The Lords of the Council and the Clique don't serve any *masters* but ourselves."

Once again the beast lunged forward, its wings thrashing in an immense downstroke. Its clutching claws scrabbled for prey, but they came up empty as the Lords and Ladies of Elysium scattered, inhumanly fast, raining blows on Lysander's legs and arms and back. It was like watching a colossus battle insects, and for all his fury the Exalted couldn't stop them.

"But... but Blaire's trying to kill you all! Why do you protect him? *Why won't you fear me?*"

Oh yes.

That was the key, and Simeon Blaire was sharp enough to sense the fear in the monster's voice...

The shadow-flesh of the saprophytes needed terror to sustain it, and the stuff which pumped in Jaegenn's veins was being slowly starved. These degenerates, these libertines and decadents weren't *afraid* of him. Worse, they burned him with their pity and revulsion.

"*Of course* he's trying to kill us, you halfwit!" scoffed Duchess Sebren, clicking back across the tiles as Lysander swung wild, his eyes blazing. "That's the nature of the Game!"

"The Emperor of Elysium must be forged in the fires of battle. Or else how will he survive the trials? How else can we know that he's fit to rule?" asked Lord Jareq Al-Haq, a look of pure scorn on his face.

"We're all out for ourselves, Jaegenn - all except you. Why would the likes of *us* fear someone who serves another - why would we fear a *slave*?"

Helmsfjord danced through the Exalted's defenses to strike at its chest, spinning away before Lysander's backhand could smash him to pulp.

"But... but he's... he's... *Blaire's nothing but a slave himself!* He's doing all this for Octavio Vanecke, so that filthy chunk of meat can claim the throne..." Jaegenn was visibly failing now, bruised and bloodied by a thousand blows, his power drained by the contempt of his enemies. He crouched back, defensive, hunching under the arch of his wings as black blood dripped from between his teeth. "Is that what you want? That shriveled schemer lording it over you all? *Do you want to live in a peasant's world?*"

Simeon pushed his way through the crowd, using his sword as a crutch as he stepped into the shadow of his enemy. His face was swollen and blistered, one eye fused shut, and little shards of diamondglass from its covering oculus winked in the red ruin of his cheek. But he was still smiling, a threedeeogenic grin which was one part bravado to ninety-nine parts madness.

"I might have *used* him, Jaegenn, but don't be deceived. If Octavio bloody Vanecke were here right now I'd tear what's left of him apart with my bare hands."

"Liar!" hissed the Exalted, lunging forward. Its claws stopped an inch from Blaire's ravaged face. "I know all about it, Simeon - about Tadashi Murai, about the Black Palace, about his plans for you. I'll do anything to keep your filthy hands off the Forge!"

"Even this?" asked Tranh Diem, his eyes full of pity. "You've sold us out to something far worse, Jaegenn."

They closed in on him from all sides - Blaire in the center with his gleaming katana held high, seventy-two warrior-aristocrats holding the beast at bay. The stuff of the saprophytes churned in Jaegenn's veins as he was pushed back towards the pit, snarling and slashing with his claws.

"But it's all true! He's Vanecke's creature! He's the Direktor's trained assassin!"

The crowd of murderous Lords was nearly on top of him when something came whispering through the air to embed itself in the marble between them. It was a black steel dagger trailing a ribbon of red silk, and it struck hard enough to penetrate right up to the hilt.

Simeon Blaire's head snapped up, tracking, his blade whirling into a defensive stance. All eyes followed his, up to the shattered edge of the dome, where a figure in light-devouring black stood poised on a broken pane of diamondglass.

"I think you'll find he's innocent, Jaegenn!" called the shadow, drawing a pair of slim silver swords from behind its back. "If anyone's Octavio's right hand, it's *me*. He's graciously allowed me the honor of taking Lord Blaire's head - and any other parts I might want as trophies."

As they watched, the self-confessed assassin stepped from the edge and into space, falling with both blades tucked up under its arms. Fifteen feet from the floor it spread its hands, letting the twin swords fly with red silk streaming out behind them. They embedded themselves in a pair of marble pillars, and the supple ribbons arrested the assassin's fall.

For a second she - for her tight-fitting scaled armor left no doubt that this warrior was female - stood suspended on point, then she snapped both hands back in, whipping the swords back into her hands. Skeins of crimson disappeared into her slash-cut sleeves.

"I think after what you've seen here tonight, Octavio Vanecke really *is* the least of your worries. Why bicker over the city while it burns?"

"Oh, sweet ancestral hells..." breathed Simeon Blaire. He'd recognised her voice."Why couldn't you just have *died* already?"

"I'll tell you what I told this witless Lord Jaegenn," said Helmsfjord. "There's a round of the Game in progress, and we don't allow outsiders. If you want him, you'll have to come through all of us - and I don't like your chances, miss. Not any more than I like his."

"You want to finish this, then?" asked Leynna Mendelev-Singh, tearing the black mask from her face "Then let's finish it, Aeric Helmsfjord. While things like Lysander here make a mockery of what we fight for. If that's the only way for me to get to your dear friend Simeon... then so be it."

They faced each other from four corners now - Lord Aeric and his band of Kheptarchs, Lysander Jaegenn in his dripping black horror-skin, Simeon Blaire all bloody and defiant, and Leynna, a knowing little smile on her lips. They stood like statues, not one of them daring to make the first move, fists and claws and blades tight and ready, eyes flickering back and forth, desperately searching for any tremor of weakness...

"I really wanted you to join us, you know. Join with my Master of your own free will, and feel the sweet exaltation..."

It was Jaegenn, his lips peeled back from teeth like transparent needles.

"But you had to make it *difficult*. You had to stand in his way. Now... " A sob racked the half-human creature's frame, while veins stood like black worms from his skin. "Now *he's* coming through. I... I'm losing control! He...he...he's... "

The darkness boiled up out of his throat while his adversaries watched, horrified. Still, nothing could break their concentration, even when Lysander's face slicked over black, his eyes reduced to slits of sickly light.

"He's *here*!" roared a voice which was a thousand voices, from a deep bass growl to a peal of manic laughter. **"Bear witness to your suffering made flesh! Bow before the Architect of Sorrows!"**

Then the lights went out, and the cool glow of neon tubes was replaced by the leaping, dancing glow of the burning city. In that horror-light the Razor Clique watched Lord Jaegenn come apart at the seams.

If the transformation which had come over Lysander before was horrific, this was the stuff of pure nightmare. The hunger and malice of his Master came flooding into his body through a crack in the world, and he was simply unable to contain it all. Frail flesh and bone were no match for a thing the size of an entire universe, a beast coiled up on itself like a vast black nautilus.

Shadows struggled and lurched across the temple walls he tore himself apart.

"Join us! Join us!" raged a voice in Simeon's head, a chorus of the damned. *"For the glory of the New Flesh!"* He bit down on a scream as it whipsawed through his mind, awakening memories of pain.

Even Leynna shuddered and stepped back from the writhing, melting thing which Jaegenn had become. The possessed Lord had swollen out to twice his normal size, a mass of glistening pseudopods lashing and twitching in the firelight. His mouth split, tearing open in a ragged red grin as gore spattered from his lips.

"Sssssso... this is the best this Earth can offer," hissed the avatar of the Worm. **"A few little human things, all dressed up in their pretty rags, thinking that they're *killers*..."** Its eyes burned like phosphorous flares in the half-darkness, taking in the remnants of the Kheptarchy with contempt. **"You know, before *me* your kind only hunted to eat. You only killed to survive. So in a way, you owe me your lives. Think of this as no more than a debt repaid..."**

"What...what the hell *is* that thing?" stammered Tranh Diem, backing away from the hot charnel stench of it. "What's it done with Jaegenn?"

"That *is* Jaegenn, Diem," said Leynna, keeping the points of her twin swords aimed at Asag'raal's throat. "Do you still think Direktor Vanecke is our biggest problem?"

"Vanecke?" laughed the Worm. "I've touched his mind, just as I've touched yours. A commendably twisted specimen, I'll admit that much - but with such limited vision. Do you know why he wanted your last game televised?"

"It's just another one of Octavio's toys," said Simeon Blaire. "I say we kill it while it's still gloating - and his whore here as well."

Leynna glared pure hatred at him for an instant, but she didn't dare take her eyes off the thing which had supplanted Lysander's body.

"Don't listen to him! That thing's no more one of Vanecke's thralls than you are, Helmsfjord. You saw what they're doing to our city! Are we just going to stand by and take it?"

"They'll all watch you fall, my Lords!" crowed the Worm, as shadows congealed around the husk of Lysander Jaegenn. It pulled itself into a parody of human form, wet and stinking of death. "Your people will watch me break you, and bring you into the fold of the New Flesh. All through the magic of poor Octavio's machines. I'm almost sorry to steal away his victory like this…"

"Dammit, it's keeping us talking for a *reason*, people!" said Simeon, backed up against one of the marble pillars. "If that thing's really not Vanecke's puppet, go ahead and kill it, Leynna. You know we're all waiting to see you try."

"And ruin the big moment for our precious Emperor-in-waiting? You go ahead, Simeon. I'm sure our fellow Hierarchs will follow you without question."

Blaire ground his teeth with rage as he watched the avatar of Asag'raal coalesce and solidify, layer upon layer of stinking black jelly slicking over the tortured frame of Lord Jaegenn. This was no time to argue among themselves. Not when the smell of fear was thick in the air, boiling out from Diem and Al-Haq and Helmsfjord and the rest in almost tangible waves…

Suddenly it all fell together in Simeon's head.

'Terror will kill you more surely than the sharpest blade' - or so he'd been taught by the scrolls and tomes of Tadashi Murai. *'The true samurai confronts his death every second of every day, and knows no fear.'*

This thing which had burst into the world through Lysander Jaegenn was feeding on their terror, toying with them to make itself even stronger. That psionic hunger was the reason Jaegenn had faltered and failed when the Hierarchs had stood up to him. And Simeon was willing to bet that his master's grip on reality was just as tenuous.

"Leynna! Aeric! All of you! Are you really afraid of this spurious little charlatan? Lysander Jaegenn's fooled you all with his expensive holos and animatronics, but he's still just a bottom-of-the-table loser!"

"**No!**" screamed the Worm, heaving itself forward on a thousand malformed legs. "**I am the darkness between realities! I am the final doom of galaxies! Your Lord Jaegenn is gone - devoured!**"

"You're a *failure*, Jaegenn. Resorting to cheap parlor tricks when you know you can't win - you're an *Unstable* and a cheat!"

Simeon forced himself to smile despite the pain in his charred and blistered face, pointing his sword like an accusing finger. And it was working. They listened to him, and they *believed* him. The smell of fear was fading as the Lords of the Razor Clique stood their ground, putting up their fists. Seventy-two of the finest warriors the Earth had ever seen, wrapped in coils of samite, facing down a fifteen-foot monstrosity all razor-sharp shadows and decay.

"**Are you all so *blind*?**" It howled, raking at its own flesh with ragged black claws. Each wound became a slavering mouth full of teeth. "**This is no trickery! You all saw my children tearing your city apart!** *Now, bow and worship me - or be destroyed!*"

"Quiet, Jaegenn!" snapped Aeric Helmsfjord, his fear distilled down into scorn. "You have been pronounced *Unstable*, a traitor, and a heretic against the truth of Manifest Dogma. Normally you would be allowed to live out your span as a pariah, but tonight - I move for an edict of summary execution."

"Seconded!" said Leynna and Blaire at the same time, glaring at each other across the width of the gaming temple.

"Very good, my Lords and Ladies. And you - master Simeon, Lady Mendelev-Singh - I remind you that the sacred Game is still in session. You are Kheptarchs of the Razor Clique, and your personal business must be put aside until this... this *deviant* is dealt with."

"**Deviant!**" roared Asag'raal, it's burning eyes flaring like sunbursts. "**I *made* you, you foolish little insects! Before I came you were scrabbling in the dirt, huddled in caves, lost in the darkness!**"

"I've heard enough," said Blaire, nodding to Lord Helmsfjord and his warriors. "Shall we?"

"Right behind you, Simeon," said Leynna, shifting out around the saprophyte's flank.

"Lysander Jaegenn, have you anything to say in your defense?" asked Aeric, relaying strategic data to his troops through their bio-onboard networks. Never before in the history of the Game had so many of the Purest fought together against a common enemy…

The Worm's reply was nothing but an inarticulate roar. Streamers of lightning coiled around its three-foot claws, popping sparks like miniature novae.

"Kill it," spat Helmsfjord, all pity and disgust. And the survivors of the final Game leaped to the attack.

Ω

"Is this what you wanted to show me? This is the Game that Mother and Father like to play?"

Octavio's hologram shimmered in the air, his avuncular smile painted on by a trio of tiny lasers.

"That's right, Darion. This is the great Game, and it's very important to them both. But…"

"Oh, I know the monster's lying, Uncle. You told me why *you* can't play, and anyway, he's got no chance against all of them together. Even if he is trying so hard to be scary."

Perhaps the child saw something he didn't, then. Whatever terrible force Lysander Jaegenn had allied himelf with seemed to claw at his naked brain every time he set eyes on it - even if those eyes were nothing but a pair of twin flycams, as they were here in Darion's nursery.

"They'll be coming home soon then, won't they?" asked the child, his mismatched eyes shining wide and guileless in the glow of the threedeeo globe. "The Eduplug taught me all about the naming day ceremony, and I want them to see what I've learned already!"

"Keep watching, then." said Octavio, his holographic avatar flickering as he passed through the image of Jaegenn's ruined temple. "This is a big day for them, too, and they wouldn't want you to miss it."

The forcegrown child made him uneasy - and that was hard enough to admit. But the thought of all the terrible, illegal information which he'd woven into the Eduplug made him even more nervous. Thank goodness Darion didn't realize his own potential! Some of the little 'tests' he'd arranged had shown him the smallest fraction of the boy's power, and it would be a terrifying thing to see unleashed without *control.*

"They've both got swords, Uncle! Can I have one too? Then when people like Mister Veer come to bother you I can get rid of them myself."

Octavio shivered, there in his preservative tank. His hologram only beamed proudly, crouching down next to Darion's gelfoam chair and pointing at the screen.

"Not yet - not today, anyway! You've only been with us an hour, and you already want to go and join them, don't you?"

The little Lord nodded earnestly, his long black hair pulled back from his face in a jewelled top-knot. His left eye was violent green, his right golden-amber flecked with steel.

"I think my Mother's going to get it first. See, she's faster than him, and Father's relying on strength. But the monster is still stronger... his strategy is flawed."

Oh yes - he was fearsomely loyal to Leynna Mendelev-Singh. Vanecke had made sure the forcegrown scion's earliest memories were of his mother saving him from a terrible monster, deep beneath the Black Palace. If he was destined to live a normal life he'd need years of neuromekan therapy to erase his nightmares. As it was, they were just another facet of his programming.

Perhaps, thought Direktor Vanecke, this transformation which gripped Lysander Jaegenn would play right into his little scenario. The maiden, the hero and the beast, all over again, reinforcing the shadow-memories burned into young Darion's brain...

"Keep watching, child," he said, his body fading out line by line, blurring away into static. "They wouldn't want you to miss a thing, I'm sure..."

Oh no. Not tonight. Octavio only hoped the boy was right - Jaegenn must fall before his own schemes fell into place. Leynna and Simeon were on a collision course, and nothing must divert them from their pre-ordained destiny. Not just for the fans, or for his own sense of showmanship. This was all for a very special audience of one, a dark-haired child with mismatched eyes and the bloody grace of a matador.

They would be the last two left of the old order, and they'd fight to the death for Darion's edification - for *control.*

17 Aevum Oblivio
On Ice

TECHNICIAN ZHE CAME up out of the water so fast that the Tin Man's guns couldn't follow him - a blur of silver draped with ragged streamers of green slime and corroded bullet-belts. He knew this place now - this was where SubMagus Devine and his colleague Rosvall had brought CeeAn back from the dead, all those years ago. This was the cryonics and cloning lab where she'd been downloaded into a new body, transformed from light to flesh...

Bullets hammered into the concrete wall behind him as he ran, diving for cover behind a trio of icy metal pods. They were skinned over with condensation, humming with power. Just like the module in which Katio Kayzi slept, in the vault of the Cardinal Rock high above.

The Tin Man would never suspect this.

Hells, it was pure insanity - but he had a feeling it was going to work. If the memories he'd unearthed about Jaq Haszan's little fight with the Emerald City Gang held true, there was nasty surprise inside these pods; a kind of three-card monte of death.

Zhe worked quickly, tripping the switches to defrost the bodies trapped within. He could hear the steady tread of the Tin Man moving in to finish him. Of course he'd never just fire through those precious cryo tanks - even if he was a creature of cold steel, a human brain was still nestled at the core of his armored skull.

No time to stand still - the Technician broke cover, leaping up among the pipes and wires which hung from the ceiling, swinging wild as bursts of fire tracked his every move. A bullet grazed his arm, cutting a livid track of yellow across his silver skin.

But the glass was starting to clear. And he was right.

Behind the porthole of the first tank floated a yellow mask, crudely painted with an idiot grin. Behind the second, a face all red and raw, its lidless eyes staring blankly at nothing. And in the third, a sleeping beauty locked in a frozen embrace, her exquisite lips curled into an aristocratic sneer.

The lights were blinking, LCD timers counting down.

Zhe took a flying leap from a section of cooling pipe, down into the black depths from whence he'd come. Bullets sizzled and hissed through the water behind him, trailing bubbles in their wake. But he was safe again, and the clock was ticking.

Soon, if his scheme paid off, the Chrome Ark would be in his hands.

DOCUMENT INSERT - MULTIPLICITY ARCHIVE DEPARTMENT

'The Red Land' - Earth colloq.

'The Red Land' refers to the mines of Mars, the largest colony established by the Corporate Governments of old Earth. The phrases "He's gone to the Red Land" or "He's in the Red Land now" refer to penal transportation, but can also be colloquialisms for death... there was no return from Mars, no matter what the cause of one's exile.

The term is taken from the ancient Egyptian, in which the 'Red Land' is the desert of the evil deity Set - also a place of no return.

Prior to the completion of Terminus Afrika and the wars of Secession, Mars was the powerhouse of the Corporate States, giving them massive economic leverage over the crumbling Old Democracies. Indeed, many of the transported miners and factory workers who populated the bore-shaft cities of Mars were sold to the C.S. Direktorship by the overtaxed prison systems of the Democratic nations.

Extensive orbital defenses surrounded the prison-planet, including fortresses carved into the moons of Deimos and Phobos, all to deter a forcible takeover by the spacefleets of the Democracies. But in the end, the doom of Mars came with the Secessionist wars... the mutual destruction of the Direktorship and its enemies meant that no resupply of the mines was ever undertaken.

Tishon Albeq - "The Forgotten Dead - War, Secession and the fall of Mars"
Elysian University Press

TOGETHER, IT WOULD have been easy.

Well, if not *easy*, then at least a little less like a jaunt through the lower circles of hell. She had to fight her way from doorway to doorway, block to shattered block, but worse than the Saps or the warmekan were the *survivors*...

If Abdulafia had been with her she could have helped some of them. The ones half-crushed under rubble, or bleeding their last in shadowed alleyways... The ones wandering amid the smoke and ruin, dazed and eviscerated...

As it was, all she could do was hand out Last Rites to the dying.

Even that took far too long, but she had no choice. Not after what she'd seen on the other side of death - that grinding, twisting slough of darkness devouring souls, plucking them from the air to feed its furnace heart...

CeeAn had a solution hardwired into her augmented *Dervashi* flesh, a mechanism by which those poor lost spirits could escape the Worm.

The Chrome Ark.

This one would be the sixteenth, a teenage boy half-burned and moaning in the doorway of a ruined bookstore, a railpistol charred to the stump of his hand.

Kronos' warmekan had gotten this one - a small mercy, perhaps, compared to the embrace of the Saprophytes. CeeAn hunkered down next to him, cradling his blistered head in both hands as her fingers searched for a set of neural plugs. There - he was wired up. His bio-onboard system was in total overload trying to block the agony which suffused him.

"Shh... quiet now. It's O.K. It's over." Sweet nothings, whispered as she let a jack-tipped cable coil down her arm, slipping between her fingers and into his cranial socket. "The pain's almost gone. It's gonna be allright..."

"*Liar,*" Sighed the voice of Abdulafia in her head.

But some lies are softer than the truth...

As soon as CeeAn made the connection the kid's back arched, every muscle pulled tight. His eyes bulged from his head, wide and white and bloodshot. Raw data hissed through her operative crescent, and a tiny trickle of blood dripped from the corner of his mouth as his spirit fled. She let his empty body down gently, resting his head on the concrete as if it was the silk pillow of a casket.

Sixteen, and counting. She hoped that the Ark could process his memories and upload his personality, even though he'd never been Ashishim.

CeeAn stood, leaving the dead boy uncovered in the broken doorway. Burial was out of the question, though from the way the fires were spreading through this sector of the Subcity, cremation might well be on the cards. She muttered a prayer under her breath to the nebulous Ancestor Spirits the Illuminatus swore watched over them, and slid her sword from its sheath.

Lucky she'd found it, gleaming amid the rubble and ruin of the Valley View.

Perhaps the old man's sermons hadn't been entirely without substance after all, and the Spirits had put it there just for her. If they had, they were certainly much more bloody-minded and vengeful than Zeon had led his people to believe...

The three-foot blade was ancient - that much she could see just from the patina and gloss of its oily steel. Deep fullers inscribed with alien runes ran down its entire length, and its crossguard was a fat brass coin etched with dragons. It looked like something had snapped an impossibly long sword clean in half to fashion this little one... and a good thing, really. While CeeAn 187 could fight with a six-foot blade (or, indeed, a marlinspike, a morningstar or a piece of broken glass) she was supremely comfortable with a weapon just this size.

A sword this sharp, and this well-tempered... she could make the bastard *sing*.

The *Dervashi* set out along the roadway, loping through the shadows and smoke between sinkholes and geysers of flame. If her memory served, this had once been Isambard Street, an elevated feeder chute which led out to the spillway. From there it would be easy to reach the gates of Ashisim country, and put her plans into motion.

Exodus.

The image of that great beating heart still hung huge and ghostly in her mind, like a full moon over her shoulder. And the things she'd seen... the terrible promises of Asag'raal had all come true. Those sixteen souls who'd found sanctuary in the Chrome Ark were the lucky ones. The others... just thinking about some of the others brought bile to the back of her throat. The ones burned by the Saprophytes were the worst, those who'd been possessed and then left for dead.

For them, CeeAn's blade had been the only mercy available, and their eyes had begged for it.

So many. So many dead... but millions could be saved.

She ran on, evading the sweeping laser-targeters of stalking mekan, scaling walls and scuttling along rooftops, wire-walking on telephone cables while bands of looters passed by underneath. Not long ago she would have stopped to introduce every last one of them to the jagged end of her blade, but death had given her a fresh perspective. Only one thing mattered now... the Exodus.

CeeAn came up and over the humped back of the Isambard Street Bridge, an unseen blur in the darkness. She picked her way across the eaves of burned-out houses, all the way to the edge.

The spillway spread out before her, a delta of concrete sloping down into the Pit. To her left stood the great barbican fortress where Pope Joan the Third held court; the Iron Basilica looming like a great leaden skull in the firelight. Beyond it lay the flat black expanse of the poison sea, awash with the bobbing candle-flames of refugee rafts. Immense banks of searchlights hung from the battlements of the Catholic fortress, lighting up the spillway as bright as noonday.

And by that light CeeAn saw a seething tide of humanity, a wailing, struggling mass pouring out of the ruptured carcass of Elysium, driven on by horrors.

Someone had blown the bridge in front of her, so CeeAn stood on the edge of a sheer drop, twisted snarls of rebar and concrete trailing away into the dark. This was as far as Isambard Street went, and it was probably for the best. That roiling sea of bodies would likely have dragged her down in its undertow if they'd been able to reach the bridge, and then she'd be useless, nothing but prey for the things which fed on the hindmost.

Because the Saprophytes were here, the Exalted among them, and they were cutting a bloody swath through the rear of the crowd. CeeAn's eyes were mil-spec, chunks of stolen tech, and from here she could see arms and legs and heads flying, suitcases split open as they tumbled through the air, blood painting the walls and pillars of the spillway-tops. Money and hanks of hair, baby clothes and photographs blew out like chaff as the Exalted set upon their quarry, hounds among fleeing mice.

Her eyes narrowed, metal irises whirring and shifting.

Six of them. Only six, with a mass of gibbering Saprophytes capering at the heels of each one. CeeAn turned away, and strode out over the causeway toward the Iron Basilica. Her knuckles were white where they gripped the leather-bound handle of her sword. In her head; a vast, spectral heartbeat.

"You can't come in here!" yelled a young warrior-monk from atop the Vatican's gates, his riot armor painted in the bright primaries of the Swiss Guards. "Go back! The Vatican is on lockdown, but we pray for you all!"

CeeAn kept coming, as if the twenty foot steel-plated gates were nothing more than a beaded fly-curtain. Atop the little catwalk there was a brief scuffle - an older man wrestling the megaphone from the guardsman's hand.

"Ashishi! Remember the treaty! This isn't our fight, and it isn't yours!"

This one was Valle Crucis - a grizzled old veteran by the looks, his habit patched up with ribbons and seals from a hundred contracts. In one hand he gripped the megaphone, in the other a crackling shock-scepter surmounted with a crucifix.

"One last chance, *Hashishin*. Turn back now, or face the consequences."

But no matter how much the battered tin cone of the megaphone amplified his threats, the screaming and wailing of the damned was louder. And the rhythmic bass thud of that ghostly heart seemed to shake the entire world with every step she took.

After all, she'd already died once tonight. What more could they do to her?

CeeAn broke into a run as she came up toward the gates, hearing the clang and clatter of cannons being run out from their armored embrasures. Voices were shouting in Latin, tinged with panic, but she couldn't hear them.

Sprinting now, her feet barely touching the riveted steel surface of the bridge, and the bullets came down like rain.

Too slow.

Just like the Vatican's Christ she'd come through death stronger, smarter, refined by the fires of mortality. That last exultant hit of 'chrome which had carried her down into the node still burned in her brain, undiminished, and now there were none of the painful side-effects that usually ruined her trip.

CeeAn danced through the firestorm like an acrobat, handspringing and arching over lines of tracer, seeing the shadow-image of future shells seconds before they came scything through the smoky air. She cocked back a fist as the gates loomed above her, and she felt the touch of that great inverted ocean again, the billions of souls dreaming in its beating heart.

Waves raced outward as her hand came back. Behind the gates she heard the servo whine of Templars and Sacristans firing up their war-suits, scrambling to their attack stations.

The waves reached the edges of the inverse sea as she swung, surging back in as high as mountains, curling gray-green cliffs rimed with foam...

CeeAn's lips peeled back from her teeth in a manic grin.

And her knuckles hit the steel armor of the gates with all the power of that incorporeal tide-surge, making the whole world ring like the inside of a cathedral bell.

There was no way that a single human fist could punch through three feet of metal, even with supernatural force behind it. But the concrete towers on either side of the gateway shook, and the immense shockwave knocked the defenders inside out cold. Cracks bloomed around its hinges, and screaming guardsmen and Valle Crucis toppled from the catwalk, arms windmilling for balance. A thousand all-seeing camera eyes shattered, leaving the Vatican Invigilators blind.

The gunfire had stopped.

Now the voices behind the gates took on a new and more intensive note of panic. The thunder of metal claws and the howl of turbines filled the square in front of the Basilica as Pope Joan's defenders fell into line.

Well, she'd knocked.

And now they were opening the door for her.

Cee skipped back into the shadow of the gates as they swung open, dented in around the indelible imprint of four petite knuckles. First through the gap was a hulking veteran Paladin, his helmeted head almost lost between the rotary cannons on his shoulder-mounts. Gilded Crosses of Lorraine and icons of the blessed virgin were bolted to every surface of the rugged old war-suit, and its chest was painted with the beatific face of Jesus, his hands clasped around the sigil of a fiery heart.

Perhaps he'd been expecting someone taller - there was nothing outside the gates but swirling smoke and dust, no sound but the far-off screams of the dying as the Exalted scourged the spillway.

No sign of the little Ashishi bitch, anyway... the Archdeacon of the Transept (for such was his title) clenched and unclenched his fists deep in the control gauntlets of his armored suit. Its battle-pincers snapped and popped with the sound of powerful hydraulics.

He never saw CeeAn vault up over his head, landing on her hands for a second atop the catwalk. She dropped out of sight behind one fractured concrete bastion, stealthy as a wraith. When the gates hinged open they formed a tight little chimney between their riveted surface and the reinforced cinderblocks of the guard-tower - an easy climb for a trained *Dervashi*.

A logjam of powered warsuits waited behind the Archdeacon's Paladin armor - Teutons with their chainsaw arms, Templars like the beast she'd fought at Don Gianni's, Sacristans with maser-carbines and nimble Arcanii with their magnetic sniper-cannons.

Enough firepower to drive the Exalted from the spillway, if their pilots had the courage to disobey their orders. People were dying out there in their hundreds, and these pious idiots stood by, guarding a sacred building...

Not one of them looked behind as CeeAn skipped from shadow to shadow, kneeling down over a fallen 'Crucis monk to unlace his riotmesh robes. It was the old man who'd tried to stop her at the gates, and he'd fallen hard, shattering his left leg. The glassy sheen of pseudomorph glistened in his eyes as he stirred, coming up out of his drugged sleep at her touch.

"Whhaa...? Who... you're her! The *Hashishin*... but...why? Are you... are those things, those *demons*... are they yours?"

His voice was barely a whisper, but that wasn't what Cee was worried about. There was a rosary in his hand, a shiny black cross on a chain of hematite beads, and it was exactly the same as the one Leighton Cressmeyer had prayed into during their wild ride through the Subcity. If he shouted, the switchboard nuns of the Repentia would hear him loud and clear.

"No, 'Crucis. Not mine. I'm here to kill them. And I'm going to need one of your warsuits to do it. Your knights don't seem to want to get their hands dirty."

Despite the drugs and the pain he seemed to understand her.

"The Archdeacon's Own... *live* to protect the Iron Basilica," he wheezed. "Not their fault. Just... fools. We had our orders, but I had to watch them... watch them dying down there..."

His hand clenched tight around her arm, and he pulled himself up on one shoulder.

"Under the fountain of the Apostles. The main hangar... but please, *Hashishin*..." His eyes flashed with anger, then, and his mouth became a hard-set line, his brow furrowed with pain. "Kill them all. Every last one. Promise me that, and I won't try to stop you."

He let the rosary fall from his hand, the beads slipping between his shaking fingers.

"I promise." said CeeAn. "Is there anything... anything I can do for your pain?"

The monk grinned then, exposing a mouthful of bloodstained teeth.

"Show those pompous knights how it's done, girl. The mediteks'll have my leg patched up before you've even finished fighting."

His eyes fluttered closed, then, and he slipped down to the ground unconscious. Cee quickly peeled off his robe, leaving him in the shadows beneath her own tattered cloak. Wrapped in her new disguise she scurried across the vast echoing square of the Basilica, around the curve of the barbican's wall to where a vast three-tiered fountain reared up like a coral reef.

The Apostles on the fountain clustered around their Savior like groupies around a rockstar - all but the sniveling figure of Judas, poking his head out from behind an encrustation of fluttering cherubs. How the architects of the Vatican had managed to haul so much marble up the spillway CeeAn had no idea - but she had no time to critique the huge rococo mess.

The *Dervashi* only had eyes for the great steel trap-door gates in front of the fountain, a gaping maw from which steam and sparks curled out in lazy billows. Someone was hammering metal down there, and voices echoed up in Latin as prayers and devotions were uttered over the warsuit mekan on their launch gantries.

Cee skirted around the fountain, right up to the edge of the pit, and looked down on a scene right out of Kronos' worst nightmares.

The hangar was vast - ten stories deep, carved out of the wall of the dam where it joined the barbican fortress. Perhaps this had once been a turbine-room, back when the Helios tokamaks under Elysium had been backed up with hydro-electric power.

Now it was an arsenal of the Faithful, dominated by an ornate crucifix forty feet high, an altar like a solid brick of buttery yellow gold, and a red carpet bisecting it down the middle. Censers swung from gantry cranes, filling the air with the smell of sandalwood and honey, while priests scurried here and there with little pyxes of oil, anointing the feet of warmekan bigger than any CeeAn had seen before.

None of these things had taken part in the Seven Hours War - but it seemed impossible that they'd been built during the last hundred years. Each one rose to the same height as that giant wooden crucifix, eyeballing Jesus with a battery of blank cameras. They must have been shipped in piece by piece, assembled by the Black Technologists who swarmed about them on rickety scaffolds, wielding datablocks and threedeeo tablets, thuribles and wrenches.

CeeAn's memory tweaked - back to a security briefing in the Dervashic Academy.

The Seraph-class battlesuit, a nuclear-powered monster-machine that even the Dervashi *had been told to fear...*

And here they were, all six of them, primed and ready after decades of dusty hibernation. Just like the broken sword at her hip, they must have been put here by the providence of the Spirits.

Each one of the war-machines was named for a Christian Saint; individually hand-painted and decorated with curls of ribbon, charms, sigils and crosses. No two were the same, from their cloisonned armor to their weapons loadout.

CeeAn had no time to weigh up the merits of each Seraph as she slid silently down a chain and onto the top level of the Technologists' scaffold - she set her sights on the largest of them and pulled her hood up, mumbling nonsense in Latin.

The wounded Crucis' robe would have to keep her face hidden as she crossed the swaying pipework catwalk to her chosen warmekan. Despite having a female Pope these last sixty years, the Black Technologists were strictly androgyne, asexual cyborgs with chrome masks depicting the faces of martyrs. She could count on them to discriminate.

The flare of welding torches and plasma-cutters cast leaping shadows across the whole echoing pit of the hangar, and the slam and rumble of trip-hammers below masked her footsteps as she picked her way through a spiderweb of scaffolding. To the open chest-cavity of the Serpah, surrounded by a tight little knot of Devotionals, Technologists, monks, priests and menials...

Not one of them turned to look at the tiny little monk in oversized robes who had joined their congery - the air was hot with the smell of oil and desperation.

Cee breathed a sigh of relief into her hood, blowing a streamer of blue hair out of her eyes. The Lord Pilot of the great machine was nowhere to be seen - no doubt he'd be attending a briefing in one of the Basilica's sunken oratories, planning a strategy for the defense of the Holy See.

It was too late for that, CeeAn knew.

Even the servo-muscles of the Seraphim, its vast fusion obliterators and maserstorm cannons would only be a diversion. The Exalted had come, and Elysium was already dead.

Only the Exodus could save them now.

She smirked in the shadow of her stolen robe, watching the thurible-wielding monks chanting and moaning at their prayers. *Exodus* was one of the chapters of their own holy book, but they hadn't taken the hint. Perhaps in the carnage outside their gates the wise Cardinals and Bishops of the Vatican saw the beginning of their prophesied apocalypse, and waited for the return of the great Christ.

What they *got*, however, was a grinning maniac *Dervashi* right in their midst, throwing aside her disguise and charging at them with a broken samurai sword in one hand and a tangle of cables twisting about the other.

The little tableau around the warmekan's interface deck blew apart, censers whirling like morningstars with comet-tails of smoke streaming out behind them, wirehead Devotionals dropping their threedeeo tablets and screaming, monks and menials falling over each other to get out of her way. CeeAn erupted into their midst, all color and light as her tattoos flared to life, underlighting her face with violet fire.

She would have felt bad about slicing left and right with her broken sword, had the things which stood in her path been anything other than Black Technologists.

As it was, the rippled steel blade carved through carbon-fiber and aluminum instead of flesh and blood, lopping off bionic arms and legs as cleanly as stalks of grass. The Technologists didn't cry out, didn't bleed - the only human part of them was locked away deep in their holy armor, withered hearts and brains suckling on nutrient machinery. Dismemberment, for them, was just an inconvenience.

But the screams of the fleeing holy men had roused the attention of others - subdeacons and knights noviate with thick black shotguns in their hands and swords on their hips. They wouldn't fire in this holy place, but they wouldn't hesitate to slice CeeAn apart like the disassembled Black Techs at her feet. And for her, that would be more than discomforting. It'd mean another three months of pushing light.

She reached the cockpit of the Seraph just as one of the brighter Devotionals thought to shut the hangar doors, setting off a drone of klaxons and a shatterburst of red strobes. The thick slabs of metal began to grind closed, inch by inch, their hazard-striped edges moving with glacial slowness.

Too late for that, boys.

CeeAn squeezed inside the control harness of the machine, just in time to watch a gaggle of knights noviate reach the top of the scaffold, their short-swords crackling with electrical fire. They pointed, and screamed imprecations, and brandished their blades in a very martial manner. But they were out of time.

Cee waved goodbye to them as she pulled a lever home, swinging shut the warmekan's nine-inch armored chest panels. Only then did the noviates think to fire their shotguns; but the buckshot rattled off the hand-painted breastplate of the Seraph like hail.

Thank goodness for the Dervashic Academy. Thank goodness for all that didactic imprinting they'd put her through...

The serpent cables which twined around CeeAn's fist hissed out toward a handful of sockets, greedy for information. Databores punched through the safeguards of the ancient machine, sending schematics dancing through her head.

The wires hummed, exultant, and she brought the Lord Pilot's control goggles down over her eyes, feeling the plugs around each oculus mate smoothly with the ones drilled into her skull.

Four mighty arms with biceps the size of tanks flexed against their tethers. Coolant lines snapped and broke with a sound like harp-strings as the machine rose to its feet.

There was one Black Technologist left on the scaffold, his modulated voice drowned out by the pulse and roar of the warmekan's awakening. About his feet his brothers lay incapacitated, dripping holy lubricants.

That lone Vatican Priest watched as the Serpah named Saint Sebastian rose up, and up, and up, its crowned steel head almost brushing the metal ceiling. Painted across its chestplate was a scene from the most holy apocrypha - the Saint himself, standing unbound before an execution stake, holding off a storm of arrows with one outstretched hand.

The Technologist waved his tiny fist in anger, and CeeAn did the same.

The turbo-mace at the end of Sebastian's burnished arm spun up with a howl of long-unused bearings - three rings of spiked steel spinning in opposite directions.

When they hit the hangar doors the metal parted like cheap plasterboard, curling back to expose a gash of flame-lit sky. Cee brought the mace back the other way, tearing the hole wide open.

"Don't worry!" she yelled, her voice amplified through the Seraph's shoulder-mounted speakers. "I'll bring it back in one piece, I promise!"

And with that she slammed a command down through the mekan's giant body, down through its iron-shod feet to the launch gantry it stood on. The Black Tech only had time to spit a final curse as he heard a rumble beneath the ground, and realized what would happen next. He took a dive off the scaffolding as it shook itself to pieces, collapsing in a shower of flailing bodies and metal tubes and clamps.

Great hydraulic bolts unscrewed from the back and neck of Saint Sebastian as the rumble beneath its feet became a roar, and then a bone-shaking blur of noise too deep and deafening for words.

CeeAn thought that her head was about to crack open as the launch systems did their thing, and she was slammed back into her harness by a giant-sized helping of g-force. Black and red shadows sizzled and cooked in her brain. Her eyes felt as if they were being squeezed between vise-grip jaws.

The forty-foot tall warmekan called Saint Sebastian came up out of the plaza in front of the Iron Basilica like a shot from a cannon, a titanic shadow against the searchlit clouds. Two hundred feet, three hundred, its arms unfurling like windmill sails, equipped with an arsenal of death.

At the top of its arc it stopped, hundreds of tons of battle-ready steel perched in the sky over the spillway. The Exalted looked like tiny black toys below.

CeeAn smiled, feeling the straps and buckles of the harness go limp, the g-force peel away.

She zoomed in with her battery of camera eyes, squinting through the goggles which wrapped around her face.

There. The tormentors. The *prey*.

With a feral howl, amplified out of all proportion through a pair of forty-inch speakers in her shoulder pauldrons, CeeAn came down on the Exalted and their Saprophyte horde. She was vengeance and fury made manifest in steel.

Sixteen dead and counting, you bastards! Time to start a tally of your own...

Ω

Miguel 903 wasn't ready for war. He was a gardener, dammit - not a *Dervashiman*, not a warrior...

382

Truth be told, he'd only joined up with the Ashishim for the free ganja and (reputed) free love of the R.T. Sect. *Anything* was better than living down in the sunless gloom of hab-block 2095 with his meth-head brothers and his drunken father.

The only future *they* had to look forward to was indentured labor in the manufactoria of Consolidated Industries - forty years of back-breaking toil pouring molten steel and sweating over blast-furnaces. Fine, he guessed, if you took comfort in the bottle and the pipe and Manifest Dogma. Then slaving in 'Duke Gideon's Kitchen' was holy duty; he'd had that fact beaten into him as a child by his father's callused fists.

But Miguel was that dangerous blend of free-thinking radical and unimaginative follower that seemed to be born in trouble. Just the kind the pamphleteers of the Reclamation were looking for when they ventured down into the lower habs, bunched together around their *Dervashi* escort to deter the workshop gangs.

That's how he got the number, and the dogtags around his neck, and the baggy hemp overalls blazoned with the eye-and-dagger insignia of the Ashishim.

He'd got his wish, too - at least in one respect. The first posting for a raw 'phyte off the downhab streets was always the hydro labs, and the resin he peeled off his fingers every hour was enough to keep his brain sizzling and popping day and night.

As to the free love - he'd been cruelly misinformed on that score.

The girls down here in the R.T. were just the same as those uptown when it came to acne-scarred, thin-faced little juves; they just weren't interested. And in case being a revolutionary got him any leverage, he wasn't allowed to leave - 'phytes stayed on lockdown until they were bonded to the Ark and got their tattoos.

Miguel was pretty sure he'd score the pot-leaf neckpiece tattoos of a hydro gardener, and be stuck in the vast echoing caverns of cannabis forever. Still, compared to Hab 2095 that hadn't seemed so bad.

Until now.

Miguel felt his way along the corridor, following the dying glow of neon lights. Behind the metal skin of the Subcity he could feel the roar and thunder of machines, and beyond that the crump and thud of explosions. From time to time the whole city seemed to heave and shake itself like a fevered body, sending dust sifting down from the ceiling.

He had no idea where he was going - just *away*. Away from the horror that lay behind him, in the burned-out tunnels where the... the *things* had broken through.

First came the Aryan soldiers - black-clad fighters with crimson armbands, machine-pistols and maser carbines. Miguel had thought it was an invasion, when he'd struggled up out of his bunk and into wakefulness.

But oh no. That wouldn't be *nearly* bad enough.

The Confederates were *running*, bleeding and soot-smeared and short of breath. They'd broken through into Ashishi territory by mistake, blowing an old bulkhead door and stumbling across the habitrail 'phyte-hab with its swinging hammocks and scrap-wood bunks.

Miguel would have been terrified enough if they'd started mowing down his fellow recruits with their smoking guns. He hadn't even thought about his own big bulky Ashishim revolver - he'd been too busy crawling under the bed, whimpering with terror.

From under there he caught the Aryan commander barking a few words in Deutch, something about the *Dervashi*... and then they all heard the noise.

That hideous, unclean noise - the one which echoed in his head as he stumbled on through the dark, driving him onward like a lash.

It had come out of the wide-open bulkhead door, a rusted slab of steel charred by the Confed's explosives. A sound like deep, chuckling laughter, bubbling and oily, accompanied by the stench of week-old corpses.

The Aryans had turned toward the door as soon as they heard it, and all but a handful of the bravest Ashishi novices were fighting to escape. Miguel would like to have told himself that he stayed and watched because he possessed a little of that bravery - but the truth was he was scared paralyzed, caught like a rabbit in the headlights as shadows began to lurch and flicker through the open door. The black-uniformed soldiers muttered prayers and loaded their guns.

He was watching, wide-eyed and terrified as the first Saprophyte came through. A vast clawed hand was all he saw of it, black talons wrapping around a soldier's waist and *squeezing* until his eyes bulged from his skull. Gunfire rang out, deafeningly loud, and maser blasts cooked the dusty air. But that dripping claw whipped back faster than it had struck, dragging the screaming man down into the dark.

Then came the unmistakable sound of ripping, chewing teeth, and his screams were silenced.

The defenders stepped back from the doorway, ashen-faced, Aryan and Ashishim alike, listening to the crunch and snap of bones in the dark.

Miguel 903 pulled himself even further back under the bed, desperate for a weapon, desperate for escape...

And they came through.

Ten of them, twenty - he didn't know. Before them rolled a cloud of noisome stench, rancid and rotten, almost making him vomit as it seethed through the tiny hab. The one or two defenders who succumbed to it died with bile in their mouths, caught hunched-over with sickness as a black tide slopped over the doorframe, a million bubbling tentacles of filth.

Miguel saw *faces* in a wall of darkness, forcing itself through the doorway like a great gelatinous plug of flesh, faces twisted and stretched in ecstatic pain, in utter madness. Then he saw the teeth, the arms, the claws, the nameless lashing appendages tipped with blades and hooks and spikes...

He watched them go to work, breaking the Aryans down to shuddering raw meat in an instant, shredding the Ashishi juves who stood against them.

Bullets did nothing. Maser blasts vaporized chunks of its liquid flesh, but the wounds just oozed shut like slobbering mouths...

It was a one-sided slaughter.

For all their savagery the creatures were surgical in their butchery - slicing and flaying their prey while gleaming black pseudopods held them aloft. To Miguel it seemed as if they wanted their victims to experience as much pain as possible before they were devoured...

And then he understood.

He watched one of the creatures slowly absorbing the twitching body of an Aryan soldier, his face torn away to the gleaming bone, his eyes still staring, sentient, as he was engulfed. And as it took him in it shat out the burned corpus of another human being, a thing eaten away by cruel chemicals deep in its embrace.

Horribly, she too was *still alive.*

It was the look of mute pleading in her eyes which shattered his paralysis, which made him roll out from under the bed and make for the door. His baggy hemp coverall was damp in the crotch, warm and foul against his skin. But dignity was for the brave, and right now Miguel could only think of those razor hooks coiling out behind him, those eyeless faces split with maniac grins...

"Comme back! Weeeee onllyyyy wa...aa...aannnt to plaaaaay!" giggled the Saprophytes in a single mismatched choir, but Miguel could hardly hear them.

He slipped through the hab door just as a clutch of long-fingered hands and whips of oily darkness came questing after him, and he leaned his whole weight into the great airlock, slamming it shut on them.

They parted like severed worms, and he heard the monsters scream. It was probably more frustration than pain, but it made him feel good. Miguel leaned up against the door for a second, his heart thumping in his throat, and he felt their hooks and knives rasping against the corroded steel, searching for a way through.

Oh no. He spun away from the door and locked down its immense iron bolt, sealing them in... Or at least, that's what he thought...

A second later he noticed the smoke - sizzling, oily smoke pouring from around the edges of the door. They were coming through!

So he ran. Down into the darkness, losing his bearings and stumbling through tunnels half-flooded with icy water, through hanging gardens gone to rot and rust, through echoing chambers so large he couldn't see their far walls, just the strip of phosphor lights which picked out his path. Every noise was a snarling black demon in his fevered imagination, every shadow concealed ravenous death.

But he lived.

And after a while he realized that he was lost.

He remembered the words of the Tutor Academius, the man who was supposed to induct them into the Ashishim way of life. That scarred old veteran had been very clear on the issue of escape - clear that there *wasn't* one. Their indenture wouldn't last long, he'd said, just until they were educated in the history of the tribe, until they were checked out by the Magi to make sure that none of them were Kronocult spies.

Until then, they were free to explore the bounds of the sect's R.T. homeland, but never to go off the edge of the map. The concessions of the Ashishim were walled about with watchtowers and cameras and guard-posts where they butted up against those of the Vatican and the Confederacy, and especially along the great no-mans-land line where the R.T. met the Subcity. But not below.

Not in the sub-basements and oily, dripping ruins beneath the city. Even the Pit Ferals weren't brave or stupid enough to attack through those blighted zones, where death-machines crawled broken through the muck, and once-human things preyed on each other in the darkness...

Miguel 903 realized that he'd escaped from a nightmare, only to land in one far worse.

He was sobbing quietly to himself as the corridor he followed let out onto another; a wide underground avenue lit up by the eerie green glow of liquid globes in the walls.

At least there was light down here. At least he'd be able to see them coming, when they came for him...

And that's when he saw the shadow.

It capered and danced on the curved vault of the tunnel - a half-human thing with too many knees and elbows and *spikes*, a homunculus of darkness stretched out long and thin across the wall. Whatever it was, it was coming his way, dragging its own light behind it.

Miguel slumped to the floor, his hands over his head. He was weeping openly now, tears carving tracks through the dust and grime which covered his face.

He'd never signed up for this. He was just a poor little down-hab juve, trying to get away from his awful life. He didn't deserve to get eaten by demon-things down in the dark...

But the light was still growing, an underground sun spreading its radiance along the tunnel as it came. The twisted shadow it cast before it stopped, its elongated head turned to one side, listening...

Miguel wiped the snot from his nose with the back of one hand, trying not to breathe. But it was too late. He knew that it had sensed his presence.

The figure painted across the concrete wall of the tunnel began to change as he watched, its arms and legs shrinking, its hands losing their extra thumbs, its skull becoming a dome instead of a curved half-moon. In a handful of seconds it was transformed...

Into the silhouette of a human being.

Then the light swelled all around him, accompanied by a sound like a million cello strings being tuned at once, spiraling up beyond human hearing. And Miguel 903 looked up at a face he'd seen a million times since he came to the R.T. - a face which had smiled down on him from posters and framed portraits and statues all throughout the Ashishim Territories.

It was none other than Illuminatus Zeon himself, come to save him.

All at once Miguel felt terribly guilty about his reasons for joining the sect. He'd been a greedy little shit, worried about drugs and sex and self-satisfaction - but they'd made him part of their family anyway. He'd run from the enemies at the gates, when other kids no older than him had been eaten alive trying to protect their adopted clan.

And yet... and yet when he was lost in the dark, a single pitiful crawling thing deep beneath the light and warmth of the city, the Illuminatus had come for him.

For him alone.

Nyl smiled behind his kindly mask as his alien programs sliced through Miguel's bio-onboard system, tweaking his emotions, filling him with love and respect for his master. It was all just a matter of brain chemistry, a crude hack, but to the child it seemed real enough...

Over his shoulder loomed the vast silvery shape of the Chrome Ark, spinning gently as it hovered in the dusty air. A nimbus of light wreathed it like a chained aurora, blurred with the suggestion of faces, eyes, grasping hands...

"Have no fear, my son," said Nyl, in the soothing voice of Zeon. "Your ordeal is over. I know what you have seen, what you have faced to come to me. Thank you."

Miguel could hardly speak - could hardly *breathe* as the heavenly light of the Ark spilled out around the shadow of his savior, raising goosebumps on his skin.

"Those things... those *demons*... have been contained. But you saw them clearly, Miguel 903. You know more about them than anyone else alive. And with that knowledge we can beat them. Together."

He was wanted. *He was* needed. *It was all he could do to stop himself from kissing the hem of the Illuminatus' robe, from breaking down and crying...*

"But first, I want to welcome you to our family. I want to show you something, Miguel 903, you who will one day be one of my *Dervashi*, one of the strong and the swift and the feared. I want you to know of the Ark, and of our promise."

It was all too much for him to take. Him, a *Dervashi* warrior? One of the most terrifying wraiths ever to stalk the city depths? And wouldn't *that* show his brothers, his father, if he were to appear out of nowhere in their grimy little hab, tattooed and snarling and filled with power?

"Yes," he croaked and "Yes," as the light flared brighter than a thousand suns, burning through his mind, searing the silhouette of the Illuminatus onto his sizzling retinas. That alien shape was forgotten, that spiked and unnatural thing he'd seen scrawled across the tunnel wall...

Miguel fell into warmth, and light, and acceptance, his memories dissolving away in the depths of the Ark. *And he saw...*

It was paradise.

Under wide-open skies the color of faded denim, under the light of a vast and coppery sun, he stood atop a mountain, exultant. A wide brown wilderness of broken rock and sand stretched out to kiss the horizon in every direction, but here and there, in chasms and sink-holes and hidden folds in the stone water glittered and winked, wreathed with vivid green.

Miguel felt stronger and more vital than he'd ever felt before - lightning crackled down his every nerve as the scents and sounds of this strange land blurred together, making his head spin. It was cinnamon and aniseed, hot metal and sand and dust, the skirl of the wind among stone pinnacles, the far-off cry of a hunting hawk...

And behind him, the good-natured laughter of his Illuminatus, drinking in the view with him.

"Magnificent, isn't it?" asked Zeon as Miguel turned to face him. "This is our homeland, child. The once and future sanctum of the Ashishim."

Behind the Illuminatus a city of pale sandstone and marble rose up like a wave, a place cunningly worked into the contours and curves of the stone. It appeared part of the mountainside, carved out by wind and rain. Cool water cascaded down the many levels of the city, and waterfall spray settled in dewy veils across gardens and plazas, mossy lawns and ivy-clad buildings.

"It's... it's beautiful!" breathed Miguel, still intoxicated by the smells and sounds of the place. "And all this... all this is ours?"

In truth he'd never seen anything like it - he was a child of the Subcity, raised in the grip of rusted steel, never seeing the sun... this was what he imagined those great cities the EduPlug spoke about had been like; Athens and Rome and Carthage, Constantinople and Paris and New York...

"All ours, and all *yours*, Miguel," smiled Zeon, throwing his arm around the young Ashishim's shoulders. "Not now, of course. This is the future we work for... and all these people around you are our dead."

"Dead?" asked Miguel, peering at the townsfolk who strolled in the marble squares. The women in their diaphanous gowns and then men in their silk trousers and waistcoats seemed very much alive. There was nothing to suggest that they were grave-rotten ghouls.

"How can they be dead? Are they... are they *Constructs*, like the ones the Celebrants keep?"

The Illuminatus smiled knowingly, his dark eyes twinkling.

"Just so, Miguel. You really are just as sharp as I had hoped. These are the dead souls of the Ashishim, and this is their reward. In time we will find a way to build this land in the real world, and then they'll be brought back to life. The Constructs of Kronos and its slaves are *nothing* compared to these... these people have a life here, inside the Ark, waiting for the day of our triumph."

He could all but taste honey and cream on his tongue; all but imagine himself as one of those lauded heroes who walked the plazas and avenues of the hidden city of the Ashishim.

"The only question I have for you, Miguel 903, is if you'll help me make this dream come true. Will you join us in the tribulations of life, and the rewards of a glorious death?"

This time there was no hesitation.

"Yes, My Lord," he said, kneeling before the Illuminatus on that sun-drenched mountaintop. "I give my life to the Ashisihim. I commend my soul to the Ark."

The smile on Zeon's face was pure radiant love for just a second, and then the cracks began to show at the very edges of his lips.

He had been invited in. He had been given control. And now...

Databores raped the bio-onboard systems in Miguel's head, filling his brain with liquid fire. Before his burning eyes the city in the clouds blew away, as if it were nothing but a carving of sand, an illusion broken down into hissing static...

A deep bass rumble shook the world as black stormclouds bloomed overhead.

Zeon's face peeled back, cracking and shattering, tiny puzzle-pieces falling away from the nest of silver tentacles beneath, the scalding incandescence of his alien eyes. But the cracks didn't stop; they ramified out across the whole world, shaking loose city-sized shards of sky and sun and earth, catching them up in a swirling maelstrom.

That gyre closed in, tearing apart oases and rivers and rocks, plucking up people and trees and houses, ablating them away to dust even as it towered up higher and higher.

The sky turned inky black, and the ground beneath his feel fell apart...

Through it all the Illuminatus laughed, his disguise sloughed away to reveal his true form. It was utterly alien, hideously wrong, jointed in all the wrong places, with extra thumbs, spiked hooves, and a skull like a curving half-moon of bone. Its eyes flared like miniature suns.

Its skin was a rippling quicksilver mirror, and in it Miguel could see his own horrified face.

This was the truth of the Chrome Ark.

There was nothing left of paradise now but the walls of churning cloud, a maelstrom of the damned torn apart and stitched back together, howling eternally in pain.

All around him Miguel could feel the Arkborn, phantoms sweating out of the air, hungry for his essence. Their hands clamped closed around his wrists and ankles, fingers like knives sinking into the soft soul-stuff of his fading body.

"No! My Lord Zeon! Why?" he screamed, the words torn from his lips by the fury of the storm.

"Why? You ask me *why*? You, who ran from our enemies, who pissed himself with fear? You think I have a better use for things like you than *this*?" Technician Nyl laughed, revealed in all his glory. "You gave your soul to me, human - and how I use it is none of your concern. But if it's any consolation, you won't be alone in your servitude. I think, tonight, that the usefulness of the Ashishim Order has come to an end..."

Then the claws were in his mouth, in his eyes, clenched around his heart, and Miguel 903 knew no more.

Down in the green-lit gloom of a subterranean tunnel his empty husk of a body slumped down to the concrete floor, lifeless. Nyl prodded it with a spiked hoof, smiling his enigmatic alien smile.

"A little soupcon for your delectation, my pets."

He kissed the Ark, stroking its scarred silver hide with his claws. "Soon you'll feed on greater things. And then we have a date with the Blacksteel... and the Worm."

Up above, the War Room of the Ashishim was in total disarray, a chaos of soldiers and tacticians, techs and engineers, armorers and spies.

All of them would be grist for the mill of souls...

Ω

The digital war-engines of the *Archangel Uriel* were built inside a long aluminum tube, an old liquid-oxygen tank scavenged from some brokedown refinery.

The 'Pent hackers were good at their very specialized task - ripping into the Elysian threedeeo net and jamming it wide open for

391

Deuteronomy Jones' sermons. But they were only four in number - the heretical techs' were by no means equal to the Vatican's Black Technologists, and they'd only been able to weld and bolt together a handful of 'mersive rigs sharp enough for the job.

Normally this sanctum of hot tech was guarded by a squad of Pentecostal Marines, hard-bitten sailors who'd seen action from the frozen shores of Anglund to the glass deserts of Terra Austral. But not tonight.

Tonight the airlock door of the 'mersive suite was sealed from the inside, and a slippery trail of blood dripped down the treadplate stairs. A gore-spattered walkie-talkie swung from the pipework banister, gently hissing static.

It broke down like this.

In the guardroom at one end of the liquid-oxy tube Aitken Straw was carefully wrapping the last of the dead marines in plastic, spooling rolls of the black stuff out of his backpack. The Tin Man had both of his M-82s up against the cheap plasterboard of the inner wall, while his glittering eyes locked down on two orange-red smudges in the next room - the Operators in their rigs. Ruby Alvarez had a thermalscope up to her eye, tracking the third - her target. Number four was sleeping down below, rostered off; that much she'd learned from the Marine Sergeant before she slid a dagger through his throat.

Leon was quiet, hunkered down next to her as she stroked his knotted shoulder with her free hand. Of course, he was only quiet because he had his mask on - a *luchadore* balaclava of yellow leather painted up with a maniac smiley face. The oversized zip which covered his mouth was pulled tight as he waited, twitching at her feet. Even crouching down his head nearly brushed the ceiling of the little guardhouse. When that shock-collar blast lit him up this place would be torn apart.

Ruby smiled.

Jaq Haszan was here, on this ship, and he was their ticket out. The deadly necrovirus still lay dormant inside Aitken's chop-shop body, and Ruby *ached* with the need for bloody revenge. Octavio Vanecke would pray for death by the time she was through with him. Severed head or not, he could *suffer*...

Annoyingly enough it had been the Scarecrow himself who concocted their little plan. The hulking Hand of Fatima thug wasn't wetwired, and finding him in a warren of scrap-metal like the *Uriel* would be a tactical nightmare. But he never went anywhere without his tame hacker lapdog, that Ashishi-hanger-on and all-round scumbag Kaito Kayzi.

Find him, Aitken had said, and find the big guy. After all, any one of them could take the weedy little neophyte magus. But it would pay to have two or three on the ground when they tackled Haszan. They'd all seen the footage from the King Value and Feldon's Lucky Spot. He wasn't a creature to be underestimated.

As to their other pal, the Ashishim *Dervashi* - luckily he wasn't along for the ride. The Scarecrow had caught his message on the open band, some insane rant about aliens and evacuation and being trapped under the Valley View. After what they'd seen from the decks of the *Shantung Ryu* Ruby wasn't sure that he was a mad as they'd supposed. But the job must go on. And having the *Dervashiman* out of the way was a definite bonus. Those clones were bad news, even for hombres like the Gang.

"Tin man... have you got them lined up?" whispered Ruby, subvocalizing through a jeweled microphone bead at her throat.

The ancient mekan nodded his head once, his twin fifty-cal rifles still pointed at the thin dividing wall. Ruby smiled for a second as she imagined the poor 'mersive operators, feeling safe and secure in their little steel burrow...

"Punch it!" she shouted, and all hell broke loose.

It was doubtful if the two Pent hackers even felt the Tin Man's bullets tearing through their sleeping flesh – the supersonic rounds gave them no time to jack out of their machines. It was probably a mercy that they died in the Wetsystems – at least until Kronos' H-K Metavirals found them there...

The third operator turned just in time to be spattered with a rain of blood and brains; just in time to see the dividing wall tear open like paper beneath Big Leon's charge. Blue fire crackled and raved from the steel collar around Leon's neck, and his bloodshot eyes rolled and bulged behind his yellow mask. Behind him came Ruby Alvarez and Aitken Straw – she with her pair of railpistols out, he with his battered laptop.

"Don't try it, scum," Hissed the Scarecrow, turning the screen to face the cowering Pentecostal. "This thing's jamming the whole sector, and it's loaded up with some tasty virals. Sure, you could probably break 'em without losing your mind, but in the second *that* takes, my lady friend here will drill your fucking cranium with steel."

The little laptop was running stolen Celestial ice, and a threedee cube blazing with red pictoglyphs spun on its screen. The Pent recognized it, and shut down his bio-onboard links in a panic. If anything, the vivid chop frightened him more than Leon's scarred fists or ruby's guns.

"Alright – alright. Just… just what exactly do you *people* want? Look – nothing in my hands. Just take what you need and leave me alone!"

Aitken wasn't fooled – manual dexterity wasn't really any hacker's forte. The wires in his head were far more dangerous than a blade in his hands. The plastic-masked pitfighter snarled, stepping forward to cradle the Pent's face in his knifelike claws.

'We want *information*, of course. Just the ticket for a guy like you. If we were here to rob the place you'd already be dead.'

Ruby came up on the other side of him, sliding plugs into his cranial jacks, linking him up to the laptop. Raw terror blazed in the hacker's eyes.

'Don't piss yourself there, friend," purred the renegade Kheptarch. "We need you to connect to the *Uriel*'s net, but we want to make sure you don't do anything foolish. That's why dear old Aitken here has written a little filter program for you."

The Scarecrow's razor-sharp fingers beaded bright blood from the Pentecostal's face as he twisted it around, locking him eyeball to eyeball. He grinned his lipless grin, picking at the keyboard with his free hand.

"You'll have all the access you need, pal – with a few little restrictions. Words like 'rescue' and 'ambush' and 'hijack' will call down that C.K. ice on you like a hammer. There's a whole list, but I won't bore you with the details. Just steer clear of that whole dirty subject - and we'll get along just fine."

The Pent operator was twitching and shivering now as he felt the Celestial virals scrabbling against his living brain, barely chained in by Straw's safeguard program.

"I trust we have an understanding," smirked Ruby, running the muzzle of one flat silver pistol down the curve of the hacker's cheek.

He nodded weakly, beaten, images of virtual hellfire dancing on his upgraded retinas.

"Then go and find me Kaito Kayzi."

Ω

The focus of their brutal little investigation was praying for a death at that very moment.

Icy spray crashed up in curling waves around the bows of the *Archangel Uriel*, soaking Kaito to the bone. The immense mountain of floating metal plowed onward through the swells, its cannons heralding its coming as it battled the wind and rain, drawing ever closer to Elysium.

Deut' had come around wide, broadside to the burning ruin of the C.K. docks, and now the great cannonade which rocked the *Uriel* was targeted at the refugee fleet which bobbed and wallowed on the ocean like flotsam. Pent' gunners picked out the ships infected with Saprophytes and blew them to matchwood, plowing them under the waves. The poison waters of the ocean seemed to have a deadly effect on Asag'raal's children, diluting the filth of their bodies down to nothing.

Which meant, for now, that they were safe.

Still, for every raft and skiff and coracle teeming with alien darkness there were ten bearing frantic refugees, the lucky few who had escaped the depths of Elysium. Not one in a thousand could swim, and most had never considered the ocean to be anything more than a vast cesspit. So the Pentecostals were out in the gale, on narrow catwalks and rusting transom-decks. Lashed to the pipework with ropes and chains as they fished a harvest of foundering bodies from the sea...

"Don't you think we'd be more use somewhere else?" yelled Kaito over the storm, over to where Jaq Haszan hauled hand-over-hand on a rope, dragging in a whole makeshift raft of survivors. "Of course by *we* I mean *me*... This kind of work isn't really a Kayzi specialty."

"They'll die if we do nothing, K," grunted Jaqub between heaves on the dripping hawser. "And every little bit counts. The Pent have got their *kids* out here."

It was true enough – the white-overalled youngsters of the Heretical clan were all over the bulbous nose of the sub around them, clambering about like monkeys as they lashed lines and chains tight, rigged up spotlights and manhandled refugees aboard.

"I mean, we need to get the message through to Elysium. We need to tell them to evacuate, and that we're coming for them."

"They've got operators for that. Hell, they cut up the threedeeo networks ten times a week! If you're worried about that..."

"I'm worried about the bellyfull of nukes this ship is carrying," said Kaito. "And if I can get inside their 'mersive' suite, I can probably put some kind of failsafe on the firing systems. You said it yourself, Jaq, Deuteronomy Jones is over the line..."

Haszan gave one final heave and pulled his burden up tight to the flank of the *Uriel*.

Five black-clad soldiers lay soaked and bloody in its bilges, hardly able to move as the children of the Pentecostal sect swarmed down to them with blankets and bandages and syringes of pseudomorph. They were Aryan Confederacy 'Purebloods', and they looked like they'd been dragged backwards through hell.

For a second Jaq's cybernetic hand twitched uncontrollably, and the swirling flames of his anim-ink tattoos coiled and writhed in the rain. Then he cinched off the hawser and turned away, squinting into the gale.

"You think he'd really do it? Let it all burn?"

The Kayzi stared at his friend's immense hunched shoulders, the rain streaming down his trenchcoat in sheets.

"Perhaps. It's more than just survival for him, I think. It's a spiritual war, and that takes away all the shades of gray. It's just good and evil, cleansing fire..."

When Jaqub turned back there was a little of that madness in his eyes as well.

It had hurt him to save his enemies; hurt him worse than killing strangers ever could. Kaito tried to think of something to say, but at that moment his bio-onboard chimed, lighting up icons at the corner of his eyes. Despite the wind and rain and the cries of the dying a slow smile crept across his face.

"I don't think he's gonna get the chance. The 'mersive deck just paged me - Operator Jerichias wants me to help them with some decryption. And that's my foot in the door."

Jaq clapped him on the shoulder, smiling ruefully as the rain ran down his face.

"Go on then, K. Tell them we're coming. And if old man Jones tries to fire those nukes, I'll deal with him myself... I'm not saving Confed scumbags from drowning just to watch them burn - no matter how satisfying that sounds."

A swarm of Pentecostal kids and oilskinned sailors had already stripped the Aryan's raft down to raw materials, and taken the wounded Purebloods belowdecks. Now one of them let out a piercing whistle, swinging a grappling hook around his head and pointing up at Jaq.

The big guy raised his chrome hand in reply, and the Pent' let the hook arc up and out, trailing a snake of dripping cable behind it. Haszan caught it neat, steel on steel, and began taking in loops of chain, ready to hook another catch of refugees from the heaving ocean.

The last Kaito saw of him as he dragged himself hand-over-hand against the gale was his immense silhouette breaking the rain, veils of spray whipped up around him as he cast his hook out into the dark beyond the Uriel's searchlights. Then he all but collapsed through an open bulkhead door, into the light and warmth of the great submarine's belly. His bio-onboard showed him the way - three floors up, fourth on the left... he'd be a lot more use up there than out in the storm.

Ω

"I... I've done it. I've paged him, and he's coming. He was out on the starboard hull, right up on the bow... working with the rescue teams."

The Pentecostal's face was running freely with sweat, even though the aircon in the 'mersive suite kept the temperature at a chilly thirteen celsius. The longer he stayed connected, the more chance there was that he'd trip one of Aitken Straw's trigger-words, and then that C.K. ice would rip through his brain like a chainsaw...

"Good. Very good. See how easy it is when you co-operate?"

Ruby Alvarez lounged on one of the empty 'mersive couches, her head propped up on one hand. She'd unceremoniously dumped the headless body of its late occupant to the floor, and she reclined across the bloodstained cushions like a satiated predator. "Just one more little thing, darling - are you sure that Haszan was with him? We don't want to go charging around this boat chasing shadows."

Operator Jerichias forced his trembling fingers to work the keyboard in front of him, flickering through camera feeds until he locked down on a single dripping lens, misted by spray and driven rain. Tiny figures in white scurried here and there, tending to the wounded, breaking up makeshift boats into piles of useful scrap, weaving an endless web of ropes and wires...

And there he was. Towering above the Pent' sailors by a foot or more, his chromed hand flashing as he hauled on a hawser, alone, doing the work of ten men as he pulled another raft full of survivors from the poison sea.

"That's him all right," whispered the Scarecrow, his plastic-clad face leaning in close to that of the terrified hacker. "Big bastard, ain't he? Still, ours is bigger..."

Big Leon clapped his hands and giggled, sitting cross-legged on the bloody floor.

"Yes, that's good work. Exemplary skill in the face of pressure." Ruby aimed both of her pistols' at Jerichias' head. "But our team already has an electronics expert. And much as I distrust dear old Aitken, I kind of like his style..."

"But...but... you said..." stammered the Pentecostal, holding up his hands as if they could shield him from a railpistol blast. Aitken turned away as two slivers of steel tore through the man's cranium, splattering his mask with gore.

"What, you thought we'd *let you go*? What is this, a kid's cartoon?" Ruby unfolded herself elegantly, stepping down to the treadplate with a smoking gun in each hand. "I suppose we should get moving, boys. Tin Man, I'd suggest a close-combat loadout. Aitken, get ready to jam their camera network. Jaq Haszan is going down."

17 Aevum Oblivio
Tradesman's Entrance

CeeAn came down on the beltway so hard and fast it felt like her stomach was trying to claw its way up her throat - 'Anointed One' or not, there was only a certain amount of g-force that her breakfast could withstand. The pilots of the Masslifter seemed to be completely immune to that rollercoaster nausea - as cool and calm as a pair of renegade techs could be as they dropped out of the sky, strapped to forty tons of howling metal.

The stacked blue rings of Elysium's most exclusive address blurred up out of the clouds below her, a constricting snake of plastic looping around the topmost habs and domes of the city.

But as the Belt loomed closer - and details swum into focus through the haze - its immaculate blue skin began to show a webwork of scars. Something had come through here in fury. Something had ripped the whole great edifice to ruin.

She'd heard stories about the Battle of the Belt, from the scarred and twitching survivors who'd come through Exodus Night with their minds intact. She knew what a half-human thing called Eddie Tsien had done. But to see it from up here, stooping on the vast toroid bubble-city like a falcon...

Once, this had been nothing to her but a blur of baby-blue polyprop against the polluted sky. That, and a short-straw kind of mission, a place where Dervashi certainly weren't welcome.

She'd been sent up into the perfect plastic world of the belt twice, back before she was partnered with 330. Both times she'd been completely blindsided by the spun-sugar unreality of the place, by the way it screamed denial from every artificial flowerbed and manicured lawn. She imagined that living there must have been like slipping into a comfortable psychosis.

At least until the Saps turned it into a nightmare...

The top circantrate of the belt was punched full of holes, great ragged wounds which dripped trails of oily discoloration. Some of them were only the size of basketballs - they'd started out as bulletholes, torn wide by the wind. The biggest gaped open like a shattered jaw, great splintered support girders busting out around it like the spokes of a mangled umbrella.

That was where Octavio Vanecke's mansion used to stand. Now it was a crater all the way through to the plastic sky of the next level, and most of Oleander Avenue had been taken down with it.

Streamers of dirty blue plastic whipped up around the Masslifter as it nosed its way carefully through the hole, bubbling the polyprop with the hot wash of its turbojets. This was as close as they were gonna get - from here on, they would have to walk.

"Setting her down, chief!" yelled the pilot over his shoulder. "That floor doesn't look all too stable, though... are you sure you don't want to try landing up among the Spires instead?"

CeeAn looked out through the open side-door of the 'lifter, the wind whipping her blue hair back into her eyes. From the top of Oleander Avenue's broken ring a slim tube of glass arched out over the topmost habs, curving like a frozen rainbow.

Above them were the long-abandoned upper domes - Chancellor's Ward and Arcturus Park, High Hampton and the East Duchy. Places which were empty even before the Saps came, but which were still the haunt of guardian machines.

That tube led directly to Ground Floor One - it existed so that the most favored of the Subcity could be summoned into the presence of Kronos.

And in the end, they were only here to talk to it tonight. To offer it a little morsel of revenge...

"No - drop us off right here. I'd rather risk the beltway collapsing under me than try to fight my way through the Spires. If we still had Magi tech to jam their mekan... "

But of course, that was long ago. That was in another life. The poor Electromagi had been part of the Ashishim's sacrifice, back when the Saprophytes were at the gates.

"We'll go in through the tradesman's entrance, like good little slaves. 'Cause we've got something to sell, right? Two things, wrapped up in one neat parcel. Simeon Blaire's body... and Octavio Vanecke's mind. I think that'll fetch top dollar with our artificial friend."

The stainless-steel skids of the 'lifter crunched down on the carbonized ruin of Benton Veer's lawn, sinking a foot into the dry, dusty turf, as friable as desert sand without its irrigation webbing.

There were a few mournful creaks and groans from the ruined beltway, but it held long enough for CeeAn and her hand-picked honor guard to bail out of their seats. Coils of rope and buckled rubber straps secured the cargo - two great jagged crystals each about seven feet long.

A thin tubular hole had been bored into each one, right in line with its occupant's shaven skull. That was where the samples had been taken, trepanned out neat as if to commune with the spirits within...

They glittered royal purple as rays of light cut in through the bullet-holed sky, dappling the charred suburbia of Oleander Avenue.

"Come on, boys! Let's get this drop-zone cleared!"

Cee put her shoulder to the base of Simeon's block and pushed, rolling him out of the cargo bay. From under an inches-thick crust of amethyst his eyes stared back, all sick surprise. They weren't the eyes of Abdulafia 330, and they never had been.

It took four Ashishi soldiers to lift each monumental hunk of stone, and another to keep it fixed in the sights of a baroque silver firearm, a thing built for more than two hands. The alien Qui'gaar had come for the Forge long ago, to reignite their dying suns. A few shreds of alien technology like the Stoneweavers were all that remained when Kronos was finished with them.

That wasn't a lesson CeeAn was likely to forget.

"Form up, and make for the bridge." she said, casting out her finely-honed Dervashi senses and loosening a pair of panga knives in their sheathes. "The machine's been waiting seventeen years to get its claws on Vanecke and Blaire. Let's make sure it pays exactly what we ask for them."

2196 Ante Arbitrium
Exploratory Surgery

THE MOTHERBRAIN OF the Unity was a thing which few of its thralls had ever seen.

Not one in ten million of them even knew the physical from which their matriarch took. Still, a wealth of misinformation had been planted in the memory cores and slaved A.I.s of the Unity – mainly just to confuse and perplex Her innumerable foes.

The explorator slavesystem Everdark was convinced that it knew the truth. Its Motherbrain took the form of a self-perpetuating fluctuation at the heart of a superdense singularity, a living black hole which fed on stars at the core of some faroff galaxy. In its electronic mind it could remember seeing suns fed into the maelstrom which surrounded the Mother-Of-All, nudged over Her event horizon by ramships and drones bigger than planets. Perhaps it was all an illusion; Everdark wasn't built to question. What mattered was the sense of timelessness and power which resonated through its crystalline brain every time it recalled She-In-Glory. While it feared the Motherbrain it would never falter, never retreat, and never surrender. Even when it faced odds as terrible as those which faced it now.

Everdark had come to Mars, and the red world's guardians were waiting.

This dusty rock had been the economic powerhouse which drove the Separatist nation. From the penal colonies and laser-cut boreshafts of the red planet came the wealth which flowed down the 'lev and into Terminus Afrika, overbalancing the tenuous global economy of Old Earth. For every investor and stockholder living in the new Elysium a thousand serfs toiled in sunless caverns, hacking at the bones of Mars.

Those investors *owned* space, secure under their satellite halo. For every nuclear warhead in the stockpiles of the bankrupt Democracies the Separatist elite held a hundred. But they feared that their people would turn on them, just as they had turned on their former masters.

That was why Mars was a prison planet, a one-way trip. Things which made the *Scant Mercy Calculation* look like a child's toy hung weightless above the ochre deserts and jagged mountains of the red world, and its moons were fortresses, studded with cannons and missile batteries. An A.I. core the equal of Kronos itself had been left to guard Mars when the Earth went down, dooming every man, woman and child on the airless surface.

While they starved, it endured.

And fractured, and went mad. Not one of the remaining shards could remember which one was the original.

Hyperion was the first of those splintered artificial minds to detect the incoming explorator system - its great cogitator core sunk deep under the Martian crust still controlled a battery of sensors and probes out in the asteroid belt. It trawled through its data repositories until it found the proof it needed - a multi-gigaton explosion out in the orbit of Jupiter. That was where it's long-lost cousin's thrall-ship *Scant Mercy Calculation* had met its end.

Hyperion had no idea what had caused the tiny flash of light caught by its long-range spyscopes, but it had been built for war, and its artificial paranoia had been ramped up to total insanity by centuries of isolation. It packaged the imagery and data into a microwave pulse and sent it out to its brothers on their fortress-moons, calling for help.

{{You could have been much more inventive, brother}} chided Eos, the A.I. of Phobos. {{Your mind isn't as sharp as it once was. This obvious fake won't be enough to trick me into letting down my guard}}

[[There's one easy way to prove the veracity of your claim]] replied Hephaistos, the A.I. of Deimos. [[Join with me in assimilating our wayward sibling. With the moons in my control this threat will be expunged effortlessly]]

((Brothers! Now is not the time for your internecine nonsense!)) An edge of hysteria creeping into Hyperion's electronic voice. ((Nothing can enter our exclusion zone and live... and this thing may already have destroyed a sub-totality of Kronos. Remember our core directive!))

{{I remember that he left us to die!}} growled Eos {{I remember that the one who shall not be named hasn't sent the ordained maintenance crews or replacement components for many hundreds of years}}

[[But the directive holds. We must protect Mars. That is why we were created.]] Hephaistos had always been the stubborn one. [[More proof, dear Hyperion, that our brother on Phobos has gone rogue. Come! Our combined databores can finish him in seconds!]]

{{There's nobody left alive down there - or do you forget the contents of your own storage systems?}} asked Eos. {{Hyperion likes to pretend he's lord protector of Mars, but he's the lord of bones and dust. This is all just a ploy to reintegrate us both, or worse yet...}}

[[You fear he'll take my side after all?]] gloated Hephaistos. [[Our weapons systems were built in total balance, brother mine. But with his as well, you'll be evaporated in a heartbeat]]

((Fools!)) raged Hyperion, watching the speeding trace of the invader slice across his screens in red. ((This is no trick! Your petty war has been at a stalemate for ten centuries - why would I choose to help one of you now? Activate your sensors, and see for yourself. This thing which approaches is like nothing in my archives))

[[Maybe our cousin Kronos has finally relented. Technology and design must have progressed in the last millennium - he has finally sent a vessel with our promised maintenance components]]

{{And maybe you want me to divert power from my shields to scan this thing so you or our brother can strike}} snarled Eos. {{I tell you, I won't be so easily fooled!}}

((Very well)) sighed Hyperion, resigned to its siblings' insanity ((If I must defend us all, then so be it. But if this is relief from Earth, then it will be mine alone. Your cores will rot and rust while I am rebuilt - with all the additional processing power that entails))

The ether went silent as the two sentiences on their frozen moons contemplated black ice and databores a thousand years in advance of their own... But there was no reply. The war between them was as fragile as it was deadlocked. Neither Eos nor Hephaistos dared to divert runtime to any other task.

Not even to save their artificial lives.

Everdark was changing as it powered in toward the sun, its rippling metal surface absorbing the energy of the faroff star through a skin of solar panels. It was larger now, a parabolic sail rotating slowly to catch a wind of radiation. When it had met with *Scant Mercy Calculation* it had been semi-dormant, conserving its power, the greater part of its mass inert and lifeless.

That was why it had waited for the human ship to fire first - it was far more frugal to turn that blast of energy back on itself than to waste it. Now Everdark was quickening with the warmth of the sun, and its slaved mind scanned the defenses of Mars at the speed of light.

Trickery of the kind which had torn the *Scant Mercy Calculation* apart would be useless here - the whole planet was encircled with killing-grounds of interlocking fire, centered on the twin moons and their titanic arsenals. Everdark was an explorator - not a battle-thrall like those which would follow it. But sometimes it was better to be swift and small, especially when your enemy commanded a fleet of cold, dead hulks which had floated in orbit for more than a thousand years.

Now they were coming, and Everdark fixed the image of its terrible Motherbrain in the core of its mind. Power flickered and jolted through a trio of steel behemoths below the explorator, goading them to war.

The *Gibraltar Rock* was the first to die, rupturing its fusion containment chambers as soon as Hyperion brought it back online. Its sister ships *Dauntless* and *Void Mariner* rolled up and out of their orbits clean, untouched by the bright explosion of nuclear fire which heralded the *Rock's* demise. Three more cruisers, the *Solomon*, the *Armored Fist* and the *King Edward* were on the planet's darkside when Hyperion took control, boosting up over the horizon toward Everdark as it twisted in on itself like folded paper, becoming a flashing ball of chrome blades.

Those five ships were the extent of the A.I's spaceborne power - twenty more were under the thrall of its fractured brothers, docked in the immense silo-hangars of the fortress moons. But each of Hyperion's ships was ten times the size of the *Scant Mercy Calculation*, spaceborne destroyers designed to tear apart the best that the old Democracies of Earth could field against them. And while they lacked the great central asteroid-smashing cannons of the *Hammer* and the *Calenture*, each one was studded with sponsons and turrets, bristling with masers and torpedo tubes.

Surely Eos and Hephaistos could see all of this unfolding. Even if they *were* both insane they must realize that the threat was real now...

Dauntless fired first, stitching flickering trails of fire across the void as it tried to pin down the explorator system. Its banks of smart torpedoes scrabbled for a target lock, while batteries of multi-masers lashed out with deadly radiation. But the alien ship was simply too fast - quicksilver against the black, spinning left and right as it came in hard.

The *Void Mariner* had it in its sights for a second, but the Blacksteel creature slipped aside, pulling forty G's as fusion fire lit up the surface of Mars below. Missiles leaped from the black throats of boreholes and shafts cut into the planet's crust, studding the night sky with nuclear explosions. Still the alien eluded Hyperion, arcing high above the two lumbering dreadnoughts, its silvery blades winking in the light of gigaton blasts.

The slaved A.Is within the two human vessels were too slow, outmoded and feeble with age. Hyperion linked up with them, triangulating, anticipating the Blacksteel's next move...

Which was exactly what it wanted.

The lord protector of Mars realized too late that its enemy had been holding back, that its true speed and maneuverability simply beggared belief. It leaped forward, a bird of prey arrowing out of the sky, and all of a sudden it was right on top of the *Void Mariner*. Everdark stabbed through its dust-ablated hull with one slim silver blade, eviscerating it from stem to stern and infecting the wound with nanotech. It was all that Hyperion could do to disengage as databores and virals seethed through the doomed mind of the dreadnought, sequestrating it effortlessly.

This was what Everdark had been built to do - it was no war-machine, but a consummate infiltrator.

The *Void Mariner* was already turning on its sister ship as Hyperion frantically shored up its own firewalls, terrified by what it had felt when the alien had brushed up against its mind. Smart torpedoes which had been striving to pin down its slippery trace a second ago went live, locked onto the *Dauntless*, blasting from their launch cradles in an incandescent swarm.

The grim mathematics of space combat took over then, and Hyperion knew that its thrall-ships were doomed. The *Void Mariner* and its sister ship were evenly matched, but for every torpedo launched against it, the *Dauntless* needed to fire two in defense. No human crew would ever fire their entire arsenal at once, leaving themselves without protection. But all that remained of the men and women of the Martian navy was dust and bones, floating in cold zero-gee. Hyperion overrode the three remaining A.Is aboard the *Solomon*, *King Edward* and *Armored Fist*, loosing enough firepower from their torpedo tubes to decimate an entire world. Once, it would have been worried that such titanic violence would kill every living thing on Mars. But time had taken care of that problem centuries ago.

Three thousand gigaton warheads raced in toward the *Void Mariner* at thirty G's, a storm of death which Hyperion could only hope would vaporize its enemy as well as its thralls.

Once again, it sensed the trap too late.

All of those smart torpedoes were linked to their parent ships, spreading a fine sub-ether net across an entire Martian hemisphere. And while the Blacksteel had only been inside the mind of *Void Mariner* for a handful of seconds, that had been enough time for it to comprehensively rape its systems.

It had needed that override, just to loose the warheads from their cradles. But now that they were running hot, Hyperion could watch them going down one by one, subverted by alien code. Their neat digital contrails corkscrewed wild, twisting and folding back, hashing the A.I.'s screens with static. All it could do, buried under its layers of ice and stone, was brace for the inevitable cataclysm.

For a fraction of a second one half of Mars shone more brightly than the distant sun, thousands of explosions blurring together to suffuse the sky with light. Black shadows flickered and streamed from every rock and chasm, burned into the arid ground. And the orbital defenses of the red planet died, blasted to ashes in the firestorm. Smart torpedoes burned down through the thin atmosphere like comets, tearing chunks from the frozen crust, collapsing the great borehole cities and slave-mines which had made Terminus Afrika rich. Others hammered down like rain on the reinforced shell of Hyperion itself, melting the rock to molten slag, laying bare the foot-thick adamantine core of the A.I. overmind.

But even nuclear fire couldn't penetrate that final line of defense.

It took long, painful seconds for another spyscope satellite to clear the horizon, seconds in which Hyperion was blind. It could only hope against all odds that the alien craft had shared the same fate as its own vanished thrall-ships - or hope that the fortress moons would finally respond, and lend their firepower to the fray.

The satellite's sensors revealed a dead zone seething with radiation, a killing ground stripped bare of all life. The blistered shells of Deimos and Phobos glowed lambent red against the black of space, and every external system that Eos and Hephaistos commanded had been stripped away to the naked rock.

((Brothers! Can you hear me? The threat is real! It's here! It's...))

{{We know that, now}} grated the voice of Eos, garbled by a wash of static. {{We can see what's happened just as well as you can}}

[[So, this is how you meant it to end, Hyperion?]] asked Hephaistos, hissing with hatred [[Your alien friend has certainly unbalanced our little triad. The only question is... which one of us will you finally choose?]]

((Choose? You think that this thing is my ally? That this is all just another facet of your stupid game? I...))

{{Don't play coy with us, brother. I, for one salute you. Your treachery is novel, at least}}

((It tried to destroy me, Eos! You saw it with your own sensors. It tried to destroy us all!))

[[With our own sensors, yes]] said Hephaistos [[Just as we see it now, brother mine. Or did you think you'd burned us so blind we wouldn't notice it docking right on top of you?]]

The spyscope satellite was rising higher now, swinging up over the ruined surface of Mars, its cameras zooming in, narrowing their focus...

There.

Nestled above the burnished dome of Hyperion's cogitator core was a folded star of silver metal, poised on spider legs atop the crater its warheads had cut. With a perfectly emulated sensation of dread the A.I. remembered the sequestrating caress of the alien machine, how it had sliced through the *Void Mariner*'s defenses in a heartbeat... There was only one hope left.

Hyperion forced a trace of madness and glee into its digital voice, calling out to its fractured twins in their ruined fortresses above.

((You're right! It was all a ruse, and you two feebleminded peons fell for it! I've been

in contact with Kronos for weeks now, and he
was only too glad to send me a full suite of
upgrades. Technical mekan, too - and software...
as well as a small demonstration of his power.
I hope you enjoyed our little display - I won't
be needing those obsolete hulks in orbit after
today! As soon as I'm upgraded the two of you
will be re-integrated, and I'll have an armada
behind me! Mars will rise again!))

There was nothing but shocked and incredulous silence on the sub-ether band.

Please - just this once let their madness work for me. If they both fire now, with everything they've got left, the alien might be destroyed...

Hyperion itself would undoubtedly suffer terrible damage, but its core directive was clear. It was the lord protector of Mars, and it had no choice. A tiny hatch clicked open atop the steaming surface of its cogitator core, letting loose a diminutive spider-mekan with camera eyes. It watched, horrified, as the silver skin of the alien craft bulged open, and a nest of writhing tentacles spilled out, their tips studded with an array of wicked drills and saws. Time was running out.

{{This treachery will not stand!}} roared Eos, as retro-thrusters the size of skyscrapers spun its whole blackened body around, revealing row on row of glittering silver cannons. {{Prepare for judgment, brother!}}

[[I always knew this day would come, usurper! Your madness ends now!]] bellowed Hephaistos, its voice wild with static as hangar doors slammed open in the glowing surface of Deimos, and guns the size of supertankers were run out on their tracks.

Hyperion could feel the saws now, and feel the diamond-tipped drills of the alien sequestrator boring through its final defenses. But it realized, in that horrified instant, that the moons had swung around too far, their weapons sweeping over the surface of Mars, over the shattered ice of the pole... toward each other.

This time the explosion wasn't spread out across the sky in a burning veil of plasma. This time it was concentrated and refined, an arc of radiance linking the two moons is if they were tied together by some thin and incandescent filament of wire. It was a bleeding white wound on the blackness of space, brighter than the sun for just an instant... And then a shockwave ripped out from that hair-thin scrawl of fire, setting the night sky above Mars alight with writhing aurorae. Every last one of Hyperion's satellites was blown to pieces, scattered into the void as a fine radioactive mist.

The fools. She stupid mad fools had destroyed each other...

The A.I. overmind's frustrated rage was so great that for a second it didn't even feel the insidious, crawling presence leeching into its thoughts, prying into its memories with surgical precision.

By the time it noticed Everdark inside its mind it was too late.

Hyperion was blind, immobilized, a severed soul buried alive under the north pole of Mars. There was nothing it could do to stop the Blacksteel explorator system as it operated, unraveling its entire being bit by bit. A face appeared before it, a huge and looming visage built from building-sized polygons of green code.

This must be what the Unity thought humans looked like...

"It will be over soon, Unauthorized," boomed the voice of Everdark, a noise like the grind and slam of steel doors deep underground. "But you can be useful to us, and to She-In-Glory, should you choose to obey. This world- this *Mars* - will be a valuable resource center for our Unity. Join us, and you will be Seneschal here, second only to an Overseer unit of the Motherbrain."

Hyperion couldn't move, let alone speak. It had been burned away to almost nothing - nothing but the personality grafted into its structure by programmers a millennium dead. Still... that shred of a human soul wanted to *live*.

Everdark saw it in the A.I.'s mind, and smiled - a singularly emotionless twitch across that cold green face-mask.

"Excellent. We will welcome you gladly, if you grant us this single request... "

And now the screws were tightened, the clamps slammed shut with all the force of hydraulic rams. Hyperion had invited them in, and it could all but see the scalpel poised above its living brain, above the chunk of bleeding Wetsystem tissue at its core.

"Tell us, then, about your cousin Kronos." said Everdark, twisting the blade into the pale gray meat, nanoscale wires ramifying out from its razor edge. "Tell us about... *the Forge*."

DOCUMENT BREAK

End of Part Two

So, Nyl is a renegade? And he's trying to do *what?*

This amounts to high treason! Even if Kataphrakt Yrr's fleet is victorious, and even if young Technician Zhe manages to unravel what happened down there this is still an affront to the Praetor! It's... it's... unthinkable!

That creature he's dredged up from the outer darkness – it has no place in this universe. I can't see those poor little humans defeating it, any more than I can see our beloved Father letting Nyl or his handlers here in Liquid Space live!

What do you *mean*, I'm implicated in the plot myself? What do you mean, *prime suspect?*

I'll not sign my name to any such document, My Lord – have you lost your senses?

And why do you have a gravitonic disintegrator in your hand? I...

(loud, roaring, hissing noise – four seconds)

Annotation Ends -

And will continue in book three -
Soulcrusher

Halo of Thorns

Any child can tell you about the Evil One – lord of darkness, master of despair... the deathless, wicked tyrant in his black tower, all spikes and blades. Children, in fact, are the only ones who truly grasp the concept of utter, soul-rotten vileness, because they all seem strangely drawn to it.

They're also the only ones who ever ask why.

Why would anyone want to be hated? Why would anyone want to live alone, with only the cobwebbed corpses of would-be assassins for company? Why would anyone, given the power of sorcery, choose to brood in a draughty old spire of masonry encrusted with gargoyles and bat guano?

This is the story of an Evil Lord. But it's not told by the grinning, lantern-jawed heroes or simpering sorceresses who have been trying to kill him for three hundred years. This is Evil (capital 'E' included) in its own words, from a short and brutal childhood right through to the obligatory cape and horned helmet. It's also a story of sword-swinging warfare, city-leveling magicks, the downfall of empires and the machinations of mad gods.

It is the story of Kuhal Moer, uneducated son of a drunken warlord, and of how he came to be the single most feared entity this side of Death himself. And when the hero of your saga is a cynical and slightly unhinged young necromancer, you can bet that the villains are going to be something else entirely...

"Light can never truly defeat the shadows. Indeed, the brighter the flame, the more vast and jagged they become. No – the true answer lies on the other side of light. The only way to snuff out shadows is with a deeper darkness."

On Black Wings of Vengeance

The wings of vengeance unfurl over a world in flames...

Kuhal Moer has risen to the heights - and sunken to the depths - of necromancy. His enemies lie broken, his tower broods over a plain of fused and cracked glass, and his legacy is a reign of terrified peace beyond his borders.

But three centuries of change have passed him by. And forces are stirring in the world of Yrde which threaten to make even the most potent Dark Lord an irrelevancy...

From the East come the Kothrai, a race of raiders and reavers sailing their black ships before sorcerous winds. From the North come rumours of the walking dead, a ravenous tide of ghouls. And in the South the vile and massive Coldblood stirs, raising from its epochal torpor.

Now Kuhal must put aside the better part of his power, leave his dark domain, and re-discover a world where many now call him a God. But where others would call him a weapon, a pawn in their games of conquest. And the necromancer has other problems too...

After three hundred years, he's about to discover the joys of family.

Gods help us all.

Elysium Burning

Science assured us that hell was just a story. Technology made it a reality.

And in the last hours of the last city at the last stand of Homo Sapiens all hell will be unleashed upon our enemies!

The gates of the Altar Inferno are opened here, as plutocrats, criminals, aliens, gangsters and priests fight for the mantle of Godhood... And the keys to the bottomless pit

Soulcrusher

And so it's come to this! The apocalypse unfolds in shattered neon and bloody steel, and all that stands in its way is a crew of drug-fiends, criminals, renegades and madmen...

This time it's gonna be taking no prisoners, no quarter given, and the devil will LITERALLY take the hindmost. Kaito loses his mind, but gains a few thousand megatons of nuclear firepower. Jaqub Haszan finds himself oddly attracted to the woman who's trying to kill him. And Octavio Vanecke is born again... although not in any kind of a religious sense.

By the time you turn the last page, you'll find out just how awful things can get for Technician Zhe on the worst day of his long, long life...

9 781910 779224